Paint

Paint

Grace Tiffany

Tempe, Arizona
2013

Published by Bagwyn Books, an imprint of the Arizona Center for
Medieval and Renaissance Studies (ACMRS), Tempe, Arizona.

2 3 4 5 6 7 8 9   14 15 16 17 18 19.

For Amy

If I were to describe for you what an extraordinary effect his words have on me! The moment he starts to speak, I am beside myself: my heart starts leaping in my chest, the tears come streaming. . . . I stop my ears and tear myself away from him, for, like the Sirens, he could make me stay by his side till I die.

Plato, *Symposium*

1

The boy is ill-clad in coarse woolen breeches, a linen shirt, and patched netherstocks. His wrists protrude three inches beyond his sleeve-ends. The loose sole of his hobnail boot makes a flapping sound as he races after her in the garden, yelling insults that are new to her, like "Polly PENcilpate!" and "vile *parve mulier!*" and "Prune Powderstuff!" At least, Emilia assumes these are insults. They have the tone. Her own taunts are sturdy, workaday London railleries she's learned from her male Bassano cousins. She cranes her neck to look back as she runs, and hurls curses in his direction. "Codpox! Cullion! Turkey-dog infidel! Shake your ears, ye malt-arse cunny-face!" She is quick indeed, but the dooryard is tiny, and she's small for ten; the lad's legs are longer than hers. He's gaining on her. She hikes up her skirts and sprints, her braid bouncing, as the *flap-flap* grows louder behind her. He is laughing as he goes. He's a relative, she's been told, though she's had the luck never to see him before today. He's got a wooden sword stuck in his belt. He holds an inkpot in one hand, and with the other he clamps its lid down tight against spillage. Perhaps he has done this before.

Flap-flap. "*YAAH-HH!*" The boy's laughter opens into a yell of savage triumph as he gains another yard on Emilia. *Flap-flap!* But she's reached the gnarled apple tree by the high wall and knows from long practice how to swing herself instantly into its branches. She's up, and climbing as high as she can, now laughing herself. He skids to a halt and stands looking at her, translated on the instant from wild bear to canny thinker. There she sits on a stout tree-limb, a puzzle with feet which dangle five feet above him. He can't follow her up without dropping his ink.

Coolly she gives him the *figo*, thrusting her thumb between forefinger and middle finger and shaking her fist. She wonders, *Whence the ink?* The pot's not one of theirs. Does he carry it around from place to place? She twists now, and hangs from the tree's thickest branch, holding the hem of her smock skyward for modesty's slim sake. She jeers at him, contorting her freckled, upside-down face. She creates a chant out of thin air, and delivers it sing-song. *"Drink your ink! 'Twill make you stink! So I think!"*

The boy unscrews the lid of the pot, grabs six inches of her dangling braid, and inks her hair black.

"Son of a whore!" she yells, whipping the blackened braid away from him, not caring at the moment whether her mother overhears, or the neighbors do. Hooting, he runs back into the house with his lidded pot.

She pulls herself upright on the branch and sits in the tree for an hour, crying with anger. She unplaits her hair and tries to wipe off the ink with apple leaves, but the black only spreads farther and stains her hands, her face, her smock. When she finally drops to the ground, sniveling, and stamps into her mother's kitchen, the boy is gone.

"What did they want?" she bellows.

Margaret Johnson is slicing carrots and dropping them into a boiling pot. She looks up with her customary frown of concentration. Seeing her daughter's face and clothes, she wrinkles her brow more deeply. "What have you *done*, Melly?" Her voice is sharp.

"What did they want?"

Emilia's fierce rage blows the wind from Margaret's sails. Her mother opens her eyes wide, then frowns again mildly as she reaches for another carrot. "Those two? The boy's father was one of my brothers, though he's long dead. His widow's settled in Charing Cross, and she's remarried. The stepfather wished to ferret out money from the family, for that one's raising."

"He should leave him home. He does not advertise himself."

"What can you mean?" Margaret raises a shoulder to wipe perspiration from her chin. "In my parlor that boy was quiet and reverent, with a most courtly bow. A trifle patched in the sleeve and frayed in the jerkin, but that's no fault of his. You might learn graces from *him*, Melly." She shoots her daughter a meaningful look as she drops the last piece of carrot in the pot and wipes her hands on her apron. She's too tired to scold today. She says without rancor, "If that smock weren't falling apart and ripe for the ash heap already, I'd beat you for those stains."

"Those stains are none of my doing."

"Whose, then?" Margaret starts to stir her soup with a large wooden spoon. She expects no answer, and gets none. "At any rate, we can do nothing for the lad. A hoyden and a baby girl are enough for me, and I no longer have a man lugging gold uphill from Whitehall. I sent the stepfather on to Roderick; *he's* got a few pounds to spare." She lays the spoon on a table and wipes her brow with the back of her hand. "And you, in the muck! I meant you to get firing for the stove. I've burned the last stick." She peers closely at Emilia. "You look like a blackamoor. What *is* that muck?"

"*Ink!*" Emilia marches upstairs, rubbing her cheeks with the hem of her smock.

"Have I not *told* you, Melly, not to tamper with ink unsupervised?"

In her eleventh year, and her twelfth, Emilia tampers with ink unsupervised. She's not a hoyden, really, just a London girl like others of the parish. When he lived her father was an artist, a highly regarded musician at court, who earned enough to lodge his family in a city house. But he was a craftsman, too, who mended and made instruments. All the fathers of St. Botolph Bishopsgate are well-paid mechanicals, and their wives — including common law wives, like the now-widowed Margaret — do not cosset their daughters. They give the lasses coin and send them out into the world in pairs, or alongside their brothers, to buy bread at the baker's and geese at the pannier's, gingham and calico and pins from the peddlers at fairs, and ale from the taverns. To skip, scuff shoes, throw sticks, and hurl pebbles as they go is ordinary for such girls, still wild in their childish androgyny, for all they are dressed in sober smocks, aprons, and caps, like doll-women.

Emilia's no different from the other young maids, except in this ink addiction. She wonders, after her strange interlude with the ghastly cousin in the garden, whether something about her attracts the black stuff. She doesn't drink ink, as she bade that boy do his. Nor does she willingly spread it on her body. But she knows her letters, and when she can find paper and a sharp goose quill, she writes. What? Fairy stories, nasty scraps of doggerel with rhyming swear words, letters to God. The paper she uses comes, unauthorized, from her father's store of scoresheets, and the ink comes from his desk drawer. To hide the fact that it was she who was stealing it, and not some intruder, she once broke a window in his study at night, leaving Baptista to rant and rave the next day, hurling sticks of firewood at his quick-dodging wife and daughters and puzzling loudly over what thief would purloin a stack of paper and leave untouched the box of silver coin that stood beside it. To further conceal her larcenies, her habit, once she's composed and read over her scrawlings, is to burn them in the hearth when no one's looking. The house in St. Botolph is small, and lacks secret places to store her work, which is, anyway, never quite good enough.

Emilia was only seven when her father's heart failed him in the street, right on the stoop in front of their house. But she can still hear in her mind the mixture of complaint and braggartry that always marked his homecomings from royal court occasions. Baptista would collapse, puffing, on the settle in the parlor. "*Mi stanno lavorando per la morte!*" *They're working me to death!* This, after shuffling home at the tail end of three days spent blowing dinner music for some guffawing Dutch diplomat, floating downriver from one of Elizabeth's palaces on a crowded, filthy barge, and toiling up three hills to his house, all the way bearing a sack of recorders. "*Basta, basta, basta! Mi stanno lavorando per la morte!* Look, Meg!" He shakes a sleeve. "They give me crimson damask livery, *amore*, but they won't wash or replace it after a nobleman gives it the puke. Now! Some supper!"

Her mother frowns in vexation, twists her lip, shakes her head. She pinches the rich sleeve and bends to examines it, then straightens and sighs. "I can guess whose duty this will be."

Baptista stretches and lets loose a groan. "Forty years of service for four English monarchs. What am I given for this slave's labor? The wine levy, a pair of ill-fitting gloves every New Year's, and twenty pence a day."

Margaret pats his shoulder. "That is not all. You have immunity from arrest as a queen's servant. You can riot with apprentices on feast days, my darling."

"If I would, I could not. I'd be tooting for Elizabeth with the troubadours. I should have been knighted by this time." He is slowly tilting toward a new position on the settle, sideways and horizontal. "Signor Baptista Bassano, *un caviliere.* Supper, Meg!"

Her mother clucks as she brings him a pewter mug brimming with his favorite ale, a Southwark brew called Left Leg. "What good would a knighthood do us, Baptista? You could not bequeath the honor to your children, even if we were church married. Even if they were boys."

He mutters, drinks ale, and is pacified. In twenty minutes he is flat horizontal and snoring.

Even if they were boys, thinks little Emilia, who has listened, scribbling with stolen ink under the stair. She likes this word, so she mouths it. *Boys. Boys.*

After the sad evening when Baptista drifts down dead like a yellow leaf seeking the ground, her mother develops ailments of her own. She is distracted, and Emilia, after her chores at home are complete, wanders the parish unchecked. Baptista was a petty household tyrant, to be sure, but his rules had bound them, had made them a family. Without them, the women of the household drift apart. Emilia's little sister Angelica plays dolls in the dooryard dirt for hours on end. Margaret alternates between utter collapse and domestic mania, lying in bed humming or wearing out her back and knees scrubbing pots and floors. Emilia patrols the neighborhood seeking scandalous conversations on which to eavesdrop from various climbable perches. This is how it goes for years, but things change when Emilia reaches adolescence. She stops climbing trees. Her colorful swearing at calamities continues, but only in whispers addressed to herself, or shrieks muffled by pillows behind closed doors. She helps her mother clean house, and hauls Angelica inside and gives her a scrub.

She stops writing, as well. At her mother's urging, she practices the lute. There is one in the house, of her father's making. Music is her family's heritage and livelihood, but Margaret is thinking only indirectly of those things. As a woman, Emilia will not be invited to make one of the consort at Elizabeth's court, though that's been peopled mostly by Bassanos for decades. However, as a lute-playing woman, she may make herself a gracious addition to some noble lady's privy chamber.

This thing becomes a necessity when, after a week of agony, tended night and day by her eldest daughter, Margaret Johnson dies of the smallpox. Emilia, now seventeen, remains untouched by the pox despite her close nursing of her mother. On the sixth day as she sits by the bed there blooms in her like a dark, heavy flower the knowledge that her mother will not recover. Emilia kneels on the rush-strewn floor during one of Margaret's last lucid moments and begs and receives her blessing.

For weeks after the night Margaret breathes out her spirit in a last rattling gasp, Emilia's undone by grief. Her cousin Augustine, eldest male of the Bassano family, takes charge. The St. Botolph house is leased out. Young Angelica is sent, crying, to serve in a gentlewoman's house in Lambeth. And Emilia? She will come to Elizabeth's court, to live a nomadic existence traveling among eight royal residences and forty noblemen's houses, as an under-servant to one of the queen's women, young Lady Penelope Devereux Rich.

And so, a green grape of a girl, she rides in a cart downhill to a wharf at Thames-side, where she climbs listlessly into a flatboat. Accompanying her are a traveling trunk, a lute in a case, two oarsmen, three other random passengers, and a liveried servant of the queen. The liveried man looks at her sidelong now and then and smiles through his youthful beard. She wonders why he bothers. She feels like a clam. She wants to tell him so, but clams can't say they feel like clams. Her salt tongue has gone missing, silenced by pain for her losses. A half-smile for the youth is the most she can muster. She feels silence descend on her, closing her in.

Their barge glides through London's merry middle. She can see from the river the playhouse flags to the south, and, on both sides, the docked penny wherries. She hears the hawkers of skate and eel bawling out their prices on the wharves. Riverbirds caw and carts rumble on the bankside. This is her place, or at least it's a place she knows. But she's bound away from it, toward a world that's new, or new, anyway, to her. Whatever language they speak there, she'd stake five pounds on the hazard she doesn't know it.

2

Three months later come the Midsummer Revels at Nonsuch Palace. Knights, earls, and ladies flit under the outdoor canopies, circling the bright-burning torches like colorful silk-winged moths. Emilia's tapping her foot, watching the dancing. Her prop, the Thames-traveling lute, lies on her lap under her inert fingers. By Lady Penelope's sufferance and by Augustine Bassano's indulgence, she is sitting with the musicians, though she's not practiced enough, and not male enough, really to play with them. On a stool next to hers, her curly-haired cousin Alphonso Lanier holds his recorder lightly, with love, never missing a note. Every now and then, when a tune is familiar and simple, Augustine nods at her and she strums a few chords. This has happened twice in the past two hours.

She likes sitting in a place where she's not expected to talk. Since she came to the court, a stone has lodged in her chest. It's a spherical stone, about an inch in diameter. Sometimes it flies up to her throat and sticks there, impeding the flow of speech. This happens when the wellborn maids alongside whom she serves discuss in her presence banquets she hasn't attended, or sports like fencing or tennis of which she knows nothing. Or, even more disconcertingly, when a well-dressed man in a velvet cap pinions her with his eyes and advances toward her, his lips parted to utter some modish salutation, his smile broadening at her blushes. These gallants all smell of aniseed. They keep the fragrant stuff in buttoned pockets of their codpieces, and take it out brazenly in pinches to place it under their tongues, staring languidly at the women while they do it. She never knows where to look.

There will, at least, be no attacks of stopped throat tonight, here among the musicians, where she keeps still, half-hidden behind the violist, like the shadowed statue of a nymph, or a girl at the edge of a painting.

Her lady, Penelope Rich, whirls by the consort, her dark blonde hair silver-bound and her jeweled hands raised. Twenty pairs of men's eyes follow her, but she pays no heed, as she laughs up at the smiling face of the baron Charles Mountjoy, who clasps her waist tightly. She's in love with Mountjoy. Her boldness fascinates Emilia. Penelope's married to a midlands lord who owns an ample estate, but she insists on living at court, submitting her two children to the royal nursery for raising, rather than suffer a dull and, by her account, loveless existence with her husband in windy Warwickshire. Lady Penelope didn't choose her marriage. But she has chosen her lover, and her lover is here.

Emilia inclines a little more toward the light, then shrinks almost instantly back into shadow as tall Henry Carey, the Lord Chamberlain, dances by. She isn't quite quick enough to avoid his eye, which catches hers over his brocaded shoulder and widens with interest.

"I'll propose you a game, virgin," Augustine jests out of the corner of his mouth. "Try to tell the ladies here from the men. *Farfalla uomini!* Such butterflies! Now, Pietro."

The drummer strikes a note, and the recorders start up again together. After a half-measure, the cornets and sackbuts follow.

Study it, she tells herself determinedly. But study what? Were there a real place for her in the consort, she'd practice her instrument. She would become a lute-master — "lute-mistress" is no word — instead of simply a skilled amateur. There is and will be no such post for her, of course. So rather than scanning music or fretwork, she studies the world that, since she arrived, has unfolded before her.

It's a universe whose system's too complex for simple parsing, less a subject for natural science than a moving work of art. She watches its surface: the manner of a curtsy, the cut of a farthingale, the raising of a fan, the flash of an emerald, the arching of a penciled brow in an upturned, smiling face. *Listen.* To what? The elaborate song of quick conversation. Voices *a capella*, the pace *accelerando*, the *cadenzas* of raillery, cascading from the merry heights down to deep, mock-portentous *basso profundo*. This ceaseless court chatter may be foolish — so Augustine thinks, finding everything foolish that isn't his music — but the talk is not formless. The shape of the discourse is improvised, drawn and redrawn every moment, but a structure is there, in the intricate web of jest and reply.

She knows she, Emilia, isn't dull. She *has* listened, and after ten months at court, she's sure she could play the game as well as any young woman. And she is good, with her head resting on a pillow at night in the ladies' chamber, imagining, or with pen scratching paper in the letters she writes to her sister Angelica at Lambeth. Jesting with her family in the intervals between their numbers, she's at ease. She can spin puns like a moth spins silk. But she can't keep up otherwise, otherwhere, among the courtiers and the women of court. She wishes she could speak like Elizabeth Throckmorton, who has hooked with her beauty and wit so great a fish as the handsome sea voyager Walter Raleigh. Or like her own lady, radiant Penelope Rich, whose witty disdain inspired anguished sonnets, still read and discussed, from the all-admired knight, Sir Philip Sidney. Sidney, slain four years ago by the Spanish in Flanders, and protesting beforehand in a hundred poems of the thousand deaths meted out to him by Penelope's dark, sparkling eyes.

But Emilia can't speak like Penelope. She's not born to the manner, and shyness unstrings her vocal chords. She emits meek, feeble chirps and laughs tinnily. *Who's talking?*, she wonders, then realizes it's herself.

She leans forward again on her stool now, as the recorders bring their song to a close. Is that real cloth of gold winking through Lord Hunsdon's cut sleeve?

"*Melly!*"

Startled, she looks to her left. Augustine is gesturing with a movement of his head toward the music on the stand before her. "*L'amor Dona Ch'lo Te Porto.* You know it, yes? Come in with us in the chorus."

She plays badly. Augustine winces and blows more loudly, and Pietro rolls his eyes. She doubts they'll invite her to sit with them again. Yet none of the dancers seems distressed. A space has formed in the middle of the floor around a very young man, indeed a boy, a youth with long golden hair, who is tossing his head as he circles his partner, his left hand on his hip, his right hand raised. His face is fresh and beardless. Magnetlike, he draws the eyes of men as well as women. The lady with whom he dances looks at least as young as he, younger even than Emilia. Fifteen, perhaps. But a world of knowledge sits on her brow, and she wears her finery like one born with a right to it, moving gracefully in her emerald bracelets and blue-green sarcenet gown like some beauteous lizard, showing her skin and scales. Emilia's seen her before. She serves the queen, and is an earl's daughter, one more Elizabeth in a court strewn with Elizabeths.

She watches as the pair take one another's measure, and gasps when the young man suddenly seizes and kisses the girl's wrist, then releases it without disrupting the rhythm of their dance. "Bessie," he mouths. The girl smiles.

Emilia has stopped playing to watch, and now the song ends. The young man bows to the girl and, to her surprise, turns and bows to the consort. As he straightens he notices her, Emilia, half-shrouded by Augustine. His eye brightens with curiosity. She looks down in embarrassment, then looks up to find him gone, hidden in the gallimaufry of colored sleeves and skirts and head-dressings and hose.

Well. She has sowed some slight mystery. She's accomplished in that, at least.

She's aware she's a puzzle to most of the bright folk who people the palaces. Likely each pair of women whispering behind a jeweled fan is assessing her. *What's she? A Bassano? What's that? Ah, the consort.* Augustine and his fellows laugh about it one day and grumble about it the next, the fact that the denizens of the court world are never sure what to call or how to address the musicians. "We are the invisible gentlemen," Augustine says when alone with his consort. "We come closer than nine-tenths of the nobles to the body of the reigning monarch. That should count for something, in a country where two barons once fought for the post of Groom of the Stool." Laughter and nods. His point is well taken, among players and musicians packing props and instruments alone in a banqueting hall. Still, Emilia knows they *are* invisible, unseen though seen. The minstrels don't pile off barges lugging their instruments, but fly in magically from some otherworld of fairies and elves.

What, then, to call a girl who has come to court to fill a place little higher than a chambermaid's, but who bears in her veins Bassano blood?

Most find it best to walk blindly by her, and not call her anything at all.

"What is it about an un-blue eye, Emilia?" Lady Penelope asks her the next evening, from a cushioned seat in her chambers. Penelope's voice is low and soft. Her eyes, now glistening with drops, are even darker than Emilia's. *In color black why wrapped she beams so bright?,* Philip Sidney wrote.

Penelope picks up a small brush and begins applying white powder next to the rosy spots of fuchus on her cheeks. "An eye that is black. It drives some Englishmen mad for possession." Penelope's hair is wound into a complicated pile of braids pinned tightly to the back of her head. Emilia herself has arranged the tresses this morning. "I think it has to do with Armada fever," Penelope adds. "Could you bring me the pencil, there?"

Emilia follows her mistress's gesture and sees a small, sharpened stick of kohl at the corner of the cosmetics table. The kohl is lying on a torn printed woodcut, and she picks up both woodcut and pencil. "What is this etching, lady?" she asks, handing the pencil to Penelope.

"Ah, something clever. Look." Kohl in one hand, Penelope turns from the mirror, taps the paper, and asks, "What do you see? A young girl or a hag?"

Emilia studies the drawing closely. At first she sees nothing. Then Penelope, running a slim and nail-painted forefinger down some lines of the woodcut, shows her that from one angle the picture yields the silhouette of a maiden, while from another it shows the brooding profile of an old woman. "It caught Nancy de Vere's eye in her husband's book of emblems, and she tore it out."

Shameless to tear a book, Emilia almost says, but stops her tongue. Nancy de Vere is an earl's wife. Penelope might not welcome a servant's mockery of a woman whose standing at court is on a footing equal to hers. Before replacing the woodcut on the table Emilia glances at it once more. Though crude, it's clever, as Penelope said.

"You may have it if you like."

"Thank you, milady," says Emilia. She folds the paper and hides it in her placket.

"Nancy grew tedious with it." Penelope leans close to the glass, outlining the corner of her right eye, pulling her skin to the side to tighten it and raise the eyelashes, as Emilia watches with interest. "Nancy! Testing gentlemen with the thing was her only pastime for a fortnight."

"Testing? How could they pass?

The lady shrugs. "I know not. Half the gallants saw one thing and half saw the other. The truly obtuse saw neither." Penelope has forgotten that her maidservant, by this odd reckoning, would number among the obtuse. "Men see what they desire or what they fear. And this, *this* is the point!" Penelope suddenly points her pencil aloft like a torch or a sword, and widens her eyes like a clown's in an interlude. "The Spanish Armada! You have hit it!"

"*I* have?" Emilia says, smiling. "What can you mean, my lady antic?"

"The answer to my question. Why do some Englishmen chase dark eyes? Because what is feared is also desired. Instance? Englishmen want to capture Spaniards. Failing that, they'll pursue women who look Spanish."

"Ah! But the English *have* trounced the Spaniards, not two months ago."

"O, but the Spaniards are elusive. They are out there still, sailing in their last boats, with their black eyes of menace and their olive skins." Penelope makes a scary face in the mirror, and Emilia laughs.

She gets an idea. She visits the castle kitchens, where she finds in a pantry a mortar, a pestle, and some sheets of dried cinnamon paste. She takes all these things back to her room, and stows the tools and the spice in her smallest trunk. She locks the trunk and hangs its key from her neck by a cord. At her first opportunity, on a night when Penelope is with Mountjoy and the maid with whom she shares a room is abed God knows where, she begins her experiments. These continue for weeks.

To convincingly color her skin with cinnamon dust takes only a few combinations. It is harder to darken her hair. She purchases powders and potions from the apothecaries and clothiers who frequent the gates of the palaces, and tries a variety of washes, some of them created to dye clothing. One or two of the mixtures make her head stink, and, mortified, she hangs back from the courtiers and other waiting women in humiliation until the smell fades. At last she arrives at an odorless watered inkwash customarily used for the blacking of netherstocks. She wears a torn, cast-off pair of Penelope's gloves to apply it. The wash doesn't fade, and she need only doctor the roots each six weeks. Like the other ladies of the various chambers, she's consistently kept her hair pinned and capped in company, and none could definitely swear, when the alteration's complete, that Emilia Bassano has changed its color. It wouldn't be strange to have done so, though it would be odd to have dyed it black.

Penelope sees what she's doing, but says nothing. She only touches Emilia's cheek now and then, less in affection than in sly curiosity. She looks at the point of her finger afterwards, and half-smiles.

When the court is next visited by booksellers, Emilia buys a small volume of Italian phrases designed for the Continental traveler.

Her silence, given color, is restful now. By the gold chain fastened to her belt, she can lift a fan to the bridge of her nose, hiding her face and revealing only a smooth, golden forehead and eyes which belladonna has made soft and fathomless. She's become a picture of herself. She is Italian, and short phrases more than suffice. *Ché bello!* How beautiful! *Mi perdoni.* Forgive me. *Non capisco.* I don't understand.

After one frightening interchange with a diplomat fluent in five languages, she learns to avoid the more well-traveled courtiers. For the most part, when she's not performing duties for Penelope, she keeps to her books, and to herself.

3

A palace is its own town. When the queen is in residence, each royal place, Greenwich or Whitehall or Nonsuch, is peopled with citizens of every rank, from lords in their velvet apartments to armorers and blacksmiths who lodge by their outlying forges, from satin-skirted women who hold the queen's train to pantlers and wenches keeling rusty pots by the wells of kitchen gardens. Emilia's business with laundry women and bookmen, with sellers of ink and cosmeticians, is helping familiarize her with these palaces' more secret regions, but she is still learning which halls to step in, what corners to avoid absolutely, what places to visit only when wearing a veil. The tangled passageways are like labyrinthine streets. Some corners harbor night watchers.

One evening, soon after her Italian metamorphosis, she is carrying towels to Penelope's chamber at Whitehall when she hears footfalls in the passage behind her. Before she can turn she is turned involuntarily and spun to the wall. Hands, dry as snakeskin but strong as steel, pin her and raise her skirts. She tries to push forward, but a velvet knee pushes her back. It's dark, a space in the hall well between the lit torches that sputter in their sconces, and she cannot even see the looming face that menaces her. A hand has pushed her way into her mouth. She bites it and tries to scream, but the hand stays in place, gagging her until the airlessness is worse than the pain she now feels below. She sees flashing spots, feels herself going limp, prays frantically to a God who is elsewhere. And then, just as she thinks she will suffocate, it's over. The man steps away from her, freeing her mouth. Air rushes back into her lungs. She falls to her knees, gasping, feeling sticky blood on her inner thighs and a red pain in a place so secret, so far inside, she didn't know it existed. *Damned fool!*, she curses herself, as though it's her fault. Her hands are still gripping the gold-stitched towels.

"*Pig!*" she tries to cry, but she can only say "*Puh! Puh!*"

He looms there, a tall shadow. Why won't he go? Now he is bending toward her, gripping her elbow, trying to help her stand, whispering "milady," as though he thinks himself chivalrous. She strikes at him, but he holds her off at arm's length, saying, ridiculously, "I love you, my beauty. *Ti amo,* by God."

At once, hearing him speak aloud, she knows his voice, and thinks, *Of course. Naturalmente.* She has heard this great man murmuring Italian phrases in her wake more than once as she and a bevy of women passed knots of privy councilmen in this or that palace garden, men who stand with casual grace in their silks, testing the weather of the day as they test each other's weather, weighing the chances of international tempests, domestic storms. *Bella donna. Molto bella.* He is that one. Henry Carey, Lord Hunsdon. The Lord Chamberlain, of the cloth of gold that peeps through his sleeves of slashed scarlet.

She breaks from him and stumbles painfully down the passage. Her room is empty, and the ewer by the washbasin is full. Good. She throws the towels helter-skelter on the bed, locks the door, places the basin on the floor, and, with shaking hands, pours water into its bowl. Then she squats painfully and scrubs herself for half an hour, spasmodically, almost ritually, trying to get clean.

Lady Penelope pales under her paint of rosy fuchus. She has been applying the color with two fingers, but stops to embrace Emilia, leaving a spot of red on the white towels Emilia has arrived holding and, again, cannot seem to put down.

"That one is a bastard, a knave, and a rogue," Penelope says fiercely. "When no one is looking, he's a rampaging bear. I say it though he is my kinsman. The family has stories. I grew up hearing them. You are not the first, I can tell you. And even when he was a child he took whatever he wanted — toys, clothes, any sort of food. A neighbor's pony. He put things back when he tired of them, usually broken or spoiled. Mary Boleyn indulged his disposition because, she said, he was like his father in everything; couldn't be gainsaid. And then she would leave the rest to guess which father she meant. She was a little proud of it, my grandmother said. Nay, more than a little."

"Which father?" Emilia dully repeats.

Penelope looks hard at her. "You have never heard the story?"

"I . . . ."

"But you know he's the son of Mary Boleyn. And that Mary Boleyn was the sister of the queen's mother, Anne."

Emilia nods. Against the towels her knuckles are a slightly darker white.

The lady drops her voice. "Do you also know that before Anne, and some say even after, Mary Boleyn was a mistress of the old king? Not by her own will, but by the king's. When Anne was pregnant, he called on Mary to fill his bed." Penelope's hands are still on Emilia's shoulders. Her grip has tightened and her gaze has sharpened.

"Yes, no, I . . . Oh."

Releasing Emilia, Penelope rises, opens the door, and looks down the hallway to right and left. She closes the door firmly and returns to her stool before the mirror, but this time puts her back to the mirror. Picking up a small painting brush, she waves it like a sword or a pedagogue's birch pointer, leaning toward her trembling servant. "Most people believe Lord Hunsdon is Henry the Eighth's son," she says in a low tone. "The king married Mary off to a Carey when she got royally pregnant. Then she gave birth to a future Lord Chamberlain. That man is a Tudor! And he's as canny as his kinswoman, the queen." She sits back now, then swivels to look in her mirror. Instinctively, she raises the brush to her face and briefly doctors her eye-paint. "The fox is much craftier than his mother Mary was. He knows not to flaunt his blood. Even when Elizabeth's sister, the papist queen, died, and for a week or two no one knew which way the wind would blow, your Henry Carey—"

"*My* Henry Carey?"

"Well. *He* stood back to see what would happen." Penelope drops her brush and carefully caps the open pot of fuchus. "He watched everyone who stood for anyone but Elizabeth lose his head, while he kept his. Now he's well content merely to be an *important man*." She says the words scornfully. "But she keeps him close, the queen does. I think she hoped he'd be killed in battle when she sent him to the north twenty years ago, to quell the rebellion there, but instead he brought back some Scottish heads for her perusal, like a warning. He did!" she says to Emilia's mirrored face of disbelief, shaking a rose-tipped finger at Emilia's reflection. "Heads in a bag. He's a savage under his silks. So she made him a privy councilman, and it's all honey sweetness between them now. She knows he's her father's by-blow, and he knows she knows." She selects another small brush from an array of brushes, and returns fully to her painting. "And so, one rapist begets another." Her voice, adding this conclusion, is strangely soft. "But what can be done?"

Emilia has stopped kneading the towels, but she is still shaking. *Dismiss me*, she wants to say. *Send me home.* But to where? The house in St. Botolph is leased to another. Her sister Angelica's in lowly service in Lambeth. Emilia's next closest relations are here, at court, playing recorders and lutes and drums and cornets for the pleasure of the queen. What is home?

Penelope Rich regards her own face. She touches an eyebrow. "It's the eyes," she murmurs. "Your eyes. Like mine. They put some men beside themselves."

Emilia draws herself straighter. "Lady, at least your gallant poet Sidney respected your chastity."

"Ha! This is what fools think, because of a few agonies set down in rhyme. 'Respected' is not the word I would –" She stops, seeing, in the mirror, Emilia's trembling lip. Laying down her paintbrush, she turns back and grasps her servant's hands. "Those poems were right, after all. I *am* a heartless statue. To *think* what you have just endured, and I must prattle! But listen to me. You are not betrothed. Do you love anyone? Are you in love?"

"I am not, but, lady —"

Penelope grips her hands more tightly. "Believe me when I tell you that nothing can be done about this. As I said, you are not the first. The queen knows about Lord Hunsdon, and looks away."

"Why does she so?"

"Because she fears him. It's as I said. He's her half-brother, and everyone knows it. Long ago, there was a contract forged between the royal pair of them, spoken or unspoken, I know not. But ever since, he has what he wants at court. Has it heedlessly. And yet . . . ." She puts her hands in her lap and looks keenly at Emilia. "You say, after, he tried to help you to rise? And said *ti amo?*"

Emilia dabs her eyes with her sleeve. "I did not think him courteous for that."

"Of course not. He's a bastard, I have said, in manners as well as in fact. It is only that . . ." She glances again at her own eyes in the glass. "I have seen this . . . *mode* of passion before. Perhaps it's nothing more than lust, after all. But I think he believes himself in love with you. You must consider that."

Emilia makes a face. "He's old."

"Good. Likely he'll die. Before then — and even after — why shouldn't you reap the harvest of his amorous dotage?"

"*What?*"

"Too poetic? Forgive me. By harvest I mean benefits."

"If the benefits is to be waylaid in hallways –"

"This is a man who can choose from many women."

"Would he would choose someone else, lady! And he is new married."

Lady Penelope makes a sound of contempt. "Yes, and to a young wife, to boot, a mere decade older than you. *My* age. But it's no love match. A matter of families, like the marriage I was thrown into. You, he wants for his mistress. The office may not be onerous. Even if you hate him, you should agree." She holds up a hand to stop what she imagines is Emilia's objection. "Love can wait."

"Who would love another man's whore?"

"Another man's *mistress.*"

"What is the dif—" Emilia stops herself, seeing a warning light kindle in Lady Penelope's deep brown eyes.

"There is a very great difference, Emilia. A chambermaid may be a whore. But a lady with a thousand pounds a year? Anyone may love such a lady. And so, if it's love you want, make yourself ready for it. Better to be a definite woman than a green girl who knows nothing, and says nothing."

So. The lady has noticed her shyness, and finds it a flaw, as Emilia herself does. Emilia's natural color rises to her cheeks.

Lady Penelope doesn't notice her blush. She is opening the top drawer of her table, rearranging the boxes and tins within. "Marry, how do you think *I* learned to come out from behind a pearl fan? To be something more than the beauteous portrait of a maid? Not from being paraded about in sonnets. To be a . . . *person* takes some practice, no matter how you get it." She speaks with a mixture of pride and disdain. She stares at herself hard in the mirror, then suddenly slaps her own cheek. "Ha! *There's* color." She picks up a brush again, and this time dips it in vermilion paste. She begins on her lip. "Henry Carey is nothing to laugh at. He's sixty-five, but a hale sixty-five, and he's a soldier, first and foremost. A brutal one."

"I know to my cost, lady."

"He will not stop ambushing you, in any event, and if you protest, nothing will come of it. You'll be called a whore and turned out into the road. On the other hand, if you play his game a little —"

"How can I play it a *little?*"

"Let him bespeak rooms for you, or even a house. Let him buy you velvet gowns and a cockatoo."

"I do not want a cock —"

"A lapdog, then. Anything! The Lord Chamberlain is besotted with your Italianness. Those accents you affect have done their work better than you —"

"Milady!" Her face burns, and the sore place in her center radiates pain through her abdomen every time she shifts her position, which, in her agitation, she does frequently. She wants to soak in a tub. She wants to be far away from here, back in St. Botolph, in the house that is no longer hers. She wants her mother. She should not have interrupted her ladyship, she knows, but anger, shock, and despair well up in her throat and overwhelm restraint. "Lady, I *cannot* speak quick, as you do. I am no lover of affectation, but if it is thought that I come from Italy — less is expected of me, in that way." Her cheeks are flaming. She looks down. "I am allowed to be quiet. Or to think before I speak."

Lady Penelope meets Emilia's eyes in the glass. Her expression is skeptical, but amused. At last she speaks again. "Emilia. I give you the best counsel you will receive in this matter. You've read twelve romances where violated virgins protest to the king and the culprits get their come-uppances. But this is the palace of Whitehall. In my three years here I've not see any female but the queen come off well by pointing fingers and bel-lowing accusations. And the queen, you must know, is a goddess."

Emilia buries her fingers in the towels, looking down at the cloths' white fullness scarred with one angry streak of vermilion. Penelope speaks true, and Emilia knows it. Queen Elizabeth's storms are hail and tempest and the eruptions of Vesuvius. Elizabeth is entitled to say what-ever she wants, at whatever volume.

"You, my sweet, are a mere woman," Penelope goes on. "And you've eaten of the tree."

She looks up frowning. "*I* have not —"

"Tomorrow he'll be sending you gifts of contrition, a pair of embroi-dered sleeves, a packet of sweets, tra la. Receive them. Let him redeem himself. Grant him some feigned affection. 'Twill be easy enough. In a week he'll be your slave, for a time. Long enough for your position at court to be assured. He can do more for you than I can. Be a mistress. It's com-mon enough here, and the world cares not." Lady Penelope says all this while gradually lowering her voice's pitch, and at her last statement her voice sours a little. As she speaks she is spreading oil of cloves over her cheeks, her red and white, smoothing the same patch of skin over and over, almost as ritualistically as Emilia scrubbed her own blood from her thighs before seeking refuge in her lady's chamber. Emilia watches, entranced in spite of herself and her pain, as Penelope picks up a third brush and, for a final layer, dips its soft bristles into a small bowl of crushed pearl. This garnish will make her face shine in torchlight like a goddess's. Still painting, the lady, also transfixed by her image, repeats her incantation in a voice low and fierce. "Cares *not*. Cares *not*. Cares *not*."

4

Castoreum, rue, and nenuphar, ground and mixed with the roots of lilies. Nenuphar is rare, but when it cannot be found, blanched almonds will serve, and there are always plenty of those in the kitchen stores. Margery Braithwaite, a brisk palace midwife who also assists the cooks, pockets handfuls of the stored almonds for a fee, or, when she can, steals them outright, and brings them to this or that lady's chamber according to demand. She runs a tidy business, every week of the year.

It is Margery, not Lady Penelope, whose advice Emilia seeks in this bitter business of child prevention. Margery is the counselor of choice to the queen's ladies, who know how it enrages the queen when their unmarried bellies swell. As for Lady Penelope, she grants counsel freely to Emilia, but she lacks the unmarried women's concerns, and knows little of their preventatives. Twice a mother by her hated husband, she admits to all who ask that she would welcome another child, one fathered by the love of her heart, the twin of her soul, the Baron Charles Blount. Emilia tells Penelope she is sure Blount will get one. She has, after all, read in Galen, the great Greek philosopher and physician, that love speeds pro-generation, while, on the other hand, a woman's body grows cold and refuses to conceive when she is gripped by anger or fear, as in cases of brutal ravishment. Penelope responds to this piece of foolishness with a hearty laugh. "I've some news for old Galen," she says.

Emilia decides to be careful.

When it comes to his personal schedule, Henry Carey maintains a soldierly discipline for which she soon becomes grateful. He visits her only on Wednesdays, unless he is absent then on business of state. So she does not need to bother with the pessaries every day. This is well, because the ground castoreum produces an itch which is only partly soothed by the baths in which she immerses herself straightaway upon Carey's departures, lowering herself into a copper tub filled with water mixed with lentil juice, vinegar, and sengren (also purchased, with silver, from Margery). Mandrake and henbane are also proposed in the herbal Lady Penelope has lent Emilia, the little book whose pages she avidly turns, noting not only these recipes, but others which promise to produce glistening nails, damask skin, and a face that mocks portraiture. Emilia has acquired vials of opium and ground mandrake, but is a little afraid to use them: the mandrake because it is, puzzlingly, recommended as both a facilitator and a preventer of pregnancy, in two different parts of the herbal, and the henbane because she can't quite bring herself to push something inside her that is known to cause the death of chickens.

She hates Carey with a pure, non-negotiable hatred, unalloyed by any gratitude for the luxurious rooms he secures for her at the palace, for the coat of arms suddenly granted the Bassanos, for the sapphire earrings in her jewelry box and the satin gowns in her wardrobe, or the gallantry with which he publicly acknowledges her, now "Lady Emilia," at court. Or the time she enjoys, now she's released from most of her earlier duties, to read and to write; to pen the satirical descriptions of court characters that make the musicians laugh. She is amazed, but not flattered, by the tiny portrait painted of her by Nicholas Hilliard, the famed miniaturist, whom Carey commissions for the work. The three-inch oval shows a dark-haired, unsmiling face clamped between two enormous, puffed butterfly wings of hair above and a stiff neck-ruff below, like a pinned insect. Hunsdon keeps the picture hidden in his chamber, which she thinks is for the best. *It's a phantom,* she thinks. *And with him, so am I.* She feels hollow, as though she is all outside.

But yes, there are benefits. She's darkly amused by the regard and admiration that shine forth on her now from the eyes of the men, young and old, who surround Henry Carey, Lord Hunsdon — men who wasted little time on her tongue-tied self before Hunsdon raised her status. Lady Penelope was right. For Hunsdon her heart is sour ice, but he has brought her a rich part to play, has taken her from darkness into the main light of day. They fill her with contempt, these male courtlings who give her speaking looks only because Hunsdon acknowledges her, but she prefers their calculated regard to her former invisibility. And there is one among them who seems genuine and unaffected in his courtesy; who was, in fact, now that she thinks on it, courteous to her well before her ennoblement. The young, golden-haired earl of Southampton, Henry Wriothesley, gives her on their encounters the same look of interest he shot her way when he first saw her two or three years ago, cowering in the shadow of her cousin Augustine during Midsummer Revels at Nonsuch. This is the young, golden-haired earl of Southampton, who is still a mere teenager. His frankly appreciative expression mixes ardor with innocence. *I like you*, it says, *because beauty likes beauty, and because I like everyone.*

The women of court have passed from ignoring to slighting her, a fine but discernible difference. Is this progress? She can't be sure, not knowing just where she is going. Still, having known small friendliness from these women before, she's armored against their disdain. It's not, anyway, universal. There is middle-aged Margaret, Countess of Cumberland, who will hear no gossip and is sweet to all. Emilia has Penelope still, and one day Queen Elizabeth, passing her curtsying form in an antechamber, greets her by name, almost kindly. Hunsdon keeps his wife Anne in Hertfordshire, outraged, Emilia hears, and fuming at the lack of respect accorded her. Henry's first wife, twelve years dead, gave him more than enough heirs, two sons now grown. But the young Anne lacks children; is occasionally pregnant, and always miscarrying. Young Anne Morgan entered into the match with Hunsdon expecting all sorts of honors that did not accrue: a position with the queen, a high place at court. The father who arranged the marriage several years ago has died, and Anne's mother is now busy petitioning her sons for portions of his estate for herself. No one but Anne Morgan seems concerned for Anne Morgan's interests. Emilia has stolen what was rightfully hers. Anne showers her husband with letters of aggrieved complaint.

Emilia hears all this not from Henry Carey but from Margery, who served Anne Morgan's family exclusively before an expansion in ranks among Elizabeth's serving women increased the value of Margery's various services at court. Margery is loyal only to her accounts. Now she moves between Hertfordshire and London like a shuttlecock, as busy facilitating Lady Anne's pregnancies as she is preventing Emilia's. Freely she reports the lady's distresses. Emilia feels, on occasion, dull pinches of guilt when she thinks of Lady Anne Morgan Carey's frustrations, but the remorse is as shadowy and remote as the lady herself. She, Emilia, can imagine nothing better than to be sovereign of her own time at the lovely country manor Margery describes in detail, to be mistress of her oak-shaded walks, with nothing to do but read and write, and another woman to perform for her the labors of a marriage bed shared with a *senex*, albeit a vigorous *senex*.

I work for Lady Anne as well as for Lord Hunsdon, she thinks, with slight bitterness. *She should send me money, too.* As for the rights imparted by marriage — well, what was marriage, after all, but a ritual enslavement for females? So her mother always told Emilia and Angelica, while fondly patting Baptista's bald head as he sat scribbling musical notes or carving wood for a new recorder. *And that is why I never married you, my sweet*, Margaret would add. So it is, so it has long been, for many of the musical Bassanos, awash in their own borderless world of notes and melody. They maintain casual arrangements with their effective spouses, and have to be urged by friends to set down bequests in contracts, lest they leave what is due by natural right to their heirs and mates undesignated, to be seized by the queen. Not one of Emilia's male relatives, even old cousin Augustine, sees a thing of value lost by her improper jointure with Henry Carey, Lord Hunsdon. What they see are their new coat of arms in the heralds' books and her pearls and sarcenet. Both of these sights please them. When she appears glittering before them in a palace banquet hall, they congratulate her with their eyes, wink, and go on playing.

For all that they disgust her, she is gratified by their blessing.

Her hair grows darker still. She increases the proportion of ink to water in the inkwash. Thank God Hunsdon does not speak Italian. Does he know she had a mother named Johnson, and was born not ten miles from Whitehall palace? He wouldn't want to know, and anyway, how would he? All her invisible relatives at court play some version of the Italian game, though half of them really speak nothing but English, and the rest an Italian so bastardized it would never be understood outside the family. They are not likely to disclose details about her upbringing. Hunsdon, of course, sees what he wants to see: a dark beauty of southern climes, to whom he can write poems in imitation of Petrarch. Their conversation is thus agreeably limited. To his Petrarch, it is not difficult for Emilia to play the beautiful Laura. Distant. In fact, dead. Her performance in his bed is just that: a part played in a chamber, which makes possible the part she now plays in the world. With this in her mind, she finds that he does not repel her.

But she also finds that the pessaries aren't infallible.

5

"Mandrake, henbane, and rue," Margery says, when Emilia tells her. Her plump face is unperturbed. This has happened before. "No more quailing from the henbane."

"Quailing? Is this a pun, Margery?" She manages a smile. "It's a fowl one."

"What do you mean? Into the bath with you. You'll drink some, to boot. It will flush out the babe."

Emilia winces. "No."

Margery drops the pan of water she is carrying. It lands on a table-top and splashes. "Will you be stubborn? He cannot marry you. And the longer you wait . . . ."

Tears fill Emilia's eyes, but still, she shakes her head. "I cannot."

"Then why did you ask me here, to your rooms? For word-play?"

"I know not," Emilia whispers. She has no remarks to make.

Margery gives her a hard look. Then she waves a hand at the Turkey rug that hangs from the wall, at the tapestry with its Eden scene, at the rose-colored gown Emilia has left draped over a wooden-backed chair. "Into the road with you," she says. "You may bid farewell to all this."

"He won't put you in the road," says Lady Penelope, unplaiting her own hair, then running her fingers through its shimmering length. "*I* won't permit it. But what will you tell him?"

"That I need someone to play a husband's part."

The lady gives a harsh laugh. "He'll say he's been doing that." She looks curiously at Emilia. "The henbane won't kill you, you know. You're not a chicken."

"Nor is the child, and it's meant to kill *it*."

"*It*'s much more like a chicken than you are. Are you certain you won't?"

Emilia stares intently at the silk roses on the tips of her shoes. Then she looks up. "Margery called it a babe. She said, 'Flush out the babe'."

"Ah." Lady Penelope studies both their faces in the mirror as Emilia rises to begin combing her dark gold tresses. "Do you know, I nearly killed my first son."

"What?" Emilia stops combing, her hand suspended inches above Penelope's head.

"What else can I call it but killing, now that he's a lad? My husband is a cold knave who'd a mistress when he married me. She's quiet. He dislikes *talkative women*. When I raised my voice to him once, in the first month of our marriage, he struck me over the mouth. When, a month later, I found I was with child, I locked myself in my chamber and screamed. I knew a baby would ruin any chance of annulment. So I swallowed a compound of rue and — lord, I don't remember what. Something I found in that herbal."

Emilia slowly resumes combing. "And?"

"It ran out of both ends of me for two days, and the boy was born seven months later. The healthiest child I've ever seen." She beams. "Whene'er the lines on my face creep —"

"You are twenty-eight. You have no creeping lines."

"Because I paint them with tincture of onyx! You've seen me do it. I *need* to do it. I would despair, but then, I regard the boy. Both of the boys, now. They *glow*. What must we look like to such children? Hags?"

Emilia laughs. "Not hags. Like mothers. Your children do not mind wrinkles."

"No more should we, when we are old. Ouch!"

"A knot, lady."

Their eyes meet, smiling, in the mirror. Lady Penelope says, "I will speak to the queen. You will be granted your toy husband. And then you will have your real child."

There comes the necessary marriage, the swearing of eternal fidelity, a ceremony made in haste, the banns waived by ecclesiastical permission issued at the behest of the notable Henry Carey. Emilia pins up her ink-darkened hair. She stands, promises, and is promised to. Neither she nor her cousin Alphonso consider themselves hypocrites. They are joined already by a family bond, and neither has had any reason in life to link formal marriage with the governing passions of life. Alone with her, he calls her "coz." For each of them, the marital vows are words that, like some poetry, mean something other than their literal sense. The promise beneath their promises is a pledge. They will give each other a face to wear.

The day after her wedding a gift arrives at her door, brought by a page in Hunsdon's maroon livery. "A wedding present from Lord Hunsdon," the boy explains, and bows. "Give you good day." As he patters down the passage, she unwraps the silver-papered parcel. Inside is the Hilliard miniature and a pair of velvet pearl-sewn shoes. Is there a letter, a message of good wishes? No. Nothing. What underling did he send to buy the slippers? In a fit of disgust, she walks quickly down a palace passageway and throws them from a corner window, down, down, into a low garbage ditch.

"You threw *what?*" Alphonso says that evening when she tells him. "*Pearls* in the *garbage?* Ill-bethought, Melly. You'd not have done so had I been here."

"You weren't here."

"And won't be, in a moment. I'm for the Bel Savage Inn. There's a torchlight play. Would you give me another angel, angel?"

Alphonso flows out through the doorway in a wash of perfume, rattling his coin. She sits broodingly for a quarter of an hour. Then she rises and swathes her head and face with a veil. She slips out a rear entrance of the palace with a torch and, a holding the veil to her nose, retrieves the slippers from the top of the ditch-pile. No one sees her leave or reenter the private apartment she's been given to share with her new husband. A little water clears the shoes of their stains. She stores them in a wardrobe, for future use or sale.

The pregnancy is bad. Emilia is bedridden for much of it, nauseated for almost all of it. It's no better when she rests than when she doesn't, so she forces herself to walk to keep her blood flowing, and ignores the titters and whispers of courtiers she passes in the hallways and on garden paths. *Being with child, as you see, she was for color married to a minstrel.*

When her day comes, Alphonso is miles away, attending the queen with the rest of the consort at Richmond Palace. Emilia is alone, save for Margery. She labors twelve hours in delivery, loses blood, and is fed opium. After that, the pain grows less sharp-edged. She seems to float above herself, to watch, from the ceiling, her own pale face as Margery holds something to her nose. "Mandrake," Margery murmurs. "*This* will bring him." At once she is back in her head. Then her brain begins to spin. She closes her eyes. As though in a dream she hears Margery say something to a girl who's arrived with fresh towels to stanch the afterbirth, when it finally comes. The two are far away, standing at the foot of the great carven bed that was Penelope's wedding gift to her. How long have those women been talking? Why won't the baby come? Her dizziness increases, and there's a rushing in her ears. Through it she hears Margery's hurried direction — *To the kitchens, the far pantry, beyond the barrels of millet. A knife, a bowl, and three cloves of garlic* — and the closing of a door. And then there's a sudden slide, a helpless tumbling into a darkness too black for any thought, too thick to be pierced by even a dream of a baby's cry.

She wakes to a room filled with grey daylight. Alphonso dozes in a chair by the bed.

"Alphonso," she tries to murmur, but she can emit only a formless sound.

He starts, and his eyes fly open. "By God. Emilia! You live. You barely breathed! Margery thought . . . ." He grasps her hand. "But I am glad, coz, so glad, even . . . ." His smile is wan and tired.

The room is entirely quiet. She sees, in his eyes, the thing he does not want to say.

"Where," she asks, "have they buried him?"

It's autumn before she's herself again, or what looks like herself, or what looks like the self she's created. She sits at her stool, aproned like an alchemist, and regards her face in the mirror. She spreads water of cloves evenly over her nose, cheeks, forehead, chin, and neck, then rubs the liquid gently into her skin. Next comes the darkening dust, which she now keeps in a cedar box carved inside and out with images of the Madonna and Child. This box, a gift from Alphonso during her pregnancy, was to have served as a wish-holder for mother and son, to be filled over the years with birthday gifts of silver, snippets of hair, anniversary rings, and other keepsakes. As it happens, it is perfect for cosmetics.

After applying the face-dust, she lines her eyes with a kohl crayon, then, with a thinner pencil, attends to her brows. The portrait complete, she wraps her tools and powders and pastes and washes and vials in rags and silk napkins and restores them to her trunk. She locks the small chest, then drops the key down her bodice. She's replaced the simple cord that first held the key with a gold chain.

She sits down lightly on the bed, lifts her grey satin gown, and bends to roll up her stockings. These are dark crimson, the gift of Lady Margaret, Countess of Cumberland, who took it on herself to give each of the married musicians' wives a pair this past New Year's. *Thank you, Lady Margaret.* Rising, Emilia retrieves her pearl slippers from the wardrobe, and steps redly into them. She belts on her purse, and wraps herself in her cloak.

A page knocks on her door, and she gives over her trunks. Only one more thing to do. From a drawer she takes a sheaf of poems written her by Lord Hunsdon, what seems an eternity past, when he first sought her as his mistress. It is almost mid-morning, when Hunsdon, she knows, will pass through the cloistered walk next to a side courtyard, on his way to meet with queen's council. She goes out.

From around a corner she hears his step. She is waiting. Her hands are shaking, so anxious are they to divest themselves of these half-plagiarized lines, the usual courtier's mish-mash, trite numbers stuffed with tired conceits he thought fine inventions. *Dark beauty of the south, / With rose lips stop my mouth.* He's a soldier, not a writer, and these poems prove it. But that is not what galls her. Had the lines been composed with love, rather than lustful fantasy; had they been written to *her,* and not to a dream . . . But they weren't. And so she is avid to purge her life of these, his last traces. *You did not put my name in them,* she will say. *Most economical! You may bestow them on the next lass you menace in a dark hallway.*

He appears. She steps forward, opening her lips. But Lord Hunsdon doesn't acknowledge her or even turn his face. He continues his brisk walk to council as though she's not there. He's straight as a cannon's ramrod, too important to look to the left or the right. *I come, my queen!*

She throws the poems, so-called, at his vanishing back, then watches as they flutter like moths and settle on the stone floor of the passageway. She stares at the scrawled papers for a moment, wondering whether she might somehow, someday, turn a profit with them. *No,* she concludes. The verses are not pearls, and besides, they're unsigned.

As she decides this, a gust of cold wind picks up the pages and sends them in various directions, down the passageway, through the air. She watches them vanish like fall leaves. Then she goes back inside for her traveling trunks.

6

E milia sits on the marble bench in the middle of the garden maze, turning the pages of her tiny octavo volume of philosophical aphorisms. To do so isn't easy, blocked as her fingers are by fleece-lined leather gloves, but if she took them off her hands would freeze. The dark season of Advent has dawned, and today is especially damp and chill. Her toes are already half-numb inside her ill-chosen bright velvet slippers, the ones sewn with the tiny seed pearls, the pair she rescued from the garbage-filled palace ditch.

Gradually she becomes aware of voices, and stops reading to listen. Two men are walking the green beyond the hedges.

"Let's in!" calls one, as clear as a Christmas bell. "In here!"

She stiffens. It's her host, Henry Wriothesley, the young lord of this manor. His footfalls grow louder. He's entering the maze, along with a companion. She listens tensely for several long minutes as their quick voices and crunching steps move closer, then fade, then approach again, coming once very near her, the snorts of laughter and the sounds of boots hitting the earth no more than two yards away. She can't distinguish their words, but the general murmur pours over and into her ears, a babble and a hum, a river of dialogue, its twin currents now parallel, now mingled, now briefly stalling in eddying pools of laughter.

Her nerves are as taut as a rabbit's. She knits her brow, trying to hear more, even as she works to devise some greeting to offer the men should they reach the maze's center and find her sitting darkly there. *Buongiorno, signori.* And after that, what? Nervously she fingers the small key that dangles from her gold neck-chain.

Henry's voice rings again, at the closest range yet. He says, "My dear old tutor is translating him into English."

She stares blankly at the page before her. *Nothing that is human is foreign to me, quoth Montaigne.* She sees out of the corner of her eye the gap in the hedge which opens her haven to the bent green passageways of the maze. Henry is the Earl of Southampton. He owns the estate. Has he not penetrated this evergreen puzzle before?

"Ho! Over here," the earl says now, some ten paces to her left. "I . . . ah . . . think. No. Yes." Two pairs of boots tread the earth on the other side of the single hedge now dividing her from these English Jasons. "Or, no, by God's sonties! Not. *This* way."

She poses, holding her book with one hand, keeping the other curled in her lap. She braces her body and arranges her face in a Mona Lisa smile.

But the pair don't appear. Several heartbeats later she hears, amid laughter, from a little farther off, Henry's companion coarsely exclaim, "Frot this folly!" There come a crash of branches, some doglike yelps, and a thud. The same fellow yells, "Plague on it! Tore my hose to shreds."

"And you tore my hedge!" Henry shouts. "Be sure, hireling, you'll have a lighter purse for your presence this week."

"My presence or my presents? Which?"

"Witch? I?"

"Which eye? The right one."

"That's I. But I, a witch? *You* have the witch eye."

"Aroint thee!"

Both men are laughing so hard they can barely talk. Some alteration in their timbre and volume confirms they've entered the open air. Their voices start to fade in the direction of the house.

She relaxes and shakes her head. She herself solved the maze's puzzle on her first morning here. But then, she wanted to solve it.

The next day is drizzly as well as cold. Emilia goes out anyway. She knows her best exit by now. It's remote, a servants' portal at the side of the manor. The door lies beyond two large gathering rooms on the floor below her chamber, noisy parlors which she has no choice but to pass. The big rooms brim with laughter and the music of enthusiastic speech, the notes of recorders, virginals, sackbuts and lutes, and the slap of cards on tables. The gentle guests are challenging one another in the game of the season, primero. Snatches of dialogue float into the wide hall where she walks. *My lady Arbella, you have hit it! A very palpable hit! Ah, is't so, sir? Would that you yourself had, as you say, hit it, at Newington Butts last St. Michael's Day. Ah, but lady, on that day your eyes made my hand shake so I could hardly hold the bow. . . .* And so on. Emilia is now a shadow of herself, gliding darkly by doorways. When she passes, voices falter or fall silent. Women's painted lips curl, or part, or tighten, and men lean to the left so their eyes can follow her caped back. She grips the sides of the cape with two lowered hands so it billows behind her. She walks without stopping.

In the lobby she pauses, letting the cape flutter to rest. This place is a cavernous, high-windowed vault, filled with light that falls down from the old clerestory, preserved from the days when Tichtfield was a monastery. The light illuminates oil paintings of the earl's recent ancestors, as well as woven tapestries and fine cloths depicting his favorite tales from Greek myth. She hears a door close above her, and looks quickly up at the second-floor passage that opens on one side to overlook the lobby. No one's in view, but you can never know, in a palace, in a mansion, who is watching you from behind a corner. She adjusts her face, trying not to stare at the pictures like a mechanical's daughter. The images are fine, if lurid. There, in a tapestry, the god Jupiter blasts the mortal Semele with a lightning bolt, while with a powerful left hand he rips from her their infant child. Emilia shudders, and turns her eyes to the wall opposite, where hangs another tapestry. Its picture, like the other, is not like the painted Biblical scenes of lesser households, Moses in a basket or the Prodigal Son's return, but a second one drawn from Greek myth: a kneeling Narcissus who gazes, besotted, at his lovely reflection in a pool. The bare-breasted nymph Echo holds her arms out behind him, plaintively and possessively. Narcissus has clearly been created to resemble young Henry Wriothesley.

She steps backward to see the picture more clearly. Her slippers make a whispering sound on the hard floor, a polished geometry of black and white tile. A shadow flits across the tapestry. Once more she glances up at the corridor above, and again sees no one. Most likely a hawk or a gull has flown past the high window. Still, she feels spied upon, so leaving the tapestries, she clasps her cape close and goes outside. She skirts the moat that stretches in front of the manor. *The moat is ten years old, and built for show,* Henry laughingly told his guests two evenings past. Certainly it would have stopped no armed French besieger from circumnavigating the house and clanking in through the workers' rear entrance. She rolls her eyes at the moat, and moves across the green. Feeling equally evident here, in the wide open, she continues her walk until she reaches a copse of trees. No other strollers are in sight on this cold afternoon, too wet for the hunt or for falconing, so she is alone, a black form against yellow leaves, starkly visible from any uncurtained window. *Look at me, then. From afar.* She straightens her posture, and subtly adjusts the silk-lined hood of her cape. Gazing vaguely into the middle distance, she strikes a pose to satisfy spectators, should there be any. *The maid in mourning.* The breeze catches her cape and blows it behind her like a dark sail. She begins to glide along the line of poplars and elms. *The caliph's exiled daughter. We have no such tall trees in my country of hot sand and baked air.*

A pin is poking her through her starched stomacher. She straightens, trying to deflect its point. She's aware of her slimness, the result of a sick stomach that plagued her a full three months after she gave birth to her child, three months after what happened to him happened. For much of that time it seemed her appetite would never return. The sole benefit of the queasiness was, her loss of flesh enabled her quickly to fit into her best gowns again once she felt lively enough to wear them. As an enhancement, before coming to Tichtfield she spent a pound to have a brown woolen cape dyed black. Now the stark color outlines her trim waist against any background: green branches, stone, sky. She knows she's fit for the viewing, yet she cannot escape the discomfort of her conspicuousness. The grand pile's windows unnerve her with their cold, blank stare. After a minute or two she leaves the wood's edge and moves across the green to the safety of the patterned hedges. There's a new, broken gap in the hedge from the two men's boisterous exit the day before. She avoids it. As she did yesterday, she threads through the evergreen maze like a needle, bending herself toward its damp center.

She has brought a different book today. Inside its cover she's penned sentences, which she now recites to herself in a low murmur, seated on the hard stone bench. *"Comme é bello!"* How beautiful! *"Non ancora."* Not yet. *"Il mio ex tutore lo sta traducendo in inglese."* My old tutor is translating him into English. This overheard comment delights her. Can a person be translated, like a word?

A weak sun has emerged, and she's grateful for it. In the gloom she's had to squint at the page. The belladonna wash that softens her eyes leaves a residual blur that sometimes makes them swim. She must use it less often.

Tired of the lesson, she flips pages, scanning the poems in the book. *Love. Dove. Take my glove.* Her cape is furred and her own gloves good, but still, she shivers. How many days can she frequent this maze? The air has turned wintry. She's about to rise and go back to her room for her copy of Plato, to read by the window, when she hears a branch break. Like a startled deer, she looks up.

A man is standing in the aperture of the hedge, bearing books of his own in the crook of one arm, and brushing pine needles from his cap with his other hand.

7

He scans her face, her trim, black-clad body, and her tense fingers poised on her book. She's had no time to prepare a half-smile, or any special expression, and now feels her face frozen in startlement. He meets her eyes. "A silent woman," he says with interest. He smiles. "Italian?"

"I am, *sì*."

"I meant your hand-wear, lady. Your gloves." The man bows.

She looks down at her hands, feeling a blush begin. She recognizes his voice. It's a country voice, not a Londoner's, and not a gentleman's. He is Henry Wriothesley's companion from the day before, the man who crashed through the hedge and swore.

"Can you speak English?" he asks.

"No. *Parli Italiano?*"

"I, lady?" He laughs, at his ease. He takes off his cap, rubs his forehead with the heel of his hand, touches his hair, replaces the cap. She sees a scratch on his forehead, and guesses he got it from breaking through the hedge. He takes a step toward her. "May I sit?"

She nods, though without waiting for her permission he is already lowering himself onto the wide stone seat. *Country manners*, she thinks primly. His movements are quick and spare. He places his own books neatly beside him, on the side farthest from her. She wonders what he reads, but doesn't quite know how to ask. He is still talking. "I do not speak Italian. I have not even enough words to tell you so. Nor can I read it. I wait until everything is Englished. And everything in the world will be Englished, before long. Can you understand this much of my speech?"

She furrows her brow. *I am straining to follow you.* A careful nod. *Yes, I can just make out your meaning. But do not tax me.* "I . . . speak. But not well," she says in the dimly remembered accents of her father. She is practiced in speaking low, without too much movement of the facial muscles. She has learned this habit from Penelope, who is forever cracking her lip paint with her deep, full, body-and-face-shaking laugh. To preserve her paint Penelope strives to suppress this merry tendency, at least on formal occasions, or in the presence of the queen or higher nobles. Emilia has studied her mistress's method, and is now much better at what they all call "freeze-face" than is Penelope herself.

"You are Emilia Bassano, are you not? Of the court musicians?"

"Of their *famiglia*."

He doffs his hat again briefly. "William Shakespeare." He pronounces it "Willum." His second bow is more spare than the first, a mere duck of the chin. Brief and serviceable. He has a habit: a quick, rough smoothing of his hair with his hand, front to back, just after he removes his cap. Then, again, the cap's back on his head.

She nodded. "I am pleased, Will'm —"

"Will suits me. And where is your home?"

She blinks. "The Bassanos are to England from the north of Italy."

He smiles more widely, charmed, it seems, by "are to." He is not especially handsome, neither flesh nor fowl, this nor that. With one bare gold ring in his ear, he resembles a gentleman pirate. His dress, like his words, is better than his accent — a fur-lined cape, velvet trunks and doublet over a cambric shirt, a cobweb collar, watered silk hose, silver-buckled boots of neat's leather. A fine wool hat. *Hireling*, Henry Wriothesley called him yesterday. But Henry has been kind to the hireling. Will's gloves are kidskin, and, from the look of their stitching, more finely made than hers. All these details she takes in with a sidelong gaze as she deftly closes her book, hiding her Italian jottings. She has the strange thought that she should sit on the book.

"You read . . . ?" he asks, glancing at the volume.

This is easy to misunderstand. "I can, yes. Better than . . . to speak."

Reaching crudely, he seizes her book and flips open its cover. Seeming not to see her notes, he glances at the frontispiece, the title, the author's name. He closes the book and hands it back to her. "I would not read that."

"No, not good." She puts the book to the side and lays a casual hand on it. "The poems are . . . how do you say?"

"Execrable."

"How?"

"Execrable. *Your smile is heaven, your frown is hell. Thy hands of snow, thine eyes like suns.* Ex-e-cra-ble."

"Esscrabble."

He laughs. "From the north of Italy, you say. From what province, the Bassanos?"

"Venice." She blinks again, leaving her eyes closed a fraction of a second longer than before, to show her dyed lashes.

"Ah." His hair is auburn, his eyes grey-blue. At the mention of Venice, something peculiar has happened in the depths of those eyes, a shift, as when a door opens far back in a house, almost out of sight. "Venice, Venice, Venice," he mutters. "And music. Lady, do you play?"

"I . . . can play the lute. And also, the —"

"Virginals, I will guess. So all ladies do, or try to do. Tell me, why do they call them that?"

She knits her brow again, in real puzzlement this time. "Call them ladies?"

"Ha! Forgive me. I will speak slower." His voice is light, thin, almost papery, like the brown leaves the wind blows about their feet. "The instrument. Does this name, virginals, come because only virgins can play them?"

She shakes her head firmly. "No." Looking into his eyes, to the half-opened door deep within them, she releases the slow, sly smile she's practiced many times before her mirror. "No," she repeats. "*I* can play them."

He laughs.

A very palpable hit.

Should she try to tell him she knows something about him already? That she overheard him and Henry wandering the maze yesterday, and bursting roughly through the hedge-branches? How did he find the center today, after yesterday's failure? Did he follow her in? She didn't hear a single footfall. Is he a bird? Can he fly? She wants to make a jest of the thing, but isn't sure how to manage one. And he flusters her further by leaning toward her, with his eyes trained on hers.

"You smell like a cinnamon stick." He reaches a finger out to touch her face. "Will you allow me?"

She won't. Her gloved hand flies up to deflect his. He catches her fingers, then kisses one of them. Bold, not to say elegant, for a country fellow! He's practiced this gallantry somewhere. But his next words are prosaic, as he looks approvingly at the gloved hand he's caught. "Lamb-skin, fleece-lined, dyed black in Flanders at two pair a pound. Or was the currency ducats?"

She nods, and is silent. Lady Arbella, back in the house — whoever she is — has wit. Emilia has only this mute beauty, for brief or long-range spell-casting. At the moment, however, the beauty, or the dark dress, or the interesting hand-wear, seems net enough to hold this Midlands fish. She is surprised at how much she wants to keep him here, talking. She has not known the depth of her tedium and her loneliness at Tichtfield.

Mockingly, she quickly pulls her hand back, leaving him holding her empty glove. He has words enough, and she expects he will offer some amorous sally turning her gesture into a metaphor of chastity, or else of lightness. But he only holds the glove, frowning intently at its seam.

"I hope, on my close examination," he says, handing it back to her, "you did not pay *more* than two ducats for these."

8

They have left the maze and are walking the rim of the wood when abruptly he asks, "Where is your husband?"

She cannot help it. She thinks of the woman at the well in the gospel story, which everyone knows. *Are you the Christ?*, she wants to say, with blithe, witty blasphemy, but she can't, or at any rate doesn't. He'd say something even more clever in reply, and then what? Say too many words, show too much wit, and you are expected to keep on at it. It's exhausting, even terrifying, and often, in the end, humiliating, when invention utterly falters.

"He play at court," she offers.

"His name?"

"Alphonso Lanier."

"What plays he? Games of chance? Primero? Or Barley break? Not the fool, I hope."

She smiles thinly. "Is in the queen's consort. He is playing, how do you say, the *registratore*."

He looks at her oddly, one eyebrow cocked in amusement. "He plays a register, in the consort? He registers? He is a clerk of the exchequer, in the consort?"

She shakes her head vigorously, blushing again. Carefully extricating her arm from his, she mimics the playing of a recorder. "Like a *flauto*."

He claps his hands. "Ah, the recorder! Very good. And you? Do you play?"

This question has so many possible meanings it stymies her. She makes a half-smile, the Mona Lisa expression, calling it now into use. She knows Mona Lisa's compelling face from the print hung in Lady Penelope's palace rooms. Penelope tries to do the Mona Lisa smile as well, but, as with the freeze-face, Emilia does it better. To her half-smile Emilia now softly adds words. "I, play? Not the recorder."

"Only the virginals."

"And *luto*."

"Yes, the lute. Wondrous. Will you sometimes play for me, lady?"

"Perhaps." She steps delicately over the corpse of a fieldmouse. He looks down at the carcass intently, and is still looking at it, head craned backwards, when they are three steps past. "Do you believe maggots are formed by the action of the sun?" He takes her arm. "Some say so." Now he squeezes her arm with his hand. "You do not think on such things."

She thinks him passing bold for so low a servant. In the week she's been at Tichtfield she's heard mention of him, Henry Wriothesley's near constant, eccentric companion. He is spoken of. *A journeyman, from Warwickshire. The father's a glovemaker, and he's one of those knaves who steal plague bills off city walls to write on their backs; he's got ink-stained hands. Plucked from the scaffold, too, I mean the one in the Rose playhouse, though poetry's his practice now. A private soldier in the scribblers' army, all marching in search of an earl's patronage. They know Wriothesley's the witty one who throws gold in the air and loves a sonnet.* Yes. But Will Shakespeare, unlike most of the other fortune-seekers, has truly got the earl's patronage. He's here at the Wriothesley estate, and, as she's also heard, he's dancing the pavane at midnight, whacking horsehair tennis balls in the palace's game-court like any Frenchified nobleman, and eating pheasant and truffles nightly at the supperboard. He and Wriothesley are as tight as a brace of conies. She imagines Will Shakespeare's success has something to do with the talent he's showing now. He can do a kind of mimicry of courtesy speech and gestures, even while saying outlandish things, all the while keeping his brows arched and his tone faintly exaggerated, as though he knows he's feigning *gentilesse* and doesn't care if others know. As a trick, it amuses.

"How is it you have come here?" he says, pushing a branch from her way.

"Lord Henry have . . . ." *Frot.* It is beyond her, to describe in halting English the general invitation to her family, sent to her oldest cousin, Augustine; the letter that urged her and any other Bassanos who might slip the queen's court to bide at Tichtfield Manor, Southampton, through Christmastide, and to bring their lutes and recorders. This would be too many words. "He want Bassanos to come," she says plainly.

"To play! The musicians!" His boots crunch the earth. She has worn sturdier slippers today, but she is slight, and they make only a light sound on the bracken. "Are the musicians at Tichtfield your family, then?"

"No." *For a laughter!* For all his gracious inviting, it would have been a triumph indeed for Henry to net even a single Bassano, of the family who for fifty years have crafted their own fine instruments, and who since the time of Henry the Eighth have formed the chief consort at the English court. Young Wriothesley has money enough, but his situation with the queen has grown precarious, and the Bassanos, though they are only minstrels, are yet too politic to be rented by dangerous noblemen.

He nods, seeming to read her thought. "The Bassanos are shrewd. Unless you are nameless, and have naught to lose, 'tis best to give a wide passage to rusticated earls."

She is silent.

"They're not sent to the country for nothing. A wide passage."

She touches her black-clad breast, and feels the bump of her key underneath it. This, the key-touching, is becoming a nervous habit.

"A wide passage most particularly to those rusticated earls imprudent enough to sport in the queen's very hearing with the name of her dear dead mother."

Emilia stiffens slightly. She's heard about this. Everyone has. At Richmond Palace, at the queen's supper board on All Saints Day, young golden-haired Henry jested that Tichtfield was a gift to his grandfather from Henry the Eighth sixty-five years before, when that king was trading manors for votes approving his divorce. Not content with this for bad tabletalk, Henry Wriothesley had added, "His *first* divorce." The casual remark was construed by some as a suggestion that King Henry the Eighth's marriage to his second wife, Anne Boleyn, had been invalidated after her death, a posthumous second divorce granted. And if that second marriage was illegitimate, perhaps the fruit of that marriage, namely Elizabeth, was also . . . .

Emilia nods briefly at Will, and looks up through a clearing in the branches overhead. She sees, against the grey pewter sky, the crow that flies cawing above them.

Will follows her gaze. "Look you, an omen."

They come to a large, flattish boulder, and he sits. "Here." He pats the rock, and she obediently sinks down. "To my theme again. Henry Wriothesley's mistake. Anne Boleyn, that witchy lady, you know, was perhaps not implied as Henry's topic, but no matter, since she was inferred."

Emilia softly hums a fragment of the tune *L'amor Dona Ch'lo Te Porto.*

"I have heard she had eleven fingers, and lay with Lucifer."

She stops humming and averts her face. *Please, leave this topic!* The fellow will say anything. Henry Wriothesley's a diplomat to him. For all his imitation courtesy, Will Shakespeare has clearly spent little time in the houses of the great. Even here, hidden in the woods, she, Emilia, late of the queen's court at Whitehall, is not fool enough to laugh at this last jest. She shifts uncomfortably on the boulder, and notes, from the corner of her eye, that his eyes follow the line of her body as she moves.

He doffs his cap and rubs his forehead. The scratch on the skin shines, livid. He replaces the cap on his head.

She touches the cloth above her hidden key.

"Henry has hired wondrous *musicisti,*" she safely says. In fact, she thinks the recorder players Wriothesley has hired to be of the second tier, though they sound well enough. Two of them were Augustine's students in London at one time or another. She remembers them from Bishopsgate, and at least one of them, she knows, would remember her, if she greeted him and called him by name. Which she won't. The musicians are servants. She is a guest. She is the lady Emilia, to whom fine, blue-eyed Wriothesley bowed when they met at court just after her wedding.

"*Musicist*—? Ah. Musicians. But he has not hired your husband, though your husband is well qualified for his hire, not being a Bassano."

She's a little flattered by his persistence on the subject of her husband, of her having one. She had begun, before today, to wish Alphonso had accompanied her here, even if he did nothing but play music until one and sleep until noon. A husband would give some color to her solitude in this place. Alphonso, however, is bound to play for the queen, from Whitsunday through Christmas Revels, every day and night through the Feast of the Epiphany. It's a better engagement, for both of them.

"No," she says, folding her hands in her lap. "He is not here."

They are shielded from wind in the forest, but a breeze shakes the tree-tops, and a pinecone drops at their feet.

"Looks," says Will, pointing. "Another omen." Cap off, rub, cap on.

He switches tacks now, gesturing vaguely toward the world outside the wood. A weak ray of sun shining through pine branches catches a mother-of-pearl—or a real pearl?—button on his sleeve, and the button winks at her. "And what think you of this frightening mansion of Tichtfield?" he asks.

She laughs. "You not like?"

"Not *like* the granite abbey patched with new marble? Like a scarred old face daubed with white lead? I would prefer its original majesty."

Majesty. A strange word to bestow on a monastery. Is the queen's face his simile? With a poet, who can tell? She shies away from the perilous conceit. "Henry also is . . . not like?"

He takes off his cap and punches it idly, like a boy. "No. The house likes him not. Old stone and new make an unhappy marriage. It was the notion of his mother, the countess, to import the columns and statues from Florence. She persuaded her wild prodigal of a son to spend the money, since in that habit he excels. Now she would persuade him to marry and live in the pile." Hat back. "And that's why I've come."

"To marry Henry?"

Another hit, she would have thought, but the sally seems to make him uncomfortable. He pulls at his lace collar. "To rhyme him into a sober life. I sent her a poem that she liked."

She marvels at the cleverness. A crowd of London poets is chasing the son. This one splits from the pack, and writes to the mother.

"Now I am to compose sonnets in praise of the conjugal state."

She knits her fingers together. "And this, you do?"

He frowns thoughtfully. "In a manner of speaking, I am doing it. My theme is not marriage, precisely."

"What, then?"

He suddenly pins her like a moth with his sharp grey gaze. "Have you children?"

She is surprised. "I . . . have a son."

"He is at court, then."

"No. Is . . . ." She can't bear to call her babe what the midwife called him. That was "dead." And so she voices what Alphonso calls her illusion. "He is raised apart."

He nods as though he understands this, though she doesn't see how he can. "I have a son," he says. "He is eight years of age."

Does he think this topic seductive? She waits, but his gaze has fallen inward now. "Eight," he says softly, as though to himself. Then he raises his eyes and smiles into hers. "I ask," he says, "only because I am writing poems about sons. For the countess, and for *her* son, Henry."

"Ah?" She waits. Unexpectedly, he's discarded his satirical tone.

He grows briefly impassioned. "Our beauty wastes as it must, but that of our sons renews it. Our own lives will shrivel, but our children's faces resurrect us. This is the notion." His eyes glow. "Do you not think it so?"

She does not wish to disappoint him, but she's deflated by this idea. Children reviving parents? During her pregnancy her face spread with bloat and she developed circles under her eyes. In the ninth month, hanks of her hair fell out during washing. At first she thought this was due to the hyssop and camphor treatment she'd begun to apply to it, and the darker treatments, and left her hair alone, but still, it came loose. Later one of the ladies at court told her the same had happened to her when she bore her second child. Emilia's hair grew back, but she still aches to remember the months of sickness she endured even after the birth, and also her sallowness, the anemia and the grief. It took her a year to recover her one weapon and lodestone, her beauty. She does not think a woman could ever write a poem such as "Willum" describes, rejoicing that her child's fresh face replaced the fine looks sacrificed in the bearing of him, or that a child's youth provided a kind of happy substitute for a parent's aging. Unless, of course, she lied. But then, that was what many poets did, and buttered their bread thereby.

She thinks all this, but what she says, in her mildest voice, is, "*Il bambino* is . . . an investment."

He smiles warmly. "Yes. An investment in tomorrow. That is the conceit."

She considers what she knows of investments, of money and trade. The lease on Italian wine imports, granted for life by the old king to her father Baptista, accruing into a sum inherited on his death by Margaret, his wife by common law. The sum then passed down to Emilia and her sister Angelica when Margaret died, with Emilia's portion administered — not well — by Alphonso, her husband. The hay-tax stipend accorded Alphonso. "An investment that yields . . . *interesse*?"

He regards her admiringly, and claps his gloved hands three times slowly in mock applause. "Yes. An investment with *interest*. When we have children, we get back something for our nothing."

For whose nothing?, she wonders. *A man's?*

"Do you know something of interest?" he asks.

"I know many things of *interesse*." Interest, *interesse*. Another point won. She sees, again, the shift, the door opening far back in his eyes.

"And what do you know of interest?"

"Much." The word acquires an extra syllable in her speaking. *Much-a.*

"It is of interest that you hail from Venice." His smile broadens. "*Shine* from Venice, I should say, since I hope you are not made of ice."

These poets.

He taps the flat stone rhythmically. "Ven*ice*, where money pours like golden rain. So full of *interesse*, this city is."

It occurs to her, of a sudden, just what it is that intrigues him, and what the general script may require of her. "Yes." She bestows on him her darkest, most Oriental stare. In her eyes, softened and darkened by belladonna drops, there lurk — in a vague confusion she knows is seductive — the deserts of the east, the spices of the Indies, heaps of saffron, sticky sherbet, reddish henna, the fleshpots of Egypt, a voice from a mountain, cloves, a handful of sultana nuts, the ark of the covenant, and the hanging gardens of Babylon.

"I am a Jew," she says, almost too faintly to be heard, holding his gaze. His grey eyes widen, and she continues. "We . . . have to . . . *fuggiro*. To fly Spain and the Inquisition. That is how we come to Venice."

9

Back inside the manor, having climbed one of its numerous stair-cases, she closes her chamber door, runs to her high bed, places a pillow over her head, and yells into the bolster. She chastises herself in a mingle-mangle of Italian and English. "*Catso!* 'Tis *fuggir-AY! Fuggir-AY*, unspeakable whore!" She still has the old adolescent habit, when strongly vexed, of cursing herself in the harshest terms she can muster, naming herself *cagna* or slut or *puttana*. It clears her mind for thought.

At this moment she needs to do it, to calm herself. Some canny alert-ness in that young poet's gaze, and, more, the liveliness of his speech, has unsettled her deeply. The man was a clown, and yet, like the wise clowns who cavorted among the great in the palace interludes, he seemed to look into, behind, and through her, absorbing what light she gave and returning very little. Since Hunsdon, at Whitehall and Greenwich and Richmond Palace she's learned to run swiftly around corners to avoid courtier-poets, those canny strivers who listen to others' speech with ears as sensitive as dogs' ears, pouncing on any phrase that can be played with or worried like a bone, going on and on with their overstrained word-games until you want to thrust daggers through their felt-covered chests. But this man hadn't pounced, nor overplayed. Rather, he'd lis-tened and prompted. *And what do you know of interest?* He'd put *her* to the test. Then he'd stored what he'd casually gathered from her stutter-ings, in that shadowy room behind his eyes. Like a spy or a profiteer, he collected speech-scraps. This alarms her. What did she tell him? What will he do with the intelligence?

She rocks back and forth. At length, feeling herself beginning to suffocate in Henry's fine linen, she throws the pillow to the floor and rolls onto her back. She pulls her key out from her bodice and touches it, consciously this time, as though for luck. Then she hides it again. Con-templating the room's ceiling, she comforts herself with the recollection

that, during their stroll back to the house, Will Shakespeare proved himself ignorant of Italian. Every phrase of it he attempted came out sounding like Latin. *Good*, she thinks. The *bella lengua* is her screen, her hedge.
He won't burst through it.

After a moment she rises, takes paper and quill from a drawer, sharp-
ens the pen's nib with a small pocket penknife, and writes to Alphonso.
She begs him to send two tins of beeswax and bear's grease and another
pot of vermilion, posthaste, to Southampton, out of his own supply. She's
paid for it, after all, she reminds him.

She signs and seals the letter. Then she sits by the window and reads
thirty pages of Plato's *Symposium*, in English translation.

The poet is not present that night at the supperboard. She's disappointed,
as she's powdered and perfumed her face and neck, lined her lips with
kohl, penciled her eyebrows into perfect half-moons, and dressed her
hair with silk ribbons. Further, she's put on a dark purple gown and
tied on slashed velvet sleeves lined with satin, and is wearing, again,
her pearl-sewn slippers. She earns admiring glances from many, and
after the fruits and ices are served, one or two witlings address her with
the practiced introductions that always hang weights on her answering tongue. Yet her dark southern stare from behind a jeweled fan, followed by "*Como?*," proves an adequate response, and she is thrice asked
to dance the pavane, which she is not so bad at.

The other women hide behind their own fans, speaking of her, not to
her. But to this she's accustomed, as to an old song.

She sees Henry Wriothesley across the room, scattering light, teaching the torches to burn bright. A circle of laughter surrounds him. He's
kicking up his scarlet-clad legs, demonstrating a wild *morisco* he learned
in France. Everyone loves Henry, with his sunny smile and his Flemish
silks and his long blond locks. Even the queen likes him, though she's
prudently punished him this season. He knows it, and is not overly dismayed at his rustication. As for Emilia, she feels herself, upon her return
to court society after her long illness, to have swum fully into Henry's
view for the first time, after having lurked for years at the shadowy
edges of palace rooms, and at the margins of his appreciative adolescent
glances. It must be her marriage, coupled with the recently awarded Bassano crest, that makes her now clearly appraisable, like a portrait new-
framed and hung on a wall.

She calls to mind an episode from three months past. She was slipping into the queen's presence hall behind Lady Penelope. Henry Wriothesley, standing amid a knot of men, turned at some noise and looked at her, channeling the full radiance of his blue eyes on her face for several beats of her heart. She stopped where she was, arrested. Instinctively, she raised her fan. Wriothesley had smiled at her before, but had never done what he did next. He made a leg and bowed deeply. She nodded, turning scarlet from her hairline to the edge of her bodice, and, doubtless, below that edge. That being all there was to the moment, she scurried after her lady, who, from behind her own raised fan, rebuked her. "What a fool you just made of me! I was sweeping across the room chattering to no one, because I thought you were still on my tail. Then I looked back and you were staring at Wriothesley."

"*Perdonami*, lady."

"Not to say he's not worth a goggle."

"*Sì*."

Some two months later came the invitation to the Bassanos to pass Christmastide at Tichtfield. Though Henry Wriothesley is always extravagant in his courtesies to the consort, the invitation, like his bow to her, was unprecedented, and she wonders whether the things — the bow and the invitation — are linked. In any case, she has shyly hoped to know Henry better in Southampton, at Tichtfield, and is surprised to find her purpose strangely diverted by the poet. First he distracted Henry, and now he's distracting her. She wishes she had the audacity to approach the earl, but she knows if she did it today, she would bend her wit to find a way to ask about his missing friend. Where's the *poeta* tonight? Where will he be tomorrow?

And, as well as an eight-year-old son, has the *poeta* a wife? It would seem to follow, or rather, to precede.

"I do."

They are strolling the large kitchen gardens behind the manor. He seems neither happy nor sad about being married. He does seem, however, disinclined to discuss Mistress Shakespeare. But he welcomes the talk about sons. "Mine looks like me," he says, as though this were a marvel in this decadent age. "Does yours look like you? Do you expect to have more?"

She evades the first question and chooses the second. "Is not like. My husband is not . . . much husband." She pauses. Should she reveal this? She plunges. "Not for women."

He frowns, but doesn't comment. She doesn't think she needs to explain Alphonso's nature. That, he will understand. The world he has come from, the theatrical cosmos, is a place of shape-change, where men paint their faces and turn into women. There, a high degree of amorphousness is permitted, even when plays are done. So Alphonso has told her, at any rate, and Alphonso's half a player, as are all the court musicians, who earn part of their pay performing at the court masques and comedies, and even, when the purse is right, at the city playhouses. Alphonso consorts with youths and men to whom feminine behavior of all kinds either comes naturally or has been learned by art.

What Will may wonder is why, and under what conditions, she might marry into such ambiguity. Only for show? She was pregnant by whom, then? And was *that* man still in the scene?

"Your wife," she says, seizing the dialogue. "She is *bella*? And is in London?"

"She is *much* wife, and she lives in Stratford. Now." It's his turn to wriggle into a new subject. "Is it true there are no virgins at court past the age of thirteen?"

She laughs. "There is one."

"O, of *course*. *That* one. The goddess." He rolls his eyes. "But I mean, the others. Those who serve." A sparrow hops by them, chirping. He cocks his head. "Omen."

"Who tell you this? About virgins? Henry?"

He waves a hand archly, dismissively. "I have been to court, lady, you know."

As a groom of the horse-boys' chamberpots? She looks at him narrowly, and sees that his eyes are twinkling.

She has brought no fan to raise today, but she wears a man's hat that shadows her face. This, with a pair of green stockings, was her marriage gift from Lady Penelope, one well approved by her new husband, who pronounced men's hats for women the *only* fashion in London today. She pulls the brim down a touch. "So, there, you steal maidenheads? In *il corte*?"

"I had brave plans, on my visit to court, but lacked the time. I was hobbling about with a stick, an old *senex* in a play. My hair was full of talc and my face was painted all mustardy-yellow. I did not cut a fine figure. But I had eyes, to survey the scene. The ladies I saw did not look like virgins, I'll tell you straight."

She laughs. She thinks she dimly remembers an old yellow-painted clown cannily surveying the crowd, one of the motley crew of players at a court entertainment a year or two before. Did the calculating clown have Will's eyes? Anyway, his assessment of the ladies was apt, if not original. What price maidenheads at court? Half the young women discarded theirs in their first year of service there, bartering a virtue for a pair of embroidered sleeves, a vague promise of enduring love, and a sonnet. She herself never knew such a nest of sluts before she was replanted at Whitehall. There was certainly nothing to match it in her mother's parish of St. Botolph, that place of narrow streets full of houses governed by seamstresses and grocer's wives.

But she will not speak to Will Shakespeare of St. Botolph.

Will circles a patch of lemon grass. With a stick he's picked up, he taps the ground as though seeking water or replaying the part of the yellow-faced *senex*. But he doesn't look old. He looks like a boy who's slipped over the wall into a gentleman's orchard, looking for windfalls and causing random damage.

"Perhaps, though" — *tap, tap* — "it is not possible, only scanning the outward frame, to know a virgin from a woman who isn't. Could we weigh a lass, before and after the event? We think a maidenhead a heavy thing, but it weighs nothing. It *is* nothing. Do you agree, Lady Emilia?"

She looks carefully down.

"Ah, but if the lass *conceives* . . . . Then we know something. Though we don't know it all."

To this she responds with a stony look, which he, looking closely at the soil, appears not to notice. He's clearly fishing for the name of her child's father. This means that Henry Wriothesley, if *he* knows — and doesn't everyone know? — hasn't yet shared that intelligence with Will.

He squats and writes something in the dirt with his stick. She squints, trying to read, but he is already rubbing it out. He says breezily, changing his tack, "I think it matters no more whether our queen is a virgin."

Gods.

Using his stick, he launches himself back to a standing position. He watches her for a reply. She drifts several feet from him and sits on a marble bench, averting her face.

"I see I must ask you outright, Emilia, you of the advanced Republic of Venice, where the prostitutes roam with their bubbies exposed, whether you think it a thing of any moment whether England's divine Astraea, its eternal Diana, its great Gloriana — I mean —"

"I know."

"— whether she ever descended into the mortal vale like gold-raining Jove secretly to busy herself between ordinary sheets, like everyone else." He knits his brow in abstraction, as though engaged in a debate with an Oxford don. As if this were as likely a scholarly topic as any other. "Has she danced the sword-dance? Belike she has. Would she dance it again? It doesn't matter. She is vigorous still, surely, the queen, and might lie on a featherbed and kick the roof-thatch, but she's well past the age to bear a son. Poor soul! I saw her close, when I was there. Her face is pox-pitted and twisted by toothache. If I was mustard-yellow with stage paint, she was dove-coted, she was, smeared from chin to forehead with white lead to cover the blemishes, though ceruse does the skin no good. I met a surgeon in Bedlam who tells me it's poison. So she does herself harm to do herself good, like a marmoset that eats its tail."

She has raised her hands to cover her ears. "Stop," she whispers. Truly, he *is* new to this life. She's been five years in the cloistered court, and was a girl when she last heard discourse so free.

He comes close to her now, and kneels by the bench. "You. Silent lady, you. Ho!"

She turns her whole body away from him, still covering her ears.

"Come, Emilia. Do you think I'm such a fool as to —"

"But you *are* a fool." She drops her hands. *Every revels needs a jester,* she wants to say. *Is that the true reason you're here?*

"I know how to do tricks with my voice. You could hear me, there on that bench, but no one else possibly could, not even if he were crouching behind that hollybush, there." He points to a spike-leaved, red-berried clump of green that stands some four feet away from them.

She says nothing.

"Or listening behind an open window, there." He points behind them to the back of the house, in the direction of the kitchens. "But no windows are open at Tichtfield, because it's turned true cold December today, and we see our breath, look" — he blows out a puff — "and because all the gentlefolk who aren't hunting or hawking, both sports in which I do not participate, are inside drinking and listening to those-who-are-not-the-Bassanos play their sackbuts and cornets."

She stays silent.

"And their recorders and lutes."

Silent still.

Faint on the wind, as though summoned by Will's imagination, comes the bell-like baying of hounds on the chase.

"What . . . ." she says hesitantly. "What is an earl's . . . work?"

Will cackles. "*Work*'s a good English word, but you must mean some other."

She raises both hands suggestively, Italian-like. "Perhaps. I mean . . . ."

"Office? Duties? At one time an earl was a sheriff. But now we have sheriffs. Sheriffs guard borders, and collect shillings from folk in taxes and tolls."

"And earls?"

"Spend them. Come. Walk and talk." He takes her elbow and raises her. "I'll teach you English. Then you can speak." And he does it, strolling with her past the garden boxes and patches, naming each green herb that they see. *Rosemary. Rue. Fennel.* Here in the south, near the ocean, the plants still thrive, though it's full December. Relieved to be chatting about saner subjects, she goes willingly, and repeats the names after him with a soft accent. *A-ross-marie. A-rue. A-finnil.*

"And henbane. Avoid that."

O, yes.

He stops at the far, trellised end of the garden and looks at her square. "Do you know how I found you yesterday?"

She raises both eyebrows. *How?*

He points up and back. "That tower, at the corner of the house. I first saw you inside, in the lobby. When you went out, I ran up to the top of that tower and looked out. I had a bird's-eye view of everything. I saw the track you took. I saw you wind through the hedges. I drew the path in my mind, and then I raced down and followed it."

She looks back and up at the tower, then back at him. It had not crossed her mind that the whole of the maze, its pattern, its secret center, might be visible from the manor's heights. "I am . . . ."

"A-*mazed* is what you are." Laughing, he waves his stick as though it were a wand. "Amazed."

They leave the kitchen garden, but neither one of them wants to revisit the maze, which has now lost its allure. Instead they walk in the orchard, past bare trees wind-shorn of their apples and peaches. Every moment she thinks he'll return to the subject of her questionable husband, or her missing child, and she marshals words for an answer. But he doesn't. He talks about trees. "O, for a high oak," he says. "They grow taller in the north. Here the soil is too sandy. Too near the sea."

As he says the word a gust of wind rises, and she thinks, for a moment, she can smell the salt air.

"But you will know nothing of oaks," he goes on. "Naught flourishes in Venice but money and moss." With his hands and his voice he now paints a picture of a towering oak, full-leaved and green. "A sacred English tree. I see this oak in a clearing, near a comfortable stone house. The oak is peopled. Gathered at its base are a circle of philosophers."

"English philosophers?"

"Why not? Or poets. Or playwrights. Or lawyers, who can tell? People who like words. A holy society of priests and priestesses of the word. They are clad in black, black stripes on their sleeves, like Cambridge scholars. They are merry and sorrowful."

"Which?"

"Both. They are merry and sorrowful. And all have books. They read from them. I see . . . ." He squeezes his eyes shut and taps with his stick like a blind man. "Is it a young man, joining the group? Yes, it is."

"Who? You are this young man?"

"I am an *old* man of twenty-eight. A veritable senex. A father of three, one of them a son who is my power and strength. Or will be." He steps on a fallen branch, cracks it, and opens his eyes. "And you, as I take it, are . . . fifty? Sixty?"

She smiles. "Twenty-two."

"Hum. Henry thought you were sixty."

She laughs outright. "This" — *Thees* — "be courtesy talk?"

"I know little of that kind of talk, lady." He picks up a windfallen apple. The fruit's half-rotten, and he hurls it. It sails well beyond the rim of elms that borders the wood. Country manners, and a country throwing arm.

He takes her elbow with that arm and turns her back toward the house. "Come. Let's in, for the music. And for the courtesy speech you require. For that, you must go to Henry."

She purses her lips. "He must teach *you*."

He laughs oddly long at this. Then he says, "Well, if it please you, Emilia, I will ask him to."

10

But Will seems unlikely to ask Henry Wriothesley anything. Some spell between them has suddenly snapped. Or no, not broken entirely. Yet the magic that binds them appears to be strained.

The poet's new excess of time these past few days bespeaks the change. And then there is supper, where Will and Wriothesley now sit apart, exchanging no glances, not speaking to one another. Will is well down the table the night of his afternoon stroll with Emilia, attending to his sauced venison, saying little, in fact, to anyone, and barely sipping his wine. His habitual place at his host's side is filled this night by a flamboyant soldier-knight Emilia recognizes from court and is surprised to see at liberty. She knows that this knight, like Henry, has recently been rebuked by the queen, much more severely than was the earl. The man's been punished for his potency. He is Sir Walter Raleigh. He's gotten his Elizabeth Throckmorton, of the queen's privy chamber, with child, then secretly married her. But the secret is out.

The air around the supperboard is heavy, redolent with the scent of wax from twenty burning tapers. Up table Raleigh is speaking low to Wriothesley, but not low enough. He hasn't Will Shakespeare's professed trick of selectively aiming his voice. "And my Lizzie still in the Tower!" she overhears the knight say at one point, with angry intensity. "*She* only let *me* out to manage the business of the gold from New Spain."

"Mined gold? Bought gold?"

"Bought!" Raleigh shows his teeth in a short, barking laugh. They are white in his black beard, and only one is broken, chipped at a slant so it looks sharp and wolvish. "Bought with some English blood on the lawless sea. Since I'd funded the voyage —"

"With her money —"

"Taken from us, she thought I were best to divide what we'd earned." Raleigh saws into his meat with his knife and spears a reddish hunk.

He lifts the hunk to his mouth and says, chewing, "That way she could escape blame for . . . . " The rest is unclear, until "gave her the bulk of it, in any case. Still she swears she'll keep Liz and our child locked up til year's end." He picks up a spoon and toys with a fig on his plate. His hands are brown, and even from yards down the table she can see they are seamed with scars. "I'll spend Christmas with my new bride under guard." *Murmur, murmur.* ". . . how to bear a grudge."

Feeling eyes on him, Raleigh abruptly stops talking, glances downboard, and catches her look unaware. At once she lets her eyes blur and cloud. She has weakened in her abstinent purpose and used the belladonna drops again this evening. Now she blinks once to disperse them, letting dim mystery displace the sharp light of her curiosity. She gives Sir Walter her most beguiling half-smile. The knight's face unfolds, shedding its narrow defensiveness, opening into suggestive admiration. He murmurs something to Wriothesley, who glances over at her and then says something to Raleigh. She ducks her chin, raises her fan, and looks away, in any direction.

Any direction happens to be toward Will, who has now stopped eating entirely. His sparsely bearded chin is propped on his hand, and he is regarding her from his seat, some five or six places down the table.

She does not expect the shock she feels in the center of her body as he slowly smiles, then almost imperceptibly winks.

She goes alone to Henry's library the next day, and glides silently in. Her first day in this place she spied a man there with his back to the door and a stack of volumes resting on a table before him. That spare, wiry man was paging, searching magpie-like, book down, choose another, moving with speed, grace, and economy. She knows now it was Will.

Henry's gone hunting today with Sir Walter, his own hounds, and a pack of his own followers. Raleigh has no followers at the present time. They've all shipped, in a manner of speaking. They are following the winds of the queen's favor to some other port. As far as Emilia can tell, Will follows no one, though she knows his purse is filled by the earl. At any rate, she suspects he does not hunt in woods, and wherever he wanders he will end here, again, in the library, with the books.

She is ready for him to see her. She wears dark blue wool and, yet once more, the pearl-sewn slippers. She's brought her lute. She arranges herself in the carved and cushioned windowseat behind the lute's burnished mahogany bowl, and plucks its strings. Softly, she sings. *"L'amor dona ch'Io te porto . . . ."*

It is not a quarter of an hour before he appears in the doorway, like Odysseus unbound from a mast. He nods and makes his brief, smiling bow. "Lady."

She nods in return, then drops her eyes again to the neck of her lute. She continues to sing.

Will seats himself near her on the windowseat and folds his legs at an angle, one ankle on the other knee. He has nothing in his hands today. He listens well. She finishes her song, thinking it strange that Italian syllables can leap so trippingly from her tongue when the English ones falter and clunk. He keeps silence for some moments as her last note dies into a vibration on the air.

He opens his mouth to speak. She's ready for his question. She thought long last night, and chose the words to use to tell him about her past, about her lost child.

But what he asks is, "How do Jews live in Venice, lady? Do they lend money? Do they sell clothes? Do they lend clothes? Do they sell money?"

"Ah!" A half-laughing, bemused exclamation.

He leans forward and touches her knee. She feels, again, the jolt, and stiffens. "I am sorry, lady," he says. "You lack language. I forget myself." He leans back against the mullioned windowpanes. "As for your family, they are musical Jews. Did they become Christians in England? Did they attend synagogue before then, speaking Hebrew, revering the Law, worshiping the God of Moses? The *I am that I am*?" On his tongue, the phrase sounds like this: *I am that iamb.*

She's a trapped rabbit again, glancing furtively from left to right and back again. She says, "Aye. I . . . *sì.*"

His eyes light up like twin lamps. "Tell me what they do. Tell me about the *shiva.*"

"That is . . . ."

"The mourning ritual, is't not?"

"*Sì.*"

"And the men are circumcised." He shudders theatrically. "How do they do *that*? With a carving knife?"

"Ah . . . ."

"But you could not know. Surely this rite is hidden from the women."

"*Sì.*"

He makes a face. "Monstrous frightening, it sounds, but there must be some art to it, else there'd be no little Jews and Jewesses. Though I reckon there's a fair proportion of accidents. I'd not trust *my* son to a knife-wielding rabbi. Or is it the rabbi does it?" He leans forward again, his hands on his own knees this time. His cap is far back on his head today, perched at a rakish angle, and she can see that the scratch on his forehead is nearly healed. "But tell me of the *ghetto*. I hear its houses are four stories high."

She must get beyond *sì, sì, sì*. "*Seven* stories," she corrects. "And all like *palazzos*."

He leans back again and laughs, appearing to take this for an irony. "Then those houses must dwarf the other dwellings of the city. Do folk fall from the top floors? No, do not tell me." He's made himself wince. "I will fear for the children, running about near the windows, up there." He says this pointing forward and upward as though the buildings she's described were in front of them, visible, conjured. His gesture is so convincing that, fleetingly, she turns her head to look at the air. "What about the sons?" he goes on. "What of the daughters? Are they allowed to roam the — ah, no fields. No plants but moss, no roads but canals. Do they cavort in gondolas? Are they merry little sluts, like English girls?"

She shakes her head. "No, no. Jewish maids kept close. They see nothing."

He looks keenly at her. "And you? You were kept close?"

In broken English, she tells the tale. How her father locked her in a room every day and made her read the Books of Moses.

He interrupts. "Girls are taught to read, then?"

And she had expected a wooing! Why doesn't he take out a pencil and paper, and get it all down? "Ah . . . not most," she stammers. "I am taught. But only the Bible. Stories of . . . ."

"Esther. And Rahab." His hands are clasped together now, the fingers knit. He wears no gloves today, and for the first time she sees his fingers are stained with something. He notices her looking, and glances down. "Glover's dye, that will never wash out. And some ink. Pray, go on."

She meets his eyes again. "The windows are shuttered. I cannot look out."

"You dare not. Because only a painted Jezebel would look out a window." He unknits his fingers and rubs his stained hands with glee.

"*Sì!*" His face is full of merry humor, and she warms to the spirit of the thing. She recounts her acts of defiance, ticking them off on her fingers. Sneaking out of the ghetto with a Christian servant woman to sample roast pork. Selling a jeweled ring of her mother's to buy a monkey, which she hid in the attic and fed with lychee nuts until it escaped over the ghetto rooftops. Once she herself escaped during Carnival, dressed as a boy, and lowered herself four stories by means of a rope of tied bed-sheets so she could attend a mass. She stops then, seeming to struggle for words, and uses her hands to show what happened next. She was captured, and beaten by her father for professing belief in the Holy Trin-ity — she makes a swift sign of the cross — but she did it all again the fol-lowing week.

"Your musical father? He beat you like a drum?"

"This was . . . before he is musical."

"He was converted? Translated?"

"We all do. Are. When we come to England."

"You all were. Excellent!" he says, straightening and clapping his hands. "*Most* brave." What is he applauding? Her valor? Her piety? Her performance? Some trinity of these? She doesn't care. She basks in his approval. She has told a tale well.

"And now your family is at the English court. Ennobled."

"Not noble. But we have . . . ." She sketches in the air with her hands.

"A coat of arms? You have a coat of arms?" For a fleeting moment, a look of envy crosses his face. "What is it? Here." He fumbles in his cloth-ing. As it turns out, he *does* have a pencil and paper. He offers both to her. "Can you draw it?"

She lays aside her lute. Crudely, she sketches the Bassanos' new crest, the image designed by Cousin Augustine. Three silkworms hang-ing in the air above a mulberry tree.

He gazes down at it in fascination. "Marry, that's *odd*," he says admiringly.

~

Lord Henry seems not to know or care how many guests are in his house, as long as they're satin-clad and can dance a galliard. His mother, the countess, is a rare, faintly frowning presence among them. She spends most of her time at the estate of her second husband. And why should she not? She has no power here. Tichtfield belongs to Henry, who is his father's heir, and he fills it with people who please him, or seem likely to. The crowd ebbs and flows. Now that Emilia's met Will, who's become a sort of confederate, she's finding it easier to drift among the silken moths, to practice the arts of concealment she learned in Elizabeth's palaces. She moves out of the hallways into the rooms, though she stays a silent figure at the edge of the group, raising her fan just in time to deter gallantries from fellows with slashed sleeves and rose-tipped shoes or curled hair. What was it Augustine called them? *Farfalla uomini.* Butterfly men. She remembers Augustine yelling *farfalla!* at Alphonso once, and Alphonso then rising from his bench at the supperboard and fluttering back and forth, his feet capering nimbly, smiling blissfully and flapping his sleeves of scarlet brocade, until even strict Augustine laughed.

What would Will make of Alphonso? Will has not returned to the subject of her husband, her child. Is he waiting for her to renew the topic? Are they on to something else? For now, she and he seem involved in a nameless game, both gliding along the rims of rooms, listening, catching each other's eyes. She sees him, and comically raises her fan. He grabs a sheet of music from a stand and half-covers his face. She sits on a joint stool in a corner. He stands in the opposite corner and speaks in a low voice. He says, "Can you hear me?"

She nods.

"You are the only one in this room who can."

This cannot be true. A woman in gold-dyed taffeta, standing next to him, has turned her head and is regarding him strangely.

He keeps on. "I read Lucretius the philosopher today."

She lowers her fan and raises her eyebrows. "In Greek?" she mouths.

"I cannot read Greek. A translation. Lucretius says the world is made of tiny atoms that collide and dance, and that no god created them. How do you suppose he knows this? Has he spoken to this no-god?"

She would challenge this absurdity — Will's, not Lucretius's — but is given no chance; his words flow on without a stop. "Do you know, when I was your age, that is to say, about twelve years, in Stratford-upon-Avon, some folk used to think me mad?"

She smiles and nods encouragingly.

"Mad! Only because I slept in graveyards."

The taffeta woman moves away from him with a withering backward glance. Emilia raises her fan to just under her eyes.

I have not slept among tombstones, she thinks. *I have not gone so far.* Though this isn't to say there weren't Bishopsgate folk who thought her one pin short of a game of bowls as well, back in her own youth. At fourteen, she was the only maid in the region who mouthed words to herself as she bustled about alone, watering the herbs, performing her chores, visiting the chandler's shop or the greengrocer's stall to make purchases for her mother. How could the neighbors know she was only writing penlessly, sounding out phrases?

He's suddenly at her elbow, gazing at her so keenly that she's impelled to turn her face half-away. "You have eyes of mourning," he says.

The belladonna. It is working, softening her gaze, darkening the pupils. She blinks. He swims in and out of her view. His own eyes are suddenly veiled and distant. "You mourn for all these painted poppets," he says in an undertone, as though to himself.

"I, mourn? For *these*?" She tilts her head toward him as she speaks. She is wearing an Arab perfume, given her by Penelope. It, or something, rouses him from his reverie, and again he regards her keenly.

"Let us mourn their lost faces," he says, raising his eyebrows. His own face is a tragic mask. "Because God gave them one, and they make themselves another. Poor faces! Can they breathe beneath their dolls' masks? Noses, lips, cheeks, all dead and buried. Crying out like fearful ghosts."

She stares. *The townsfolk thought me mad,* he said.

"But *you*," he continues. "*You* shun the white powder and the pale plaster. Mere creation shines forth in your face. It is excellent good, when God is the painter!"

He is peering at her sharply. He's discarded his tragic look, and now a smile tugs at the corner of his lips. Is he mocking her? She steps out of the torchlight, her face still half-shrouded by her fan. But she holds his eyes.

For a week Emilia vanishes from Tichtfield. It's only partly a stratagem to keep Will's interest. Mostly, she wants money. She doesn't require cash in Southampton, at gold-raining Tichtfield, where Henry Wriothesley seems bent on creating a true second court this season, an improvised holiday scene to rival Elizabeth's. Henry pays for everything, but Emilia won't be a guest in his house forever. So she thinks it wise to secure at least part of her husband's hay-tax and consort fees before year's end. She doesn't know what Alphonso will spend it on otherwise, but she knows he'll spend it.

She's three days at court, where she and Alphonso merit rooms. Elizabeth has removed from Whitehall to Nonsuch Palace, outside of London in Surrey, where the scene is less manically festive than at Tichtfield, and the music far better. The fortunes of Raleigh are all the buzz: Raleigh, now spending a dank Christmas in the Tower with a wife who hardly knows what she's stepped into, and is too pregnant for the annulment it's rumored she craves. Penelope Rich shares all the news. The topic of Raleigh has eclipsed that of Wriothesley's rustication.

Emilia distances herself from the gossip, looking for Alphonso, but she finds it hard to speak to him. When he's not playing in the consort, he's asleep. However, on the third night she finds him drinking jovially with the flautists, after they've all supplied three hours' music for a play. By the end of their interview, she's wheedled funds from him. She lays the money by with Augustine for safekeeping. The next morning she attaches herself to a party that includes two carpet knights newly dubbed for sharing their yearly incomes with the queen, the wives of these knights, and a group of players. They all launch themselves on foot or on horseback for Southampton. Lady Penelope's lover has lent Emilia a mare.

On the cold road, as her horse picks her way daintily among the frozen ruts left by the corn carts, Emilia broods. Before departing Tichtfield she left a letter for her host with a serving maid, explaining her plans, though she's sure her plans mean nothing to Henry. It was a matter of courtesy. She said nothing to anyone else. She has pleased herself, these past few days, in imagining Will's wonder at her absence. She rides now, shrouded in black wool, and for the hundredth time conjures a vision of his puzzled face searching fruitlessly for her dark, vague eyes across Wriothesley's game-filled rooms. The knights' wives who ride next to her chatter for miles about their new manors in Kent, the damask tablecloths of one, the Venetian glassware of another, the wall-hangings, the plate. "We've commissioned an oil of the Holy Family for the south wall," says one. "With our faces and young Richard's as Joseph, Mary, and the infant. Have we not, Charles?"

"Wife, we have." Her husband straightens the purple feather in his cap.

"A knight of the Square Table," whispers the player riding behind Emilia. He makes a motion of slapping down cards. "Valiant at primero." He and his fellows smother their laughter.

Emilia pictures the Holy Family. She remembers that Will has a family, a wife in Stratford whom he never mentions, a son whom he praises nearly each time he speaks. And it's Christmas. The thought suddenly strikes her, nearly makes her pull up her horse in the middle of the high road.

Why should Will not have left Southampton, as well, to be with his own?

Suddenly she's anxious beyond words. Her heart can't tell whether to stay full or deflate like a pricked balloon. The heart can't know, until she's in Tichtfield. Now she wants to urge her mare to go faster, but the caravan makes its own pace. The players have brought a wagon for their costumes and scene properties, but most of them are walking, enlivening their journey by singing carols. *"At Christmas we banquet, the rich with the poor! Who then but the miser but openeth his door? At Christmas of Christ many carols we sing, and give many gifts in the joy of that King."* One of the players sings "we *sin*" instead of "we *sing*," and accompanies the phrase with a crude gesture.

"Sirrah, you have achieved blasphemy as well as bawdry," calls out one of the knights, and the player bows. These men, like Henry's musicians, are actors of the second tier, not full members of the company that now dazzles fine audiences at Elizabeth's court with interludes and comedies. Because they are second-rate, they are free to travel south, hoping to earn a first-tier wage at Southampton. You would think they'd be more anxious to get there, but they're warmed by a bottle of wine they keep stowed in the wagon, and seem as happy to dawdle as Chaucer's pilgrims. She'd charge forward alone, but for fear of highwaymen and the fact that she doesn't know the route.

They must stop at an inn to eat and feed the horses, and then there's a pesky delay at Stokebridge, a matter of tolls and disclosure of identities, since they're bound for a port town. Are there any priests among them? "She's a nun," the bawdy player quips recklessly, gesturing at Emilia. The toll agent grimly surveys her dark hair and eyes. He comes close. "I've ne'er seen hair so black. Art Spanish?"

"She's Italian." It's another of the players, who knows Alphonso. "She's musical."

The agent looks bemused, as though one or both of these adjectives is unknown to him, but he waves them along. The knights and their ladies, who've paid scant attention to Emilia before this, regard her suspiciously for the remainder of the ride.

It's so late by the time they reach Tichtfield that most of the great house's windows are dark. They ring a bell, and sleepy grooms appear to walk their horses. They enter as a group, then go their separate ways, the players led to meaner lodgings in the rear of the palace, she followed by a porter, walking towards the ornate central staircase. Two men are playing Ruff and Trump and singing rounds in the lobby. *Hey, ho, nobody at home.* She's not heard that song since childhood. As she approaches, the pair break into a new catch.

> *The Dutchman for a drunkard*
> *The Dane for golden locks*
> *The Irishman for aqua-vit*
> *The Frenchman for the —*

At the song's climax one man pushes the other off his stool. The falling man kicks out and catches the other with his foot, and they both land on the floor laughing.

At first Emilia thinks they are Will and Henry, and her heart beats hard in her throat. But as she comes closer, she sees they're some new guests whom she doesn't know. She touches the key under the broadcloth of her gown, and slips past them unheeded. She's in a fever, and doesn't know what she'll do. She walks up a flight of stairs and down a passageway to the same chamber she was given in November. She's followed by a page who bears her traveling trunk. She gives the boy a groat, and he vanishes.

Ah, me. Should she walk the hallways with a candle, knocking on every door, surveying this warren of rooms in search of the place where Henry's stowed Will? She imagines the various couplings, licit and illicit, she'd disclose if she did. What would be worse, to look everywhere and find Will gone, or to find him with . . . someone else?

Madness, the whole notion. She must go to bed, even if she can't sleep.

In her room she lights a candle and strips off her traveling clothes. She dons a loose, gauzy gown and peers at herself in the mirror. This morning, full of hope and excitement, she prepared herself to meet him.

Amazingly, her face has withstood the wind and the weather. She looks her most darkly beautiful. But to what purpose, her painted loveliness? To dust a pillow?

She snuffs the candle and climbs shivering under the blankets. The windows of the room are curtained as well as closed, but through them she hears an owl hoot, not far away.

A quarter-hour passes. She turns restlessly in her bed, feeling the weight of the counterpane.

A soft rap sounds on her door.

She rises on the instant. This knock, that a moment ago was a dream, seems now a thing that was always inevitable. She walks carefully across the cold floor without pausing to light the candle. She opens the door a crack and peers through. In the dark hall she sees the outline of a man, but cannot tell if it is he or the other. "Who is't?"

He leans forward, letting his face be lit by the bars of moonlight shining through the small window at the end of the corridor. It's Will, in his shirt. He whispers, "I passed a fat monk's ghost in the refectory. Did you hear the owl hoot?" He touches her wrist. "Come with me. Lurk and haunt."

She takes his hand and kisses it. Laughing softly, he cups her chin, then enters her room and closes the door.

11

" *Traduzione*," she says. "*Converzione*."

"Yes?" He looks at her expectantly.

They woke this morning to snow falling outside. The world was white when Will pulled the curtains open. Soft cotton wool lies on the green and the hedges. Even inside, the house-sounds are muted. Not that the pair of them have sought noise and company. It is late afternoon, and they've not left her room. A discreet maidservant — well, perhaps she's discreet — has knocked, has brought them cold meats in custard coffins, glasses, a flagon of wine.

"Is . . . your language."

"English?"

"*Your* English." What she means, and seeks crude terms to describe, is that Will's words, released into air, translate and convert themselves. She's been listening, and has noticed the phenomenon: words assuming all their possible dimensions, analogues, referents, and futures in the moment, making these audible, as well as visible to the mind's eye, available for use. This is what she means. *Hail. Shine. Golden rain.* Is he even aware that he does it? She wants to ask him.

"Your words have . . . ." She shapes a polygon with her hands.

"O, I see. You wish to dance the morris." He rises, naked, and takes a stance, arms raised.

She laughs. "Your words have many *sides*."

"Many *signs*? Here." He begins to mime various actions: a man pulling a rope, a conner testing ales. Then he lies on the floor-rushes and crosses his wrists over his lower abdomen, hiding his cock. "What is this? I know you know it."

"A . . . corpse?"

"No, no. *This* is corpsing." He raises his arms and crosses them at the elbow over his chest. "The other was a rabbit on a spit. And this" — he pulls his forearms up and makes a steeple with his fingers — "is a fish scraping implement, mark you, for haddock or bream, with a pointed protrusion for removal of scales."

She throws up her hands. "*Basta!*"

He sits. "What did you call me? No matter. However bad, I deserve it." He looks at her quizzically. "Do you know, I think Henry is wrong. You are nothing near sixty. Eighteen is more like."

She laughs. Struck by an idea, she reaches for the commonplace book she keeps by her bed. From its pages she withdraws the old woodcut, now frayed, of the young maiden who is, from another angle of vision, the old hag. She hands it to Will. "You have seen it?"

"Not I," he says, gazing down.

"Then what is you see?"

"A woman!"

"What woman?"

He hands it back to her. "A crone and a maiden."

She frowns. "But which?"

"Yes, perhaps. Or a girl."

She retrieves the paper from his hands. "But you cannot see both. No one sees —"

"Both?" He frowns at her in genuine bafflement. "I cannot follow you. 'Tis a drawing of a woman. And here, before me, I see another woman, and one who confounds me. Why, I ask again, are you fully dressed?"

"I am not." She is wearing, again, her loose-bodied nightgown. He's made love to her twice this very day, and she hasn't removed the gown. With a mixture of vanity, craft, and shyness, she rose while he was still sleeping to put it on again, and to repair her face. "I am not *all* dressed."

"You are as dressed as a Christmas goose, and that's too dressed for me."

He could not have left Tichtfield for his home in the Midlands, in Stratford on Avon, he tells her in the days that follow. He has a task to complete. He is writing a sonnet a day. She cannot read them, no. He is bound by a compact. They are Henry's poems. Let Henry share them if he likes.

After the first night, they lie nearly each time in his chamber. His room looks out on the estate's large graveled entryway to the woods beyond.

She is surprised, on first seeing the chamber, to find the place neat and spare, without crumpled papers on the floor or scattered shirts. He's been given a writing desk, a stack of paper, three quills, and a supply of inkpots, one of which she manages to steal and secrete in her own trunk. On a table by his window sit a Geneva Bible and an ever-changing stack of smaller volumes: North's translation of Plutarch's *Lives*; a book of Italian tales; Golding's Ovid, opened to the tale of the nymph Echo and the youth Narcisuss. Will never sits motionless and reads, as she herself does, has always done, for hours on end. He looks at the books frequently, taking something from this, something from that, half the time standing. He's always in motion. He keeps a penknife in a drawer, and each poem he completes he locks out of sight, or straightaway delivers up to his employer. The poems vanish, anyway.

Sometimes the two of them pass Henry outside or in corridors. The relations between Will and Henry have not resumed their prior intensity, but they are cordial. Will bows to his host and employer, keeping his face impassive. Henry gives Will and Emilia a flick of his eyes, a courteous flourish, and a knowing smile. The earl does not circulate his poet's verses about marriage and children, and if Will minds this, he doesn't show it. She has thought all poets wanted their work published to the world, but Will seems to care only that his pocket is padded.

He sends most of his money to Stratford.

For hours at a time, day after day, Will sits and scribbles. It must be he lacks all vanity. He doesn't read aloud a single line, not even a phrase, for her approval, though when he stops to rest, he lets his free speech wash over her like a waterfall. He's given up his feeble attempts at Italian, though he likes to hear her speak it. He can rarely do more than guess what she means when she speaks the *bella lengua*, or pretend to guess, as he tries to translate. Most often he substitutes his own meanings, odd constructions that amuse him. "You say the Doge bathes publicly on a balcony overlooking the Piazza San Marco? How frequently?" "Then *all* Paduan cats observe curfew?"

She finds it odd that so profound a word-skill as his would stop, like a sovereign's authority, at the borders of things English. But so it is. He can't speak Italian, Spanish, or French. His Latin is passing good, or so he claims. She'd hardly know. But Will prefers English to all languages, since it contains, as he says, "both short words and long. A *ghost* is a *phantom*. An *ossuary* is a *bone-house*." He says this triumphantly, then looks at her with his brows raised and his hands spread, as though to add, *Need I say more?*

And then he turns back to his writing. He spins words like silk.

In bed, he peppers her with more questions about Jews and Venice, as well as about the Moors who dwell in that city. She's learned that she need say little or nothing; he will answer these questions himself. If she starts a sentence, and then waits, he will finish it as he likes. A Padua, a Verona, a Lombardy, a Venice rises fantastically from the whole cloth of his thought. He has a stiff prick for Italy, that's certain, like every other English poet she's met. She thinks of Walter Raleigh's hot stare across Henry's long supper board that evening a seeming eternity before, though in fact it was only weeks ago.

She says, "When I climb down the rope of sheets from my room in the ghetto —"

"You are chased by masked men, aye, men in bird masks, all the way to the Ponte del Vecchio! You bang on the locked gates. *Santa Maria!,* you pray. Nothing happens. How could it? Prayers to saints are not efficacious, as good Master Luther knew. Cursing like a drab, then, you turn to face the predators. These, reaching the slick, mossy stones of the embankment, slip and tumble into the canal. The men flail in the drink. Heads vanish. Do they reappear? They do not. They had forgot . . ." His pause is portentous. "The crocodilian." He pinches her leg. She shrieks. His hand travels up her side and across her breasts, and rests on the little iron key that lies between them. "What treasure chest does this open? What have you, locked up in hiding? Jelly of cock-sparrows? He-monkey's marrow?"

She doesn't answer. He doesn't want her to.

She tells him she loves him, aware that the "him" she craves is a voice incarnate. She first heard what she wanted, what she wants, in a rhyming jest, a disembodied set of voices, a cadence of speak-and-reply on the far side of a hedge where he walked with Henry. She didn't know then what she was hearing. Some magic of Henry's, or something unnameable that rose between him and the other. Now the thing is in range, present in her hands, though she cannot play the part Henry played with Will. She could not speak it if she tried, she feels sure. She is his silent beauty. He is the music, both the recorder and the song, his own tune housed in his body, encircled by her arms. She seeks a natural poetry to describe what she feels. He drinks her darkness. His tongue soaks her like rain. They grow by moonlight.

She rises with the lark every morning, and leaves him sleeping.

When she comes back to him, dressed and painted, he addresses her as though she'd never left, no matter how many hours they've been parted. This is agreeable to her. She wishes he would never stop talking, and in fact, he rarely does, punctuating even their most intimate embraces with questions like, "Do you think God is dreaming us?" and, "Where learned you *that*? In Italy?"

"You have not been to Italy," she says, as they walk again in the maze together.

"No, nor nowhere." He muses, kicks a pebble. "When I first went to London five years ago, I thought to make one of a crew of sailors, going with Walter Raleigh's ship to Virginia. I wanted to cross the sea, to see everything there was to see in the wide world."

"Why did you not?"

He is silent. She is sobered and chilled by what she imagines him thinking. *I have a wife, and children.*

After a minute he says, "I went to the Rose instead, and joined some land-pirates."

At night, they mingle with the guests Will calls "the caterpillars." He darts his eyes around a room and makes sly observations even when dancing with her, which he does gracefully, surprisingly so, until he explains that of course he can dance, is he not a player? And the players must know how to do everything. "Let me show you," he says. "We are atoms. Let us take care not to collide." With her palm raised, touching his, slowly circling in candlelight to the music of second-rate musicians, she pretends she's his mirror image.

Now it's January, and now King's Day, the end of the merry season. She wakes after Will, unusually, and finds him sitting by the bed, staring at her with a gaze as intent as a hawk's. She jumps a little. What does he see? Instinctively, she pulls the counterpane up to her chin.

"I have your Christmas gift, Emilia." He places a poem on her sheet-covered breast.

At last. She has given him a pair of hand-knit silk stockings of dark grey, a pair of Alphonso's, never worn, that she brought back from Nonsuch. In exchange, she asked for a poem. Now she sticks out a hand and raises the paper to the light.

It's a sonnet, fourteen spidery lines on fine parchment. She reads slowly. The last line of the poem says, *Then I will swear beauty herself is black.*

It is wondrous, what he's done with her complexion of burnt cinnamon, her midnight eyes, her shadowy hair. It is what she expected, indeed, more than she expected him to do in this vein. Yet the poem leaves her disappointed. It's entirely concerned with her outside. She is amazed that she cares, when her outside is practically all she has presented to him, but she does care. A tear starts in her eye, and she deftly catches it with the sheet-corner. Moisture and the black kohl from her eyes stain white linen. *No weeping.*

"*Grazie,*" she murmurs.

He is touching her hair. He pulls back his ink-stained finger and looks at it, nonplussed. "I am sorry. I could not sleep, so I rose and I wrote. Now I've put poems in your hair." That stare again, like an interested eagle. "Or no. It is the reverse."

Again she's a rabbit, trembling. "The ... reverse?"

"It's your hair that's put poems in me. I've written you another, also. You shall have it after the revels."

"Revels?"

"Revels, lady!" He jumps up and raises his arms, clenching his fists so the muscles tighten. "'Tis the Feast of the Epiphany!"

Henry Wriothesley's golden foot-long locks are flying. He is spinning on a table in the middle of his great hall, carelessly kicking goose pie slices, tins of nuts, candied apples, and custard pastries hither and yon with a silver-buckled foot. The guests are shrieking and dodging. They toss bread at each other, though no one Henry splatters or bonks is so bold as to fire any foodstuffs back at an earl. Not even an earl who is bare nineteen and whirling as fast as Henry.

A glass of Rhenish in one hand, Emilia picks up her skirts with the other and runs for the room-rim, as is her wont. Where's Will? He has after all promised her that new poem after the play, which was a raucous comedy with a rambling plot involving a fool named Fortunatus and numerous pratfalls. He and she hated it. It's done now, and the dispersing audience are reeling noisily through the first floor banqueting rooms. She climbs on a chair and looks about. At last she spies her lover in close conversation with a player, the bawdy one who came near to causing her trouble with the toll officer on the road to Southampton from Surrey. *A nun, indeed.* She climbs down from the chair, places her goblet on a table amid other half-filled glasses, and navigates a slow, twisted passage among silk trunks and farthingales until she reaches an open doorway. She stands in the space, fan raised, draping herself against the doorframe. Will could see her there, if he happened to look up.

But he doesn't. His dialogue with the player continues. He is asking a spate of questions, and, by the look of things, growing increasingly vexed at the answers.

After several minutes of posing, she lowers her fan, sighs, and leaves the hall. She winds upstairs and down a passageway to Will's small room. Never before has she been a lover's thrall, and she doesn't like it or understand how it happened. Still less does she know what to do about it.

She lights candles and arranges herself on the bed. She lies reading a book of Will's, or more likely one he's brought up from Henry's library. It's a startling book called *The Golden Ass,* by Apuleius, about a man who's changed into a donkey and makes love to a goddess. With her eyebrow pencil, she jots words on paper as she reads. Trapped in her self-modeled silence, she's thus far made no attempts to tell Will what she thinks of his authors, though while he's writing she often picks them up and reads them. There are things she might say about Plutarch's idea of parallel histories, or Ovid's lovers erotically transformed, or indeed, Plato's searches for truth. But she's only echoed Will's thoughts, like a standing cliff above water. Now she's determined to alter the case. She's drafting some comments to make about Apuleius.

But when Will comes in an hour later he only nods, not even looking at her. He goes straight to his trunk and ferrets out a book, which he carries to his desk. "I must write. Stay, if you will." He adds, as an afterthought, "Sweetheart."

Sour! He's forgotten about the second poem, and she's too proud to ask for it. He is single-minded, writing, now, and tapping time. Often he does this, comes into a room and swoops down on paper and pen with the speed of a hawk on a mouse, as though some small brain-prey will flee if not captured in ink. But in general he swoops with a kind of exuberance. Today his face is narrow and set. He is less like a hawk than a hound today, racing after the cry, falling out of the pack and scrambling to regain his place.

"The book?" she asks.

"This? One of Holinshed's histories. I found it last summer in Paul's Yard." He inks his quill. "We think we are protected by our fear. Instead, fear cripples us, and makes us rather fly those ills we have than scuttle toward the ones we know not of." He pauses, begins again. "We think our fears protect us. But instead . . . Fears cripple us, and make us rather fly . . . Those ills we have than scuttle toward the forms . . . And dark conditions of all things unknown." He looks at her. "Does this sound to you like something Richard the Third might say?"

She looks at him glassily. Richard the Third was an old English king and a bogeyman, and that's all she knows about him. "Reechard the Turd?"

She hopes this will make him laugh, but her contrived mistake must echo some jest he has already heard. He doesn't respond. Still intent, he says, "You are right. Richard the Third would not say *any* of that. Not *any* of that." He returns to his paper and makes some scratches.

She goes back to her book. As she half-reads, she gathers herself for the next pause in his scribbling. When it comes, she asks in a small voice, "What said that player?"

"That someone is writing a play *I'm* writing." His voice is grim. He pauses to sharpen his pen. "You have heard of Kit Marlowe?"

She picks at a loose thread on the counterpane. "The *poeta*? But the playhouses . . . ."

"Are closed, yes, by the plague, but they'll open in spring." He tips back and forth on his stool, then starts writing again. "After Lent, they will open."

"You will return?"

"I? To be once more a motley for the view?" His voice is as dry as a biscuit. "I am a house poet. I write verses for thoughtful gentlemen." *Scratch, scratch.* "'Tis more lucrative."

She shifts. "Than playing at court?"

He says, with the merest tinge of bitterness in his dry voice, "The company for which I played was not asked to court this season."

12

"Now speak of Whitehall and Nonsuch and Richmond Palace. Tell me the fashions."

The flowers are budding in Henry's orchard. It's late March, past Lady Day, the Feast of the Ascension in the old calendar, fresh in the dawn of a new year. She has coaxed Will outdoors, tired of these weeks of his gloomy muttered scribbling and scribbled muttering, and her scheme seems partly to have worked. He's refused to budge without paper and pen, but his mood is more buoyant this morning. He sits on a bench in the sun, his writings rustling in a warm breeze and held down by his right forearm and a stone. He's named every flower in view for her English edification: pink primroses, striped gillyflowers, yellow daffodils, purple crocuses and violets.

A small rabbit appears from under a bush, freezes for a long moment, then hops in a zig-zag pattern across the garden. She taps Will's shoulder and points.

"What? Ah, gods! Yes, it's an omen, another, the most frightening of all. Now tell me, the court, the court! What do they wear? I've seen the New Men in their long hose and short trunks. But how quickly things change! You were there at Christmastide. What's the newest idiocy in ruffs? What were the colors?" With his left hand he makes a sweeping motion, taking in the flowers, the sun-dappled walks, the greenery. "Colors like these?"

She sits near him on a bench, arranges her petticoats, and begins to speak haltingly of red satin caps and azure capes and bright yellow bows and bonnets. He writes and writes. She imagines her voice as a buzz in his ear, or a rush of wind, but he asks a question every so often and she knows he is listening. He is tapping his free hand on stone. After she pauses for a long minute, he says, "I have written a play of Italy. A farce, with characters drawn from the *commedia dell'arte*. I will put you in it, Emilia, at the end. I will make you the abbess of a convent."

She laughs. "I, a chaste nun?"

"I would not punish you so. She will have lived a life in the world, before her holy retirement. She'll have been a mother. And a wife. Though disappointed in both endeavors."

"Ah."

And now, when she's not expecting it at all, he turns his head and says, "Tell me, who married you to Alphonso? Who fathered your child?"

All these months she has thought he avoided this topic only because he'd already heard some version of the tale from Henry. She has waited for him to voice an oblique comment about her life at court, to crack open a door into that murky maze, so she might slip through and delicately refine the story. But his more intimate conversations with Henry must truly have ceased, some time ago. It seems he's heard no story at all.

Well, then. At least his interest is returning to her. She draws a breath, and says, "When I am a girl, and new at Whitehall, where my cousins bring me —"

"As green as a salad —"

"A man sees me."

He cocks his head and looks at her gravely. "What man?"

"A very great man. Henry Carey. Lord Hunsdon."

"Ah! *You* are . . . ."

She dislikes the look of recognition, almost of reappraisal, that appears in his eyes. So he *has* heard something, from someone, if not from Henry. Something about the Lord Chamberlain having a mistress.

She hurries to tell him. Of Elizabeth's privy councilman, the great Henry Carey, who gifted her with his regard — if "regard" is the right word, being more a French word than an English one, for the rough fingers that grasped her from behind as she, just eighteen, bore that soft pile of towels toward her lady Penelope's chamber.

She rises and acts out the scene for Will. Here are the wrists that spun her. Here is the slamming of her back against the wall of the dark palace passageway. This is the breath in her face, the hand in her mouth, the pain at her center.

"And then I don't talk about that," she concludes.

He looks at her in silence. After a minute he says, "This is all?"

She frowns. "*All?* Is not enough? This should happen to *you*."

"Your English has gotten better. Why did you not go to the law?"
She shakes her head. "Truly, you have not lived at court."

"Oh, aye, I see." His eyes brighten with understanding. "Wickedness
buys out the law in the courts of power. Not like the town. I've read about
it. So." He sits up expectantly. With faint shock, she realizes that he is
entertained by this story. "Say more! He holds you in thrall. You do not
know enough English to ask for help. He makes you his mistress, nay,
his ladyfied slave. And he marries you to the coxcomb, and you bear the
old monster's child, and it is a prodigy, and he takes it away and hides
it — wait, Emilia!"

She is at the garden gate, opening it. "Is not story. Not a play." As she
shuts the door she adds in a tight voice, "And Alphonso's no coxcomb."

"I am sorry." He is following her to the gate. Some part of her tells
her to walk away, to end it now, this moment, but she doesn't. She waits
for him, tipping her head backwards, refusing to cry. He puts his arms
around her waist and kisses her neck, heedless of all the windows in
Tichtfield, of the unseen figures who may stand behind them. "Come
back. Forgive me, my love, I am sorry. You are right. I am a knave. My
imagination . . . . I know nothing of the court. I read books, that's all. I've
only been there once, and no one spoke to me then but a gentleman pensioner who yelled at me to stay out of the main dining hall because the
players were served in the kitchens. I am no one."

"Your play have been there, if you hasn't."

He stops kissing her neck and turns her to face him. "What mean you?"

Why did she say it? But she can't take back the words, so she goes on.
"Two days ago I have a letter from Alphonso. He say . . . ."

"May I read it? If you will."

His eyes have an anxious look. He's gripping her shoulders. She had
felt herself thawing, but now, again, she looks at him coldly. He doesn't
notice the change in her weather. He's been sporadically running his left
hand through his hair while scribbling on the bench, and it's standing
up like a rooster's crown. His doublet's unlaced and his shirt is loose. He
is marvelous, the most irresistible man she has ever seen. But *why?* And
could he make her do anything he asked?

"Do you wish me to walk with you?" he says. "To get it?"

"No. I'll get it." *I'm a puppet,* she thinks. *Or a planet.* She's moving
along an inexorable course. She wants, perversely, to see what will happen. Cursing beneath her breath, she goes.

Halfway along the passage on her return, Alphonso's letter in hand, she hears his step. She rounds a corner and comes face to face with him. He couldn't wait, of course. He's gathered his books and his papers, his quill and his inkpot, and trailed her. He looks down at the letter as though he would seize it the same way he grabbed her book of poems the first morning they met, in the evergreen maze. But he restrains himself, saying, "To my room. I've more paper there."

Why this should matter she doesn't know, but she follows him.

Seated on a corner of his bed, she watches as he reads. He is frowning. "They have done it. And they have done it wrong. My children!"

"Your children?"

"My children, left alone. I am a villain. They cannot fend for themselves."

She cannot follow his track. "Your wife?" she asks hesitantly.

"Shrew."

She straightens primly. "Is not gentlemanly, to speak of a woman so."

"Woman? What woman? I am speaking of my *children*. My paper children. My play of the shrew! It's clear they made a botch of it. To cast Will Kempe as a lover! I meant him for the servant, or for Cousin Ferdinand. And Kit Marlowe. More praise of Kit *Marlowe!* Will he not die, to please me?" He grabs a new quill from his table and inks the point. "Do you not see how it is?"

She thinks she does, but doesn't answer. She knows his question is rhetorical. Alphonso's letter is fluttering to the floor like a butterfly. Sighing, she reaches to pick it up. Will is writing and muttering again, hitting a book repeatedly with a hand more rhythmic than angry. He's like something mechanical. He's scribbling something in parts. It isn't a sonnet.

She wants to say something, so she says, after a moment, "Easter is coming."

"Good," he says, not looking up. "An end to eel pie."

She sighs. Rising, she returns to her chamber and examines her hairline. She pulls the vial of belladonna towards her, regards it intently for a moment, then pushes it away.

It has been clear for weeks that she has two rivals. When she and Will met, she discounted the wife immediately. Henry Wriothesley, that bright-faced youth, she thought the chief contender for Will's heart. But by January she'd found herself faced with this other force, darkly approaching, nebulous and powerful, a god more shadowy even than her eyes. Is it before this divinity, and not before her, that Henry himself has retreated?

Ever since Twelfth Night, Wriothesley has been much absent, while Will stays at Titchfield with Emilia and a narrowed list of guests who remain. Having served his brief term of exile, Henry's back in the queen's good graces, and as April arrives he begins to accompany Elizabeth on progresses to other lords' manors in the countryside, as she, economically, leaves her own palaces to be aired. When he revisits his own estate, and is seen at the supper board, he and Will still sit apart, as they have since December. But there is now a more conspicuous intention in their apartness, at least as this emanates from Henry. She cannot quite name what has changed. She herself watches Will, her eyes luminous and fixed, seeking a spark from her lover's. Will's gaze is hooded these evenings, his fingers softly, eternally drumming rhythms on the tablecloth, making the peppercorns jump. His fingers are tensile and strong and there is a callus on the middle digit of his left hand. Henry's eyes visit all his guests' faces, traveling everywhere, like the sun. Except Will's face, which he carefully skips. The silence between the two men is not cold, but charged. She feels, on these nights, like an onlooker to some unspoken debate.

She feels Will slipping from her like smoke.

As for Henry, she's begun to feel so invisible to him that she is thunderstruck, passing him in the lobby one April morning, to hear his "Lady Emilia. Will you ride? We are falconing today."

She stares at him, almost frightened to discover she is visible. He's cloaked, booted, and spurred. "I have . . . ."

"We will wait for your change of clothes."

"I do not . . . ."

"Ah, you've not been a-hawking? Ride with us, and watch. You've boots?"

She nods. Why shouldn't she go? She learned to ride in her first month at court, and today she was bound for nowhere, having returned, or been returned, to the aimless pursuits of her first days here, heading out for a walk on the grounds with a book. She goes back to her room, re-dusts her face, puts on her riding boots and a cloak, and pins on her head a short-feathered cap of the kind she's seen Penelope wear to go falconing. At the last moment she goes to Will's door, on another part of the floor. It's closed. She puts her ear to the wood and hears the scratch of a

pen, interrupted at odd moments by his own low voice, chanting, repeating. She raises a hand to knock, then thinks better of it. She drops her fist
and goes down to join Henry's party.

Wriothesley is all mirth and merriment as, with a dozen gentlefolk,
they ascend a hill, and three of the men let fly hawks. Henry's falcon is
well trained and gorgeous to watch as she circles, then swoops, then
returns, unforced, to his raised wrist. Her own heart strains at that vision
of liberty. They spend hours on the hillside. When they ride back, they
stop their horses in the graveled courtyard before the many-windowed
house. Grooms arrive. She is the last to ride in, and by the time she reins
in her horse before the pillars of the house the party has dispersed but
for Henry, the courteous host, who waits for her to dismount. She can
do it by herself. But Henry Wriothesley is beautiful, and as he appears
by her side, already on foot, she allows his hands to catch her waist as
she slides from the saddle. His blue eyes are nothing like hers. She has
lost her slight hat on the hill, and the wind has blown her hair loose. She
laughs, looking down, as her face nears his. A dark lock falls from its pin-
ning and brushes his face, and then she is down entirely, still gripping
his shoulders.

She and Henry come late to the supperboard. Will is not there. Late in the
evening she knocks on his door, but no one answers. She knocks again,
then puts her ear against the wood as she did in the afternoon. Once
more she hears the scratch of a quill, though, this time, no contrapuntal
voice. It is impossible that he has not heard her knock. Humiliated, she
returns downstairs for dancing and music. She stays below until well
after midnight. When she retires, she wills herself not to walk past Will's
chamber a third time. She folds herself between sheets of lawn. They are
cool, and the bed is soft down. But she can't sleep.

In the morning, haggard, she finds Henry Wriothesley in the library,
standing stock still by a diamond-paned window. In his hand is an open
book that he stares at blankly. She squints to read the engraved cover.
Plato's *Symposium*.

"Lord Henry," she says, as lightly as she can, though her heart is
hammering fiercely. "Where is the poet today?"

He looks at her. To her surprise, his usually friendly blue eyes have
gone hard and metallic. Indeed, they are bloodshot, and have circles
below them. But then those eyes soften, and his face turns sunny. He

bows formally and hands her a folded paper. "This was left for you, Lady Emilia," he says airily. "You see, our bird is flown."

Ungraciously, she bolts from the chamber and dashes outside, holding the paper. She runs and runs. Without planning it she comes to the maze, and enters the green puzzle, still running, unthinking, following the twisted path unerringly to the center. There, on the old bench, she drops down. With a shaking hand she unfolds the paper and reads. *"January, On the Feast of the Epiphany, 1593,"* it says. Under the date is written the sonnet he promised her and never gave her. It begins, *"My mistress' eyes are nothing like the sun."* She reads the whole of it. Underneath, he has signed it with his own name.

She reads the poem a second time, then a third and a fourth. Then she folds it small and places it in her bodice. She walks out of the maze and back to the house, beneath the suddenly garish sun. She enters, and winds through passageways and up stairways until she comes to her chamber. She slams the door shut and crosses the floor, kicking the fresh rushes a servant has strewn, and reaches the wall where her traveling trunk sits. With the key from her neck-chain she unlocks her treasure trove. She sorts through the kohl crayons and sealed pots of vermilion and fuchus, the eyebrow pencils and wrapped cakes of ceruse, the carved boxes filled with powder and freshly ground cinnamon, and the empty inkpots, including the half-used one she stole from Will. At last she finds, wrapped in a rag, her large vial of primrose oil. She sits on a stool before the mirror, pours oil on the rag, and scrubs her face hard, until the skin is pink and white and the cloth is covered with muddy-looking brown spice. With the other, cleaner side of the rag she rubs off her lip paint and the thick lines of kohl around her eyes. What took an hour to lay on takes only a fourth that time to remove. The process is sped by her tears.

When she's done she rises to look out the window. She can see flower beds — daffodils, crocuses, and violets, now giving way to camellias and snapdragons — and can see also the edge of the kitchen gardens, where in December Will named for her the English herbs. She hears her own voice, repeating. *A-ross-marie. A-rue. A-finnil.* As though she didn't know the names, as though Margaret her mother hadn't grown every one of those herbs in her patch of rear garden in St. Botolph Bishopsgate. *'And henbane. Avoid that.'* Oh, aye, I know about henbane.

She feels suddenly sick to her stomach, and sits still until the queasiness passes. Then she rises, fetches a handkerchief from her trunk, returns to the stool, and looks hard at her face in the glass. "I will go to Venice, bare my breasts, and be a whore outright," she sternly tells her reflection. "I'll take Alphonso, and we will be rich. The world tour's the *only* thing for two cousins who've ne'er crossed the Channel." She blows her nose. "Or even poxy *seen* it!"

She frowns, leans closer to the glass, and squints. There's none here but herself, and why should she leave off this satisfying rant? She puts the heel of her hand to her head. "Damn all London tradesmen, foul knavish jacks, damn them to pitchy hellfire. Damn most those who sell ink, and damn you, Melly Bassano, you Bishopsgate slut, for the waste of a six-pence." She touches the hairline, which is beyond correction. No matter how carefully she applies the inkwash, the black always bleeds an eighth of an inch onto her forehead. Lye will take it off, but leaves blisters.

Though she knows it won't work, she picks up the rag again and rubs it along the skin below her hairline, removing only some final traces of cinnamon dust. Then she drops the clout and rubs her skull with both hands. "*If hair be wires, black wires grow on her head*," she mutters. "Pretty conceit, were I a set of virginals, or a farthingale's undercarriage. Or some piss-poor viola with the tuning knobs athwart. Ah!" She stops pull-ing and looks at her hands with dismay. "Saint George and Saint Jeron-imy. Now *this?*"

Wound around her fingers, in shades of rusty brown and unnatural black, are two hanks of hair come loose.

13

The court is convened again at Whitehall this May. By the end of April Emilia is there. She's arrived from Tichtfield feeling a pressing need to speak to Alphonso, a need particularly to wrest more money from him, to arrive at a more permanent means of securing at least part of his pay for her uses. But he is as busy during May Revels as he was at Christmastide. He sleeps until mid-morning, breakfasts hastily when he has the time, and from two every afternoon until hours past midnight sits in a wooden-backed chair, his left leg crooked with his velvet-shod foot beneath the rungs, his right calf forward, his hands fluidly plying the stops of a recorder. He is one of seven, a group whose instruments include a flute, a viol, a drum, two more recorders, and a lute. Sometimes there is a boy to manage the sheets of music; sometimes the boy is late, or not to be found, or incompetent, and Alphonso and the others must flick their wrists quick as thought to turn pages so notes are not lost and the queen does not frown. She likes harmony and order, and has famously sharp hearing. A Dutch portraitist has begun to paint yet another oil likeness of Elizabeth, presenting her in a rich orange gown stitched with embroidered eyes and ears to signify her constant watchfulness. Elizabeth does not truly own such a gown, but she smiles at the painter's conceit, and pronounces it apt.

Happily, two days after her arrival at Nonsuch Emilia finds an exchequer's draft tossed carelessly on a pile of silk netherstocks in her and Alphonso's rooms. She immediately seizes it and hides it away. So half her purpose has been met at the first jump, and now she minds less that Alphonso's mouth is so busy piping notes that he can hardly find time to speak to her. She can wait. She has grown to womanhood watching the musicians of her extended family scramble from one entertainment to the next, gathering and porting music for ten, twenty, fifty midsummer or Christmas concerts. Some of these performances are sudden, arranged on the gad, with no time given to prepare. Others are marred by drunken knights in the audience who sport feathered caps and ornamental swords, who clink their goblets and loudly call for "Mistress Mine" or "Jack and Joan." Still other entertainments are cut short by the queen's abrupt dismissal of her consort in the midst of this or that piece specially written for her, a piece they've all forsaken their beds to rehearse. Elizabeth's outbursts are rarely prompted by any dislike of the music, which is always practiced, and approved by her well-trained ear. She is pressed, instead, by the sudden business of state, or else a courtier's ill-timed comment has spoiled her good mood.

Out of the queen's view, the musicians shrug, roll their eyes, and case their instruments. Indeed, they are grateful to rest when they can, and to eat whatever delicacies they find lying about on the tables.

"Stay, then. I longed to chat with you. I'm glad you've returned." It is the interval between songs, and her husband's mouth is full of honey-brushed Christmas sweetbreads. Having rushed from sleep to a performance chamber, tying a sleeve as he went, he is having his first meal of the day. Alphonso gestures quickly with his head at the gathered company, a rainbow display of women's capes and stitched-silver bodices, of taffeta farthingales of rose and peacock, of men's gold satin shirts winking through cut velvet sleeves. *The trunks are getting longer, Will,* she thinks. *Tight lacing at the points. Starched ruffs jutting six inches outward, like roofs, over half-bare breasts. Feathers are dyed, and felt banding is back.* The Mona Lisa half-smile is in fashion this season, and the room is dotted with ladies circulating slowly, lips under careful control, arms lowered and crossed at the wrists, eyes kept determinedly vague and mysterious.

"By God." Alphonso points a thumb at the crowd. "You have begun a mode. And now *you* abandon it."

"It —"

"Cramps the face-muscles done too long at a stretch. I remember. You told me. But it's more than that. Your gown! You've come out of mock-mourning." He glances admiringly at her dress, a rich affair of pale green with silver stitching. "You should walk. You'd shine among these popinjays. You look well in lighter colors, my feigned Ethiop. Has something made you glad?"

"No, has *not*. Is that I am —"

"You may shed your accents of Lombardy. I know you were born in Bishopsgate."

"Not Lombardy." She smiles thinly. "I told him it was Venice."

Alphonso snorts through his mouthful, holding a hand over his face but spitting a crumb or two out anyway. She primly brushes her lace. "Venice! Simply your only town for love in a boat. Next you'll claim you're a wandering Jew."

She laughs. "I thought of that before you, in fact. I did claim it. He likes a Jewess. And we Bassanos were supposed Jews at one time."

"What's a supposed Jew? It sounds like a perilous thing to be."

"I would say, it's supposed the Bassanos were Jews, once. So said Uncle Alvise. Do you not remember his tales of Bassano del Grappa, where the five brothers were born?"

"Bassano del what?"

"A paltry town in north Italy. They were Jews! Or their parents were, or their grandparents." She taps his sleeve with the stiff half-moon of her fan. "Silk-spinners, or some such thing, in Bassano del Grappo. And then the sons took up music, and turned Catholic. So I think."

"You know nothing of Italy, or Jews, or turning Catholic. With one request for particulars I could make your lies fall about your ears like a house of cards. How did she believe you?"

Emilia is less and less sure that Will did believe her. But she says, "He believed me because he also has never been anywhere."

"Did you tell her Italian women can fly?"

"I came near to it."

"Wonderful! It is you who are poetical, not she. But already you grow tired of her."

"*Him.* But no! It's only . . . . " She thinks of Henry Wriothesley's face, announcing to her that Will had left the pair of them. *Our bird,* he'd called him. *Our bird has flown.* She recalls the nights in March and April when she knocked on Will's door and received no answer, the nights when she heard nary a scratch of a pen or the rustle of a page from behind the door. He would say, the next day, that he'd been stuffing himself with cold fowl in the kitchens, or reading by moonlight in the library. Or perched like a gargoyle on a fourth-floor ledge, taking the starry view. She's not willing to say aloud where she now suspects Will truly was.

"She tires of you?" Alphonso gestures at the violist, who sits twenty feet from them, his fingers flying, snipping a length of catgut, repairing a string. "By God, I'll seek her out and thrash her with Anthony's bow."

She smiles. "I would not tangle with him, were I you. He has . . . done some labor in the country, where he grew up. He's got strong arms. I'm sure he can hit with his fists. He's not a gentleman, though he wants to be."

"Her muscles are hard, you say?"

"More than a little." Her expression sours. Her stomach is beginning to roil. This has been happening three times a day, with the regularity of a clock. She is more and more certain that, one day soon, she must give Alphonso a new piece of intelligence.

"Perhaps I would like her. Perhaps she would like *me*."

"Why do you say that?" she asks sharply.

"To make you laugh, cousin! Though it hasn't worked. Come, look cheerly. Come out of your dumps. You have knotted yourself up in false-hoods with her, and that is the source of your melancholy. Undo the dam-age. Scrub off your black lies. Find her —"

"*Him.*"

"Find her —"

"Where?"

"— and tell her that you are no gentleman, neither, no more than she. Tell her your mother's surname was Johnson, and that she had a lit-tle nephew from Hartshorn Lane in Charing Cross who wore a wooden sword and chased and roared and poured black ink in your hair."

"Ah, I hated that boy, though he gave me ideas." She is laughing again, now. "Alphonso, my dear, if I knew where Will went, if I saw him again, I could not tell him any of that. In one way this man is like Carey, God rot him. He's a much better poet than Carey, but he too only loves me — loved me — because he thought me from somewhere else."

"London is somewhere else to her, if she's from the country."

"Not any more. She's — I mean to say, he's a Londoner now. He lived there a player four years, before plague closed the theaters and bounced him to Tichtfield."

"But the plague's done its worst for the nonce, so why is she not at court now, with all the rest of the crew? Melly, I've never seen such a crowded schedule. Twenty-five new musical scores to learn. A play by Dekker in the morning, one by Chapman in the afternoon, then Greene in the evening, and this is only today's slate. God be praised it's spring."

"Why?"

"You know how spring is his only season for progresses, and he —"

"Meaning the queen."

"Yes, he loves a June progress, meandering through the country estates and letting the hosts spend the money. Lord Cecil or Lady Bedford can hire the musicians and bring up their local players for a pound. All this May merriment makes me want to weep. O, for a sad play by Kit Marlowe! The queen can't abide *her*, but she's kind to the minstrels."

"Not the queen?"

"No, *Marlowe*. Marlowe doesn't have us break into the *tarantella* every quarter-hour."

"That is *why* the queen cannot abide him."

"That, and her scandalous treatment of Plantagenets." Alphonso smiles. "Marlowe's. Edward the Second, swishing about on the stage of the Rose!" His eyes flick leftward towards a page who lurks by the refreshment tables, ogling Emilia. He lowers his voice. "We half-died laughing on the balcony, Anthony and Augustine and I. Marlowe flourishes in the public eye, down in Southwark, working, it is said, on a play about Richard the Third, and he —"

"The queen."

"— leaves her there, plotting how he may stop her little pen. Instead, for his festivities, we have the new sports devised to torment the pipers. For May week, three successive masques where music *never* stops."

"That's worse than last year."

"Lady Penelope announced she would dance in the first one, and then every other gentlewoman demanded a part, though half of them keep time worse than furry Sackerson of the Bearpit. So your beloved Lord Chamberlain commissioned two more." Emilia frowns fiercely, but he pays her no heed. "We must attend their rehearsals, and be commanded by the Revels Master" — here Alphonso straightens and mock-salutes — "who lacks only a flat cap to pass for a puritan pastor. We must sit straight on our chairs and say nothing, no noise that's not musical, not a hoot, not a fart. I'd rather freeze in the Rose behind the Admiral's Men."

"Don't you mean the Admiral's Women?"

He nods. "*They'll* let you laugh, for all their tragic grandeur. But then, the best of their company are all *here*. No slipping on icy stage-boards for the great Ned Alleyn. Who does your girl play for? Admiral's? Pembroke's? The palace is swarming with actors."

"I don't know. I don't know where he is or what he does. Perhaps he's gone home to his wife."

The suggestion seems to flabbergast Alphonso. He opens his mouth soundlessly, like a fish.

"He's a playwright as well," says Emilia. "He wrote the comedy you hated and the queen liked, that you sent word of to me of when I lodged at *Tichtfield*." She dislikes the bitterness that has colored her voice at the word. She speeds on. "The play of Kate and Petruccio —"

"That?" Alphonso finds his tongue. "Where the little boy broke a good lute over a man's head, for *his* laughter?"

"For the queen's?"

"I wanted to vomit."

"Yes, you said so, in the letter."

"But she's left the playhouses?"

"For a time, he did. He said they were black, patched, and motley."

"Things can't be both black *and* motley. If that's how she talks, she should go back to her country work."

She laughs. "He will not. I'truth, think he's gone back to the city."

"Because of thee?"

Thee. She looks at him fondly. "No, cousin." She pauses. "There's something else. Or some*one* else. Or some combination. But I'm not in the game."

"I'll thrash your girl with my recorder. If you were fine enough for the Lord Chamberlain, then —"

"Yes, and I told him of the Lord Chamberlain."

"You told her of the Lord Chamberlain," Alphonso says wonderingly. "Fie, fie."

She raises her eyes and throws up her hands in a mock Italian gesture. "Ai, ai! What would you?"

"You had to speak."

"He would have known."

"A tale of pathos."

"The alien maiden, frightened and speechless."

"The powerful baron, who'd have her way."

It is the Bassanos' old way of speaking, a family language, like a song in parts, point and counterpoint. Penelope was right; Alphonso's a toy husband, and most people know it. But just now, losing herself in this game with him, Emilia doesn't mind.

"Who was that cousin?" she asks.

"Which?"

"In days gone by. The ink boy. Sporting the wooden sword. I only met him that once. He lived near Charing Cross, as you said. But that's all I know."

"Nor I."

"I think Mama said he went off to war in Flanders. Perhaps he died there." She broods. "I hope so."

Alphonso rolls a strand of her hair between his thumb and forefinger. "Now you ink it yourself."

"Hush." She lifts a finger to her lips. "I mix the ink with rice water. It comes out as black, but much less sticky."

"The things you know! *You*'d make a wondrous player. I wish *I* were one. Then I could act Queen Bellafonte, and wear that green dress." Hearing the warning touch of a string, Alphonso grabs and drains her wineglass, then hands it back to her empty. "Again, the choir."

14

The news shocks the court a week later. The poet of poets is dead. The day is brilliant with sunshine as word from the city trickles up stairwells and through halls and rooms. The canaries caged in palace chambers are chirping riotously, maddened by the songs of the free birds flying from branch to branch outside the open casements. Voices are muted. The queens' servants speak in whispers, bunched in twos and threes in the corners of Whitehall corridors and step-landings and assembly rooms. Yes, he is definitely dead.

He was stabbed with a dirk in a public house in Deptford, all reports agree. There was a quarrel over the scot, the charge for the fare. Who would pay it? Tempers grew hot, and knives were drawn. So goes the tale. An ordinary tragedy, except for the fact that its hero and victim, Kit Marlowe, had at the time of his killing stood under suspicion of outrageous blasphemies, and was due shortly to testify before Star Chamber. Some thought — well, everyone thought — he had done covert service in France for the queen seven years before, under the supervision of her then-spymaster Francis Walsingham. A busy observer, he had, in the view of the wise, heard much in the circles in which he'd moved, and knew things about some of Elizabeth's favorites that she would not have liked voiced or committed to record. What things? This was open to speculation. Suggestions, perhaps, about the religion of the Earl of Essex, her current favorite. Imputations, even, against the queen's Boleyn relatives, including a close kinsman whom she had, after his long years of service, finally learned to trust. Or else Marlowe's head might spin in a circle while he yelled that the queen was a witch and a bastard and he himself was a god. The playwright was reckless, even mad, a loose cannon of a poet. Charged to speak, who knows whom he might have hit?

He has died, Emilia thinks, remembering Will's outrageous wish. *Are you pleased?*

She leans dizzily over her windowsill. The palace apartment she shares with Alphonso is well-placed. Near the west corner, it overlooks an apple orchard, and the scent of the white blossoms rises on the breeze. The odor is delicate, but even so it's enough to nauseate her, to cause her to turn and grope once more for the ceramic jordan she keeps underneath her bed. How can anything still be left in her stomach?

After ten minutes of heaving she lies on her mattress, spent. Her skin is damp and hot. *I must tell Alphonso today,* she thinks. She knows she can wait no longer, but the thought of tracking her errant husband through the warren of rooms on the south side of the palace, of encountering clandestine couplings and inciting embarrassed hostilities, makes her want to vomit again. She thinks, *I'll send a page.* She hasn't seen Alphonso for three days. Their chamber is cluttered with cast-off garments, velvet trunks and leather jerkins and lace farthingales she has lacked the energy to stow in a trunk or a wardrobe or even stuff in a sack for the laundress. It is usually he, a meticulous man where clothes are concerned, who straightens the place. When he does finally appear he will lecture her, shaking his head and sending his voice into trills and octaves. *Stay where you are, Alphonso,* she prays into her pillow. *Let me sleep.*

On a nightstand next to her bed lies a translation of Tacitus' lives of the Julio-Claudian emperors. Beside the stained book stand tins of powder and fuchus, bottles of musk and rosewater, and a vial of the belladonna she used just last night to soften her eyes. Brushing her face with cinnamon before supper, she accidentally inhaled a mouthful of the dust and for half a minute was breathless, choking and gasping, until all of it was coughed out of her or ingested. *"JESUS GOD!"* she yelled, forgetting herself, forgetting the open casement. She had wanted then to pitch their whole kit of ointments and powders and potions and creams out the window, to let it fall among the apple trees, to poison the fruit of Whitehall, this contrived demi-Eden. She didn't, of course. As on her last day at Tichtfield, after ten minutes spent ranting at herself in the glass she reorganized her cosmetics and repaired her face. She no longer knows how to go outside her room unpainted.

She turns her face to the wall and sleeps. Through her dreams run those Roman tales of Tacitus she read by candleflame late into the previous night, only stopping to trim the wick once or twice. She sees the Empress Livia moonlit in an orchard, painting figs with tincture of nightshade to poison her husband, the Emperor Augustus.

She wakes to a dull pain in her abdomen and the feel of sticky blood on her thighs. Half-awake, she calls, "Margery!" In her last dream she was back in the birthing bed and her child was slipping from her. Someone was taking him away, forever. "*Margery, let me see him first!*" she cried out in the dream. Now she sits up, suddenly alert.

She bends, grips her stomach, and moans, more in mourning than in pain. Her blood has soaked her nightdress, but has slowed now to a trickle. It is gone, then: her chance of holding him, her hope that he might love his child, and because of it, her. *Look in thy glass and tell the face thou viewest: now is the time that face should form another.*

"Children," he had once told her, "are the calendars of our true date. And they are the time to come." If so, her true date is lost, as is the time to come. Her hope has drained from her and stained her mock wedding sheets.

A key turns in the lock. Alphonso stands in the doorway, a recorder under his arm, his face unshaved, his hair sticking up like a coxcomb. He ebbs into the room. "God's small clothes, Melly, what's happened to this place?" He peers at her closely. "What's happened to *you?*"

In the months that follow, she does little more at night than sit in her room and read. She does her best to manage their accounts, to wrest their money from Alphonso's grasp before he has wasted it all on fripperies, on feathers and silks and beeswax for his skin and cases for his lutes, on new music, on tobacco and tinderboxes and trinkets for this or that youth from the playhouses who's caught his fancy. Half her father's legacy saved from the imported wine stipend has gone to her sister Angelica, or rather, to Angelica's guardian in Lambeth, a gentleman appointed by the queen's chief counselor Robert Cecil, who keeps her in service to his wife. The other half of the stipend was granted, through the ministrations of Lord Chamberlain Hunsdon, to Alphonso on Emilia's behalf, and she might appeal to that lord regarding its misspending before it's used up entirely, might even petition to have the grant reallocated in her own name. Perhaps Hunsdon would do it. Alphonso has the hay-tax stipend to sustain him, after all.

But she will ask Hunsdon for nothing.

During the day Emilia waits again on Lady Penelope, who is now heavily pregnant with her second child by Charles Blount, Baron Mountjoy. In Penelope's person and bearing she refutes the common saw, once quoted by Will, that God gives ladies one face and they make themselves another. Yes, she paints — they all paint — but, unlike Emilia, Penelope never pretends that the perfect semi-circular eyebrows she's etched on her brow are her own, or that the child she bears is her husband's. Lady Penelope complains openly and to both sexes that the cherry tincture of her lips has stained her good damask handkerchiefs beyond all cleansing, and that just this morning, in bed, Sir Charles bit her in his passion. "See!" she tells her ladies, pointing to the teeth marks on her neck. "The powder won't hide it!" Her husband can do nothing to protest the scandal. Lady Penelope's brother is Elizabeth's darling, the great Earl of Essex, the champion of Cadiz, who has beaten back the Spanish and will soon, it is said, sail to Ireland, to confront the Catholic rebels there.

Emilia listens nostalgically to her friend's tales of nighttime passion, and gazes wistfully at Penelope's belly. She thinks of how once, during a free morning last year, before Tichtfield, she visited a corner of the chapel where her own child lay buried. The rites for the infant were concluded before she was fit to rise from her bed; indeed, before Alphonso could return from his engagement at Richmond Palace. There was no inscription marking the baby's existence, only the flat stone on which were engraved, already, the names of Lord Hunsdon's two legitimate children who died in infancy. The stone, recently tampered with, was loose. "Yours is there, too," Margery said, holding her arm. "You can know it, if no one else does."

Emilia comes less and less into company in the evenings. She does not want to talk to Lord Hunsdon, but she cannot bear to be publicly ignored by him, or by Hunsdon's two grown sons, George and John, pasty-faced lordlings who along with their wives take pleasure in spurning her, aiming mocking looks or murmured jests in her direction. She writes news to Angelica, hoping some kind lady of her house is helping Angel in her reading, so that her sister might laugh at Emilia's descriptions of these Careys, and of other court characters. Emilia is not fool enough to share any real secrets on paper, but witty word-sketches will serve to delight thirteen-year-old Angelica.

For herself, she touches her lute, and turns her hand to poetry. Her sonnets turn longing and loss into cleverness, and she loses herself in the game of it, seeking apt rhymes, building conceits, until she comes close to forgetting the pain that launched their creation. Once she shares some of her verses with Lady Penelope, who is amazed by them.

"This word *will*," Penelope says. "You are punning. Tell me! Is it William Stanley?"

"No, lady."

"Sir William Brooke, then."

"*Nay*, lady!" She laughs along with her mistress.

"But why not? He's a spry one, for eighty. And you've tasted an older man —"

"I'faith, 'twas you who pushed me to that. Much against my *will*."

"And much against your *will*, you now have eight velvet gowns hanging in a wardrobe. Let me see. *Will*. I know. Will Granger, the boot-blacking boy."

Emilia makes a droll face. "You have hit it! No more dried stockfish for me. Nothing compares with a fresh lad of fourteen."

Lady Penelope pinches her. "You are tormenting me. Who is it? Tell me! What does he look like?"

Emilia ponders the question. It's strange, but less than half a year since she saw him last she can't summon Will's features to her precise recollection. She remembers gestures — the rubbing of his forehead, the constant movement — and words, words, words. But his face swims amorphously before her mind's eye. Vaguely she says, "He looks like a gentleman."

Penelope gives her full, deep-voiced laugh. "What are your criteria?"

Guessing games entertain her ladyship, so Emilia perpetuates this one, day after day. And she resists her mistress's urgings that she circulate her poems, in which Will is sometimes praised, sometimes derided, and never fully named. It is not that Emilia thinks the verses lacking in art. To the contrary, she knows they are too good to seem like poems she, Emilia Bassano, could have written. They show a mastery of English that is rarely hers in speech, except with Alphonso, except in her letters to Angelica, except when she jests with her ladyship or her family. She is loath to shine with pale fire, to be thought a thief of some other woman's words. Or, as is more likely, some man's.

So she hides her sonnets in a locked trunk, like the swaddling clothes of dead children. Still, she continues to write them. And she reads, and reads, and reads. Among the trinkets and oddments her husband buys her at the stalls in Paul's Yard are books. She gives Alphonso lists, and he comes back with packages tied with string. She undoes them eagerly. At night she absorbs their contents like a dry sponge. To the Tacitus she adds John Foxe's *Book of Martyrs*, *Il Principe*, by Niccolò Machiavelli, and Castiglione's *Book of the Courtier*. Though Castiglione and Machiavelli have both been Englished, she tries them also in the Italian, practicing. And she buries herself in stories of that far country, Italy: news and legends from Venice and Verona and Florence and Rome. What are real Italian ladies like? She reads of Lucrezia Borgia, who poisoned her enemies with a powder she kept in a ring, and of Francesca Bentivoglio, who stabbed her husband for keeping a mistress. She devours the tale of Vittoria Accoramboni, a scandalous woman lately deceased, who was married early and against her will. In Rome, Vittoria plotted with her lover and brother to dispense with her unwanted husband by means of a potion: concentrated arsenic drawn from apple seeds. Brought to trial, she defended herself against a corrupted justice, demanding, *If you be my accuser, pray cease to be my judge!* She brazened the thing out, and was acquitted, though everyone knew she was guilty.

Ai, Vittoria!, thinks Emilia. *Ah, the Italians!*

One day she accompanies Alphonso to a play at the Rose in Southwark, the less fashionable side of Thames. The work's a tragedy set in the Court at Castile, and is replete with vengeful stabbings by assassins disguised as wedding guests, an aggrieved father with a murdered son, and a skull-faced character called Revenge. No metaphor he; he's the thing itself. The actor who plays the grief-maddened father is tall and thin and dressed all in black. He bellows at them, bearlike, from the scaffold in a thumping iambic. "MY GUILTLESS SON WAS BY LORENZO SLAIN!" His face is covered with grease and powder. One of his hands clutches a knife that drips blood, likely a pig's or a goat's, that the players have bought in a bucket from a butcher. The man's skinny wrists protrude from his sleeves as he struggles histrionically with his captors, heaving them this way and that, in a player's ecstasy. At length he is dragged howling from the stage.

"She was the worst actor I have ever seen," Alphonso says afterward, as they sit in an eating shop, sharing ale, radishes, snails, and a mutton pie.

"Yes," says Emilia, chewing.

"I cannot fathom why they do not use painted flats for scenery, as they do in the court. Do they think the groundlings not worth the expense?"

Emilia knows the answer to this, because Will Shakespeare once told her. "Nay. They think the courtlings are too stupid to understand words without pictures."

Alphonso laughs heartily. "And they are right. But i'truth, I like the new flats. They're marvelously like life. A horizon, trees diminishing, roadways narrowing to a point. A natural perspective."

Emilia swallows a gulp of her ale. "Natural. Can anything in paint be truly natural?"

"Well, let us call it a shrewder deception."

"That's it," she says sourly, wiping her hands with her handkerchief. "Every artist's a deceiver. All that varies is the skill of the lie."

"Melly!" Alphonso gazes at her reproachfully. "Don't be bilious. You lost your poet, but you have me."

"Yes." She smiles at him sadly. "I have you."

She recognized Will in the revenge play, though she decides not to tell Alphonso this. Will played a small part, that of a painter, as it happened, himself mourning for a lost son, hired by the other grieving father, the atrociously bellowing one, to create for him a portrait of a happy husband, wife, and child—a reminder of his lost family. Ah, the grief, the tragedy! Will has, it seems, not been using the bear's grease she gave him to stay his loss of hair, or else the grease doesn't work, despite what the herbal claimed. On stage he looked balder than before. He wore his hair and beard whitened with powder. He entered and exited doddering like a *senex*, carrying his paints and his canvas. Why does he demand these old man parts? Or *is* it his choice? At the rear of the stage, just before he exited, he winked at the golden-haired occupant of a lord's box. She squinted jealously at the box. What was this? A new woman? But no. The figure raised a pipe, then blew out a puff of smoke. It had to be Henry Wriothesley.

Her heart took fire with an envy that still burns at the memory. It's a resentment scarcely quenchable by this glass of Southwark ale.

Revenge, indeed.

15

Two days later Emilia is traveling a maze of corridors in the lower regions of the palace, seeking the storerooms where fruits are kept in barrels. She is bound on an errand for Penelope, who craves limes. Rounding a corner, she comes face to face with a maid from the kitchens. Seeing Emilia, the girl palls, draws in her breath, and retreats. Crablike, she starts to scurry back the way she came, her bucket of water sloshing and spilling on the rushes.

"Wait!" Puzzled, Emilia calls after her. Then her mind matches a name to the face. "Bridget!"

The girl stops in fear, and stands absolutely motionless, like a painted statue of a servant. Emilia walks quickly to her, takes her arm, and turns her so the women face each other. She has not seen this person for nearly three years. In that time the lass has grown from a child to a woman. She is trembling under Emilia's hand. Why?

"It was the cord," the girl stammers. "So she said."

Emilia feels ice begin to form in the pit of her stomach. "Bridget," she says slowly. "Are you talking about my child?"

The girl bursts into tears. "I did nothing. Mistress Margery, she sent me for the knife, to cut the pains –"

"To cut the *pains?*"

"The pains, or the cord, I knew not which, but when I came back she took the knife and sent me away again, for more water. And you were not moving. And when I came back again, she said the boy was blue from the cord that had gone 'round his neck."

Emilia closes her eyes briefly, as though the image were visible in the air before her, and she could only in this way escape it. "Did you see him?"

"Yes." The girl swallows. "No. When I asked, Margery pointed to the corner of the room. The — it — was wrapped in some cloths. There was so much blood, in the bed, on the clouts, and I could not look. She saw how

I was, and she said I must not stay. She said she must bury him, that she would do it, that I should go and clean my hands, and change my smock. But Lady Emilia, I heard . . . ."

"What?"

The maid swallows and looks away, chewing her knuckles.

"*What?*"

Bridget cringes as though struck. "The first time, when I ran to get water, and I was far down the hallway, I thought I heard a cry. And I knew, they said in the kitchens, that Lord Hunsdon's wife hated you, and didn't want the child to live so I — please, do not hurt me!"

Emilia sees she is gripping the young woman's arm hard enough to bruise it, and lets go. Now it is she who takes a step back, a nervous hand to her mouth, as the girl says, "Lady, I must have imagined it. I am sure I did. And I left the next day, I went back to my mother in Shoreditch, I didn't want to be near Margery, it frightened me, the way she looked at me. But my mother's died since, and there was a place for me here in the kitchens, and I knew she was locked away —"

"What do you mean?" Emilia feels dizzy again, as she did on the morning she miscarried Will's child. She leans against the wall and presses her forehead with the heel of her hand. "Bridget, you've done nothing wrong, and I mean you no harm," she says worriedly. "Whatever the midwife did, you need not run from me. But you must tell me. *Where* is Margery?"

Bridget is blowing her nose on her apron. Over its hem, she looks at Emilia and blinks. "They speak of her in the kitchens. She's in Bedlam, lady, this past half year."

When the turnkey swings open the door, the limited light falls squarely on a mass of rags piled in the center of the dirt floor. The rag-heap rolls to the side and starts to howl. It is female, and human, but sounds and looks bestial, with its full-throated wail and its head of hair matted like seaweed. The turnkey dashes water from a bucket into this being's face, and she falls from bellowing to mere gibbering.

"I warned you, lady," says the guard. "You'll have nothing from her but a monkey's chatter."

With a handkerchief to her mouth, Emilia stares at the woman. "Hold the lantern," she whispers. "High, and closer." The turnkey complies. Carefully, she kneels and takes the woman's chin in her hand. She raises the face and stares into blank blue eyes.

Margery Braithwaite.

"Careful," the guard warns, just as Margery the midwife pushes her hard. Emilia tumbles backward onto the filthy floor, and the guard raises her as the midwife begins again to howl. "Come away," he says, pulling Emilia out to the hallway and shoving the iron door closed.

He leads her to the hospital portal, where the resident surgeon waits. "So?" the surgeon says.

Emilia is wiping her eyes, partly from sadness, partly in a futile attempt to see more clearly through the gloom of this place, where few torches are lit and the windows are small, high, and barred. "What will become of her?"

"She will get better, or she will not," says the surgeon. "I think she will not. It is the mercury. These women who think to practice medicine . . . ." He shakes his head. "It's her fault."

"But to stall her there, like a beast! Whate'er she's done . . . ." Emilia can hardly bear to think of just what it is that Margery may have done. When she does, her heart begins to swing closed like the metal door of the woman's cell.

She tries not to think, but she thinks. Margery divided her time between the palace and the estate of her mistress, Lady Anne Morgan Carey, the wife of Lord Hunsdon, who hated Emilia, and must have hated her more when she heard news of her pregnancy. Anne Morgan Carey had money to purchase what unholy act she would, and Margery had the means. The midwife was, at heart, a woman of business.

Now, she's an animal.

Emilia can think of nothing else for two weeks after seeing poor, ruined Margery. In the third week she goes back to the hospital, which stands hard by the playhouses on the south shore of Thames. She pays her fee, and walks past the interested patrons of the mad: the playwrights taking notes for tragic characters, the idle with appetites for shock. She shudders with pity at the chained patients, some of them rocking, some crying, some babbling or laughing with endless incontinence. All this misery can be seen from the entryway, as from hell's antechamber.

A young man approaches her, and she shrinks back, not able to tell whether he is mad, or a guard, or another surgeon. The man removes his hat, bows, and tells her he is a student who assists the physicians. She asks after Margery Braithwaite.

"That old huddle is gone," says the man, replacing his hat. "Gone yesterday."

Briefly, relief floods her. "She was released, then. Good. To her family?"

"To God."

"What?" Emilia stares at him with new foreboding.

"On her way to the baths, with the other women. On Sundays, we lack guards enough. She jumped from the stair and broke her neck."

With an effort of will, then, Emilia pushes Margery from her mind. She regrets the whole episode, including the encounter with Bridget, whom most of the other servants of the palace regard as touched, anyway. She will make herself miserable pondering a kitchen wench's murderous fantasies. She knows she is too prone already to brooding.

But a restless mind must worry something. She begins to think, again, of Will and Henry Wriothesley.

It is only a matter of time before she sees both men at court. Wriothesley has incurred new disfavor with the queen by impregnating a lady in waiting, just like Raleigh did; a thing the queen always hates. But Wriothesley has married the girl, and been Elizabeth's soldier, and remains so charming and popular that, indeed, here he is now, in the big palace gallery, watching a new play, still with his long locks, but wearing a new soldier's beard. And there before his eyes on the scaffold, intermittently, is Will Shakespeare. It is Midsummer Revels again, at Greenwich Palace on the water this year, and Will is one of a new group of men who've been summoned to play. He acts the part of a clown in a fresh comedy of which he is part author, but which is mostly credited to another writer, George Peele. Yes. Will is a motley to the view once more, despite his professed disdain for the actor's life. What's more, people have heard of him now. Emilia hears talk. In the city, he is writing as much as he is acting. He has stepped into the place Kit Marlowe once held. He has triumphed with a colossal play about Richard the Third. He is fashioning more history plays, and a lover's tragedy, and — something more than Marlowe did — some comedies as well. He does everything, does Will Shakespeare.

"Such money in it. Cloth of gold costumes!" Lady Penelope murmurs at the interlude. Eight months pregnant, the lady sits sunk in a chair, having sent her faithful Baron Mountjoy for some juice of nectarines. She is fanning herself in the heat. Emilia has let out, then expanded Penelope's muslin gown so it's twice its original width, and still it stretches so tautly over her belly that the bump of the lady's navel is perceptible under the cloth. Emilia keeps stretching to cover the unseemly knot with a silken cloth which Penelope as often pushes away, complaining, "It's *hot*."

"Let me fan you," Emilia says.

Irritated, Penelope pulls her fan from Emilia's fingers. "Marry, I'm not so incompetent. I have read that farmers' wives in Northumbria give birth in the fields and then go back to their threshing, the babes at their breasts. I think I can wave my little fan in the air."

Two ladies in front of them turn to glare, fingers at their lips. Seeing that the annoyingly talkative woman is Penelope Devereux Rich, they instantly change their gesture. Their faces slacken into expressions of bland, pleasant obsequiousness as they nod, then turn back to regard the play. Penelope smirks at Emilia, points her finger at their backs, and mouths, "*There's* comedy for you." But when she speaks aloud again, her voice is an obliging whisper. "Did you hear the poem of introduction?"

"No," Emilia says softly. "I came late." Indeed, she has spent the day debating whether to come at all. But in the end she has come, drawn against — or to? — her will, like a compass needle that must point north.

"Your Lord Chamberlain."

"Gods." Emilia has already placed herself half-behind a pillar, so as to see and not be seen. Now she slides down in her chair and shields the exposed side of her face with her hand. "Where?"

"He's their patron, I mean. This new company is 'The Lord Chamberlain's Men'."

Emilia's stomach clenches like a fist. She sits straight again, and watches blankly as the players end their song and jig. The musicians rest their instruments, and the play begins again.

So. Henry Carey is now his patron. He is at last guaranteed to perform at court, as was his wish, from November through Christmastide, at Shrovetide, and for every festivity and special occasion, and how can she hope to avoid him? If he speaks to her, speaks to anyone *of* her, the fiction she's spun for him of her life will collapse like a paper Jack in a holiday bonfire.

That night, in her bed, she lies alone, tossing in the heat. *What does it matter?,* she thinks. He's rejected her anyway. He tired of her quickly. That dark illusion she conjured for him at Tichfield wasn't sufficient to hold him more than a few months. Her grasp was finally... nothing. Air. He is pulled to his fellows, the players; to his children in Stratford upon Avon, perhaps, or even to his wife, though he never did speak of her much. Pulled back to

Henry Wriothesley. Or to some complex of all of these, some rich, bright world of clever talkers from which she is always excluded.

She is walking the grounds of Greenwich alone when she hears her name.

"Lady Emilia."

She turns. It is bright, hot morning, the day after the play. There, behind her on the path by the river, stands Henry Wriothesley.

Ah. Goldilocks. How shiny you are. She nods as he bows. Her heart beats faster for a moment as she glances behind him. Is he with Will? But no one else is in sight, save two anglers, casting, far down the bank of the lazy river. From a neighboring field come shouts and cheers. The summer entertainments have entered their second phase. A joust is being staged, knights in armor imitating Launcelot and Gawain and other Round Table heroes for the pleasure of the queen. The men charge on a cleared plain ringed by a deep, walled, water-filled ditch, an imitation fourteenth-century moat, with the spectators seated safely on the other side. The contestants must show their skill in keeping their horses within the circle, as well as in striking each other's targets. She hears the cry go up for "Carey! Henry Carey!" One voice yells, "True son of his father!" though this shout is quickly quelled. So. The ageless Lord Hunsdon is holding his own among the rest.

"I must arm myself," Henry Wriothesley says in a half-mocking tone, gesturing vaguely toward the noise. "I am in the lists against Walter Raleigh this afternoon. But sit with me a moment, Emilia." Like the flamboyant gallant he is, Wriothesley spreads his summer coat on the bank. What is he after? Herself, again? It's not impossible. There were, after all, those two shared golden hours at Tichtfield. Her motive then was two parts desire, three parts jealousy. An Italian intention to wound, as she was wounded, by Will's indifference. And Wriothesley's motive? The licensed, undisciplined passions of a rich, handsome youth. But he is married now, recently, and more plausibly than she, to the very young woman he was dancing with the first night she saw him at court, as she sat with the musicians and badly played her lute. Bessie. By all accounts he's besotted with the girl.

At any rate, Henry Wriothesley's present intentions do not seem amorous. He's fumbling with his coat. "My wife is possessed," he says. "She swears she'll set fire to this, and then to my hair."

"She is with child?"

He glances at her cannily. "A good diagnosis. Very much so. Soon to be delivered. Ah. Here." From the coat's deepest pocket he pulls a thick sheaf of fine bound paper. "I have sought you out, lady. My Bessie will not have them in the house. She's a very demon for jealousy. I thought you might want them. What you will do with them heaven knows, not I, but they're yours."

Now those same pages are dotted with candlewax from the tapers she's burned sitting for hours, reading these — what to call them? — two times, five times, ten times through. Her eyes blear quickly these days from the belladonna with which she's half-ruined them, and the scrawled lines squirm like snakes on the pages. They have twisted about her lungs like ropes, squeezing and cutting off breath.

The parchment with which Wriothesley supplied Will at Tichtfield came from the expensive stock of a London stationer, and is as smooth as fine cloth. Each poem on its page is also a fine piece of woven silk, knit tight and seamless. At Wriothesley's estate he only showed her a few of them, though he was writing several a day. Like a fool, she thought they were all either love poems with herself as their subject, or dry, clever arguments urging the glorious continuance of the Wriothesley line, in conformance to the request of his employer, the countess, Henry Wriothesley's mother. Will never showed her more than a fraction of the sonnets. Now she knows why.

The greater part of them plainly declare to any reader's eye his bottomless love for the golden one, Lord Henry the beauteous, fairer than any summer's day, his own eye's clearer eye, gracious and kind. *A woman's face with Nature's own hand painted, hast thou, the master-mistress of my passion.* No wonder the new Lady Wriothesley has threatened to burn these. Only a few poems are devoted to Emilia, and almost all of those dwell on her rampant sluttishness, and his own jealousy — not of Henry, but of her, for poaching on his territory. On Henry. For seducing, nay, *enslaving* young Henry Wriothesley, as Will would have it. She almost laughs, remembering how the young earl practically hauled her into the house and up to his chamber on the afternoon of their day of falconing; how he tore off her silken small clothes and took her standing, like a Barbary pirate. She allowed it. I'faith, she enjoyed it! Perhaps that did make her a slut, but it hardly marked her a steely tormentor, a cruel imprisoner of Will's innocent friend. *Jesu*, the imagination of that man! How could his fancy so trick his eyes, whatever he saw from a window?

And this is not all. Apart from the few gentle poems to her of compliment and affection, the ones he showed her during their first month together at Titchfield, these sonnets maligned and reviled her. They spoke, not of love, but of lust. *The expense of spirit in a waste of shame.* The shadowy allure she'd cultivated, *enacted* for his pleasure had only led him to call her a witch.

Before her lies the poem that pains her most, and the one that, because it hurts her, she cannot stop reading. The candlewax so blots the ink that some of its words are now hardly legible, but that doesn't matter. She's memorized the whole of it.

The poem is written to Henry Wriothesley, though of course, by convention, its addressee is not named. She is sure she knows when Will wrote it: during Wriothesley's absence from Tichtfield that final spring month, in Easter week, when the eye of heaven had warmed the earth and the bed wherein she lay, comfortable, in Will's own chamber while he wrote. Stretched and luxuriant as a cat, waiting for him to turn from his page and look at her. What had he to say then?

> *Looking on darkness which the blind do see*
> *Save that my soul's imaginary sight*
> *Presents thy shadow to my sightless view,*
> *Which like a jewel hung in ghastly night,*
> *Makes black night beauteous, and her old face new.*

She thinks she understands this well, and curses herself for a fool. What was she to him, ever? A shadowy placeholder for his sunny beloved. Whiling away the time at Tichtfield with her, he was always only thinking of him. Did he dwell on him while in bed with her? Impossible, and impossibly painful, to guess, but one thing is clear: in the end, he preferred Henry's real, merry daylight to her mysterious feigned night. Like Henry Carey, Will had tired of his black beauty, and in far less time. And while Carey had freed her, Will had simply discarded her.

He had never known her at all, nor cared to know.

She pushes the candle away. Then she rests her head on the fine paper and cries in hurt and rage, until the sonnet is blotched and smeared not only with wax but with wet ink, powder, and kohl. She thinks she could cut her wrists and bleed on it too, spot it red, like a stained silk napkin.

When her tears are all spilt she raises her head and snuffs the candle with her fingers. She relishes the true dark, and the pain. She throws herself on her bed and thinks, *I will kill someone myself, and then go stark mad, like Margery.*

16

Lady Anne Carey has come to court with her child. For Anne Morgan has, at long last, produced a son for her notable husband, Henry Carey, and now that the weanling's of an age to travel, she's anxious to show him off. The boy is not, of course, the heir to his father's title. He's a mere third in line behind his two grown half-siblings, Sir George and Sir John, the most visibly rising men at court next to Penelope's brother Essex. Still, the tot has his youth to recommend him, and his father's name, to boot. Henry junius is a robust lad whose fat pink cheeks threaten to repair his father's wrinkled visage. The Lord Chamberlain seems to regard this newest sprig of Careydom as a miracle, an unlooked for April in December, a little tin god on wheels. The patriarch is all smiles as he carries the crowing tyke on his strong old shoulders down the marbled hallways of Whitehall. Together father and son pace and toddle the orchards and hedged gardens, the man in his silks, the boy in his embroidered infant's gown. On fine mornings Emilia can see the two from her window.

Lady Carey herself shows small interest in her son. Having proven her worth as a breeder, she seems to think she has completed her self-appointed task, which was mainly, it appears, the elevation of her own good person in the eyes of her husband and the world at large, after the prolonged insult of Emilia. This plump little child has been carted to court as proof of her own wifely legitimacy. As for Anne, she has come because the court is where people like Anne go. She devotes herself to dancing attendance on the queen. When her little boy grabs her petti-coats she brushes him away and snaps at his nurse: "Oh, come *take* the brat, Susan!"

Emilia thinks her word accurate. He *is* a brat. It's his father's fault, seemingly. Old Carey dotes on him, allows him to reach up and grab pastries and candied figs and iced fruits and meats from the spread tables at dinner and supper, to take bites and then simply replace what doesn't please him, floury things that looked like sweets but weren't. The queen is not usually fond of children, but this one, for some reason, makes her laugh. She indulges him, which means everyone else must be pleased by him, too. He darts about the rooms among the ladies and gentlemen, crawling under women's farthingales, exciting lapdogs to manic barking, whooping loudly, red-faced with glee, waving in his hand a lark's wing or a chicken drumstick. Emilia can't decide what he's most like: a younger version of that diabolical cousin who once chased her with his inkpot, or a miniature King Henry the Eighth.

With Anne Morgan Carey at court, Emilia avoids company even more than before. Lady Anne is not content merely to freeze her with icy disdain, to treat her as one invisible. When Emilia is within earshot — and especially when she convenes with the younger ladies Carey — the wives of Sir George and Sir John — Lady Anne Carey makes pointed comments about the low-bred foreigners who infest the south of England, more and more of them each year, with their filthy habits and slatternly ways. They are, she notes, mostly Catholic. Or Jews. Or both. Emilia knows that her father Baptista converted to Protestantism from Catholicism decades before, on Elizabeth's accession, as did all his Bassano relatives. True, he kept a rosary in the cupboard, and a curious wall-mounted silver box he called a *mezuzah*. She remembers her father touching the box when he went in and out of his bedroom, for luck, she supposed. But Margaret Johnson threw both those objects out when Baptista died. So Emilia has only the ghost of a notion of what Catholics believe, much less what Jews do, for all she has heard about her Mosaic, silk-weaving ancestors in Bassano del Grappo, and for all her pretending, with Will, that she was a Hebrew. She knows Anne Morgan Carey is absurd, and knows, too, that the more thoughtful men and women of the court world also find her so. So Anne's word-bullets don't hurt overmuch. In fact, Emilia understands very well how hard it is for a jealous heart not to hate. She avoids Anne's sight when she can out of a surprising pity for the woman — that, and a preference for solitude. She does not want to think about the Careys at all.

Yet before long she finds that she must.

Her sister Angelica's guardian, the gentleman of Lambeth, has brought his ward to court this Easter to attend his wife. At fourteen, Angelica is so tall and gracious and demure that Elizabeth requests her permanent service. She is reassigned, and will wait on several of the queen's ladies. Among these, as it happens, is Lady Anne Morgan, who either has not been told Angelica's surname or thinks to enhance her insult to her husband's former lover by requiring Emilia's younger sister to empty her chamber pot.

"I will find you a better position," Emilia tells Angelica, who shrugs. Her duties are no worse here than in Lambeth, and besides, she is interested in this brave new world. She has made some friends among the younger ladies' maids, two of whom share a room with her in the west wing of the palace, where they all enjoy minimal supervision.

One night Emilia's knock on the young women's door is opened by a willowy, painted beauty, an apparent courtesan with high-piled hair, clad in a low-cut dress of yellow muslin. "I am seeking . . ." Emilia pauses. The courtesan is giggling. More laughter spills from the room behind her. Emilia narrows, then widens, her eyes. "*Angelica!*" She grabs her sister's arm and pulls her inside the small apartment, where her bedmates are seated before a mirror. One is studiously limning the other's lips with vermilion. "Stop laughing!" says the artist, suspending her thin brush in air an inch from her subject's mouth. "Hold still!"

"Are you all so anxious to be junior whores? Angelica, we will wash that from your face, now!" Emilia is shaken. Her sister is nearly as tall as she, and looks, in her paint — which is not, in fact, badly applied; the girl at the mirror is practiced — like a woman, and not what she is, a child pretending to be one.

"Everyone paints!" Angelica protests, as Emilia scrubs her face with a rag pulled from the dressing table. "Ow! Use the milk mixture, can't you?"

"Where is it?"

"There." The girl who sits painting at the table points with her tiny brush. "But Lady Emilia, I worked on Angelica's face for forty minutes!" The artist pouts. She is fifteen, and has been at court one year. "A month ago Angel was a pasty-faced beginner. Now she wears mouse-fur eyelashes."

"I warrant you think this is progress."

"I used rice powder and imported fuchus, bought with my own money, and here you are, ruining it all."

"It's you who have turned her pasty-faced." Angelica's cheeks are by this time genuinely ruddy with Emilia's fierce rubbing. The rag is white with milk and powder. "You should save your money, Kate Pettigrew.

Marry, what ails you girls? Fresh skin needs no paint. Wait til you're twenty-six, like me, and have a wrinkle or two about your eyes."

The artist makes a face. "I may never be that old. And my skin has spots. I need to cover them."

"And mine is too — *ow!* — dark!" says Angelica. Indeed, Angelica has by nature the Italian looks that Emilia — the image of her mother in all but eye-color — has achieved only through art.

"Your skin is beautiful," says Emilia brusquely. "Close your lids. *Tight.*" She has found a vial of clear stuff on the table, has raised and sniffed it and found it to be oil of cloves. She dabs some on her towel and more gently removes the kohl from around her sister's eyes. "You are all a sort of blithering she-fools. Dunces. You should be happy to show your own faces."

"No one else does." Kate sniffs, and halts her brush again. "Bella, keep *still.*"

The two of them, the artist and the destroyer of art, work unspeaking side by side for five more minutes, as though in silent competition. At the end of that time, the bare-faced Angelica looks ten years younger, and sixteen-year-old Bella looks ten years older. Emilia stands, wipes her hands, glares at all three of them, clicks her tongue, and shakes her head. "I'll leave you all to your little play brothel."

"O, *you* should —"

"Hush!" Angelica places a hand on Kate's shoulder.

"Tush and tilly-valley," Kate amends, cleaning her brush in rosewater. "Bella, you are beautiful. Now, I'll start on myself."

Before Emilia closes their door, she threatens her sister with vague punishments should she see her running about the court with a painted clown face. But she knows her words lack teeth. What can she do? Her sister is right. Everyone here paints, and Angelica is not *her* ward.

When she later tells Alphonso of the girls' games, he only laughs, fingering his new diamond earring. He says, "So that's why she asked me for some of my zinc powder."

"And you *gave* it her?"

"Why not? She would have got it somewhere. Might have been whipped for stealing from some lady's chamber. Bad for the family."

"You are useless." Emilia loosens her gown and collapses on her bed, picking up her volume of Tacitus.

"Yes, I know, my dear. Will you hand me that sleeve? And that music?"

Angelica heeds her advice to a point. When Emilia next sees her following dutifully in the train of Lady Anne Morgan and two other ladies, holding someone's lapdog, she notes that her sister has limited herself to an artful smudge of kohl around the eyes and a smear of vermilion on her lips. Emilia stands in the shadows of the cloistered passageway where they walk, clutching a volume of Machiavelli's *Il Principe* opened to the passage about Lady Caterina Sforza, Duchess of Forlì, who beheaded her treacherous male rivals to secure her own rule. She has been rereading this favorite section as she walks, and allows the ladies to sweep past and ignore her. She makes a face at Angelica, who sticks out her tongue.

Halfway down the passage Lady Anne is greeted by her husband, who has — by accident, or the lady's design? — met her at a crosswalk. From the shadows, Emilia watches as Henry Carey bows and kisses his wife, then murmurs some compliments to her companions. The married pair exchange a few words, and the group of ladies floats on, their farthingales rustling. Henry Carey regards his wife's newest maidservant with interest as she passes, the last of the group. He stands in the transept for several moments, motionless, his hands clasped behind his back. Suddenly he calls the girl back. Looking apprehensive, Angelica returns. Lord Carey touches her cheek and says something low. Angelica curtsies, then scurries to catch up with her mistress.

For a moment Emilia forgets to breathe.

"He has given me this pearl," Angelica says, taking a small ring from her placket. "And he has written me letters."

"Let me see them," Emilia says, as she appropriates the jewel.

Angelica goes to her small leatherbound trunk. From beneath some folded linen she unearths a few scrawled pages and gives them to her sister, who scans them. *Dark rose of beauty . . . . Eyes of black crystal . . . . Thine anguished servant . . . .* Emilia feels her gorge rise. "None of this is original," she says tightly.

"He is a great man. Though old. And he treated *you* well."

"Is that what you think? That he treated me well?"

Angelica looks bewildered. "But you are a lady now, and —"

"And you are an idiot."

Angelica's lip starts to tremble. Remorsefully, Emilia touches her cheek. She was eighteen when Lord Hunsdon turned his hawkish gaze on her. Angelica is a baby by comparison. "I am sorry, my angel. Please. Tell me."

"I do not know what to do. At first I was flattered, but . . . ." Her voice breaks.

Emilia begins to ball up the letters, then stops. *Evidence?* she thinks, not for the first time in such circumstances, smoothing the pages out, though her own letters from Hunsdon, full of similar over-worn tropes and tired conceits, never proved useful to her, except as a reminder of how not to write poetry. Still, she'll add these scraps of paper to the collection of more artful, more painful sonnets that she keeps locked in her chest. Perhaps one day some of it can be used to turn a profit. It would be pleasant to see someone else pay for a man's Italian fascination, besides the daughters of Baptista Bassano.

"Melly, I'm scared."

Emilia looks at her sister. Angelica is shaking. She draws the girl to her breast and hugs her, smiling grimly. "You don't need the rice powder, girl. You're pale enough."

"But what will I do? He has . . . ." She buries her face in her sister's shoulder and sobs.

"What has he done?" Emilia raises Angelica's chin.

Angelica rubs her upper lip. Emilia gives her a napkin to blow her nose. At length Angelica says, "*Touched* me."

"Where?"

"In the . . . ."

"Don't be a ninny. *Show* me, if you can't say it."

Angelica gestures generally downward, to a point between her legs. Then she indicates her small breasts.

Emilia's heart is drumming. "Touched you how?"

"Only with his hands. But he made me hold his . . . tool. It felt —"

"I of all people do not need to be told how it felt. I want to know if he has done you any violence with that ancient, wretched thing."

"No. But he says I will feel it soon. He has said it will feel *me*. He has said such things as I have never heard. He says —"

"Stop." Emilia is thinking as fast as she can. She knows without asking that despite Hunsdon's pose as smitten lover, *anguished servant,* he has given Angelica to know that she has no recourse from his supplication. And who can Emilia tell? Her single real ally, Lady Penelope, is in Devonshire now, at the house of a sister. Penelope barely survived the birth of her new child, and is recovering with her sibling rather than at the manor of her husband, Lord Robert Rich. Both her husband and her lover are at court for the upcoming jousts, which will be held two days hence, on St. Swithin's Day. But Penelope will not come to the jousting. Emilia could write to her, but the action seems likely to be futile. Far from court, Lady Penelope is in no position to appeal to the queen. And besides, exchanges of letters take time.

"I will think of something," she tells Angelica. "Our mother didn't raise you to be a wolf's breakfast."

With Alphonso she goes into the city the next day, to the home of cousin Augustine in Bishopsgate. Augustine is celebrating his seventieth birthday. Numerous Bassanos are among the celebrants, along with members of the related families, like Alphonso's clan, the Laniers. They sing and eat cakes and roast beef, and spoon sweet custards, and toast Augustine with glasses of yellow Spanish canary and Italian red wine. Emilia waits for a lull in the conversation, then tells her cousins of Angelica's danger.

To her chagrin, her story doesn't disrupt the festive mood. "But he served you well," Augustine says jovially. "And gave us a coat of arms that I like very much. Three silkworm moths o'er a mulberry tree! I fashioned it cleverly, do you not think? Perhaps she'll be a great lady, too, like you."

"I'faith, she's well on the path," laughs Alphonso.

Emilia wants to slap them. "What kind of Italians are you?" she snaps.

"English ones," says Augustine.

"Even in this pallid clime, a man of *manifest ill fame* might be punished without a trial!"

"Ah, yes? In what century? Your mother should never have let you sneak off to Shoreditch to see Kit Marlowe's play of Edward the Second. Or worse yet, the revenge plays." Seeing Emilia is close to tears, Augustine abandons his lofty smirk for a more sympathetic expression. He raises his eyebrows and spreads his hands in a gesture of compassionate helplessness. "Melly, what would you have us do? Dress up as priests and poison your man at a mass? That's not how you keep a house like this one." He waves an arm clad in an embroidered green sleeve, gesturing at his fine furnishings, his Venetian glassware, the woven tapestries hanging on the walls. "It's not how you keep your head. We favor practical solutions." He squeezes her arm. "*Pallid clime?* What *have* you been reading?"

That night Emilia sits despairingly among her bottles and washes, her tins of zinc and fuchs and vermilion. Of what use have any of these

potions and paints been? *What good to make a man look at you?* she wonders. *It only brings poison, one way or another.*

She pulls open a drawer, intending, in anger, to dump its contents
out her window, to really do it, this time. The first sealed vial she grabs is
labeled "mandragora." Ah, yes. The liquified mandrake that midwife Margery held to her nose, blotting out consciousness. The mandrake that was
meant to bring her child into the world, but did not free him — any more
than did the knife the maidservant fetched from the kitchens — from
the birth-cord wrapped around his neck. Or the dark alternative — from
Margery's hand. And she, Emilia, under the mandrake's influence had
lapsed into darkness, had never seen her son, and could do nothing to
save him.

The boy had kicked lustily the very night she had lost him. In dreams
sometimes she sees a woman coming with a knife and a bowl for her
child, as for some ancient sacrifice.

"A practical solution," she murmurs, regarding the vial of cloudy liquid in her hand.

She has lived in this palace long enough to know where the armory is,
and has seen Lord Hunsdon compete in many sports, advertising his
ageless vigor and skill. So she can find and will recognize his favored helmet. She hopes to find it stored with his shield marked with the family
crest that has been adapted not rashly to claim but to suggest royalty. It
features a lion which, while not quite rampant, paces menacingly.

The armory is locked, of course. But it is dark now, in the small hours
of morning; and she herself is dark, though artificially so, in a black cape,
sleeves, and doublet, and black hose, and the one grey set of slops she
has found among Alphonso's many colored pairs. She has been a lawless
intruder before, in search of ink and paper in her own household. She
remembers how to wrap a stone in a scarf to muffle the sound of window
glass cracking. Afterward, she pulls the sharp shards from the frame,
taking twenty careful minutes to do it. With a gingerly hand, she grasps
the top of the frame and manages to slip through and inside without cutting herself, doing only minimal damage to her clothing. She has taken
Alphonso's silver tinderbox, and now strikes a light. The small flame is
enough. She sees the armor, and can distinguish the heraldic emblems
on the shields. As she hoped, the shields are stacked and stored with the
helmets.

As hazy as her memories of the childbed are, there are things she will never forget. Only a sniff of the stuff in the vial she now takes from her vest pocket was enough: sufficient first to dizzy her, then to pitch her into blackness. She remembers with absolute clarity the last moment of consciousness before oblivion.

She holds her breath and pulls on two pairs of thin, tight pigskin gloves, treated with beeswax for waterproofing. Then she quickly rubs the whole contents of the vial of mandrake over the leather inner padding of Hunsdon's helmet, and also the beaver. When the process is complete, she sprinkles the oily solution liberally with henbane.

Outside the armory, she breathes in great gulps as she holds her hands low and strips the gloves off, taking care not to touch their outsides. She pitches them into a dry well. Back in her rooms, she pours three successive pitcherfuls of water into her washbasin and scrubs her fingers, casting each dirtied bowlful from the window when she finishes with it. In his adjacent room, Alphonso snores.

It has now been five years since her time with Henry Carey ended. She is respectably married, and has returned to her original near-invisibility at court. No one thinks of her much anymore. So she is prepared for, and ready to risk, the inquiry she's sure will begin when Lord Hunsdon collapses and dies the next morning on the armory floor while preparing for his joust.

She is therefore unsettled when, from the spectators' stands, she sees her former lover, very much alive, approach his horse in a sprightly manner and mount the steed gamely. He sits in the lists, preparing to cross the bridge into the arena and ride straight toward his challenger, who's a man half his age. He holds his helmet in one gauntleted hand. What has happened? He cannot have put it on yet; cannot have held it even close to his face, unless the poison herbs have lost their potency in the air. She squints. Her vision is not what it was once — belladonna has very much taken its toll — but surely, the helmet he holds *is* the one she doctored. Good God, if it isn't! If someone else has taken it! But wait — the helmet's on his head now. His hands begin to falter and shake as he snaps down the beaver. The murmuring starts. Something is wrong with Lord Hunsdon! Now he sways in his saddle. He drops his lance in the dust, while his opponent sits his horse, staring, stock still and stunned. Now Hunsdon's mount is running across the bridge and down the course, ahead of the game, its rider slack in the saddle. The horse bursts from the lists. As the crowd rises to its feet with a cry, the charger pitches Henry Carey head first into the artificial moat that rings the field.

Mayhem and hubbub! Emilia's hand has gone to her mouth. This is not what she planned, and she's as shocked as the rest. The moat is deep. It takes nearly ten minutes and full four men finally to fish the body out, so heavy is its armor. In the process of Hunsdon's retrieval his helmet falls off and sinks to the bottom. No one notices it. It will fetch up in two weeks' time when the moat is drained, its poisons rinsed from it.

The body is lifeless. Clearly its old heart has failed. For this soldierly lord to risk the jousts at the age of seventy was brave but audacious, brazen, even smacking of hubris. Many tried to dissuade him. Could he not be content to watch the triumphs of younger men? Let his sons be his youth! But no, he could not. And pride bringeth a fall.

A herald, dressed fancifully to evoke the days of old Richard the Second's court, declares that the jousts are cancelled because of the lamentable death of Lord Hunsdon. Emilia slips from the field of spectators, well hidden among the dispersing crowd.

She sleeps better that night than she has for a year.

17

In the following days, however, she is shaken by what she has done. Not that she regrets the execution of Hunsdon. To the contrary, the timely departure of this gilded lord from the earthly stage has left her elated, lighter than air. Finding Angelica, Bella, and Kate Pettigrew in a castle courtyard, scanting their duties and idling on the next hot afternoon, she pitches windfallen apples at them, then chases them around a fountain. She yells that they are hussies, pied ninnies, and tells them they should be folding linen and filling pitchers. *"Manifest ill fame!"* she calls out, pitching three apples in quick succession. The girls hold their arms up and shriek and laugh and call her a termagant. They are all four of them giddy, aware of the warm sun bathing their bodies, as though the shadow of some hovering, predatory falcon has at last passed on. Angelica beams. Her olive-toned face is bare and scrubbed clean under her bonnet. She has decided to be a child a little longer. Emilia cannot be sad at this.

What chills her is the knowledge of how easily her plan could have gone awry. In her cold anger, her single-minded desperation, she'd thought it sufficient safety simply that the finger of suspicion should not quickly point at her. She had not paused to consider how many at court avidly read — yes, and saw staged in the playhouses — tales of Italian revenge. She isn't the only one who likes them. She told her kin of Henry Carey's horrible new lust for Angelica, told them only the very day before Carey's . . . punishment. Who else might one of them have told? How many at court might then know of Lord Hunsdon's last fascination? And the tale might have slithered back like a snake, to bite a Bassano in the tail. Then — Cousin Augustine, drawn and quartered, after being convicted of murder done to protect his family's honor? And if not a Bassano, then some hapless groomsman or armorer might have suffered for her crime, had the poisoned helm been discovered.

She shudders. Into her mind jumps an image of Alphonso in the dock, clad in silk stockings and the latest French-cut doublet of aquamarine hue, defending himself as well as he can against the charge of treasonous conspiracy. *The mandrake, milord? Simply your only plant for palsied lechers.* All thoughts of her husband run towards comedy, but still, in faith, her blood turns cold when she thinks how she might have ruined lives that were worth something, had the thing not worked.

However, it did work.

God's hand was in it, she concludes. It is only half a jest.

She is plagued no longer by Lady Anne Carey, who enters her young widowhood with surprising good humor, taking herself, her large inheritance, and her loathsome little boy temporarily back to Hertfordshire to wait until the matter of Hunsdon's estate is sorted out among her lawyer and Hunsdon's two older sons. She is gone for the nonce, with her ice-cold looks, but still, Emilia's life at court grows increasingly unhappy once more. It's tedious. Again and again in the following year she tangles with Alphonso over trivialities. One day in the new spring she sets fire to his sheets.

"Melly!" he yelps, beating helplessly at the flames with his embroidered gloves. "Jesu, you are mad!"

"Leave them! They'll burn themselves into ash on the hearth. They stink of tobacco."

"These were not *your* sheets!"

"What care I? You were to smoke that devil-pipe only in the courtyard, or elsewhere in the palace. You have agreed a thousand times, and a thousand times broken your promise. It is only luck you've not burned your*self* up."

Alphonso gazes helplessly at the smoldering cloth in the grate. "You make free with what does not belong to you."

"Oh, *do* I?" She seizes his arm. With the edge of her sleeve she rubs the skin under his eye, while he tries to fend her off. "Look, pirate!" She raises and shakes her sleeve triumphantly, pointing at a black smudge on its edge. "It's as I thought. The kohl I bought Wednesday from the Belgian importer. You 'borrowed' it, and you stink of my ceruse, to boot. And whose is this?" She pinches his diamond earring between her thumb and forefinger. "Whose, pray?"

"Ouch!" He slaps her hand. "Leave tearing my ear."

"I say, whose?"

"Yours! Got by you in payment for whoring with Hunsdon, no doubt."

"And where's the other?"

He shrugs. "Marry, I know not. Look in the sheets. But by Gis and St. Jeronimy, I forget myself. They're burnt. Likely your whore's earring is, as well."

She wants to kick him like a football out the open casement window. "Alphonso!" she cries. "I cannot live with you."

Again he shrugs. "Then do not."

Lady Penelope has recovered from the infection that afflicted her after the birth of her last child. She has committed the babe to the royal nursery with its siblings, and is seen back at court, thinner and paler than before, but still her practical self, disposed to turn her new skin tone to advantage. "I do not know what it is that drives some fools out of their heads for dark ladies," she tells Emilia, revisiting this theme she enjoys. "But this madness, after all, has never affected the majority of men."

"No." Emilia feels a twinge of bitterness. "Only poets. And poetasters."

"It *is* Spain, do you not think? Or the Moors of the south. Do English men, in this strangely Christian way, love their enemies? Love what they hate, because they think it so utterly different from them? Does this mean they hate themselves? Or do they crave the darkness of sleep? Do they desire their own deaths?"

Emilia laughs. She has wondered all this herself, but had not expected Penelope Rich to mirror any thoughts of hers. "You grow philosophical, milady."

Penelope smiles. "After the birth, I lay for weeks in a half-stupor. All manner of strange thoughts floated through my mind, and some stay with me." She shakes her dark-blonde locks as though banishing gnats. "At any rate, I wish to look fairer, but I tire of the white zinc. There are times when it makes me dizzy and sick."

"It's compounded with mercury."

"Is that not healthful?" Lady Penelope frowns quizzically.

"Some say so, lady." Emilia is not eager to seem well-versed in poisons, even to her mistress, whom she very nearly trusts. Carefully, she says, "Some do think it a boon to skin and digestion, but I fear it is not. The smell of it makes me dizzy, as well."

"Yes. Good reason to avoid it." Penelope turns to her glass. "So. My skin's grown pale enough from weeks in bed. Only the kohl and vermilion tonight, and two tiny dots of the fuchus."

Penelope's return has vexed Emilia. She is glad to see her, but thwarted in her plan to request a long visit with her in Warwickshire. How is she now to flee this gilded prison? She could persuade Alphonso to allow her to live separately, in a small house in the city, in Bishopsgate, perhaps, near where she was born. The trouble is money. It runs like water through Alphonso's hands. They owe creditors. She's solicited her other cousins for loans, but all, knowing Alphonso, are tight of fist.

She thinks enviously of Will Shakespeare, whom she has not been able to avoid seeing occasionally in court entertainments, strolling about as a Welsh wizard or doddering creakily in his preferred old-man parts. The Lord Chamberlain's patronage of their acting company, like the Lord Chamberlain's office, has passed to his eldest son with no break, and the group is more favored, more present, than ever before. Will plays no leading parts, but he's always someone, or sometimes two or three people, and she never knows when he'll pop through a door or out from behind an arras, right into her view. She hangs back from his eyeline, and doesn't seek him out. But he has every three months a new play, as though he truly were a wizard, one who could conjure whole scenes of dialogue out of thin air, and she hears he has bought his wife the second-biggest house in the midlands town of Stratford-upon-Avon.

She wishes *she* might write a comedy, with herself and him in the middle of it.

But perhaps he has done it for her, his way. Will Shakespeare has made a sensational play of a Jew, she hears, though the Lord Chamberlain's Men do not bring it to court. There is in this play a Jewess who climbs out a window dressed as a boy to escape a harsh father. She remembers the fantastic tale she told Will, back at Tichtfield; how he drank in every word and nodded, as though he were filing and storing all she said in an infinite space behind his eyes. This Jewess in the play longs to be Christian, but not deeply, not with any really religious yearning. What she really wants is a Christian lover. She is a hypocrite: an actor. Emilia burns when she hears of the play, and resolves never to see it. She had thought Will never knew her. Now she must wonder whether he saw though her all along.

Preoccupied with her fair new daughter, and with her always devoted lover, Lord Mountjoy, Lady Penelope forgets to renew her pestering campaign to discover who it is that Emilia loves. *Loved*, Emilia reminds herself, thinking that she has loved only once, and now loves no one. She is grateful that Penelope has left this topic, but wishes, sometimes, that her lady knew how painful it was to her to sit through a court performance of a merry play, not just envying the poetry, but flinching from the possible gaze of one of the actors. She is expected to be with Penelope when Penelope wishes it, and Penelope likes plays. Emilia tries always to shrink behind fans and pillars, and wineglasses, which she allows to be often refilled. But one night she is sure Will's eyes fall on her face as he bows with the players at one entertainment's conclusion. For a half-second she freezes, wondering what he will do, and feeling, in her bones and her loins, an unwelcome heat.

What he does is nothing. His grey fish's gaze swims over her face as if he does not recognize her; indeed, as if she were not there. And then, with his fellows, he's magically gone.

She feels her color rise. Angrily, she turns, and finds, some two yards away from her, a handsome, soldierly gentleman regarding her with interested sea-green eyes. His beard is cut like the ace of spades.

"Lady Emilia Bassano Lanier," he says, and bows. "I had desired to know you some years ago, at Tichtfield, when we both were guests of my lord of Southampton. But you were . . . ." He smiles. "Rarely in view."

She remembers. *Ah, yes. A hot stare at a table. When you were a bare three weeks married, and the queen displeased, and your wife paying for the match in the Tower.* But he is charming, and despite her disapproval, she cannot help returning his smile. She curtsies briefly. "Sir Walter Raleigh."

"So. You know me."

"I have read . . . ."

"Some poems?"

She does not want to disclose that she has read more than that: a marvelous report this knight has published and circulated, of a far off country beyond the Atlantic, peopled by golden-skinned natives, where he saw a three-skeined white waterfall tumbling down an emerald hill. Enthralled, she had felt she could see it, smell it, touch it. There has been no soldier who could write such prose since the death of Lady Penelope's old adorer, Philip Sidney.

But Raleigh's lifted eyebrow suggests that it is poems, not hard facts of travel, that an alluring lady should read. And of course she, like every other lady at court, has indeed read one of the handwritten copies of his lyrics that have circulated here, passing from jeweled hand to jeweled hand. In fact, she has been deeply struck by one of the poems, that begins *Farewell, false love, the oracle of lies*. She finds this a resonant, meaningful phrase, as rich as any diamond from the Indies. So she can give the hoped-for answer.

"I have!" she says, but her voice squeaks slightly, and she is immediately tongue-tied. This formula is an old one. He is someone she would like to talk to, but he is gorgeous, so she can't.

"Which ones? But never mind." He waves a gloved hand disparagingly. "They are trifles. I'll speak of you, lady. You are, I understand, of Italy?"

Italy, my refuge, which I have never seen, she thinks, with an inward sigh of relief and resignation. Hesitantly, she says, "I am-a . . . of Ee-taly. Yes."

"Aye." His gaze grows hot. He leans toward her and murmurs, "I can see another country in your eyes."

It is in some ways her doom that Alphonso makes it so easy for her to enter their chambers with whomever she pleases to bring there, and she blames him, even though she knows this is her fault more than his. On special nights of court entertainment like plays, he works until the small hours of the morning, then packs his recorder away and drinks for an hour, and though she does not mind his waking her when he stumbles in late, she forbids him to bring any friend. So some nights, like tonight, he is reliably gone, which leaves her free, and indeed, it is a wonder that she so rarely acts on her liberty, but chiefly chooses books and pens to assuage her loneliness.

Sir Walter lies fondling her now, half-asleep. They'd danced together for an hour, and she'd known she'd surrender to him in the midst of the volta, the scandalous dance of Italy, when he lifted her high in the air and her skirts whirled above her knees and the courtiers stared and smirked. His scarred hands felt like iron. He held her like a doll. When he brought her to ground, as the musicians concluded and the room applauded, they'd practically run to her chamber.

Now he has thrown off the sheet and sunk into sleep. He has a strange, blue-ink design on one thigh which, when she touched it, he said was a thing he got in the West Indies, in New Spain. She reaches to touch it again, and he stirs. She remembers his face bending toward her in the palace hall, his avid green eyes, as they danced. It was those eyes, not hers, that held another country. *But then,* she thinks, *we are all other countries.*

So how to cross the ocean that parts them? What would she say if she rose, lit a candle, and opened her drawer, then came back to the bed, touched his shoulder, and said, 'Please, read something. I have written poems, as well'? She cannot do it. Such an action, such a request, would come from some other place, some other woman who is she, yes, but not the part of herself this man wants.

For conversation, he talks to his friends. Or his wife, whom he now betrays. Farewell, false love, the oracle of lies. In the morning he will rise and leave her bed, and when she sees him again at court, she will feel shame. Now there will be two sets of eyes to avoid, here. Three, if she counts Henry Wriothesley's. Perhaps Raleigh will speak of her, knowingly, to Henry.

She falls, finally, into a restive sleep. In the morning, when she wakes, Sir Walter is gone.

She lies still for an hour, thinking. When she rises, in a mingle of embarrassment and disgust, she burns the whole sheaf of poems she's written over the past five years, including the ones on which she labored hardest, the ones she'd last night imagined showing her amorous guest. By daylight, the notion seems ridiculous. Last of all she throws into the grate, onto the top of the pyre, her verses about Will. She sees her old lover's name curling and darkening in flame, falling to ash, then rising in smoke.

That night she dreams of a bird trapped in a high dormer room, beating its wings against a closed window.

In the end she is saved from death-by-uselessness by the queen herself, who in 1597 sends all the court musicians between fifteen and thirty years of age to serve under Lord Mountjoy in Ireland, to quell the rebellion of the red-haired savages there. Alphonso is discomfited, complaining of bogs and bagpipes and vile guns, but he packs up and goes, and Emilia feels suddenly like a door has flown open. Her mood is as light as it was nearly a year before, just after the death of Hunsdon, and this time she has not had to kill anyone. With her husband gone, she need not stay at court. And she has someplace to go. Those musicians' wives who lack separate households may serve in the manors of gentlewomen until their husbands' victorious return. Emilia is invited to Cooke-ham, near London, to join the countess Margaret of Cumberland there.

Before leaving court she gathers her possessions and sells them, not hastily for poor profit, but carefully, visiting the merchants in Cheapside and Paul's Yard, striking shrewd bargains for some of the jewels and gloves given her by Hunsdon. She lingers for a long time over the exquisite miniature of her face, commissioned from Nicholas Hilliard by Hunsdon years before. Then she briskly wraps it in silk and sells it to a dealer in portraits for what would have paid a year's rent on their old St. Botolph house. For a neat sum she also dispenses with a collection of oddments and trinkets she hopes Alphonso won't miss on his return: an ivory pipe, some rose-tipped slippers, four pairs of unsnagged orange hose, his fourth-favorite set of slashed velvet sleeves, and eight sheets of music and a pile of ballads that have lain in a corner since 1590. She cannot imagine Alphonso living a soldier's life, and closes her eyes in worry at her thousand fearful imaginings. She sees him shrieking, hands over his ears, at the whistling music of a cannonball, or throwing down the sword whose use he has never mastered. She sees him chased by a blue-faced Irish tribesman with wode-smeared cheeks, who cuts her husband's fool head off and kicks it about like a ball on a green battlefield. Or perhaps he will only be tormented by some jeering career soldier who will slash his fine sleeve anew with a sword, in mockery. In a way, this vision hurts her even more than the others. Alphonso, Alphonso! Yet there is naught she can do. The queen has ordered him off.

She has, at any rate, some funds to last her the year, so she need not depend wholly on Lady Margaret Clifford at Cumberland. She lays some of them by with Augustine in trust for Angelica. The money includes ten pounds received for the pearl ring which was Lord Hunsdon's fatal gift to Angelica. After listening contritely to a stirring speech on chastity by Emilia, her younger sister — sweet and still innocent girl! For how much longer? — had wanted to climb to the highest tower of Whitehall and throw the pearl from a window. But Emilia prevented this. It was not, after all, a practical solution.

18

The first thing she notices is the tree.

The oak is the largest she's ever seen. It stands some distance from Cooke-ham House, towering over the ashes, elms, birches, and pines from which it stands apart in its own clearing, as though receiving the lesser trees' deference. It prompts the memory of Will's vision at Tichtfield, the dream he shared with her once, of the ring of dark-clad folk seated, conversing, around a mighty oak. She has many times since made that dream her own, and put herself in it, wearing black like a Cambridge tutor, one of a circle of friends with kind, vague faces, she and the rest of them gesturing, talking, paging through books, leaning avidly toward one another, discoursing under green, leafy branches.

The room she's been given looks out on the oak, and this makes her happy. She will see it each morning and evening of her five months at Cooke-ham, and never shake from her mind the strange conviction that it is sentient.

She finds she can breathe here. Cooke-ham is a well-landed manor on the outskirts of London, a stately, three-story granite dwelling surrounded by wide fields, standing on high ground that overlooks twelve or thirteen shires. As she looks out from the summit on this greening England, she finds bitterness difficult, and self-pity tedious. She wants to move along, not sideways, but upwards.

She has time, here, to stand and grow like a plant. Her duties are light. Officially she serves the countess, but Lady Margaret has many servants, and keeps forgetting to assign them particular tasks. The lady has a steward, of course, but the man is officious and myopic, moving briskly from room to room and about the grounds in his leathern hat and polished boots, tugging his chain of office and barking at grooms

and cooks. He rarely talks to the women. He seems not to see them. Left
to fashion her own duties, Emilia spends much of her time reading tales
of King Arthur and Greek myths in English to Nan, Margaret Clifford's
young daughter. Lady Margaret is learned. She can read, and has had a
tutor to lesson Nan. Now Nan sits with Emilia in the summer shade of
the big oak, on blankets stretched on the grass and secured against the
wind by books. Together the two embark on Latin, teaching themselves
its basic grammar, using Erasmus's exercises as their guide, brushing
away ants and pausing to look at small, white butterflies that dart in and
out of the high field grass.

When she wearies of Latin, nine-year-old Nan asks for stories. She
expresses herself with some flair. "Let's read about Jesus, Mary, and
Joseph riding hell-bent for Egypt," she says. "And then Joseph, when he's
kidnapped by rogues and dragged off like a heifer." To Nan, these Old
Testament histories are no more or less real than the myths of Jupiter
changed to a bull and Oedipus left on a hillside, or the tale of wizard Mer-
lin magically transporting baby Arthur to the wave-battered castle of
Tintagel. But the Bible stories are, for the most part, less saucy than the
myths, and in her quasi-reformed mood, Emilia tries to promote them.

There are more women than men at Cooke-ham. They are women
of middle years, mostly. Some have husbands at court or in Ireland, and
some are widowed. Emilia hears them talk as, in the evenings, they sit
sewing with Lady Margaret. Emilia is shy, and drifts in and out of the
gathering room bearing wineglasses and changing the flowers in vases.
No idle court gossip fills the air above the ladies' swift-working hands
embroidering pillowcases and linen napkins. Instead, the women discuss the mysteries of scripture, or of more secular writings: the courtly
philosophy of Castiglione, the propositions of Pico della Mirandola con-
cerning government. She almost physically aches to grab a needle, a
thread, some cloth, and a stool and join them. All the books she hears
mentioned have been Englished, and she herself has bought or borrowed and read each of them, at one time or another. But she has no real
thought of joining Lady Margaret's friends. She has not been summoned
for this. Indeed, she is rarely summoned at all. She is not quite of a sta-
tion to sit and talk with Lady Margaret, and is not even sure the lady
remembers her name.

As at court, then, much of her time is free. She is lonely, but finds
solitude less painful here than when she walked amid a painted crowd

at Greenwich or Whitehall, or, years before, at Tichtfield. She has left off painting a little, with few men here to see her face, and has begun to feel pleasantly invisible. She makes herself useful, folding linen, straightening rooms, hanging clothing in wardrobes for young Lady Anne and the higher born servants of the household. She writes to Angelica, and also to Alphonso, though she doubts her letters reach him in Ireland. At night, she unlocks her trunk and studies Will's poems.

Though some of the sonnets are clearly written about her, even to her, she now considers them hers only in the most concrete and practical sense. They are writings on parchment that she owns. For all she knows, there are copies elsewhere, though not, any more, in the home of Henry Wriothesley. She let them lie untouched for a year after her first night spent endlessly, achingly reading them. Always aware of them lying (yes, *lying*), glowing like dark jewels at the bottom of her locked trunk, she imagined they might burn her, actually turn her skin red, if she touched them again. What has tempted her, at long last, to revisit them now in the light of day is only partly a desire to probe her own pain, as when a tongue irresistibly prods a sore tooth. That self-lacerating instinct is there, but she's learned to quell it. What impels her, finally, is the desire to find out how he did it.

To that end, she's more interested in the poems to Henry than in those to her, and, of course, there are more of those. They are a continual marvel. *But beauty's waste hath in the world an end, and kept unused, the user so destroys it.* It's as though his thought ran ahead of the sentence like a brook, carving a way, and made a new and more sensible grammar suiting his meaning, conveying the reckless expenditure that was his subject. Conveying, yes: carrying, bearing forward, not only describing. He had written this *fast*. How else so many in so short a time? She had seen him sit and scribble as though his hand *were* his brain. Was it practice? Could she, who spent an hour on a couplet, then went back and changed it, could she ever do this?

Thou art thy mother's glass, and she in thee, calls back the lovely April of her prime. Not *like* the glass. The glass.

Emilia rises to look at her own face in the mirror. Here at Cookeham she has started a long poem, has written ten pages, and has run out of ink to soak her hair nightly in the watery wash. She has betrayed her hair for her pen, and now her reddish roots have sprung forth. She looks like her mother. She laughs at her head. She thinks of the red rage at court, burning less ardently now than in years past, but still seen, whereby women ruin their hair entirely with any odd potion that promises to dye it a color like the queen's auburn. Perhaps she, Emilia, could grow out her own hair and sell it for a wig, before the queen died entirely. She could sell it to Elizabeth herself. The world knows the queen's bald.

She tries to imagine what it would be like to be Elizabeth. The queen is the only woman she knows who, with perfect success, enacts Emilia's private yearnings: to speak her mind, to make bawdy jokes in public if she pleases, to be the maker of manners, and not manners' slave. And to write, and be read! And yet Emilia has seen her, trapped like a bird in a jewel-encrusted gown so heavy it hardly permits her to move, a tremulous hand raised to her head to adjust the wig glued to her skull. The queen can walk nowhere without a train, nay, a chain of watchful followers who scrutinize her attitudes and expressions; who can hardly tear their eyes from her poor pocked visage, entombed in its inch of white lead. Was there a woman's face beneath that paint anymore? Or had face and mask become one?

I will never live at court again, Emilia decides.

After half a year the countess removes to her estate in Cumberland, and closes the house at Cooke-ham. Emilia is not one of the small group of servants the countess bids join her in her progress north, and so she regretfully bids goodbye to young Nan, who cries to lose her. She goes back to London. She lodges with one of her many cousins while she seeks and finds a small house in Longditch, Westminster, within hearing range of Bow Bells. Longditch is a neighborhood of aspiring gentry, peopled by merchants and lawyers and customs agents. She is neither pleased nor displeased by its residents. She is drawn by the quiet.

She visits the house of the lawyer her cousin recommends, a fellow named Tanfield, who resides near the Guildhall. A servant ushers her into an oak-paneled room where a young man sits at a desk. On the wall behind him hangs a Flemish oil painting of a bowl of fruit. The oil looks original. *So*, she thinks, *these lawyers do well enough.*

Old Tanfield is away at a client's house. The young man is his son, Edmund. He is a wide-eyed youth, fresh out of Gray's Inn, who turns pink above his plain white collar every time Emilia smiles at him. She smiles wider, and he flushes pinker. A young sister dashes into the room, a pen in her hand, her hair streaming wild. The girl looks over her brother's shoulder and, for a wonder, corrects his Latin. "*Vidilicet*, not *vide*." Then she rushes through another door, mumbling something as she goes. What is his face most like? Crimson cloth, or a boiled beet? He has no inkling that he is adorable.

With Emilia, the lad closes shop and goes to visit a landlord. For a fraction of his father's usual fee (blushing all the while he is furiously bargaining), he obtains a favorable lease on the house she desires. The brick townhouse is smaller than the old dwelling in St. Botolph where she grew up, but the neighborhood is better, full of new and aspiring gentry. She furnishes the place sparsely with secondhand drapes and pewter candlesticks and some settles and hangings given her by Lady Penelope. Each of her few purchased items, each pegged stool, oil lamp, and ceramic ewer, makes her glow with satisfaction as she puts it in its place. The things are hers. For the kitchen she purchases serving spoons, a carving knife, clay mugs, an iron pot and roasting dish, and a set of old tin plates that are only slightly bent. The bed she buys new.

A letter arrives from Penelope. The lady has heard from Lord Mountjoy in Ireland. Alphonso, it seems, is a hero. He has manned a cannon and defended an English fort against Tyrone's rebels. When the powder ran out he followed his captain through a breach in the wall, braving the smoke of the field, sustaining a flesh wound, and subduing his man at swordpoint. World of wonders! In the end, Mountjoy was forced to command a retreat, but Alphonso and his captain have received commendations for personal valor. She is astonished.

Perhaps, she thinks hopefully, *this will lead to some money.*

She is at the end of her funds when Alphonso returns from Ireland, barely recognizable in his soldier's cassock and his ace-of-spades beard, announcing as soon as he steps in her door his new plan to sail with Essex to the Azores and make mincemeat of Spaniards there. He is sure of a knighthood. He has had friendly words with Walter Raleigh, who has influence — intermittent, to be sure, but always recurring — with the queen. Alphonso is gone again in a week, but she's left none the richer. As usual, Elizabeth's soldiers have been paid only with pints of ale and some loudly yelled words about England.

She manages to obtain the unclaimed portion of Alphonso's hay-tax surcharge for the past half-year. Before the weather cools entirely, she goes to Shoreditch with a kinswoman and the kinswoman's husband to see a play. Next to her, on the sixpenny benches, a brooding man sits, taking coded notes on each scene that features a wizard. He is bushy-bearded and hawk-nosed and he wears a green velvet jerkin and a square white collar. On his belt is a dagger with a silver-tipped hilt. Like him, Emilia is listening for resonant phrases and taking notes as well, with a kohl pencil, the only implement she has on her person. The two regard each other with interest. His name, he tells her during the interlude, is Simon Forman. He is an alchemist and an astrologer. He earns a living mapping horoscopes, telling fortunes by casting men's water and charting the movements of planets. She's heard of men like him. "Piss prophets," Alphonso calls them. But this one, by his garb and gear, is one of the more successful. He tells her Lord Essex is a client. For Essex, before he set sail for the Azores, Master Forman calculated that Spain would fall to England in weeks, and its king turn swiftly Protestant.

"I would like to sell my fictions, too," she says.

He laughs.

She asks him whether the stars say her husband will be knighted if he returns from the Azores.

"The stars say nothing about a knighthood," he says. "But they say you will lie with me within a fortnight."

The stars turn out to be correct, in this respect. Forman is Emilia's lover for a little more than two months before she catches him in her house with a half-clad woman from Eastcheap. They quarrel and part. She is not brokenhearted. By then she is glad to be rid of him and his arcane mumblings, his star-staring and the brooding, theatrical stare which first flattered her, but then began to enrage her. She's a little shocked, looking back, by the ease with which she slid into his embraces. This, about herself, never ceases to surprise her. And she wonders what reckless urge prompted her, when with him, to forsake the pessaries of ground castoreum, the baths in juice of lentils, vinegar, and sengren in which she used to lower herself, long ago, after each of Lord Hunsdon's departures from her palace chamber.

Whatever it was, she knows by Christmas that she is once more pregnant.

19

She names her daughter Odilia, after the English saint who stands for purity and faith. She doesn't care that some among her relatives or the flock of fools at court may see in the name her own wish to cleanse herself of so many besmirchings, from the soil of her past liaisons with Hunsdon and what men have followed. Let them say it! She's in the city; she's not there to hear. And she's happy, seeing in her child's tiny face a thousand hopeful futures.

Unlike her first, this pregnancy was a smooth sea, and she sailed through it, feeling hale enough most days to cook and clean in her little house alongside Ellen, the girl whose part-time services she's engaged for pennies a week, to do for her just before the birth, and help with the household afterward. Until the prominence of her belly made it unseemly for her to venture abroad, she didn't miss a Sunday service at St. Clement Danes, the parish church.

When her first child yet grew within her, back in the days of Hunsdon at court, she worried that she would not love it, since she did not love its father. But the grief that has shadowed her in the nine years since that child's stillbirth tells her maternity is its own argument. The eyes of the child she never saw still look at her from her dreams. So she knew, even when this new babe was little more than an idea, that she would love it fiercely.

And so it is, she thinks now, smiling down at its toothless grin, and hooking its minuscule finger with hers. *So it is.*

Alphonso adores Odilia. He is still at sea when she gives birth, but is back shortly after, his hair bleached gold, his skin bronzed by the fierce sun of the Spanish Main. He spends hours amusing the child with a watch that swings from a chain, prattling baby-talk all the while, as though that were his native language. He sews two finger puppets, a St. George and a dragon, and conducts elaborate battles between them on the edge of her cradle. He doesn't even ask who the father might be, as though Emilia might have conceived through immaculate conception. Her entanglement with Forman was so brief, she sometimes thinks she did.

Lady Penelope Rich and, to shock the world, her lover Charles Blount, Lord Mountjoy, stand as godparents for Odilia at her baptism. They bring the girl a gift of twelve silver apostle spoons. Mountjoy is pleased to grant this favor to Alphonso for his service under him in Ireland. Lady Penelope, of course, knows Alphonso is no father, and pinches Emilia repeatedly while the guests gobble cakes and guzzle church ales in her spare parlor after the baptism.

Penelope fires whispered warnings over her bow. "Is it that William? I tell you friendly in your ear, I'll publish what a slut you are if you do not tell me the first *letter* of his surname. Only a letter!"

"My lady, you love me too well to do any such thing. And besides, your name's also a flag for cannonfire. A higher and broader flag than mine."

"Ha! Is *my* scandal your threat?" scoffs Penelope. "Mistress, by now I am scandal-proof."

But Emilia will not tell her the child's true name and origin. In fact, she's ashamed of what her friend might think of her casual liaison with Forman. Though many at court covertly call Penelope Rich a whore, Emilia can think of no lady more faithful to the one man she loves. Penelope's own parents won't speak to her, and still she refuses to pretend all her children belong to Lord Rich. This is to her a matter of honor: honor to Mountjoy and, indeed, to herself. She considers Charles Blount her husband. Among friends, he calls her his wife. They have been together now for ten years.

Blount has overheard Penelope's remark. He approaches them and puts an arm around Penelope. He's brought her a barleycake with quince jelly, but she makes a face. She cannot eat it. "I'faith, I am queasy, my sweet."

Blount squeezes her shoulder and winks at Emilia. "Soon she'll swell again, like a sail in March weather. In six months, another heir. But to whom?"

"Ah, stop." Impatiently, Penelope pushes him away.

"A decade on the precipice, teetering, we," says Mountjoy, still smiling, now rubbing his hands. "How long will we keep our balance, Emilia?"

Emilia smiles and nods nervously. Her friends' position has always been dangerous, but is more so of late. Blount is not the first English commander to have failed to subdue stubborn Ireland, but nowadays the old queen is less patient with her generals, and with everyone, than she was in her youth. Penelope has described how at sixty-eight Elizabeth creaks through her palaces like a painted automaton on wheels, repeatedly asking for news of Ireland, of the Azores, of Spain. Long faded is the flush of the Cadiz victory, when Penelope's brother, Lord Essex, was the conqueror. That was five years ago. Of late, Essex has had little to brag of. On this most recent venture, he captured some Spanish ships in the Azores, but the feat netted less gold than Elizabeth expected. It seems that Essex insisted on paying his soldiers. Some of those sailors are at home now, settling household accounts, while Alphonso has bought the gold watch that he now sits pleasantly regarding. Tension has arisen between Essex and the queen. The shadow of her brother's greatness has long protected Penelope from the worst flames of Elizabeth's anger, but a week ago she, Penelope, curtsying next to the Countess of Bedford as their sovereign passed, was roundly ignored, while Bedford was warmly greeted. She has told Emilia of this, trying to laugh, but Emilia saw the paleness under her painted cheek. Brother Essex has now been sent to Ireland, in hopes that he may succeed where Mountjoy could not. More practical than vain, Mountjoy everywhere expresses fervent hopes for Essex's success.

Knowledge of all these facts oppresses Emilia, and ties her tongue. She wants badly not to offend Mountjoy, and, saying nothing, doesn't. After a moment Blount turns again to Penelope, while Emilia chides herself for a silent nitwit.

Some of the Laniers and Bassanos are seated, playing music for the child and the company. Angelica, now in Lady Penelope's service, is here, and she lifts Odilia. But Odilia begins to cry. Emilia takes her away. She is nursing the baby herself. While seated in the next room, she smells the reek of tobacco. *"Catso, Alphonso, you dog!"* she mutters. Against the rules, he's been puffing indoors. Leaning back into the doorframe, the babe a sleepy heap on her breast, she catches Angelica's eye and signals with her head for her sister to open the window. From the room she hears Augustine speaking in a low voice to her husband. "She has acceded to our request for a renewal of your services," Augustine says. "But she is not well. She will be gone soon, and then, for all of us, everything will change."

Alphonso plays the seasoned infantryman come home again, eating his beef half raw and gargling ale in the mornings. "The ground is a soldier's bed," he proclaims from the wooden floor. "Her pillow? Mud-stained boots." At breakfast he chews raw turnips and says broodingly, "Rancid leeks spiced with gunpowder, *that's* a shipboard salad." But after a week of boots-pillow and turnips he goes back to court, complaining that Emilia won't let a soldier smoke. She's not sorry. There's little for Private Alphonso to do in the Longditch house besides practice his music, and this he can do better in Whitehall or at Nonsuch or Richmond or Greenwich, since here the noise wakes the baby. At other times, the baby wakes Alphonso. It is not for him, her old father Baptista's daily chilly boatride over Thames after the entertainments have ceased, or the long walk through the streets to his woman and children. Indeed, Emilia has not expected it of him. They have never shared a bed, and at court, Alphonso has a room thoroughly to himself. Soon he is back in his silks and earrings, his English pallor restored and enhanced by ceruse, his camp life forgotten.

After a month or so Penelope writes Emilia, telling her Alphonso looks to be in love with a French flute-player, a youth of nineteen newly come from Rouen to join the royal consort. Though Emilia doesn't mind Alphonso's absences, she is forced to mind this, since her husband's gifts to the boy strain their income.

She visits the young lawyer Edmund Tanfield.

"Lady Emilia Lanier." He bows pinkly.

"I could bottle your blush," she says, "and sell it at Richmond Palace."

He turns redder. She understands shyness so well that she wants to pat his hand in a motherly way, but she refrains, fearing her touch might reduce him to stammering. Instead, she shows him her father's will and her marriage contract. She explains her difficulty, or the portion of it that matters. "Can anything be done?"

"You *crave the law,*" he says enthusiastically, then blushes again.

"Yes, of course. If it falls on my side."

"That was from a play. What I said."

"Oh, I see."

"Well." He sits, looking down at the will. "The behest from your father. You received it in fee simple. It is —"

"Long gone. But I have a child. Certainly I am due at least half my husband's stipend. May the money be issued in my name? I'll be in the street else, I'll tell you straight. I can barely pay the rent."

This is no easy problem to solve, since Emilia has never had a formal connection to the court, while Alphonso, her spendthrift, does. Ergo, the stipend must go to him. Edmund Tanfield promises to think on the dilemma, just as his little sister enters the room and begins a brisk walk through. Emilia has noted her habit of transiting thus, for no other seeming purpose than to hurl brief insults at her brother. Or perhaps this is only when guests are present. This time the girl regards Edmund askance as she passes him. "You could not think your way out of a burlap sack, brother," she says, as she approaches the far door. She turns at the exit. "Get the husband drunk and have him sign the exchequer's drafts to his wife."

The youth's pinkness is semi-permanent. "Forgive my sister Bess," he says. "She has not yet learned a lady's graces."

"And she spies on you, to boot."

The youth drops his voice. "I think no one will marry her. She's a shrew in the making." He looks abashed at himself then, perhaps for having said the word "marry."

The girl enters again, now from the far door, crossing back through the room. She has picked up some object in the parlor beyond — a nut-hook, is it, or a clock key? — to give false color to her surveillance. "The lady can budget him," she says.

Her brother taps his finger on the oak of his desk, looking gravely at no one.

"I beg you, draw up such a contract as she mentions," Emilia says, once young Bess has vanished again. "You may leave the rest to me."

"If you wish, lady." The boy is surprised. He reaches for a quill. "I must copy it out from this —"

"You have a form for such a document?"

"We have done business with several ladies in like predicament. I did not suggest it to you, because . . . . " He clears his throat as he inks his pen. He begins to write in a wavy, semi-legible line. "These women were not so highborn."

The comment startles her. She glances sidelong in a mirror that hangs on the wall, trying to see herself as he sees her. A lady? She still wears the silks and the pearl-sewn gloves of her Whitehall days. She has bought no new clothes for three years, in order to save money.

"I'm less highborn than you think," she says. "And I have fair penmanship. How much would you pay a copyist?"

~

The trick with Alphonso works. She now has enough to settle her rent, pay Ellen, and feed Odilia before doling out her husband's monthly allowance. Their new arrangement at least ensures that he'll visit the house to get money once his fascination with the baby begins to pall. But he complains bitterly, calling her a vile trickster, asking always for more, and no signed document can prevent him from piling up debts at clothiers' and milliners' shops, or losing money at hazard. Emilia needs the several shillings a week she now earns copying documents for the Tanfields, and the few more she gets composing letters for the men, who are sought-after lawyers, and busy. She would rather be writing poetry, but she has little time, and besides, to whom would she read it?

She schools herself to avoid frivolities like the plays, though most of her cousins go. All London walks over the bridge now to watch the actors at the Lord Chamberlain's Men's gorgeous new Southwark theater, the Globe. Will is climbing up, up, up in the world. She avoids his playhouse not only to save a sixpence, but because he wrote, in a sonnet, *The expense of spirit in a waste of shame is lust in action.* She envies him more for writing the line than she hates him for calling what she had thought love only lust, mere lust, after all.

But she does hate him, too.

However, temptation is strong. He draws her like iron to adamant. When she hears her neighbor speaking of a riotously funny play now at the Globe, the players being "Richard Burbage, Will Shakespeare, and some others," she finds herself leaving Odilia with her complaining sister, who is visiting, and walking straight out the door and down to London Bridge. It is as though she is someone else walking. The playhouse flag flies high on the other side, so she has no trouble finding the tall, thatched-roof theater with its walls of a white more dazzling than any ceruse. The play is in progress, but she pays and enters, edging past a nearly bare-breasted prostitute whose face is painted like a tavern sign. The woman is taking some coin from a man, and glares at Emilia, then looks quickly down and turns away.

"Kate *Pettigrew*?" Emilia says, stopping short. She has heard that the girl, Angelica's young cosmetician and bedfellow, was dismissed from the court when she fell pregnant. Kate in the *stews*? "Kate?"

But the young woman has already slipped away, and a shifting sea of faces hides her track.

Troubled, Emilia looks toward the stage, only to see Will enter in his own paint, and his motley. He's a rustic gull with money, come to the metropolis to make the world his oyster. Dressed in absurd parti-colored garments, Will affects an idiot's laugh. When he speaks, he exaggerates the midland accents for which, he once told her, he was mocked when he first got to London. She envies how carelessly he plays the fool. She forgets Kate Pettigrew. *To the devil, the devil, the devil with you, Will,* she curses silently. *Why did I come?*

The crowd is having a riotous good time, save for her and for a tall man who stands among the groundlings near the stage-corner, frowning and yelling at the actors. He does not find the play comic at all. What does he say? She edges closer.

"You move like a mechanical dungworm!" the tall man is calling out wrathfully. The target of his abuse seems to be Will, who ignores him. "You excellent piece of country shit! And use Welsh accents, not your own! Sogliardo is *Welsh,* he's not from *Warwickshire!*"

Can that be the author? she thinks, amazed. *Attacking his own play?* She squints at him. His face is large-nosed, coppery, and pocked. The visage is faintly familiar, but what calls him to mind most clearly is his form. Large. His hands arcing and diving in wrath. *By Saint Joseph, this was that actor! The weeping father in the revenge play I saw with Alphonso! And Will was in that one, too.* She shakes her head in wonderment. *The worst actor in the world, and he behaves in life just as he does on the stage.*

This final absurdity makes her laugh, though the play has not. She watches the player-playwright curse the actor Will Shakespeare, thinking, *Aye! On! Some more of it!* Will endures, not breaking his character, keeping his back to his antagonist. He doesn't forget his lines, or shift his accents despite the hurled instruction. How can he stay cool? Does he not sweat? Emilia buys a bottle of beer and a fistful of hazelnuts from a vendor, the better to enjoy the spectacle. The stage-side entertainment threatens to displace the play, so many others near her are laughing as well, and pointing at the yelling playwright. At length the scene ends — both scenes end — and the stage door closes behind the country fool Sogliardo. The tall playwright turns and strides into the crowd, receiving some applause, for which he bows, to the left, to the right.

Emilia drains her bottle. *Well. That was worth a penny,* she thinks, placing the bottle in a pocket, to wash and sell.

She stays, in good humor, to see the comedy done.

Afterwards, though she knows she should go home, she lingers by the quay, despising herself for her weakness.

And he appears, walking, for a wonder, with the tall playwright. The two are talking and laughing.

She has dressed for this, without admitting to herself that she was doing so. She wears a dark blue cape and a sable gown. She has darkened her hair once more, and dusted her face, and limned her lips, and softened her eyes with belladonna. She cannot stop herself, any more than she can stop the breeze that blows back her hood as she turns her face slightly, to show her profile to perfection.

She hears him take his leave of the playwright and approach, as she raises a hand to signal for a boat. She hears the papery voice. "May I ride with you, lady, across Thames?"

The dry voice smites her as though no time has passed. She turns on him the full force of her darkened gaze. "Will," she says softly, pretending surprise.

Will takes off his hat in the boat. To her shock, he is completely bald. He runs his hand over his head, smiling. He begins to speak as though they are already in the middle of a dialogue, one just recently interrupted. "Do you know, this world is full of people who call themselves Christians. 'As I am a Christian,' they say. But are they indeed? Are they true followers of the living Christ?"

She stares at him. Has he gone puritan, and begun hob-nobbing with the Holy Spirit? More likely he's just being peculiar, which means he is being himself.

"You gape at me. Ah." He touches his head again. "This. The better for wigs. It was mostly gone anyway." He replaces his hat. With the back of both hands he wipes some remnants of stage paint from his cheekbones. "You saw the play?"

"I did." She cannot think of another thing to say to him, after that.

"A mad piece. But listen, you. I must beg your pardon, whilst I see you. Our parting was hasty as pudding."

She affects an ironic smile. *It was* your *parting, not* our *parting,* she wants to reply. *And you owe me penance for far more than that.* But does he even know Henry has shown her the poems? She has lain awake countless nights dreaming this meeting. She has heard herself cleverly tossing his own lines in his face, showing by a smile how painless she found his paper bullets of the brain, how trivial his attentions ever were to her. "Your hair has grown less black," he would say, to which she, arching an eyebrow: "O, I am nothing black but in my deeds." Or as now, seated in a penny wherry, he: "The Thames is crowded today," and she: "Is't not, like me, the bay where all men ride?" But here the two of them are, and he says nothing so puerile, and she says nothing at all.

His blue-grey eyes are regarding her with a kindness that burns warmer than the old desire. This horrifies and shames her. She wants desperately for him to kiss her, and can see clearly that he won't. In all her stained, sorry life, she does not think she has ever made a bigger mistake than to climb into this boat.

"You are well," he says. It's a question, a bland one. Mechanically, she nods, doing her best to maintain her enigmatic smile. The wind is loosening her hair from its pins, blowing it over her face.

"Southward ho!" the boatman cries out to the waiting folk on the north bank. The ride's almost over; they're nearing the shore. Will sighs. "Emilia, I must tell you what I left untold then," he says bluntly. "I did desire thee. But I am . . ." He removes his cap, rubs his head again briefly, replaces the cap.

In love with Henry Wriothesley. Why can't he say it? Why can't she?

"Married," he says.

She's never heard anything less poetic.

He helps her from the boat. He offers to walk her to her house, but she declines. She cannot bear for another minute her own shyness with him, or her desire. Stung and bitter, she hates him more than ever, and dislikes herself for revisiting this graveyard of hopes.

Dunce, she thinks as she walks west on Lower Thames Street, past the noisy, stinking glass-house where bottles are blown, past rusty hooks and tangled strings and the bones of fish on the bank. *Dirty London! Never your town for love in a boat.* Her face and heart burn. *Idiot, idiot, idiot.*

"She's on the game," she tells Angelica bluntly. She kneels to store her folded cape in her parlor trunk.

Angelica looks pained. She stands with her hands clasped before her breast. "But can you be sure it was she?"

"It was." Emilia stands and dusts off her skirt. "She knew me, and got away before I could speak to her." She glances sideways at Angelica, who is twisting her fingers and gazing out the window, as though she could see through the respectable Longditch houses across the river and eastward into the stews. "Angel, what happened to Kate?"

"I told you, she was with child, and left court."

"I thought she had married the father."

Angela gives a brusque laugh and taps the bubbled glass of the windowpane. "I never said that. Indeed, he was married already."

"The stupid slut."

Angelica looks hard at her. "In truth, Melly?"

"Well." Emilia is at the mirror now, roughly rubbing the powder from her face with an apron she's taken from a hook. "You are in the right. *As I am a Christian,* I should not throw stones."

Odilia whimpers sleepily in the bedroom.

"Have you fed her?" Emilia asks.

"No question. And her little arse is dry, have no fear."

Emilia shuts the bedroom door against the baby's soft cries. "Then she'll sleep again." She looks at Angelica. "Can we help Kate, think you?"

Her sister knits her brow. "We would first have to find her."

"Thank you for that piece of philosophy." In ill humor, Emilia pins her loose hair to her head as she walks toward the kitchen. "Where's Ellen? Has she brought us a joint of beef? Ah, I can smell. You are already burning it."

20

They don't find Kate Pettigrew, though in the year that follows, Emilia, seeking her, attends more plays than she wants to see. She goes sometimes with Angelica and thrice with Alphonso. Once or twice she goes alone. The crowds in the arenas gasp and laugh, the players bellow their lines to be heard above the people's noise, and Emilia moves among the groundlings, treading ash and hazelnut shells, keeping a firm hand on her purse, scanning and questioning the circulating women of sale. She earns only a wealth of odd looks and a few perverse propositions, many from men who assume she, too, is a punk. Sometimes accidentally, she treads on some feet. The streets nearby the Southwark theaters are lined with bear-baiting pits and stews, and she searches these sites, as well. She and Angelica are loath to enter the Southwark bordellos, but they inquire of the surprisingly fashionable women who stand outside them. The London flesh-peddlers have long been the first to start new modes of dress which only later appear at court along with the Paris fashions. Emilia sees Angelica taking interested note of the mannish, squarish headgear atop fire-red feminine heads of hair, of striped sleeves protruding from half-laced bone bodices. Among the colorful harlots whose throats are dressed with paste diamonds and rubies, they find half a dozen Kates. But none is called Pettigrew.

"She cannot have vanished into thin air." Emilia and Angelica are strolling toward the south entrance of London Bridge after a sixth disappointing visit to Southwark. Emilia shades her eyes against the sun that slants through the beeches' yellowing leaves and scatters splotches of light on the riverside path. A man on a barge hoots at them, yelling some vague, crude invitation as he poles his freight along. Absently, Emilia raises a fist and gives him the *figo,* then thinks, as she drops her hand, that she has lately been spending too much time among prostitutes. She says to her sister, "Can she have changed her name?"

Angelica is pensive. "I would have, were I her."

Emilia steps delicately over a pile of dog droppings. "What were her parents?"

"She'd no mother she could remember. The woman died birthing one of her brothers. The family lived in a village outside Surrey. She had a stepmother she hated and a passel of siblings." She knits her brow, struggling to remember. "Somewhere back in time the family farmed the land, but lost their holding when a lord enclosed his whole estate for sheep grazing. And her father got trained up as a shoemaker then. He made slippers for a woman who cleaned ladies' gowns at Nonsuch, which is how Kate came there. But after she left home the father never wrote and she never visited them. At court now, no one knows her. Or they pretend not. It's as though she'd never been."

A second season of fruitless seeking ends when the air grows cold and the playhouses close their doors. Emilia declares the pair of them beaten. Regretfully, they say a prayer for the downtrodden Pettigrew and stop their search.

These days, more and more Londoners are whispering what it is treasonous to speak aloud: that the queen may soon die. Emilia remembers Augustine's warning to Alphonso, delivered *sotto voce* in her parlor at little Odilia's baptismal party: that when the queen was gone, things would change for all of them. Augustine meant things would change for the Bassanos and the Laniers, and the queen doesn't anyway die this year. But the lives of Penelope Rich and Baron Mountjoy change anyway, in a way no one expects, after Penelope's brother, Robin Devereux, renowned general and Earl of Essex, does the unthinkable. He bursts into the queen's inner chamber and views her without her paint.

Hubris indeed, bordering on madness. It is bad enough already when a letter from Ireland reports no rebellion broached upon Essex's sword, but a vile peace treaty sealed between the earl and the wild warring chieftain Tyrone. The queen expresses her fury in a responding letter. Essex races back to England to defend himself, and opens a door that should have stayed closed. There sits the old queen, bald and shivering in her nightdress, her feet soaking in a bowl, her yellow limbs wasted, her back hunched with age, her wrinkled, mottled face full of pits from the smallpox she bested in her youth.

"My sovereign!" Essex cries, drawing his sword. The queen's ladies cry out in horror. The queen only gazes impassively at Essex through the windows of her eyes, regarding with interest this image of her own bold youth, or of someone's. A guard who's raced in after the striding earl now leaps to seize his arm. But there is no need. Essex means only to offer his sword to Elizabeth, and now does so, kneeling before her. And there the tableau. Essex kneeling, head bowed, strong arms lifted, holding the sword. The closed-faced queen seated with her bony hands in her lap. The palace guard watching warily, poised to intervene. In the margins of the scene stand the wide-eyed women, their white faces turned toward Essex, their forms like wax figures carved in attitudes of interrupted service: wig-combing, powder-mixing, opening a casement to clear the room of chemical fumes. One especially pale lady stands bearing in her hands an artist's palette of vermilion, kohl, and ceruse, as though she is come to offer savory tidbits to the male guests.

That lady is Penelope Rich.

Master-mistress of all occasions, Elizabeth laughs after a tense moment, making light of Essex's intrusion. The women glance at each other sidelong. They know her smile is part of her mask. The queen waves Essex out, promising him a timely hearing.

But once the ceruse and the fuchus and the perfect half-moon eyebrows are back on her face, she turns her reddened cheek from him like a disdainful mistress, leaving him to freeze and fry in his house in the Strand. He writes her letters. He writes her poems. He hears nothing from her, while her counselors successively strip him, day by day, of all his courtly offices. Earl Marshal. Master of the Ordnance. Master of the Queen's Horse. Privy Counselor. All these titles are transferred to his old rivals, or to new men, up and coming men, of whom he's barely heard. For nearly a decade Essex has been Elizabeth's darling, and by year's end he is no more than a private citizen.

Desperate, Essex rides out of his courtyard toward the palace, meaning to fall on the place like lightning, to cut his way past Lord Robert Cecil, past Sir Walter Raleigh, past all the rival suitors who stand between him and the painted incarnation of his ambition. He will make his lady understand his worth. He never gets past the end of the Strand. Royal guards, poised to spring, lie waiting for him outside his house. They interrupt his progress. Now he lives in the Tower.

Lord Robert Rich, Penelope's husband, doesn't wait for Essex's execution to throw Penelope and her children out of his house. He keeps the plate, furniture, curtains, and significant cash dowry she brought with her upon the marriage — the part of that dowry, that is, that remained after he'd paid his own family's debts and bought jewels for the then-resident doxy. Rich has been smoldering for years, a cuckold so obvious even he can see it, his wrath held in check only by his fear of Essex's arm. Now the wind is on his side. He keeps the two adolescent boys he knows as his own, and shoves the rest of them out.

Penelope sends her servants packing, with little more than her thanks and some small gifts and good wishes. Lace handkerchiefs, velvet purses, an ivory Indian comb, goodbye. Now nineteen, Angelica comes permanently to Emilia in Longditch, Westminster, crying at the loss of her mistress and of the beautiful peacock men of Whitehall and Richmond Palaces, of her hope for a glittering match with one of them. At court, Penelope is given clothing and jewels and children's clothing by the other mistresses of the queen's bedchamber, who, after slighting her for years, are struck by the knowledge that they love her dearly. She risks the queen's displeasure by moving herself and her young ones directly into the Devonshire manor of Charles Blount, where she and he live like man and wife. Luckily for the pair, Elizabeth in her old age lacks the vigor with which she once pursued the more conspicuous erotic offenders of her ladies' circle. In the past, Penelope was pardoned because the queen loved her brother. Now she escapes notice because the queen can no longer travel more than one vengeful track at a time. The path Elizabeth presently walks leads toward Essex's death on a scaffold. From now until the last day of her life, she will never really see anything else.

"Charles is appointed a judge," Lady Penelope tells Emilia. She is grim, but dry-eyed, and Emilia understands why she is tearless without Penelope saying it. Her erstwhile mistress knows lives are self-shaped by choices, and that her brother has chosen his. "My husband is trying to urge leniency" — by "husband" she does not mean Robert Rich — "but the best he can do is persuade Lord Cecil to spare Robin the drawing and quartering." Penelope shakes the folds out of a damask gown, then grasps a corner of the cloth and examines it critically. "Torn. I've worn it half a hundred times. But I can patch it where no one can see."

"I'll do it, lady, at home." Emilia takes and refolds the gown. Two children younger than four circle them, toddling and tripping and rolling on the floor-rushes. One grabs a glass letter-opener from a table and begins to chew its edge. Distractedly, Penelope takes the tool from the child's fat fist. The other child stops to poke a forefinger in the many-colored mixes of his mother's painting table, then slides the finger on the table's surface, smearing blue and green paste on the hardwood. Emilia crosses to the table, wipes the boy's hands with her handkerchief, and gives him a glove to play with instead. Her own child is home with Angelica. She has come to Devonshire at her own expense to help Penelope settle in.

"Have you seen him, lady? Robin?" She corrects herself. "Lord Robert?"

"I tried, twice. They deny us entry to the Tower." Here Penelope does blink rapidly, tilting her head to keep the tears in place. "Ah! My eyes sting."

"'Tis the oil of cloves."

Penelope deftly wipes the skin just above and below her eyes with a ragged cloth she lifts from her table of cosmetics. "Do you know, he is my brother, but he's little more than a stranger to me. We were raised apart. I never met him til he was a man, or not that I remember. I will tell you this, Emilia — I feel less grief for his fall than fear for the rest of us who bear his name."

"Yet you tried to see him." *Even after most of your family rejected you.*

Penelope looks briefly haughty, shaking out another gown, this one of rose satin. "That was a matter of honor. And loyalty. I owe something to his protection, though, i'faith, I'm not sorry to be put out in the cold at last."

"This manor looks warm," says Emilia softly, gazing at the silk sheets and the velvet draperies.

Penelope laughs her rich, deep laugh. "Yes. I exaggerate. But we could lose it all in a day. Charles is risking his neck to speak on Robin's behalf."

"Is Lord Robert allowed to see Charles?"

"One interview only. As for the rest of us, Robin's not let even to write. I suppose it would only endanger us the more if he did, but imagine it, for him! All alone in that damp Tower." Despite her claim that she doesn't grieve for her brother, she has again paused to wipe the delicate skin below her eyes. "He's only been allowed his confession. And that, if I know him, he makes only so she won't take the family estate from him, as she's taken everything else." She sits on the bed, still wiping her eyes with the cloth. She smiles sadly. "Though it must be said it was she who gave it all in the first place."

"She did not give him his life," Emilia is bold enough to say.

"That she did not." Penelope nods, balling the rag in her hand. "That, God gave him. And now he has thrown it away."

The crowd is thick in the London streets on the day of Essex's beheading. It is February, and cold, but the folk are well wrapped, and as always they love a spectacle. From her window Emilia sees a gallimaufry of citizens go past, a mix of lawyers and apprentices and gentlemen and baker's wives and even a priest of the church, all talking with great animation. She forbids Angelica to venture forth, knowing the rowdiness of crowds, especially when blood is the argument. Her cat, Mumbleclutch, yowls outside the door. When she opens it, as the cat darts in, she hears this phrase from the road: "Some players from the Globe are in it."

"Ho!"

The blue-capped apprentice who spoke stops and walks toward her, his face a question. She pulls the door shut behind her. "What said you, sirrah? Of the Globe players?"

"Oh." He tilts his cap and bows. "That some of them may hang for it, lady. They say Shakespeare's men put on a play for Essex's men, to urge the rising, the night before Essex tried to kill the queen."

They say. "Essex did not try to kill the queen," she corrects, though she keeps her voice low. "What play? Was he in it? Will Shakespeare?"

"Marry, I know not the title. Some old history. And Essex sat in a box and watched it, and clapped when the king was brought down. So they say."

"What I meant —" She stops herself. The boy is twitching, so anxious is he to rejoin his fellows on the march to the scaffold, and it will do her no good to perform a curious interrogation in the street. Besides, the air is freezing. "Get you gone." He turns and dashes. She goes back inside and shuts the door hard.

Angelica is patting Mumbleclutch, who sits in her lap, purring. Seeing Emilia's face, she asks, "What's the matter? You look like a sheet."

She raises fingers to her cheeks and pinches the skin, saying, "I don't hate him enough to want him dead."

"Hate him? Why should you hate Essex at all? Was he your lover, too?"

Emilia drops her hands and darts her sister a sharp look. "Not so saucy, mistress! You've been at court too long a year. If *you're* still a virgin, I'll eat Mumbleclutch for supper."

Angelica shifts in her chair, dislodging the cat, who lands on his feet and saunters toward the kitchen. "O, I am virgin still, and likely to be so always, here in good Westminster." She looks peeved. "There's naught to do here. No one to marry, and no one even to see me, since you'll not let me go to the plays."

"Then take off that paint. It does *me* no good."

"*You* take off *your* paint."

"What can you mean? I wear hardly any these days."

"Ha!" Angelica leans forward and points accusingly. "You've a quarter-inch of blacking lining your eyes. You look like Bull's-eye the Lord Chamberlain's dog."

"I thank you. A well-chosen insult." Emilia crosses the room to look at herself in the small mirror. She hasn't inked her hair for years, and now it's all a natural red-brown the queen would have envied. Of course, the queen likely envies anyone's hair. And Emilia's face? She uses powder only sparingly, but Angelica is right. She cannot seem to leave off the kohl. To her view, her eyes look small without it.

Behind her Angelica slides off her stool onto the floor, where she sits amid the rushes with her legs sticking straight out like a child's. She sighs loudly, theatrically. "Can we not go to the —"

"*No.* We will not make the Devereuxs' tragedy our sport. Though, marry, I *should* take you there, to Tower Hill, if you so long to be a gadabout. It would fix you." In her life Emilia has seen one execution, that of a Jesuit proselytizer, tried, sentenced, and done away with during her second year at court. Attendance at his due punishment was mandatory for all Elizabeth's servants, and she and some others she knew went, and suffered nightmares for months afterward. "If I took you up there, it would cure your longing for entertainment. You'd run home and hide under the bed." She kneels to pick up Odilia from her low cradle and kisses her. The smiling baby's skin is impossibly soft and fresh. *Did I ever have skin like this? Did I glow like an April?* Odilia babbles and coos and says her one word, which is "cod."

"There are no men here," whines Angelica, who has now collapsed backwards on the floor, where she lies like a felled soldier.

No men. A problem to be solved, indeed. Emilia lays Odilia down. She bites her lip to keep herself from agreeing with Angelica.

Angelica twitches her hands and feet. "We never go anywhere!"

"I will take you somewhere. I promise. But not today."

The next morning finds London subdued after its executional orgy. Ellen the maidservant appears in cambric skirt and apron, to sweep the floors and take temporary charge of the baby. Today Emilia has allowed Angelica a thin line of kohl, but no fucus or ceruse or eyebrow pencil. "Hypocrite," Angelica says. Emilia simply hums in reply. Together the women walk toward Gresham Street by the Guildhall.

"I have copied five contracts out," Emilia says. "These will bring the Tanfields five pounds, and us five shillings."

"The Tanfields have the better end of the stick."

"Peace." Angelica is right, of course. "You're walking in the middle, girl. That's a good way to get flattened."

"At court, the ladies have a new way to get money for cosmetics and caps. Gentlemen give them jewels and gold coins for piercing their ears. You take a sharp needle and plunge it into the lobe so quick and hard it goes right through. Though once I tried it with a Frenchman, Sir Gervaise, and I quailed, so the needle stuck about halfway. So he shrieked and ran about the room, but I said he still should pay half a crown —"

"If you continue with this story I will leave you in the High Street, square in the path of that carthorse that is now barreling toward you."

Angelica jumps to the side, waving road-dust from her nose as the horse trots past. "Frot this street!"

"If you want to be a gentlewoman, speak like one. Come, walk quicker. I will present you to a young lady you may like. She's rude, like you, but much more clever."

Bess Tanfield is not in sight, however, at the lawyers' domicile. Her brother tells Emilia that his sister, now aged fifteen, has begun hiding herself away in odd parts of the house, composing bits of philosophical poetry and scenes for tragic plays. He seems ashamed to confess this. "I told her of your offer of lute lessons. She says she lacks time for musical study. But I will put the case before my father."

The young man is not a constant shade of rose today. Instead, there ripple across his face a series of dawnlike hues, from red to pink to a nearly translucent pallor that makes him appear shocked, but still somehow ardent. He remains standing, though Emilia has comfortably seated herself across from him. "Would Bess let me read what she writes?" she says curiously, placing her neatly copied contracts on the desk.

He doesn't answer. He is transfixed by something behind her. She follows his gaze and sees what's at the end of it: her sister, affecting complete lack of interest as she looks at the bowl of fruit in the oil on the wall, yet angling herself to display profile and form to advantage.

Emilia says brightly, "Master Tanfield, know Mistress Angelica."

Angelica nods. Edmund bows deeply, but remains speechless, staring.

Emilia sighs as theatrically as Angelica did yesterday on the rush-strewn floor. "My dear sister enjoys the plays. Alas, she has none to accompany her to the Southwark Liberties."

Proving the axiom that all lawyers love plays, Edmund's face lights up and his tongue springs to life. "Shall I take you to a city comedy, Mistress Bassano?"

Angelica shrugs. "I've seen all of Chapman's at court." Her voice is a study in tedium.

He wilts a little. "*Twelfth Night*, then, when it's next at the Globe?"

"With the boy dressed as a girl dressed as a boy!" Angelica's world-weary mask drops and she claps her hands with delight. Edmund Tanfield brightens again.

Off they go, thinks Emilia. *I might have scripted it.*

21

As it turns out, no player is punished for the Globe performance of what Emilia discovers was Will Shakespeare's *Richard the Second* on the eve of Essex's arrest. Thanks to the well-rehearsed tradesman's accents of the actor called to testify, the players are judged too menial and thus surely ignorant of statecraft to have taken any knowing part in events. The members of the court of Star Chamber shake their heads and let the men go.

Emilia devours the tale as she hears it from her wayward husband, who visits the house in Longditch, Westminster, sporadically to sleep off a city drunk and visit his ladies. Alphonso is the only person she's ever told of her hurtful pass with young Shakespeare, back when they *were* middling young, though this doesn't mean Alphonso's the only one who knows. There is Henry Wriothesley, at the very least, who first read and then gave her the sonnets. She hasn't told even Alphonso about the sonnets. They're still locked in her trunk, a hidden beauty and a private bane. She has long ceased to read them in the way she did that first awful night, as if they were mere colored panes (*yes, colored pains*) through which she might, if she squinted, see something real: true history, a man's heart, some things that had actually happened. But the verses afford no natural perspective. She's written enough sonnets herself, since, to know love poems are never like that. Like all stained glass windows, they use what *is* natural — a woman, a young man, the sunlight — to illuminate themselves, their own images, and not to open a view on the untidy world outside.

Still, after tending Odilia, giving penny lute-lessons, fair-copying for the Tanfields, and patching her own and other ladies' sleeves, by the late-night flame of a candle, she's been trying to write like him.

Were the words all I loved in the first place? she wonders. *Are we anything more than words?*

She is English, like good cousin Augustine, whatever Will Shake-speare believed or pretended to believe. So she also thinks of the fine parchments marked with his scrawl in practical terms, as protection against future rain.

Everyone loves the plays except Emilia, who goes only when she's coerced, usually by Angelica and her new ruddy-faced squire. Partly she fears seeing Will again, or him seeing her, though she wonders some-times whether, with her hair grown red-brown and her cinnamon dust forsaken, he would know her now if he did. Her shyness and wounded pride are a piece of her hesitance, but its main portion is her disdain for the throwaway nature of poetry on stage. She hears beauty in the playhouses: strange shocks of words as well as of swords, complex locu-tions, dazzling metaphors the ear can't take in all at once; speeches that take long thought to work out, that require consideration from different angles, over time, as she has considered Will's sonnets. It amazes her that playwrights would cast out their liquefied gold as though it were dirty dishwater, hurling it at lords' boxes full of idiots who wish only to gossip and gamble their way through the two or three hours of stage traf-fic, and who only put down their playing cards when they see a poisoned skull or a sword dripping pig-blood. How can any writer tolerate this?

It is only, she concludes, that some men *must* write verse, and can make the occupation pay no other way than to drop their lines in front of whoever will pay. She can't fathom the thing otherwise, though the poet she'd known best always was, whether willfully or no, mysterious on this point during their months together. He professed disgust for the playhouses, and the desire to write "for thoughtful gentlemen," all the while trying his best to dress like one. Yet half the time at Tichtfield, even at the start of their time together, when she peered over his shoulder she saw he wasn't writing sonnets at all, but dialogues, all the while mutter-ing things like "Alleyn? No. Not that hand-sawyer." Then he'd wave an arm, or jump up to test whether lines could be sung while juggling.

One day, while shopping for eggs for Odilia on Cheapside, the thought comes full clear just as Bow Bells strikes the noon hour, as if the insight were rung into view. *He used Henry Wriothesley and me as a cause to send him back to the players. Not to his country wife, as he claims, but to London. He made* us *the traitors so he* could *defect.* The sudden knowledge stops her cold in the middle of the road, where she stands, jostled unheeding by housewives and tradesmen and carters, as the bell's twelve strokes toll themselves out. *Marry, that's it! He used me poetically. To give his ambition some color.* But was that the perfect way to put the case? No. Better to say he inked her black to make himself white.

And now, at last, Queen Elizabeth is dead, finally withered completely within the painted shroud of her body. They bury her, and almost overnight, plague visits the city, as though to keep the new Scottish monarch at bay in the north. Progressing down from Edinburgh, James the Sixth of Scotland, the First of England, is stalled at York, so fearful is he that the pest will strike him and his queen and his young. So London is kinged *in absentia.* The streets flowing out of the city are crowded with the horses and wagons of the moneyed, all fleeing to their country manors. In the town, the first red crosses are nailed to the doors of the sufferers, to warn neighbors and tradesmen away.

There are no cases of the pest reported in Westminster yet, and no formal announcement that plague conditions reign. Emilia hollows out onions and stuffs them with cloves for the pockets of her sometime serving maid and Angelica and herself. She sews an onion into Odilia's gown. The little girl is hale and fat, and has outlived many a sickness on her street. It's Angelica who worries Emilia. For the past day her sister's been listless and complaining of cramps. Emilia's reasoning mind tells her that it happens every month to Angelica, that this time is different only in the degree of high performance of Angelica's pains. After so many visits to the playhouses, Angel knows how to put a delicate hand to her forehead, to moan for three beats to indicate inward distress.

Emilia leaves her sister abed with a moist towel draped over her forehead and a skin of hot water to press to her abdomen. "I'll be back in three hours," she tells Ellen. She doesn't say where she's going. She arrived at the decision only last night, after hearing from a neighbor the rumor that playhouses will be closed by week's end.

Will Shakespeare has written a play about skin color. Alphonso has told her it contains a character named Emilia.

It is pure will that drives her into the playhouse. If she listened to reason, she'd stay out. But she has silenced pesky logic. This time, there is not even drink to blame, as was the case with fine Walter Raleigh, whose green eyes and tattoo and scarred soldier's hands she will never forget. Nor are the urgent desires of the body her chief driver in this. It is, instead, vanity.

Alphonso, so foolish in every case of his own, is wise, she knows, in hers, when he advises her to stay home. "I'll not see it again, for all it was brave," he tells her the night after his own cross-river journey to see *Othello*. "Nor should you go. You get killed on a bed."

"Killed! Indeed!"

"Alongside others. Don't think you're the only one, mistress."

"Does he have me Italian?"

"Everyone's Italian, as per custom. Save the Moor."

"Am I beautiful?" She bats her kohl'd eyelashes at the indifferent Alphonso.

He looks thoughtful, and fingers his earring. "I lingered about the tiring house, trying to meet the boy who did you."

"Will Shakespeare's no boy."

"The boy who played you, you slattern!"

She slaps his hand hard. "You'll pox yourself, one of these days. Or pox some young innocent."

"Innocent!" His laugh is sour. "I've met those boys."

She examines his face in the sunlight. Alphonso is no longer pretty. His once-fair skin is mottled from drink, and his golden hair is thinning. His life has soured. The lace collar he sports is irretrievably frayed. Disappointed in his hopes for a knighthood from Elizabeth, he has left court, and now lives at the houses of friends, while he hopes for a renewal of his musician's post under James. It has all changed, as Augustine warned. Alphonso haunts taverns now, and goes to the plays.

She looks out the window at the stream of foot traffic in the road outside. Clothes are getting darker in this part of town, and hair shorter, even while the locks grow longer at court. The puritan pastors are having their influence in the town.

"What ever became of your flute player?" she asks Alphonso.

"So bawdy, again."

She clucks her tongue. "I mean your young man of the consort. Gervaise, was it? With the half-pierced ear?"

An expression of disdain crosses his face. "Speak not of her. Betrayed me, and married a woman."

She turns smiling from the window. "O, perverse!"

"So say I. Sir Gervaise the Perverse." Alphonso raises and lowers his hand in a mock dubbing. "I'll knight her, if they'll not knight me." He looks at her and his face softens. "Melly."

"Alphonso. Do you think they will print it?"

"Print what? That play? How should I know? If they do, it will not be for years, when it no longer brings crowds. Just now it's fire new."

"Well. Hmm." She sits on a stool. Her gaze turns cloudy and inward.

He looks at her narrowly. "*Don't* go. I'll not go with you. She's a cold fish —"

"Do you mean Will?"

"Yes. I've met her at court. Not apt for a lover."

"Why?" she asks lightly. "Did you try him?"

"It isn't that." He frowns and leans forward, rubbing a small hole at the elbow of his jerkin. "Emilia, that heirless, hairless bitch of a queen wouldn't knight me, not for service in Ireland and a ball in my arm. But your Will —"

"He is not *my* —"

"Whosoever's Will she is, she's been granted a coat of arms. I saw it sketched in the herald's book, for all to see. A proud falcon gripping a spear, or perhaps it's a pen made to look like a spear. Intentionally ambiguous. And the motto below is rich, I tell you." His voice assumes sonorous gravity. "*Non sans droict.*"

"Not without . . . ." She wrinkles her nose. "Mustard?"

"Not without *right. She* has all the right in the world, she. "

"Will, you mean."

"Yes. Look to see *her* a knight next. *I* could have drawn your poet's device. A chilly fish rampant, in some stage paint, *gules.*"

She laughs, but Alphonso keeps frowning. "Melly, she's not for you. You should forget her, not stir things up."

She knows he's right. Will is a man of smoke.

But now, two days later, thinking that the play's last performance may come any afternoon, Emilia has taken herself off, forsaking her daily cares to dig again in the grave of lost love. She knows that all plays are incarnated dreams. And she's sure Will never knew *her*, never truly, and all she's likely to see is a refashioned memory of what, even at the first, he only imagined. But none of that matters. She is lonely enough to give way to herself, and she goes.

From a planked bench in the six-penny seats, smelling the sweat of all London, she sees, then, the new use Will has made of her darkness. And it's worse than before. Now blackness is soot, pitch, grime, filth, muck, coal dust, the color of hell. The ashes and ink on the face of the Englishman playing the Moor are not only dirt in themselves. They stand for the shameful thing Will has made of her in his poems, her stain now expanded, leaking outward to darken skin. What shame? *Lechery. Betrayal.*

And this character, Emilia? She is a lady in service, a worldly foil to her fair and innocent mistress, Desdemona. Emilia's a thief. She steals a magical silk handkerchief that was spun by holy African moths. Her virtue is lighter than air. She's a secret slut. She might "do't as well in the dark." She would do it for her husband's ambition, would "make her husband a cuckold to make him a monarch."

Emilia thinks of herself, who gained silk gowns, pearl slippers, diamond earrings, and a crest for the Bassanos by surrendering her body to Lord Hunsdon's rage for Italian women. She thinks of Alphonso, who hoped for a knighthood by the influence of Raleigh, the most prominent court soldier after Essex. For a laughter! Raleigh had lost all sway with the queen during her final year, following his second fruitless trip to the New World. He'd come back with no gold, been sent to the Tower, and escaped harsher punishment only by Elizabeth's death, which for him came in the nick of time. Given his troubles, did Raleigh even remember Alphonso's petition, much less his own night, years past, with Alphonso's wife?

But it's not a soldier's remembering that matters here. It's a playwright's. Emilia storms from the Globe before the play's climax, deeply insulted, sure that Will always thought her a whore, certain, as well, that someone — Wriothesley, no doubt — must at one time have told him of her interlude with Walter Raleigh, and that Will has made his own profitable sense of it, to bring Londoners to his stage.

On the long walk home, she tries to persuade herself that it might be otherwise. Her name is just one Italian name in a play filled with Italian names. A play is a play is a play. But she cannot rid herself of shame. She feels dirty, exposed. She kicks up the mud in the lanes as she scuffs along, not trying to avoid the dirt. The filth. The muck.

At the corner of her street she hears a pounding. It grows in volume as she nears her house, and she welcomes the harsh, hard sound, a drumbeat to match the rhythm of her heart. She comforts herself with the fantasy that she will hide in an attic and scribble satire. *I will take a man's name, and do it. I will mock his own choruses, who invite the audience to dream a galleon, since the stage is too poor to provide one. I'll—*

But all plans fly from her head when she sees it: the man on her stoop, his nose and mouth masked with a handkerchief. He is hammering a final nail into the red wooden cross on her door.

22

The sequestering is the worst of it. If she could walk to the river and look at the boats, or rent a horse, ride to Devonshire, and throw herself into Lady Penelope's arms, or run wild in the fields and swing from the trees, then the nightmare might start to recede, to be pushed back by new details, new faces and voices, new moments of day. As it is, after her first days of sleeplessness and unbroken sobbing, she must wake into absolute quiet. In the Longditch house, the silence is barely broken by the sounds of passing pedestrians and cart wheels in the street outside and the hammering of new crosses on other women's doors. These noises come to her muffled, because the city's plague laws demand that the windows of the afflicted stay closed, even though, as is usual in times of the pest, it's high summer and the indoor air is stifling. For six weeks the families of victims may go no farther than their dooryards, and may linger there only for brief tossings or burials of refuse or offal, or the drawing of water from cisterns. They are reliant for food on the kindness of friends, who may leave bundles and letters on stoops, but may not enter the homes, lest they carry out plague to the already suffering city.

Alphonso rises to the occasion. He appears thrice a week, looking tenderly through the window and brushing his lips with his hand for a blown kiss. He leaves baskets of bread and cheese, of salt pork and fish, red apples and bottles of ale and canary. In the baskets are handwritten notes. These say, "The day will pass," or, "The souls of the innocent go directly to heaven. So said the pastor," or "Coraggio!" or, less tritely, "The playhouses are closed. Naught to do out here, anyway." *Simply your only husband for plague patter,* she thinks, and almost smiles.

When her weeks of confinement are ended, it is October, and the plague, like the sun, has abated too. In these two months the disease has taken a tenth of the city. Public gatherings are still forbidden, unless for church services. The playhouses will not reopen til spring, but the weather is turning cold anyway. It will soon be too chilly for outdoor acting.

Emilia should be plumper, since she's been denied for three fortnights the freedom to walk or climb anywhere but up and down the stairs of her small house. But she is gaunt. She has eaten little. She knows she must, but she can't. For six weeks she has sat listlessly, sometimes strumming her lute, or writing a few words, or reading some passages of scripture or philosophy, then stopping in futility and despair. Now free, she walks slowly through Westminster toward Gresham Street. The populace has visibly thinned. *Walk. Walk.* One door in five wears a red cross. There is a ghostly undertone in the neighborhood, a muffled keening almost below the threshold of hearing. It comes into the street through the cracks in the house-walls, like the moan of the wind, though, unlike wind, it blows out from within. Some red crosses are being taken down by the surviving inhabitants of marked dwellings, pale men and women who look like ghosts, newly released, as is she, into their impoverished worlds. Hollow neighbors' eyes meet her own hollow eyes, and tired heads nod.

Two doors down from her house she sees a woman sweeping her steps, moving weakly but with a purpose, while her husband grips her arm and tries to guide her back indoors. She knows them. The man is Jack Horne, an importer of Indian spices. "Can you speak to her, Mistress Lanier?" Master Horne calls to Emilia as she passes. He is unkempt in his clothing and hatless, and wears a ragged beard. He looks at Emilia helplessly as his wife sweeps stubbornly on. "She is deaf to me. I fear she's gone mad. She was smitten along with the children, and has recovered, but she's still so weak I think she will fall."

Emilia approaches their gate. "The children?"

He clasps his hands together. "The cart took the second one two weeks ago. Since then she has not ceased her housewifery, twelve hours a day, until she collapses in the evening. Like the dead." He frees his hands only to wring them anew. "She wakes at dawn, eats a little porridge or bread, and then is on her feet again, or on her knees, with a dust-clout or a broom. The house has ne'er been so spotless —"

"Let her work, Master Horne."

"I must?"

"Yes. Leave her be."

He nods, in a daze, his hands still clasped before him, and turns doggedly to follow Mistress Horne down the steps and up again, in the clean-swept track of her broom.

The Tanfields' household has been spared, although Edmund has lost an uncle, an aunt, and four cousins who lived on an adjacent street. He tells Emilia this, but his voice is tinged with worry, not sadness, and she knows he is thinking of someone else.

"She is ten pounds fatter." Emilia sits, saying this. "All she's done for six weeks is cry, drink wine and eat sweetmeats, and complain now and then of the cramp. You won't like her now, but she's feeling less spleeny. She's well."

His face floods with relief. He is about to say something happy, but he checks himself. He has known of Emilia's grief since August, since the week it happened, when she sent him word by Alphonso. "It is . . . ." He stops again, blushing this time in awkward sympathy rather than shyness. "I know you did not expect it."

She looks steadily at the floor. After a moment she speaks in a low voice. "When I left the house she was laughing and smiling and bouncing on Ellen's knee." *Poor Ellen.* The maidservant was confined for six weeks along with Emilia and Angelica, away from her own family. Yet none of the three of them, she, Ellen, and Angelica, in the end contracted the pest. Perhaps they'd all been safer inside.

Emilia continues. "She went so quick, Angel said. One minute laughing, then, in a moment, sluggish. She showed blue marks under her arms. In two hours . . . ." She holds a gloved hand to her mouth, willing herself to think of something else, anything else than the tiny, mottled corpse she'd been forced to wrap and hand over for the plague cart. She'd wanted to bury Odilia in the yard, and had screamed and fought the deathman, but Angelica and Ellen had subdued her, had taken the little wrapped bundle from her hands. It was as if they were taking her heart. She'd turned away, rather than see the small thing placed on the heap of lifeless bodies.

She forces her mind back to this present day, to this place of business and her current purpose. She clears her throat. "I am not the first woman to lose a child, and I won't be the last." She hears herself speaking rotely, like a bereaved woman in a play, and notes bitterly how incommensurate these words are to her sorrow. She has lost not one now, but two. Before Odilia came, she thought foolishly that she'd paid her due. She shakes her head again, to banish feeling. "Now, my household needs means. Have you copying work for me, sir?"

"I can find some."

A knock sounds on the door. Without waiting for an invitation, Bess Tanfield enters. Mistress Tanfield has no sense of dress or of fashion, but has made an effort to look genteel. She wears a fine pair of black velvet sleeves, though she's ripped the lace trim without bothering to resew it, perhaps without even noticing the tear, and her bodice and skirt don't match. How old is she now? Seventeen? Eighteen? Near Angelica's age, though the pair of them are in most ways like lemon and honey, or day and night.

"Lady Emilia, I am sorry Odilia died," Bess says bluntly.

This undoes her. Emilia buries her head in her hands and sobs.

She had thought that her tears were spent, but these new ones flow for nearly half an hour, during which time Bess, having shooed her brother from the room and closed the door, sits patting her shoulder. "I can imagine your sorrow," she says softly, like a woman grown.

"I thank you, but you can*not* imagine my sorrow," Emilia says, dabbing her eyes with lace.

"Not *know* it, that's true. But perhaps I can begin to . . . *imagine.*" Emilia can hear the girl trying to master the debater's tone in her voice, striving for gentleness. "Listen," Bess says. "I have a poem —"

"Poetry changes nothing."

"So you may say, but listen." She starts to recite.

> *Grief fills the room up of my absent child,*
> *Lies in his bed, walks up and down with me,*
> *Puts on his pretty looks, repeats his words,*
> *Remembers me of all his gracious parts,*
> *Stuffs out his vacant garments with his form.*

"I think it must be like that," Bess says in conclusion. "Is it? A little?"

"It is *precisely* like that." Emilia is suddenly angry, and even, absurdly, jealous. "Did *you* write that, Bess Tanfield?"

"Well . . . no, I did not. I only remembered it."

"Then it was written by someone who lost a child."

"I think he must have. It was in a play."

"*You* go to plays, as well? A child like you?"

"I am not allowed, but I . . . well, I crept out once, when my father was away, and went with Ned and Angelica."

"Ah. And your brother says *you* write."

"Yes." She folds her hands in her lap and assumes a dignified look. "I write tragedies."

"What can *you* know of tragedy, little maid?"

"I can read, and I have my own fancy!" Bess says with some heat, then looks chagrined. "Forgive me, Emilia."

Emilia smiles unfeignedly through her tears. "I forgive you with all my heart." She rises and puts on her gloves. Fine black wool they are, and sewn with pearls, but worn at the fingertips now. Bess has risen, too. "You, like your brother, are kind." Emilia kisses her. "Edmund may wish to deliver his contracts in person to our house, for fair copying. Next week, if he will. If you wish to come, too —"

"To see that pair bill and coo?" Bess sniffs. "I think not."

"I was about to say, though the theaters are closed, there are often plays at Gray's Inn near All Saints Day. If women can be smuggled in, I think I know two who will manage it."

Bess smiles. "Will you make one of us, lady?"

"Not I." Emilia says at the door, as she tightens her gloves. "I have done with the stage."

I am done with all stages, she thinks in the bleak months that follow. She avoids the endless glittering pageant of court, as well as the grittier public entertainments. But she is lonely for company. She frequents the stone parish chapel of St. Clement Danes, now twice or thrice weekly, and sits nearly motionless on Sunday mornings, letting the words of the sermon wash over her. She rises for the general confession, and for the readings. For six weeks she hated God and all his houses. But coming out of her own house, she finds she has nowhere else to go.

Sleeping is bad, since she dreams that her child is alive, then wakes to the nightmare of her absence. Only once, on such a morning, does she muffle her head and scream into the pillow until Angelica and Ellen come to calm her. After that, she allows herself no indulgences. For this pain, screaming's no cure. But changes of scenery help, a little. At least now she can leave the domicile, where the cradle, a gift from Lady Penelope, still stands in the corner, too fine to be chopped for firewood, too generous a gift to be sold. Thrice a week she walks by the stalls of Paul's Yard, looking for bargains, looking for books, seeking the consolations of philosophy. She adds a translation of Boethius and a thick Geneva

Bible to the small store of volumes in her study. The Bible is second-hand, returned and discounted for some defect in the binding. She turns to it, first pondering the psalms, then rereading the stories that thrilled Nan Clifford, her young charge at Cooke-ham House. Jacob, Isaac, Abraham. Rachel, Rebecca, Sarah. *Then Sarah said to Abram, thou dost me wrong. I have given my maid into thy bosom, and she says that she has conceived.* The maid was Hagar, made to go in to Abraham, made to bear his child, Ishmael. And then the pair of them, Abraham and Sarah, sent Hagar away to wander in the wilderness. Emilia weeps when she reads this, though she does not know why. It must be that she is weeping always now, that she is a constantly flowing stream, that there are only brief intervals of dryness.

God sent an angel to save Hagar and Ishmael. *Where was my angel, O God?* she thinks, when she next wakes in the night.

She can think of no reason to thank God, but still, she prays without ceasing. She's never really prayed in her life before, at least not in the way the flat-capped pastor of St. Clement Danes urges, *letting the Holy Spirit give words to the heart.* That was a new thing, though an hour on a hard pew was old. Margaret Johnson always herded her daughters into parish church services, braving the slights of women who knew she wasn't legally married to Baptista Bassano. Margaret preferred those weekly insults, the averted eyes, the whispers, to the fines for missing church. She had been, after all, practical, more so than her eclectically religious husband. Emilia recalls Margaret's brusque hand tossing Baptista's mezuzah and rosary indifferently into the trash the day after his funeral. The look on her mother's face had bespoken no precise, godly wish to purify the house of trinkets, but a more general Protestant disdain for clutter. All through her life, Margaret Johnson had liked her house plain, and shown herself uninterested in any world she couldn't see. With her as their model, Emilia's and Angelica's youthful prayers had been as perfunctory as their Sunday visits to the Church of St. Botolph.

But things are different now. The world before Emilia's eyes is so lacking in grace or justice that she craves only dark, night, and an unseen presence to comfort her, to tell her her babies are somewhere other than moldering in the cold ground. She has nightmares. She sees babies in grave clothes, and a heap of rags in the middle of a black box. The heap suddenly raises a head and starts to howl. She bends with a lantern and peers. Mad Margery wears Emilia's face.

To fend off the dreams, she prays long each night, and in time the night-mares fade. She longs for her mother, but is comforted, still, to remember she has her mother's blessing. Is Margaret Johnson aware of her grief? Is God? Morning by morning, Emilia comes to feel that it may be so, that it must be so, that if there is a hell, there is surely an answering heaven, that the world's shuddering blows are something more than a bad dance per-formed by thoughtless atoms. That there is, at least, an audience to her suf-fering, and some sort of script for it. *What is heaven?* she asks the darkness. To her mind's eye appears a tall oak tree, with soberly dressed people of both sexes and every age speaking amiably in the shade of its broad leaves. They hold books in their laps. A house stands, not far away, with candles of welcome burning warm in its every window.

O, I see, she thinks, with a trace of humor. *Heaven is Cooke-ham.*

She bends at her desk, closed in her study like a silkworm in its cocoon. She begins again to write.

23

It is more than a year of thrift, of lessons on lute and virginals traded for shillings and pence to the daughters of London merchants and aldermen, of fair-copying contracts and mending ladies' sleeves, before Emilia can be persuaded to show her face again at Whitehall.

One burden has slipped from her shoulders. Angelica has married her Edmund. London is litigious, the Tanfields prosper, and now her sister turns true angel, sending packets of sugar and sacks of oats and occasional legs of mutton to the house in Longditch. She and Alphonso don't starve. Thanks to Edmund as well, they have managed to hang onto the hay tax stipend, and Alphonso can sometimes be nagged into repairing instruments in his brother Innocent Lanier's workshop in Mark Lane. This brings in the odd shilling or two, though his steadier wage from the consort won't return. The new monarch has been besieged by so many Scottish and English petitioners vying for posts that Alphonso's request for renewal has been lost in the general cry, though most recorder-players and lutenists with the surname "Bassano" continue at the court of King James.

Some artists are even luckier. William Shakespeare, riding a rainbow, now has for a patron the sovereign himself. George Carey, son of old Henry, is dead six months from some surfeit of carnal merriment, and the new Lord Chamberlain is of a puritan stripe, and dislikes plays. Throughout the realm public plays are now barred on Sundays, which was the players' most profitable day of the week, but this is no matter to Will. The new royal family loves the plays, and James has made Shakespeare's company the King's Men, and licensed them to play in every palace from Hampton Court to Whitehall. Each man jack of them is given four yards of scarlet cloth for livery to wear on occasions of state. Between performances they parade redly about London's fine houses in the king's train, bearing scrolls and cups and looking purposeful and important, for who better than actors to do this? So Will's in the ascendant, even while poor Alphonso's star has drooped. He's lost his foothold at palaces, and is once more her sometime co-resident in Longditch, though he visits court often enough, when invited, now and then, to make one in a consort because a Bassano is sick or a production so elaborate that thirty musicians are needed. This is the case now as, Twelfth Night approaching, he rehearses the fifth recorder's part for the *Masque of Blackness*.

She herself doesn't care about the *Masque of Blackness*, though Penelope, who's been asked back to court to serve James's queen, Anne of Denmark, will dance in it, and though the masque's mechanical under-pinnings are the talk of everyone in town who listens to court gossip. Dreaming of Cooke-ham, Emilia finds she is less and less able to abide spectacle and pageantry. She stayed home the day King James gloriously entered the city, though she read, as a kind of author's exercise, every line of each sycophantic welcome poem sold in print. As for Whitehall, the years that have etched those other lines, in her forehead and face, have only increased her fear of encountering Will.

But more than this, she dreads Alphonso spending his pay before she can get it. And to get it, she must be in the scene.

"That is he," whispers Lady Penelope, huddling with Emilia behind a tall painted screen. She points to a sandy-haired man in an embroidered skullcap who has just doffed his crystal-buttoned jacket to kneel and adjust a water-driven gear. The actors in the masque have seen the trick before during numerous rehearsals, but still, they gasp on cue as the gear turns and works the fantastic prop: an artificial sea produced by pipes shooting water in front of a painted landscape. "That's Jones," says Penel-ope. "A wizard, by my troth!"

Emilia rolls her eyes, though she takes care Penelope doesn't see her do it. Inigo Jones is the man of the season, the mind that spawns all the moving tableaux and flying serpents and colored smokes that delight the Jacobean court. And he has a certain genius, if you like shows for children. But that is what James's court does like. Looking around at the ladies giddily comparing their feathered costumes and diamonds and paint, Emilia feels a sudden sympathy with the new dour Lord Chamber-lain and with the puritan pamphleteers, who declaim against the spec-tacles that distract from the Word. *From all words*, she thinks, wondering whether amid all this glitter and optical splendor, anyone will listen to the poetry.

"Is the poet present?" she asks.

Penelope shrugs. "He was *omni*present when we practiced. He's as loud as Jones is quiet. Inigo tinkers and builds and repairs, while big Ben blusters. You'd have liked to see him swell like a turkey cock and almost yell at us for forgetting our lines. But he could not, of course. He's a brick-layer's stepson. He must bow and be courteous to grandeur. So he bel-lowed at Jones instead."

"And Jones . . . ?"

"Ignored it." She laughs. Her teeth show stark white against the glis-tening black of her face. She is holding her darkened arms awkwardly out like a dancer's, scrupulously careful not to stain her dress of azure and silver. "I ache! I cannot touch anything."

"What *is* this, lady?" Emilia delicately touches her arm. Her finger comes away smudged. "Is it pitch?"

"Coal dust, laid down with primrose oil to stop it going up our noses."

"Heavens, my lady!"

"I know. Charles thinks it's horrible, but you would not believe the con-test among all of us this time, to paint ourselves up and down like blacka-moors. I told Mountjoy, the more I can do to please the new sovereign, the better." She drops her voice. "I'm going to petition him for a divorce."

"What!"

"*Sshhh*. What else should I do? Mountjoy and I must marry, or what future for our children? We cannot leave them bastards."

Emilia drops her voice to a whisper. "But lady, only kings can get divorces. And even they must spend a great lot of —"

Penelope waves a black-backed, pink-palmed hand in a dismissive gesture. "Tush and tilly-valley. We will see." Her dark pupils shine. "We will see."

"Places!" comes the call.

"Haste, Emilia. Get you to a seat. Charles has saved you one. And *say nothing.*"

Emilia smiles as she turns to go. "That's a skill I have long prac-ticed, lady."

Penelope moves stiffly to join the other daughters of Niger. Lady Herbert, Countess of Derby. Lady Elizabeth Howard. Lady Susan de Vere.

All wear curled, pyramidal black wigs stuck with bright green feathers. Their necks, ears, and wrists are bedecked with white pearls that gleam against their pitchy skin.

Jesus Christ and Saint George, thinks Emilia. *Black women on stage, for a scandal! Cinnamon and cloves were nothing to this.*

Charles Blount, Baron Mountjoy, gestures at her from the rear of the large hall which is quickly filling with lords and higher gentry. Emilia slides from behind the painted screen barrier, noting the seated musicians, glancing at Alphonso with her eyebrows raised in a question. "Not here," Alphonso mouths as she passes. Her shoulders sag with a mixture of relief and disappointment. Keeping her eyes carefully unfocused, wishing to catch no one's eye, she edges through stiff farthingales and capacious puffed sleeves toward Blount and the four-legged joint stool he's saved her. She feels very plain. She has sold every jewel Lord Hunsdon ever gave her. She is clad in a dress of pale brown silk with a lace stomacher, a gift from Angelica, and from her earlobes dangle a pair of gold earrings bequeathed to her long ago by her mother. Over her arm is a simple woolen cloak. No necklace and no bracelets adorn her neck and wrists, and her hair is dressed only in white ribbons. Odd how her lack of brilliance makes the men ogle her, and the women stare. Despite her efforts at invisibility, their interest is evident; she feels eyes on her back. Perhaps she'll start a fashion. *O, lord, sir, 'tis all puritan garb this season. Deuteronomy's your only wear at Whitehall.*

But no. A godly trend in clothing, or in anything, is unlikely, to be sure, if this masque is an indication of the new royal family's tastes.

She sits next to Charles, wearing an unfocused smile and wishing she could think of something besides money. *What can this have cost?* She's torn between wonder and contempt, regarding at the end of the vast room the paintbrushed landscape of woods and fields, the machine-fed waterfalls, the huge orchestra, and, in the adjacent room, just visible, the stacked tables, laden not only with sweetmeats and honeyed pastries but with boars' heads, stuffed herons, roast capons, twelve breads, and what look like a hundred French and Italian wines. She thinks of the carpenters, the costumers, the perfumiers, the more than two dozen musicians. *What price? Three thousand pound? Four? Five?*

These thoughts remind her of Alphonso, of his pay, and her mission. She looks again at her husband. More musicians have seated themselves, and from this distance Alphonso's form is almost lost among a crowd of sackbut and flute players, drummers and lutenists, and other recorders. He looked pale, she remembers. Has he been drinking?

Just then a tall pair of silver sleeves drops down on the stool in front of her, and she can no longer see her spouse.

The music starts sweetly. An auburn-haired boy of some twelve or thirteen plays the first note on his recorder, a high C that lingers so resonantly that a brief hush falls on the audience. Emilia closes her eyes in unexpected pleasure.

"Henry Carey," whispers Charles Blount. She opens her eyes and looks at Blount quizzically, frowning. Why name *him*?

"I mean the younger. The son," explains Blount. "He's with his brother John at court this season. You knew his mother had remarried?"

She gives a short laugh. "I know nothing."

"The new queen found her a rising Scottish lord."

"As long as he's rising, Anne Morgan will be happy."

"So she seems."

Emilia is honestly glad of the news. So companionable is Charles Blount that she wants to tell him about the guilt she's harbored with regard to Anne Morgan since she dispensed so handily with the lady's first husband. The mad temptation amuses her, and scares her a little as well. She had best drink no wine this evening.

"Since ladies can dance in the masque, he asked whether he could perform as well," Blount says.

"Who?"

"Her son. Henry Carey the younger. He plays the recorder."

World of wonders! As Carey's meaning becomes clear, Emilia turns her eyes back to the auburn-haired youth, who is still tooting sweetly on his pipe. She pictures the boy as she last saw him: a red-faced puny, taking a bite from a savory he'd hoped was a sweet, then spitting it out on a lady's gown, howling displeasure, as his father looked on adoringly. What had the lad been then? Three years old? Four? The time!

"His infancy was not promising," she whispers to Charles.

"Some sprouts do grow." Charles bites his lip as Emilia looks down. Both know he has spoken without thinking, having forgotten Emilia's stillborn son, a Carey sprout who did not grow. There is naught Charles can do to repair the remark, so he says, "Mark the music."

The music pleases the king, that's plain. James presents a third spectacle in his own right, clad in scarlet and ermine, silver-shoed, red-haired under his heavy crown, raising his arms and shouting out "Good!" from his raised chair of state in the room's center. The watching gentry ape their sovereign, cheering each new fountain burst and leaping fake African as if they were apprentices at a bear-bait. *These make Elizabeth's courtiers seem sedate,* she thinks, amazed. She has chosen not to wear a mask like some ladies do here, since masks, she has noted, inspire curiosity regarding the face beneath. But she cannot resist an old habit, lifting a fan and holding it over her nose, for secrecy.

Not here, Alphonso had mouthed as she passed him. Will's not here. But she still scans the room, scouting for danger, and hoping, a little bit, to see him. *Him.* When she spots Henry Wriothesley smiling and applauding some twenty feet from her and Blount, she shrinks into her chair and raises her fan an inch higher.

She turns her eyes leftward and spots, hulking by a far pillar, the masque-maker. She knows it is he, though it was years ago when she saw him before, yelling invective at Will Shakespeare for mis-speaking some comic stuff of his at the Globe. The dark, lanky man stands with his arms folded, glowering at the masque's painted display, beating the fingers of one hand lightly against his sleeve, mouthing his lines as the amateur players speak them. These play their parts, indeed, better than Emilia herself expected, but the cries and applause of the audience at every visual wonder come close to drowning the actors' words, as she'd feared they might. The performing ladies seem hardly to care. They want only to show themselves in their headdresses and gowns. Politic Penelope wants to impress the sovereign. Emily watches her strike a pose at the apex of a pyramid, her blacked arms raised under a painted silver moon.

"This, the black, was the queen's own idea," Charles Blount whispers in her ear, and for a confused moment she thinks he means Elizabeth. Then she remembers the new queen, James's wife, that mother of many children, Danish Anne.

"Where is she? The queen?" she asks curiously.

Discreetly, Blount points. "There."

Emilia looks back at the masque, following his gesture to another black-faced, silver gowned, sable-wigged woman, who is now kicking up her half-bare legs before a giant paper seashell.

The new queen is dancing in the masque.

When she glances back at the pillar, shocked, the poet Ben Jonson is gone.

~

"Cousin! Cousin!"

She has no time to speak with any Bassanos now, does not recognize this voice anyway, at least not in any connection with her family. She has grabbed her cloak from the joint stool and rushed behind the screen again at the masque's conclusion, trying to find Alphonso before, or at least while, he is given his money by the royal exchequer's functionary. But the yelling behind her grows strident. *"Cousin!"* The voice is so commanding that she slows in spite of herself and looks behind her. She squints. Is she seeing aright? Unaccountably, Ben Jonson is rushing toward her, waving a high hand. "Cousin Emilia Bassano!"

Something in his action of pursuit tumbles the spring of an ancient memory, and she turns instinctively toward a twenty-foot painted wooden palm tree, intending to do — what? Run for it, and scramble up the thing? But he reaches her first, and grabs her upper arm like a trained bear performing a courtesy. She drops her cloak in surprise. He turns her to face him. He is as strong as he is large, and though she pulls back, his grip doesn't loosen.

"You are Meg Johnson's daughter, are you not?" He lets her go finally at this, and steps back to bow, in apparent afterthought.

"How did you know me, sir?" Emilia rubs her arm.

"Why, Lady Penelope Rich pointed you out. She said you wished to know me. I told her you already did!"

"Lady Penelope is mistaken, sir."

"But you remember me?"

"I do, Master Jonson, though I never would have, without your urging. I see you still delight in pouring black ink on ladies."

His eyes narrow and glint. *"You* weren't a lady."

Her fist itches to smash his nose. "I had hoped you'd died in Flanders," she says lightly.

"Very good! Let's continue in this wise, merry banter over wine, mutual jovial insult, *et cetera*," he says, trying to seize her arm again. But this time she eludes him. She takes off her heeled slippers, briefly considers throwing one at him, then, recalling their value, takes both in one hand and runs. She hears, growing louder, Alphonso's voice speaking on the far side of the false palm tree. He's involved in an argument. "Eight recorders are *not* needed for the dancing, coz. A glass of Rhenish for me, in there, and then I'm for Southwark." *Stop him, God, please!* she prays. He must have been paid already. As she rounds a second palm tree she sees him standing with her cousin Anthony, Augustine's son. Behind them, packing his recorder in its case, stands Henry Carey the younger.

"Alphonso!" she says, sweeping past the boy. "*Alphonso!*" But just as she speaks a tremendous crash sounds from the next room, and all heads turn, even hers. The guests have swamped the food tables, and the trestles have collapsed. Now capons, pies, and breads lie scattered among the floor amid broken glass.

She takes advantage of her husband's moon-eyed distraction to leap at him. "Give it me!" She has the strange, disorienting sensation that she has just seen her mother, Margaret Johnson, or else herself in a mirror. Is there a mirror on the wall, behind Alphonso?

"Back, virago!" He holds her off, laughing and staggering. "Come, all, shall we dive into the press? Who's for pheasant in glass-shards?" Yes. He's drunk already.

"Anthony, leave him," she says, trying to unbend Alphonso's fingers from around what looks like a piece of gold; a noble, or an angel. "Don't tempt the Fates. It's a wonder he played his part through without error."

"I *always* play my part through without error." Alphonso wriggles. "Help! Help! Termagant! Witch!"

Intent on her purpose, Emilia is shielded from shame by her vague awareness that around her, other silk-clad ladies are wrestling with other men. Palace guards are attacking guests who are pocketing silver; the whole court has gone mad. At last she unclenches his fingers and finds that what she'd thought a clutched coin is nothing but his pearl earring. "Alphonso!"

"What would you? It came loose when I combed my hair. It fell in my lap during the masque."

She throws the pearl to the floor in disgust. Alphonso makes a noise and dives after it. He catches the palm with a heel and the pasteboard tree rocks, then topples, missing the pair of them by inches. Immediately an armed, bushy-bearded gentleman usher appears and seizes Alphonso by the jerkin. The usher pulls him up like a rag doll, grabs Emilia's arm with his other broad hand, and propels the pair of them from the hall.

"Marry, so brusque! But I'm going!" Alphonso flails like a marionette, trying to refasten his earring as he is marched. Though half-pinioned by the usher, Emilia is able to pull from her husband's pocket a coin-stuffed purse. By this time they are all in view of two huge wooden side palace doors, which two other ushers are opening.

"Out!" The bush-bearded usher gives her and Alphonso a push that sends Emilia sprawling. But Alphonso doesn't launch. He's clinging like a burr to the usher's elbows, saying, "I will betake myself elsewhere. Only let's hold between us a firm correspondence, a mutual friendly-recipro-cal kind of steady-unanimous heartily leagued —"

"*Off* me! *Off*, poltroon!" The usher is turning furiously from left to right, trying to dislodge Alphonso. Emilia thrusts the purse into her bod-ice, hikes up her petticoats, and sprints for a far door. Alphonso whoops as the usher finally shakes him to earth. From the floor he yells, "Halt! A thief and a harpy!" She flies down the steps, then stops in the shadow of a gold statue of the eighth King Henry mounted high on a horse. Standing on tiptoe and peering through the horse's legs, she sees a risen Alphonso straightening his clothes and bowing to the door-guards. The guards are laughing now, even the bush-bearded one, and they bow back. Then they all begin a contest of courtesies, making deep legs and elaborate hand-flourishes; foppishly kissing their fingertips and waving them skyward. Alphonso outdoes them all, and is applauded. She lingers, fascinated, watching her husband. He seems now, by his gestures, to be trying to persuade one of the guards to lend him his coat.

She is gradually wilting with relief, seeing he's not going to give chase and wrestle her in the palace courtyard. *He must have kept something in another pocket,* she thinks. *And no doubt he's grateful I took the rest.*

She slips from behind the horse statue and treads the soft green lawn to the palace's outer gates. But once outside them, hard, freezing stones on her soles remind her she is still in her stocking feet. *Ai, catso!* She's lost her pearl shoes in the scuffle, and her cloak is gone, as well. She is afraid to walk alone in London at night, but what remedy? It's cold, at least, so most of the coney-catchers and roaring boys will be plying their trades and brawling in taverns, not looking for game abroad. At any rate, she cannot stay here, shivering in the shadow of the palace. She bends and rolls off her stockings, then balls them and stuffs them into her bod-ice. No use ruining them. She sets off for Longditch.

It is past three when she reaches her house and longed-for bedroom. Her feet are scratched and sore, worn out and half-numb from the long walk on the stony, refuse-strewn streets. Twice she was approached by rogues, but each time she threw fistfuls of pebbles at them and babbled in Italian until they backed off, thinking her mad. Her throat aches now, and so does her head. Drunk with exhaustion, she falls on her mattress, dislodging Mumbleclutch. She sleeps, and dreams nothing.

She's awakened by the sound of a man's heavy tread and what sounds like the scrape of a stool on the floor below. She sits upright, thinking, *That's not Alphonso.* She gets out of bed. She was too tired to draw her curtains last night, and now morning light streams freely in the room, illuminating the dust motes. She looks in the mirror. Her hair has come loose, and she pins it up hastily. The skin below her eyes is smeared from the kohl, and she dabs her face with oil, rubbing off the excess crayon. No time to repaint. She pulls a bodice over her smock and steps into her frayed house slippers.

From the stairs as she descends she sees Ellen in the kitchen. The girl is unwrapping the latest food-package from Angelica. "Ellen, *who's in there?*" Emilia hisses, gesturing towards the small parlor, the home of her tiny library and her trim desk with the folding panel.

Ellen drops the package and scampers to the stair. "Lady, a man came who said he was your cousin."

"*What* cousin?"

Ellen spreads her hands in a helpless gesture. "He gave no name. Yet I could not say him nay. He called me a housefly and brushed right past me. When I told him you were sleeping, he said he would wait. He asked if you had books. He's been in there thirty minutes —"

But Emilia is already across the floor. She stops short in the doorway of her study.

Ben Jonson does not even look up. In his hand is the draft of her poem on Cooke-ham House, and he is frowning and reading.

She feels as though she's been seized and stripped naked. "*Put it down,*" she orders.

He glances up in surprise, then stands. Again the perfunctory bow. "Cousin! We were interrupted last night. I thought to encounter your husband here, to speak to him about .... musical arrangements. But he is from home?" He looks at her hopefully, scanning her from top to toe. Yes. She's heard of his relations with women of the city, and doubtless he's heard of her flaming past. Maybe Will has told him of her. She remembers the pair of them walking and laughing by the Southwark quay while she posed by the boats like a dolt, angling for Will's eyes. The two must be friends. Perhaps they hunt women together.

Still, Jonson's words and his predatory look are nothing she hasn't encountered a thousand times before, and they do not offend her. It's the meaty hand gripping her poem that's the violation.

She crosses and rips the pages from his paw. She's too raw for courtesy. "What do you want, sir?"

He looks at her thoughtfully. His eyes, like hers, are dark, though his sit closer together. His nose is large, and looks to have been broken at least once. She remembers her itching fist, remembers him inking her braids in childhood, and isn't surprised. He's an ugly man, but his presence is as arresting as it is provoking.

Suddenly he grins, and unexpectedly she feels her anger start to ebb. He admires her in the ordinary way, that's certain, but there's another thing in his gaze, a thing she can't name, but welcomes. She's only vaguely seen it before, and then only in fantasies.

"I want," he says, "to know why you have put Philomela in a pastoral poem. The raped, tongueless maiden who's turned into a nightingale? She's fitter for tragedy, surely. This mixing of genres disturbs me, yet it seems intentional. Your Philomela becomes the phoenix fourteen lines down. Do I read you right?"

24

It was the paint that ruined the poetry, he tells her in the hour that follows, introducing a theme he'll revisit, with a dozen variations, through the months and years to come. Yes, his poetry was killed by paint, and by the twenty-foot waterfall. "Here I have labored weeks o'er my beautiful child, a thoughtful allegory of men and women, here the white chalky cliffs of Albion, most masculine, posed against the mystical darkness of Africa, that's the woman of course, with her wildness —"

"So England is male?"

"*Britain* is the word now, *Britannia*, for our outlander king. I know not whether *he's* male, if I may say it friendly in your ear, but yes, *Britain* is male, civil, shining white under the sun, orderly in its empire, encompassing Scotland and Ireland too — well, a little trouble about Ireland, I confess — and the darkness of all women everywhere is like Africa, a foreign thing, untameable. Their savagery —"

"Women are savage, then."

"— in their appetites, yes, well known, the woman's silvestrian quality, but theirs is a *divine* savagery, which the poem celebrates. We find them —"

"We?"

"— blessed by their dangerous gods. Self-sufficient, in their way, and wholly *natural*. And this idea, so clear in the words of the poem, is now muddied and obscured by five giggling ladies smeared with black paint, cavorting like stage devils before two painted palm trees and butchering my *meter*. Not that their voices could be heard above the waterfall."

"I thought Lady Penelope held character well," Emilia says loyally.

Yes, she thinks later, again and again, months after her first meeting since childhood with Ben. The outrageous cousin with the jettisoned "h" has handed her a lost puzzle piece, the key to a door. He's put the case clearly at last. *Paint ruins poetry.* She thinks of the chattering gallants she sees in the playhouses, men who leer at the ladies, ladies who leer at the men, people who shut their mouths only to gape at patched clowns and bewigged Juliets and bloody severed heads thrown down on the stage with a thud. Deaf to the verse. And she thinks of herself in years past, floating with practiced mystery through palace halls and manorial grounds, powdered with cinnamon dust and striped with vermilion. A beauteous portrait that licensed shy silence, that discouraged her own self from speaking. Self-painted. Self-silenced.

But I always wanted to speak, she thinks. *And to laugh a belly-shaking, paint-cracking laugh, like Penelope.*

Now, with a quill as a brush, she has painted in words her lengthy description of Cooke-ham. Her distance in time and space from that manor gives her, she thinks, a natural perspective on the place. She has striven to bring into view hidden truths that the house, now distilled in her poem, contains; things else invisible. There, at Cooke-ham, as Ben saw, was Philomela, a ravaged bird, finding refuge and a writer's song among the place's trees and gardens. Once she'd sat down in her study that morning, primly pulling her bodice tight and forgiving Ben Jonson because he understood, because he was *interested* in what she wrote, she'd spilled her thoughts to him for half an hour, barely stopping. She intends a new kind of poem, wherein kindness, welcome, sufficiency, and love are incarnate in the description of a real, recognizable place. That is Cooke-ham House: not some imagined Arcadia or lost Eden, but an English country estate, wherein she, the poet, once physically dwelt, whose views she took, whose walks she walked. Its tallest oak was its bulwark, a shelter and gathering place for scattered thoughts, for minds teeming with questions. A specific tree, a specific, named house, signifying friendship. The tree and the house, the natural and artful combined.

She has told Ben, more than once since, how she misses her simple scholarly community at Cook-ham, how she remembers herself and Nan Clifford seated for hours in the shade of the summer tree, reading the Bible, reading Ovid, practicing Latin. Dear Nan, who had waved at her from across the room at James's Whitehall during the Masque of Blackness; Nan, now herself awash in the tumbling court world, a new servant of the Countess of Derby.

Do better than I did, Nan, she thinks.

After Ben's first visit — interrupted, at last, by Alphonso staggering home from the taverns of Southwark, clad in the ale-stained cloak of a Whitehall guardsman — Emilia writes with the sense of an audience. One morning, emboldened, she sends her poem, now complete, via paid post to the Cliffords.

Ben has approved her choice of family. "First the noble name, then the printer," he tells her that afternoon, as she, he, and Alphonso salt oysters in a Westminster ordinary. "Acquire powerful readers, who beget other readers, who know other writers, who know the printers. You should not approach printers without such a prelude. Especially not you, a woman. You might even begin by circulating your poems under a different name."

"What name?" she asks, frowning, holding a shelled oyster in mid-air.

"Ben Jonson," Alphonso suggests.

"Harlot, you blaspheme." Ben shakes his finger at Alphonso, but looks sternly at Emilia all the while. "Do not even jest about sullying my reputation with your crazed conceit of winter tree branches as women, their green hair gone grey with time."

She frowns and pops the oyster between her lips. "I thought you admired it!"

"I admire the poem as a whole. But when I read that line, I wanted to vomit."

Emilia laughs. "I thank you for refraining. For me, I am savage and wild, and I will keep the line."

Ben shrugs. "As you will." He lifts a plate, tips it, and pours eight oysters directly into his mouth, then washes them down with a half-pint of ale. She and Alphonso stare, transfixed by the gluttonous display. Ben rises then, dabbing the juice on his jerkin with a stained pocket handkerchief. He adjusts the big sword he wears everywhere. A livid "T" shines redly on the back of his thumb. It's Ben Jonson's brand: a scarlet badge commemorating a sojourn in Tyburn jail, where he was briefly lodged the first year of the new sovereign's reign, for mocking Scotland in a play he wrote with his sometime friend and collaborator, John Marston.

"I'm off to Paul's, ladies," he says, bowing. He strides forth, leaving her frowning again in his wake.

"He won't help me," she says to Alphonso.

"No. She won't."

Ben won't. And yet he *has* helped her, more than she can measure.

She sends another copy of "The Description of Cooke-ham," with a few shorter lyrics, to Lady Penelope, and to Lucy, the Countess of Bedford, whom Ben for some reason admires. She half-considers asking Alphonso to show them to Henry Wriothesley when her husband is next called to court, but quickly decides not to. She's ashamed to trade on her past with that sun-faced earl, and, besides, the trick might not work in her favor.

"Poetry grows whorish," Ben complains, at their next tavern meeting. "I hate selling myself in a foul coupling with Inigo Jones, that scanderbag rogue. But the *pay!* Ah, perhaps it was always thus."

Months pass. On occasion she forces herself, now, to court, where she receives commendations: warm messages from Lady Margaret Clifford of Cumberland, delivered through her daughter Nan; even, once, a friendly nod from Lucy of Bedford. She spends hours preparing herself before each occasion: refashioning her dresses in the new style of lowered bodices and raised skirts; dusting her face, not heavily, but with a bit of light powder; tracing her lips and her eyes, and dressing her locks. Those who only partly know her will think she colors her hair. This is just what she doesn't do, anymore, of course. She wears her natural locks, grown out full in their original shade.

At first she has thought Lady Penelope best positioned to shepherd her poems to a patron. During the first year of James's reign, Penelope looked to have gained more from her connection with Mountjoy than she'd lost through her relation to Essex. After Essex's fall, Mountjoy went back to Ireland and did, at long last, what neither he nor Essex had managed to do before, namely, crush the rebel Earl of Tyrone. In recognition of his achievement, King James has named Charles the Earl of Devonshire. But Penelope's divorce petition has scandalized the court, who prefer masks of virtue. Though she has finally triumphed among the civil justices — whose authority is increasing, a fact King James seems not to realize — Queen Anne has since banished Penelope from her service. Penelope's subsequent wedding to Blount was a modest London affair, attended by Emilia and a few other guests, and conducted in defiance of canon law by Blount's chaplain. Now the married pair stay outcast in Devonshire, happy thus, but for the toll so much childbearing has taken on Penelope's health. In her late forties now, Penelope's face is lined and her dark-gold hair is greying. She is fat, and goes out of breath quickly. She suffers from troubles of the womb.

The world has forgotten Lady Penelope, and Penelope is fast forgetting the world. Once, when they were both still at court, she urged Emilia to circulate her poems, but she's not thought about that for years. And greetings and nods from the Countesses of Bedford and Cumberland are very well, but Emilia cannot eat them. Walter Raleigh, England's soldier-poet, is a friend to writers, but he's back in the Tower, for something he said that frightened King James. *And besides,* she thinks, *asking his help to a poet's livelihood would be too whorish even for me.*

To hell with a patron, she thinks. She visits three printers in Fleet Street: Isaac Jaggard, Richard Field, and Thomas Thorpe. They will not assume the risk, they tell her. A woman's name on a volume is scandalous.

"You have printed a poem by Queen Elizabeth," she reminds Jaggard.

He smiles his condescension. "Come back when you are queen."

Thomas Thorpe at least looks at the Cooke-ham poem. He scratches his ink-blotched face as he stands reading at the front of his shop, while busy printer's devils run back and forth behind, setting type and noisily blacking it. "It is good," he says, when he finishes. "It is *very* good. But I am burdened already, short of paper for the new year's run. We've bought three plays from the King's Men. And a woman as author . . . hum. The city censors are alert to scandal. Were you to come back next year, with a change of name . . . or offer work of this quality, penned by a *man* . . . ." He looks at her pointedly. He's suggesting, as Ben did, that she offer her poetry under a false name. She nods and leaves, vexed.

At least Thorpe didn't laugh at her.

Stillborn verses, inert in their locked coffin of a drawer. How will she live? Alphonso is called to court less and less. His fingers shake with palsy. The shakes hurt his playing, and the Bassanos can no longer trust him with delicate repairs. Sometimes he hurls his recorder to the floor with disgust, saying, "What's a musician unless she play?" She fears he is poxed and knows it and won't say it, lest putting words to the symptom make the malady real. But it's real anyway. He's sallow, and subsists mostly on bread and small beer, and canary when she's willing to get it. Her heart tears at his misery, yet she rails at him, in fear for them both. She can no longer pay Ellen, and has dismissed her. She has borrowed from Ben and Angelica, and from every Bassano and Lanier in London. She has so many debts that she and Alphonso are no longer invited to family gatherings. She's too proud to disturb Penelope. Yet she has no more funds for the rent.

She is wandering Paul's Yard one day, looking at books she can't buy, when she hears her name. She turns her head, and he's there.

Her first thought is how foolish she's been to think that here, in London, among the bookstalls and eating houses and stationers' shops, she could avoid him forever. Her second thought is how old she must look at thirty-eight, and how strange to him, with her auburn hair. Though he recognized her, and from the back, at that.

Her third thought is that he looks older himself, and thin. His face, too, is lined, and he has lost a tooth on the upper right side. He wears plain brown wool, a stiff buckram shirt, and a round, laceless collar. His nails are trimmed, but cut crudely, as though he's done it in a hurry with a penknife. Now that he's a gentleman, he's no longer trying to look like one.

He doffs his cap and bows. She sees he's bald, still shaving his head. This time, however, it's her head that's notable. "Lady, your hair!" he says wonderingly. "Emilia, you are translated!"

And unexpectedly, her years of pent anger free her tongue for a barbed witticism. She says, "*Truth needs no color, with his color fixed; beauty no pencil, beauty's truth to lay.*" She does not even bother to deploy an accent, as she still did—seven? eight years before?—during that cursed boatride with him across Thames.

He looks surprised, but says only, "Hmm. Well. What make you here, lady?"

"*I make nothing. I am not taught to make anything.*"

"*As you like it,* then. Will you do nothing but parrot my lines?"

"What make *you* here, Will?"

He waves a frayed book. "I seek practical bargains. A used edition of Greek romances."

With your wealth? she almost says. Rumor runs he spends it on nothing but houses and hoarded grain in Stratford. Witness the laceless collar. *Thrift, thrift, Horatio.*

"Romances," she says, reflecting.

"Stories of long-parted lovers, for the stage. A bargain in the market of cast-off merchandise."

"I know something about that."

He only looks at her through his endless grey eyes. But she will not let those eyes' power silence her, this time. She has begun, and will continue. "Marry, tell. You put me in mind of a thing I've read. Let me see."

She taps her lips. "Ah, yes. *That love is merchandized whose rich esteeming the owner's tongue does publish everywhere.*"

He regards her steadily. "You have read this."

"Yes. It's some trash I saw somewhere. I forget where."

After a long moment of gazing, during which she holds her own, barely blinking, he says, "Will you walk?"

Unspeaking, she continues to look steadily back at him. She wants to say no, to smile politely and say she has someplace else to go, to perfect this encounter by turning and walking away. Her figure, seen from behind, is still a perfect hourglass. Let it be seared into his memory! But she can't do it. She is hopeless, eternally hopeless, with him. In plain wool with brass buttons, thin, aging, and bald, he still holds her with those fathomless eyes of old. She must confess it, must always know it. The years between his brief appearances are mere interludes. She spends them building cardboard towers that a glance from him quickly topples. How false it has been, her hope that inked words could be loved separately from the hands that bred them, the body that housed them! It's as though his poetry were his face.

They go to her house. Cap in his hand, he enters warily, though their coming has been his own suggestion. Alphonso, for good or for ill, is in Sussex. For what's now become a rarity, he's been invited by Anthony Bassano to make one of a summer consort at Syon House, the Earl of Northumberland's southern palace. She is alone with Will in her small, spare Longditch parlor.

He sits, somewhat stiffly. She offers him wine, good Rhenish, which he politely refuses. Does he think she might poison him? She pours some for herself. "Art a puritan now, like the new lord chamberlain?"

"That one," he says thoughtfully, fingering his cap. "He's not like the old one." He looks at her apologetically. "Superior in some respects."

She shrugs, and sips. "I have heard he dislikes all entertainments, but prefers masques to plays."

"Have you, pray? And why does he so?"

"Because in masques it is at least women who play women, where in plays 'tis the boys who dress as females, which is against Deuteronomy."

He gives a snort of laughter and punches his cap. "Faugh! The hypocritical rogue! Why, I saw him one day in a woolen jerkin tied at the points with linen sleeves. An ungodly mix of two fabrics in clear defiance of Leviticus nineteen, nineteen. 'Twas a sin against fashion, if nothing else, and one that outraged me. I wanted to denounce him before the brethren; I could barely contain my zeal. Now, Emilia . . . ."

She cannot help it. She has put down her wine and taken his face in her hands and is kissing him. He sits clutching his hat while she crushes the full, soft weight of her body against his rigid form. Then he melts. The cap falls to the floor as his arms close around her.

When they wake in the morning light he seems distracted. He looks at the shadow of a chair cast by early sunlight on the wall.

"Master William," she murmurs sleepily, "you lied to me."

He turns a puzzled gaze on her, as though she's pulled him back from a great distance. "*I* lied?"

"Yes. You lied. You told me once you wanted to write no more plays, only thoughtful poems for gentlemen. Poems to be read in meditative circumstances."

He props himself on an elbow and rests his head on his hand. "Aye, I did. But it wasn't a lie, only a mistake. I believed it when I said it. Now it's all changed. Now I flat distrust thoughtful gentlemen."

"In truth?"

"Essex was a thoughtful gentleman, was he not?" He plucks at the counterpane. His eyes light up, but he doesn't look at her, precisely. He's looking inside himself, or at nothing, or at everything. "I have a new ambition. I will write plays that keep the audience from thinking. Fireworks, flying gods, perhaps even animals — things to watch." He says this not bitterly, as Jonson might have, but as though he has unveiled the best notion of his life.

"So you love it there, now."

"Where?"

"In dirty Southwark. It's not a fool's paradise."

He laughs shortly, caressing her shoulder and making her shiver. "O, yes it is. As is the world. Do you want to know why I love it?" He smiles at her. "I used to flesh out whole scripts and imagine the playing of them, when I first came to London and saw plays at the Rose and the Bel Savage. And when finally a thing I wrote was put on the stage it was all wrong, not what I foresaw, the players, even the best ones, like pirates, saying things their *own* way, adding things *extempore*, misreading or plain forgetting — it drove me into a fury. I had birthed the things, and I could not make them . . . *mean* what I wished."

"Not like a sonnet."

He looks at her warily. "You have it. But here was the odd thing. In the end, to confine words to a page — as in a sonnet — did not satisfy. Not to know what the unleashed child would *do* in a crowd . . . . Well. 'Tis a paradox, but the loss of mastery was livelier, in the end. You never know what will happen up there, on the scaffold, no more than you do in a Southwark tavern."

"You know folk will get drunk."

"Aye, but *then* what? What will they sing? What will they plot? Will they dance? Who'll be arrested? The audience, if the play's good, and that's *it*. The life of it, real life, bodies sweating, flesh and blood, and tongues that speak in the moment, forgetting their lines, or remembering them and saying them in a way you would never have expected. Or wanted. It's terrible sometimes. It makes you want to kill the players, and then yourself. But other times . . . ." He falls silent for a moment, and she listens hard, willing him to keep talking. The door in his eyes has opened again. She sees the light shifting. What does he see? She's heard stories from Alphonso and Angelica. Richard Burbage, the King's Men's leading tragedian, falling from the balcony and landing on his feet without breaking the meter of a blank verse speech. The jester Robert Armin reaching up to catch a crabapple aimed by some imp in the crowd, seizing it just before the thing knocked his cap off, taking a bite, making a face, then hurling the fruit back and hitting his target full square on the nose, and all the while making the petty battle match the words of his witty song.

"There was a night," says Will. "Nate Field, the youth, he was our apprentice, and was playing Cleopatra. In the end of the play she lets an asp bite her, to poison herself."

"I've read about that," she says drily.

"Well. You can guess we don't use a real snake, of course, just a sausage casing stuffed with linen and sewn shut. But an enemy of Nate's in the company — and he's got a few, I'll warrant you — that knavish lad put a real snake in the basket. It was only a garter, but Nate's from Eastcheap. A neighborhood not thick with snakes; not real snakes, anyway. It might have been a viper, for aught he knew. He took out the thing and it was alive in his hand. I saw his eyes go wide. I was the doddering fellow who'd brought it in, just left him the basket and exited. I didn't know about the trick, though I should have guessed something was afoot, from all the lads smothering their laughter in the tiring house beforehand. The snake was wiggling; its little forked tongue was flashing. I could see it through the curtain of the discovery space after I went off. And what did Nate do? He held the snake to his breast as if it were any baby, so it would seem to bite him as it should have. 'Give me my robe, put on my crown. I have immortal longings in me!' I'd never heard the crowd so hushed. And the snake . . . it stilled! 'Dost thou not see my baby at my breast?' And the snake was curled at his breast, playing *its* part while Nate played his." Will shakes his head in wonderment. "Nate charmed the snake!" He meets her eyes and smiles. "It's like that. Do you see?"

And she does. She sees the whole scene. She is afraid to speak, not out of shyness now, but from fear he will stop talking and resume his old habit of listening, saying just enough to probe, to spark her own revelations or glamorous lies, just when she wants to hear more of his. So she says simply, "Yes."

But he falls silent anyway, his eyes going hooded again, as though he himself is the snake, and she has to say more. "So you will write plays of miracles? The flying gods and the fireworks?"

He smiles slightly. "Plays of spectacle. And miracles, yes, but the spectacles are not the miracles. These only set the stage for the *wonder*."

At the word his voice changes, trembles slightly, as though he has amazed himself. Her ears tingle. The voice raises in her that old, odd feeling of awe, as if the sound he's left trembling in the air is the word incarnate, not a mere sign but the very thing it bespeaks.

"The wonder?" She dislikes that she's translated herself into his echo, so she adds, "Do you believe in such things?"

His eyes have gone distant again, but his mouth twists in a faint smile. "This depends on the day."

"What, then, is your wonder? The thing your spectacles make way for?" She reaches for his shoulder, hating that his action of turning makes her gesture seem grasping. But he is turning, has turned, and is now rising from the bed, now crouching to find his breeches on the floor. She can no longer see his face. He is only a quiet voice, answering, or rather, not answering. "A wonder indeed." And then he pops up and is there again, sitting breeched and bare-chested, looking at her once more, as if through the famed glass of Galileo. She feels she's performing a minimal part in someone else's story. She's like one of the players, whose schedule is so full they can memorize only their own cues and parts, and come in and off stage knowing naught of the great shape of the play to which they are, nonetheless, esssential. Will had once told her of this common practice, and had added drily, *As in life.*

"But what wonder?" she asks again.

He crosses his arms over his chest and looks down at the floor. He says softly, "That a woman could forgive. That is the wonder."

Does he mean her? Her heart floods. *Forgive? I would forgive you anything if you would stay one more hour,* she wants to tell him. But she doesn't trust her voice. She says instead, "And you will put this miracle on stage."

"I will try."

"The poetry of a read page is a small thing, by comparison, to that."

"Let us say it is something else entirely." The cautious look has returned to his eyes. "But to speak of those sonnets."

"You made me a whore in them." She reaches up to touch his narrow chest.

"You thought I wrote of *you.*" Smiling, he deflects her pinch with a wiry arm. "Perhaps I did, and perhaps I didn't. But you *are* a hobbyhorse." He pushes her. "Let's see if you rock."

"You know that I do."

"Bawdy, my girl."

"What must I forgive, then? That you called me the *bay where all men ride*?"

A pained look crosses his face. "There was no name in any poem I wrote. These were games, the sonnets, you should understand. I cannot remember those days."

So. William Shakespeare's memory is faulty. Do all poets lie so brazenly? She will raise this question, now, and make him answer. She feels freer with him here, in her house, than she ever felt at Henry Wriothesley's mansion. At last she can talk to him about what he loves, and about what she loves. She will tell him her thought: that some poems are portraits, or stained glass windows that make their own worlds. But as she opens her mouth to speak, he says, "You say that you have them, fair copied? Those sonnets?"

A remembered statement clangs in her mind, an apologetic explanation heard in a boat on Thames. *I am married.* She remembers how those words fell on her ears like a knell, or a sentence of death.

And suddenly, she knows why he is here.

On the heels of that insight, while her heart turns to ice, she decides what she'll do.

Thomas Thorpe looks as though he's been pole-axed. He actually staggers. "Where did you come by . . . ." He cannot finish the sentence. He lays a finger on the stiff parchment like a pilgrim touching a relic.

"The writing is his. Here is the signature, under this poem." She points to the first sonnet Wriothesley delivered to her, on her last day at Tichtfield. "You see the hand is the same as in all the others." *A woman scorned hath no limits. Her rage is her strength, and her cure.* "You desire further proof?"

He shakes his head. "No. I know his hand and his autograph. I own prompt books, if I want to compare. And this sonnet, *When my love swears —*"

"*That she is made of truth, I do believe her, though I know she lies.*"

"I have printed it before, myself, in a miscellany, ten years ago. He himself let it go, and one other. The rest . . . they are his. I can't doubt it. But *where —*" He checks himself. "Tell me not. You have them. You would sell them. The less I know, the better. His name on the title page. But this you have written, below it?" He points to the dedication she has printed underneath Will's name. *To the Only Begetter of These Ensuing Sonnets, Mr. W. H.* "Who is W.H.?"

"A scheme of my own. A game, you may say." After laboring in thought the night before, the sour jest came to her. "W" for William, and "H" for Henry Wriothesley. Herself excluded. She guessed that *he* would know what it meant. But Thomas Thorpe doesn't need to.

Thorpe's thinking of something else, anyway. The eccentric dedication is a small matter in comparison. "I have dealt with Master Shakespeare," he says cautiously. "By rights I should speak to him first."

She waits, her hand on the poems. Field and Jaggard are just down Fleet, a few shops away, and he knows it. At length the London tradesman makes up his mind. "I should do so, but I won't." He looks at her squarely. "And now, we will bargain."

"A moment." She picks up the poems, walks to the door of the shop, and makes a brief gesture to someone standing outside. Returning, she replaces the paper between herself and the master printer. Thorpe, who has nervously watched the progress of the sonnets to the door and back, now lays a reverent hand on the top of the parchment sheaf, stroking it gently, gone from pilgrim to pagan priest, as though what he touched were not an inked page, but some magical silken cloth embroidered with rare and cunning design.

Edmund Tanfield arrives at Emilia's elbow, like a pink-faced Arabian genie. "This gentleman is authorized to bargain on my behalf," she says briskly to Thorpe. "I will add only one stipulation to whatever he may allow. That is, *no Blackletter.* I want the text readable at a glance, not awash in ancient curlicues. The poems must be set in Roman type."

The printer smiles. "Mistress, in my shop, there is no other kind."

"I'm glad of it. Now, Master Thorpe, will you point me to your Machiavelli? The newest English edition, so please you."

That Christmas she boasts a goose and a currant pudding and a blazing Yule Log which Alphonso's tremor does not prevent him from lighting. Her presents for her husband are several: three sheet-music pieces from Italy, a velvet jerkin, and a cleaning brush for his recorders. Their debts are paid, and they are merry. A knock on the door brings their expected guests. In walks Bess Tanfield, now styled Lady Elizabeth Carey, as her father has lately married her to a high-placed member of that family, a viscount, no less. The viscount is off hunting with the king, and Bess has come to Longditch with Angelica and Edmund and the Tanfields' new baby boy. For Alphonso, the guests bring two bottles of canary, and for Emilia, a gift more enduring: a copy of Montaigne's essays, in an English translation by John Florio, one-time tutor to word-mad Henry Wriothesley. It's her second gift of a book. This morning, from Ben Jonson, she received a package via messenger from Penshurst, a patron's estate where Ben's lately been living. He has inscribed to her one of his own copies of Horace's *Satires.*

And the better to read these books? "Behold!" Bess pulls from her pocket a pair of spectacles. She's had them made by a glazier. "Little windows to magnify the word. Only try them!"

"I've seen a pair of these in a shop." Emilia puts them on and gasps. "By God, Alphonso! You've three buttons gone today."

"Do I?" Her husband looks down. "A careless seamstress." He cocks an eye at her. She can see his every crease and wrinkle, the hairs at his temples, the line where the brownish dye gives way abruptly to a quarter-inch of grey.

"Let me not look in a glass wearing these," she says.

"I have some as well," says Bess. "Melly, are they not wondrous?"

"Wondrous past hoping." Emilia kisses her. "Thank you, Bess."

But Emilia's best gift is her own, to herself. In a second-hand shop on Cheap last week she found a small oil, and has hung it from the wall in the parlor, just above the settle. It's a painted landscape. In the painting a road winds up a hill and diminishes to a point on the far horizon. A well-lit house stands on another hill, surrounded by fields and by trees, the tallest among them a stately oak towering well in the foreground. Now, through her new spectacles, she can see every detail of its trunk, and each line of its broad, green leaves.

25

The surgeons can't name her illness. But then, with women they never can, or else they deliver so many conjectures that all become finally meaningless. The medical men glide gravely in and out of her darkened chamber, holding bowls, vials, leeches on trays. Her strength ebbs, and they can do nothing. She has run the course of her sex.

A woman was beautiful, with killing eyes that lanced men's hearts. She danced in jeweled slippers at fifty palaces. Now, after dealing so many fictive death-wounds to poets, she herself is felled by a real malady: a disease of the bowels, of the stomach, of the womb. Her face has fallen, her breasts are flaccid, her abdomen swells, and everything hurts. There is a pain down there, somewhere. It doesn't matter where, or what it is, since they can't cure it. Penelope Devereux Rich Blount is dying.

"Too many children," she murmurs. "What was the sentence you taught me, Emilia? *Mi stanno lavorando per la morte!* They're working me to death."

To be with her, Emilia has rented a horse and ridden all night, accompanied by the servant of Mountjoy's who appeared breathless at her door in Longditch the day before. Now she kneels by the bedside, holding Penelope's hand tightly. "Is that what they said, lady? The doctors?"

"'Tis what *I* say. I was never right after the eleventh. But hush." Penelope lays a finger weakly to her lips. "Don't tell that to my Ruthie. Foolish girl, she's been sobbing for three days already."

"Of course I will not, my dear."

Penelope sighs. "All my pretty chickens. How will they fare?"

"The ones who aren't Riches are Blounts now. Acknowledged by everyone, whatever the canon law says."

Penelope gives the merest nod, then closes her eyes, exhausted. She stays silent for a long time. Her head bowed on the bed, still gripping her friend's quiet hand, Emilia begins to think her lady won't speak again, that she has ridden all this way for this touch and these brief sentences, and that she must now somehow make herself rise and go to fetch Charles and the children. But then Penelope opens her eyes. "You must tell, Emilia," she says clearly.

Emilia raises her head. "Tell what?"

"Who it was you loved. 'Tis my deathbed wish."

Emilia swallows, dry-mouthed. She can't do it. Even for Penelope, she can't. She says, "'Twas Prince William of Orange."

If merriment could restore her lady, this would have been the cure. But Penelope is weak, and the laughter that starts in her is quickly translated to groaning. "Oof," she says, as Emilia holds her. "Wipe my eyes. If you'll not tell, you must grant me something else."

"Name it, my darling."

"You must forgive me."

"For what?" Emilia smooths Penelope's hair and straightens her pillow.

"That I urged you . . . ." The sick woman pauses. They have given her tincture of opium, and she drifts. In a moment she's back, after a frowning struggle with her meandering mind. "Lord Hunsdon. That monster. I should not have added *bawd* to my list of titles, advising you . . . . . Yet I thought it was best — no, hear me." Emilia is shaking her head, saying "Don't speak of it," but Penelope raises a finger. "I must tell. I was all bitterness after they packed me off to . . . Lord Rich. A thousand-pound knave, he. I thought the best bargain a woman could make was for silks and jewels, and love might come when it would. I didn't know what love was, I mean I was only beginning to, then. Later I . . . knew. I wish it for you, Emilia."

"I love you." Emilia is weeping. "I love *you*."

"You'll forgive me?"

Emilia snorts, laughing and crying. "Yes! I did what I did. No one made me do it. And it didn't destroy me. Besides, Henry Carey was paid in the end." Emilia has never told anyone *how* he was paid, though his death is her proudest achievement, her best piece of poetry. She'll not speak of this, either, now or ever. "I forgave you long ago," she says fervently. "Does that please you?"

"It does. I like not to have . . . done harm." Penelope makes a wan smile.

"Nor I." Emilia pauses. "Well, unless it is harm for a greater good."

"A greater good." The words come slowly, heavily. "I've achieved little in that sphere. What mark have I left on the world? There she goes, a renegade's sister, and a play-goddess in poems. A gilt star for a Christmas pageant. What mark is that?"

"You've left more than a *mark*. You are in my heart, and in everyone's who knew you. Knows," she quickly amends. "And you leave something living, flesh and blood. You leave children." Emilia kisses her hand, then holds Penelope's fingers against her cheek.

"Yes." Penelope smiles. "I regret not a one of them. Not even Ruthie."

Once outside, Emilia gently closes the chamber door. Charles Blount is seated there on the floor, his head against a windowsill. He's clutching a Bible, and has misbuttoned his coat. "Ah, God," he says, rocking. "Ah, God."

She crouches to touch his arm. "Your wife is a woman of poetry. Go in. Read her the psalms. Here." She removes the Bible from his grip, turns some pages, then points. "This."

Mountjoy draws a ragged breath and reads. "*Thy wife shall be as a fruitful vine by the sides of thine house: thy children like olive plants round about the table.*" His voice breaks at the end of it, but he masters himself, and pulls his body heavily up. "I thank you." He bows a stiff soldier's bow, and goes in to Penelope.

And what mark make I? she thinks desolately, in the weeks and months after Penelope's funeral. *No children, me.* She knows there are enough people in the world, and tries not to be bothered by this old grief, by the thought that her own body will no more, will never, exfoliate into new life, yielding a face bearing some print of her face, a heart bearing some print of her heart. Is it only vanity, the desire to self-perpetuate? In Plato's *Symposium*, Socrates says some give birth in body, and others in beauty. But what is it to give birth in beauty? She has clung to the thought, has imagined that for her to conceive beauty was to engender poetry. *But how if no one reads my ten paltry poems, Cooke-ham, Eve's Argument in Her Own Defense, for Loving Knowledge?* She tries to distance herself from the sorrow with irony, reminding herself that there are not only enough folk but enough poems in the world, and that, as for fame, she has a whore's name in some sonnets that *are* read, if she wants to claim it.

She doesn't, of course, and the sonnets have sold so widely that a fashionable game is to guess the identity of William Shakespeare's dark, sultry lady. The pastime is second in popularity only to speculation about the name of the fair and beloved young man. A year has cooled her anger, and now and then she feels guilty, wondering how Will is taking it, seeing his love translated into her merchandise. But remorse disappears when she recalls his voice asking after the sonnets on that last, bright morning in her Westminster bed. His question still twists like a knife in her heart. She evaded it then, and turned cool, and he turned cool also, and gave her, again, the appraising look she'd seen in his eyes back at Tichtfield when she first mentioned the name of Lord Hunsdon. Soon after, he put on his shirt, washed his face, and walked out of her house. He gave a last, brief bow that seemed mocking, as his bows always did, then turned and disappeared into the morning, going towards the busy city without a look back. Vanished like smoke. Perhaps he was bound to find Wriothesley his old dear and inquire, in wounded tones, whether his long-ago parting gift had indeed ended up in Emilia's possession.

Now he'll know.

He came for the poems, only for the poems. I quoted them at him, and he guessed that I had them. And I threw myself at him on the settle, she thinks in disgust. Aloud she mutters, *"Putana!"*

She has anyway burnt her bridges. *Tit for tat, and that for thee, Will Shakespeare.* She has heard nothing from Will since that brittle morning, nor expects any word, not a bitter word sent by letter, not even a formal word sent by lawyer. For what can he do to her? What crime has she committed? The pieces of inked paper were her possessions. Wriothesley gave them to her. No law can arraign her.

And the sonnets are mighty, squeaks the dispassionate part of her mind. It can squeak only, being as small as a mouse. *Masterworks should be read by all.*

Her own poems are not masterworks, and she knows it. But they are as good as what many men write, and more, they are original, and she wishes at times she had pushed Thomas Thorpe to print them as part of her bargain with him for Will's sonnets. Pride kept her from that. But with pride differently placed, with more faith in their worth, she might have pressed her advantage.

She wishes, at times, she was more like Ben Jonson. But she's not as single-minded. While she lost one child to the plague, Ben lost three. Now he lives apart from his half-deranged wife, who will not lie with him for fear of birthing and burying more, and he spends twelve hours a day writing verses and plays. "My children were my poems," he has said to Emilia. "Now, my poems are my children."

"And your plays, cousin?"

"My stepchildren."

"Your masques?"

"Ah, ah, ah! Must you remind me of *Jones*?"

She goes to Ben's new city comedy with Bess Carey. Though a married woman, who by custom should be freer in her movements, Bess must sneak through a window and ride a horse into town to escape her husband's vigilance. "He can't beat me," she tells Emilia, on their walking way to the Whitefriars playhouse. Bess is wearing a high-crowned man's hat. The headgear is the latest fashion for women, and she has brought one for Emilia, but Emilia's head is smaller than Bess's and her hat slips down over her brow. Annoyed, she pushes it up. The pair of them hike their skirts against the mud, passing loud vendors and crafty beggars, skirting a small crowd gathered before a puppet show presenting the parable of the Prodigal Son. "He would not dare to strike me," Bess says. "My brother would have him for action of battery, for all he's a lord, and I know how to give evidence. I'll tame him in time, I'm sure of it."

A mountebank on their left calls out, "Face-physic for ladies!" Not turning, Bess raises her left hand and gives him the figo.

"But do you love him?" Emilia asks, hurrying to keep up with her friend.

"I love his manor."

"His manner?"

"His house. I've a library. He never goes into it. I've filled it with books, and I write there. He thinks this harmless enough, and for the court masques and dances that make him jealous when I go, I care not to attend them more than once in a season. Those women! Those fops! I care only for the plays. If I can go to five a year, it's enough. Melly, I've almost completed my tragedy."

"A new one?"

"Yes. Mariam, the Queen of Jewry, and her cruel Herod. 'Tis all about women and husbands."

"What will *your* husband say?"

"He'll say naught, if it's played to acclaim."

Emilia stops short, and her hat once more slips down on her brow. "You think to *sell* it?" She resituates her headgear. "To be read?"

"To be *staged*," Bess says determinedly. "I've shown it to the King's Man Richard Burbage. My idea came from his *Othello*. From Shakespeare's play, I mean, that he played in. I told Master Burbage which lines." She recites them from memory.

> *But I do think it is their husbands' faults*
> *If wives do fall. Say they slack their duties*
> *And pour our treasures into foreign laps,*
> *Or else break out in peevish jealousies,*
> *Throwing restraint upon us? Or say they strike us?*

Bess is good at this, at playing a player, her eyes flashing, her hands raised and shaken expressively at "strike us." Suiting the action to the word, not sawing the air. A pair of basket-toting laundresses have stopped to listen.

> *Why, we have galls, and though we have some grace,*
> *Yet have we some revenge. Let husbands know*
> *Their wives have sense like them.*

The laundresses cheer, and Lady Elizabeth Carey, Viscountess of Falkland, bows to them. She grips Emilia's arm. "Come your ways. We'll be late."

Emilia allows herself to be hustled along, though she's growing breathless at Bess's pace. "You should do as Ben says, and speak in one of his masques," she pants.

"Ha! I'll not prance before nincompoops and popinjays."

"But those lines weren't in *Othello*. I have heard that play."

"Did you stay til the end?"

"Ah . . . no."

"The lady's maid says it to the lady, late in the plot. The woman who steals the handkerchief. What is her name? Arbella? Aurelia?"

"Emilia."

"Emilia. *That's* comical. Like you! She turned to the audience saying it, and all the wives in the playhouse cheered. You should have stayed! William Shakespeare can do anything. And he knows everything."

"He doesn't know as much as he thinks he does," Emilia says after a moment, to say something.

"Shakespeare? Are you mad? He knows everything. What ails you? You look ill. Step up, Melly! This, *this* is why I love tragedies."

"Because they make us walk fast? Slower, pray, I'm not as young as you are. You are aware, are you not, that it's Ben's new play at Whitefriars? It's no tragedy."

"Yes, I know. I must take what's on offer. It's not every day I can sneak through a window."

The play is called *Epicoene, or, The Silent Woman.* But of course, there are no women on stage, silent or otherwise, only high-voiced boys in curled perukes. None of these costumed lads match the title's ideal, they are all so busy chattering folly and vanities. The male wits of the play deride them as wives who live without husbands, who form a "college" and gab endlessly of authors they have not read and would not understand if they had; who paint their faces, who chase men with the aggression of tigers, and who have, worst of all, the audacity to age. *Autumnal faces!* How can a man look at them? *Pieced beauty!* Such women paint and perfume and oil their lips and present their pictures to the world, and not themselves. A foul feast of falsity! They *practice any art to cleanse teeth, repair eyebrows; paint, and profess it!*

"I don't understand," murmurs Emilia. "Should women paint? Should women not paint?"

"'Paint and profess' is good," muses Bess, scratching a note in her little commonplace book. She carries a pencil always, both for eyebrow improvement and to record impressions, as Emilia did once, before she tired of writing words that went nowhere.

"Let's find Ben and kick him in the stones," Emilia whispers. "I hear he's in London again. Come, let's out, and hire a coach."

"Is it your habit to see plays in parts? We'll stay for the finish."

Emilia wants to attend to the dialogue, but is distracted by the gaudy show of the patrons in other boxes. It isn't the six-penny patrons who disrupt the play. It's the gallants, the moneyed ones, who hoot and lean from their boxes over the scaffold, waving their slashed velvet sleeves. She squints. "Are those not the other Careys? Your husband's cousins?" It is they, she is sure. Some fifty feet along the playhouse wall, Anne Morgan, Lord Hunsdon's widow, occupies a box with her two sons, Henry Carey the younger and another boy whom she guesses is Francis Montgomery, Anne's child by her current husband, the Scot. Bess has told her of the new son's existence. The lads and their mother sit alongside Lucy, the Countess of Bedford. Both matrons are laughing heartily at the play's

mockery of painted women, cheering on the painted boys who are playing them, though in fact those player-boys' skin is fresh, and the wom-
en's skins look like well-doctored dough, sprinkled with flour and dotted
with fuchus cherries. And the boys in their box? Francis Montgomery is
too young for a playhouse, though, for an irony, he's little younger than
the boys playing Madame Haughty and Mistress Otter before him on the
stage. The young Henry Carey now looks eighteen or nineteen. He has
grown like a weed since she saw him playing the recorder at Whitehall.
She knows that John Carey, Lord Hunsdon's final son by his first wife, has
lately died of a fever. This turns Anne Morgan's boy, Henry, into Carey's
heir. Does the youth feel his fortune? Does it scratch? He is pulling at a
lace collar.

Suddenly, seeming to feel her group stared at, Anne Morgan turns
and looks straight at Emilia. Abruptly, Anne changes expression. She
seems alarmed, as though menaced by a phantom. *And she has seen one,
in a way*, thinks Emilia, shrinking back into the recesses of their own box,
out of the public view. "Behold Lady Anne Morgan Carey Montgomery,"
she tells Bess. "She looks like a cherry dumpling."

"Hush! Mark the play."

They stay to the end, and by the last act Emilia is laughing as hard
as anyone, though she's been far from light-hearted all day. Under her
smiles she still feels Penelope's death like a stone in the center of her
body. And she is always uncomfortable, these days, in public, expos-
ing herself to others' eyes. To be seen is bad, to be recognized, worse.
She's acutely and sadly aware these days of having lost her looks. *Blasted
youth, ugh.* When she peers in the glass now she sees her own mother, a
woman greatly beloved by her children, yes, but not someone Emilia had
ever cared visually to imitate, a housewife who died grey and tired while
yet in her forties.

Later, alone in her house, she broods again on Will, and on the lines
from *Othello* that Bess remembered so well and declaimed in the street.
Will. The man is unfathomable, a will-o'-the-wisp, as false, as colorless
as water. She has imagined him. She had thought he imagined *her*. She
was a mere dream to him too, she believed, and is discomfited to find the
truth more complex than that. Once she considered it the jest of all bitter
jests, his writing a poem that praised her darkness as though that shadowy color were realer than "false compare." *My mistress' eyes are nothing
like the sun.* He hadn't known how utterly put-on her color was. Yet when

she was with him last, he showed no real surprise at her paleness, her auburn Englishness, beyond his initial exclamation at her hair. *Emilia, you are translated!*

Now she must think that that strange sonnet, and indeed each sonnet he wrote about her, was only a cloudy mirror. ("You thought I wrote of *you*," he had said in her bed, and smiled.) He must always have known she pretended her dark mystery, or guessed it. Her trouble with English, her stories of Venice, the artificial night of her hair and eyes: none of it had fooled him. He'd glimpsed the self behind her screen. What self? A woman with gall, and grace, and vengefulness. And years later, in that play she'd hated so much, that tragedy from which she'd walked, seething with anger, before the last act, he had let her speak her bitterness. *Yet have we some revenge*, his Emilia said. A prophecy, as it turned out, since she, Emilia Lanier, has certainly had hers.

Has he written of her, or has he written her?

26

She attends another masque at Whitehall, in the gorgeous Banqueting Hall with its ceiling of painted cherubs. Nan Clifford will dance a part in it, and has warmly invited her by letter. Emilia misses Nan, and does not want to say no.

"You'll want to witness this one, Melly," Ben cackles. "Get you to the cunnycourt. Here you will see courteous instruction of the nobility polished to a fine art. I've a secret collaborator in this."

"Not Jones?"

"*Jones!* He's not secret *enough*. Yes, he built the scenery, but I don't mean Jones. I've another partner in this. A savvy fellow, who will help me instruct a queen."

This queen, James's Danish Anne, cannot command enough revels which place her at center stage. This will be the eighth such entertainment since her husband assumed the throne. King James and his son are absent at a Warwickshire hunting lodge this evening, but he has left orders that to please his wife, the masquers should proceed with *The Masque of Queens*, in which Ben Jonson and Inigo Jones have made Anne and eleven of her women into royal warriors bearing spears and clad in painted armor and plumed helmets. First, against a painted silvestrian backdrop, there come dancing and frolicking the comic anti-masquers, rustic Arcadian farmers played by common actors. Then the crowd claps to see the spectacle of two male courtiers welcoming the descent via pulley of the crowned, enthroned, and sceptred queen, followed by the entrance of her dancing ladies. The men situate the queen carefully in the middle of the *platea*, then kneel to flank her wooden throne, as the women chant praises to *Penthesilea, brave Amazon*, flitting like butterflies back, then forward, then left, then right, never crossing before the seated wife of the sovereign. Nan Clifford speaks and dances her part beautifully, to much applause.

But after Nan leaves the floor with the lesser nymphs, the applause dissolves into a collective gasp.

By the plaster shrubbery behind the throne, a grinning skeleton has appeared. He comes closer, and from above and behind he menaces the queen, who turns and raises her hands in mock terror. One of the kneeling courtiers runs away in well-feigned fear, while the other stays frozen in his kneeling position. Emilia squints. The remaining courtier appears to be tall Henry Carey the younger, great Lord Hunsdon's last son, last seen in the Whitefriars box with his mother, Anne Morgan Carey Mongtomery. Young Henry has sat with the recorders in the antimasque, and now joins the masque proper.

The skeleton jumps into the foreground and begins to caper, as the rich painted foliage is rolled away, giving place to a second scene: a laboratory stocked with vessels and dishes of ominous-looking, strange-colored powders. The skeleton kicks up his heels, showing winged bone-feet. In a raucous voice he starts to sing.

> *Mercury am I, the god of thieves and queens!*
> *I conduct all to death. And what's my means?*
> *Fell vanity, my potions, and bad skin.*
> *I am the god who poisons all the pocked,*
> *Inviting them to Charon's boat, that's docked*
> *To take such freight of ladies who would sell*
> *Good health for beauty. Hear their funeral knell!*

The skeleton god is trotting back and forth before one of the front-row spectators, Lady Susan de Vere, who has risen and begun to scream. She is trying to hit the skeleton with her half-moon fan. Cries of shock and disgust mixed with some barely suppressed snorts of laughter come from various parts of the watching crowd. Emilia watches, spellbound, thinking, *Ben's a lunatic.*

Evading Susan Vere's fan, the skeleton turns his winked, black clad form and wiggles a bony bum, to audience cries of "O, foul!" "For shame!" "Ah, God!" "Out on the poet!"

"*I am the knight Quicksilver, who will slay —*"

"*Avaunt thee, knight!*" The queen has risen and is waving her scepter at Mercury. "*For I turn night to day!*"

The skeleton reels as if from a body-blow, then staggers with a wolv-ish howl back through the shrubbery as the audience cheers wildly. The queen drops back onto her throne with a proud smile. But her smile doesn't last. A snap of overstrained wood is heard as she hits the seat, and her expression turns to one of startled dismay, though, soldierlike, she keeps on speaking her part.

> *Fineness of soul renews our eyes and faces,*
> *Virtue grants outward beauty all its graces!*

Her scepter held high, she orates valiantly, while her throne starts to tilt to the left and her helmet slips over her brow. Henry Carey, unfortu-nate lordling, tries to brace the throne with both hands. He's sweating so hard that his paint drips from his neck onto his starched lace collar. His head is still bowed before his sliding sovereign, as Ben's script and court protocol dictate. As he looks down, the youth tries subtly to knock the royal chair back on its legs, but the bad leg suddenly breaks off, leaving the Amazon queen perched at a dangerous slant, her face half-hidden by her helm.

Emilia bites her lip and looks anywhere but at the playing area. She turns her eyes up to the fat, torchlit angel-babies who soar on the painted ceiling, then ducks her head and buries it in her hands. Though her heart goes out to the valiant boy trying to save the doomed throne, she is shak-ing with laughter, she can hardly suppress it, she must fly from this place. She jumps up and scurries out the door, abandoning protocol.

Some fifty feet down the passageway she comes to an open door that gives into an antechamber, where the anti-masquers are still strip-ping off their paint and their rustic attire. She stops, still covering her mouth to muffle her laughter, unable to resist a peek. Her eyes meet a profusion of bare legs, cocks, and bums reddened like devils' by torch-light. She thinks she sees Will among the men, unbreeched and bending to pull on his strossers, but she can't be sure. As she cranes her neck for a better view, she finds her vision blocked by stocky Ben. The masque poet is walking in a tight circle, tugging his hair and yelling at the skeletal Mercury, who has just taken off his skull-mask to reveal a pale, sweaty, sharp-bearded face that's quite as irate as Ben's. Next to Jonson's bulk the man looks all knees and elbows.

"You kicked the throne, Marston!" Ben bellows. "You kicked it!"

Marston bares a row of ragged teeth and shakes a bony finger. "I'm not such a fool! I was off stage when the thing broke, you saw me yourself."

"You were dancing in front of the *queen!*"

"*Not.*" The man Marston shakes his head vigorously. Drops of sweat fly from his hair. "I was well to the side, I took care. Marry, 'twas *you* who wrote the anti-masque into the main masque, and now you would blame me for —"

"Aye!" Ben kicks a promptbook, which flies across the room and hits the wall five inches from an iron sconce. The torch flares with the breeze and the shuddering of the wall. "You muckhill!" Ben scoffs. "You're never at fault, though at all hours halter-worthy. But you'll make your sin good when you kneel in the epilogue. Kneel and *grovel.* Don't think I'll visit Tyburn again for your trespass —"

"*Mine?*" Marston's face has grown paler, and two dots of color flame on his cheekbones. "You base-born —"

"*I* am base. Much! Your father was a malt-man, and your mother sold gingerbread in Christchurch."

"O, *did* she so!" The skeleton mask comes hurtling through the doorway into the passage, but misses Emilia, who saw it coming and is already racing again down the hall towards the nearest exit. The angry playwright voices fade behind her. In her mind she hears Penelope shrieking with merriment.

Ah, my dear, do you see this? she breathlessly prays. *Were you here, my own Amazon, we'd both be cast from this palace, to run mad with laughter in the Strand!*

She is hosting a poets' supper, at Bess Cary's urging, in her parlor in Longditch. Alphonso declines to attend, saying, "There can be too *many* words." He is tired, and hides in his room with a lute and a jug of hippocras. Ben arrives with six bottles of canary and seven of Rhenish. He has loudly complained of the presence of women, for all that she is the host and Bess Cary has supplied all the cates and four braces of conies. But he's there, at the door. He can hardly have said no to so grand a potential patron as the Viscount of Falkland, met here in proxy through his wife. Ever fatter, Ben lumbers bearishly to a seat, pours a flagon of canary, and broods over the failure of *The Masque of Queens.*

"You should be glad you and Marston weren't jailed," Emilia says.

"'Tis Inigo Jones should be jailed. He designed the throne."

Emilia shrugs. She can't commiserate. She's too vexed by the success of Ben's *Silent Woman*, the Whitefriars play she witnessed with Bess. For all its good humor, it was the worst kind of city comedy, the sort that encouraged women to laugh at their own sex, thinking others, never they, were the targets of the playwright's satire. And the play was not kind to men who liked clothes and who trilled when they talked. She is sure that Ben meant Alphonso by his Amorous La-Foole.

But what irks her more than these stage insults is Ben's failure to argue her case to a printer.

After a glass and a half of canary, she speaks. "What think you of painting, Ben Jonson?" She has done her skin lightly for the occasion: only a slight dusting of powder, and the merest touch of vermilion on her lips. A limited anti-face. Her eyebrows are her own, though she has not, could not, abandon her beloved kohl. "What say you, man? Are false colors not a help to our autumnal visages?"

He is gloomy, staring into the depths of his wine, but he stirs himself to a gallantry. "Lady Emilia, your face is eternal April. No adulterous art should corrupt it. *Give me a look, give me a face, that makes simplicity a grace —*"

"Nay, I think the adulterous art a help to our *autumnal visages*. Or a help, at the least, to you who are so cruelly forced to regard us." *In vino veritas.* She sips more wine, and smiles brightly. She thinks, *My eyebrows are my eyebrows, and my voice is my voice.* Bess Carey is smirking, and the dapper, lace-collared lawyer across the table from Emilia is smiling behind his hand. He is another guest, a known poet, and a longtime friend of Bess and Edmund Tanfield.

The air is sparking. Ben stirs, rallying his energies for argument. "Ladies." He nods inclusively at a third guest, a young man seated beside him. "In my writings I have praised paint when it is *necessary*. Only then. A pocked or a —"

"*Necessary!*" snorts Bess. "Are you so beautiful, Ben? Where be *your* paint? Had I your face, I'd throw myself in a dust-bin."

"Ah, but Viscountess, I do not claim to be beautiful. You'll not find me leveling my pockmarks with a nutmeg grater."

The whole table winces, and Emilia suppresses a shriek. Her hands fly to her ears. "God in heaven, Ben!"

"I said I would *not* do it. I do not aspire to loveliness." He raises an oratorical finger. "Nor is loveliness of face expected in a poet. I am that which I am."

"Blasphemer," says the poet-lawyer, and winks at Emilia.

"I am so much myself that I have even refashioned my name."

"By throwing out an 'H'?" Emilia shakes her head in scorn.

"I did not like the letter. 'Twas wholly superfluous. Indeed, 'twas wasteful."

Emilia cuts a strip of meat from a roast coney and drops it on Ben's plate. "Put this in your mouth, and stop talking. A wise man I know tells me there can be too many words."

"I have read the work of a prating pastor," says the young man at Ben's elbow. His hat is tall and velvet and topped by a gold feather. It's Francis Beaumont, a rising playwright whom Bess met two weeks before when she, escorted by her coerced brother, made a shocking appearance in the Pomegranate Room of the Mermaid Tavern, where players and authors were drinking. There she bested Master Beaumont in "Wax Flapdragons," a game of her invention, in which each contestant must swallow a half-pint of ale without drowning a lit candle-end floating in the tankard. She won.

"*You* have read preachments?" Bess asks Francis, arching a perfect half-moon eyebrow.

"Believe it, Lady Falkland! I held the godly tract upside down, trying to find the sense of it. Was it encoded? I could not tell. But here is what it said. Painted women must beware, when they come to heaven, that God not look at their face and say, 'I never made *that* one.'"

Emilia leans to refill the man's glass. Through the floor from above drift three slow, sweet notes. Alphonso is plucking her lute. She points upward with the bottle. "That tune. *God* didn't write it. My father Baptista did." She gestures toward the oil landscape above her settle. "And the picture, there. God never made *that* one. Should we toss out my father's music, and scrub that canvas bare?"

"Excellent," says the lawyer poet. "Of course we should not. Art is a golden world of its own sufficiency."

"Bravo," says Bess.

"Do you quote Philip Sidney?" asks Ben. "That man was a scholar by art and a fool by nature."

"O, o, good." Francis Beaumont mimes the writing of a sentence in a tablebook as he mouths, "*A scholar . . . by . . . art, and . . . a fool . . . by . . . nature.*" A light cuff from Ben nearly knocks him from his stool.

"I think better of him than do you," says the lawyer, as Beaumont straightens his high hat. "But for ladies' painting, this argument of the pastor must be *countenanced.*"

Beaumont laughs. Ben groans. "Jack Donne, leave my presence. Sail off to Virginia. I hear you've invested."

"And how have I offended you?"

"With your shallow word games. You are worse than Will Sh —"

"Why?" asks Emilia. She enjoys interrupting Ben, to watch him turn naturally purple at the effrontery.

Jack Donne the lawyer leans toward her. "Why? Because a painter paints canvas, but keeps the face God made for him. A painted lady would supplant hers. Lady, it is not a scrap of linen, but your *face.*"

Ben claps his hands. "Excellent! You are redeemed. I'll write a sonnet instantly in praise of you."

Below the tabletop Mumbleclutch sides along the wool-stockinged calves and the neats'-leather shoes, hoping for a falling morsel of chicken or rabbit. The others at table are laughing, but Emilia looks at Donne's serious eyes and thinks, *This fellow means what he argues. His word games are no games. And does he say right?*

27

Paint kills truth, she repeats to herself in the days that come. Men may disagree on the point, but Master Jack Donne has struck a chord in her. *Paint kills truth.*

On impulse, the day after the poets' supper (which Bess pronounced a great success, after the last drunken author departed singing "The Ballad of Chevy Chase" at two of the clock), she packs a crate with her long-hoarded bottles and vials, her tins of fuchus and onyx and rice powder, her pots of vermilion and ceruse. She hires a carter and goes with him to sell the whole kit to the Admiral's Men at the Fortune playhouse. They will not take the belladonna that has clouded her eyes and given her squints. It's of no use to them. But they buy the ink wash and the fuchus and the eyebrow pencils.

Will she miss any of it? She has hardly used these greases and powders and potions for years, painting less rather than more as she ages, in reverse of the current custom. But her cosmetics have always been there, near at hand in case of need, beauty in a box, weapons in a trunk. They were like her locked chest of sonnets, her treasury filled with Will's dark, magic poems, which she cherished for years like fine silken handkerchiefs. Now all her treasures are sold. *I will paint no more, forever,* she swears. The tale of a life — of woman's laughter, lover's heartbreak, mother's anguish, sister's rage — is truly told in a crease, a line, a wrinkle, a scar. She'll wear a face, and not the picture of a face.

She keeps one stick of kohl.

Unexpectedly, it is Angelica who sparks her return to writing. It is not that Angelica reads, though she knows how. She has a second child now, and as a mother has developed a practical concern for household budgets.

Last year Edmund, compelled to explain the sudden influx of money into the Lanier household, told her in a general way of her sister's past tie with William Shakespeare, and of the bartered poems. "I swore her to silence, but I *had* to reveal it," he tells Emilia. "The questions wouldn't stop." Angelica is thrilled at her sister's cleverness, and a little awestruck at her shadowy fame, which eclipses — or at least augments — even the Lord Hunsdon scandal. She is now convinced that every woman named "Emilia" in a play by Shakespeare or by someone who knows him is a staged portrait of her sibling.

"Melly!" she crows, returning from an expedition to the Fortune or the Cross Keys Inn. "Today you were a murderess and a witch!" "Melly, usually you're some sort of whore, but Ned and I saw you today in a comedy as an old abbess, spending your time in seclusion and study."

"A lonely fate for me, sister."

"No, no. After twenty years or so she's happy. A long-lost son comes to fetch her out, and she catechizes everyone in town."

"Excellent."

Angelica pesters her recurrently with a question. "Melly, the money from the sonnets will not keep you forever. You must write some in return, and keep the thing going. Like Sir Walter Raleigh —"

"Who?"

"How sharply you speak! O, you've lain with him, too. That must be it."

Emilia has jabbed her thumb with a needle. As she sucks the thumb's tip she says through her teeth, "Yes, I've lain with him, and with King James as well. Also with Prince William of Orange, and the pope. You spout nonsense, mistress. What do you know of Walter Raleigh?"

"That he has a poem answering another famous poem. Riding on the fame of the other."

Emilia lays aside the skirt whose hem she's been stitching. "Who told you this? You cannot have read either poem."

"Why not? I'm not such a fool as you think. But you're right. I haven't.'Twas Bess who told me about them. And she said that afterwards, after he wrote it, Sir Walter Raleigh's poem was read by everyone."

"Of course it was after he wrote it. Could they read it before? And it wasn't read by everyone, because you didn't read it."

Angelica waves a gloved hand dismissively. "And so I think you must write sonnets back to William Shakespeare. Why not?"

Emilia can't help but smile. "'Tis a brave idea, Angel." It is in fact an ingenious notion. She's amazed that her sister produced it. But there are barriers Angelica can't see. "It cannot wash, alas. The cases would not be alike. Walter Raleigh was famous already when he undertook his reply to Christopher Marlowe. The poems were fine, both the first and the reply — you see, *I've* read them — but it was Raleigh's name that gained him an audience, not Marlowe's. He is a person. I am none."

"That is ridiculous," Angelica scoffs, and walks to the kitchen for a raspberry tart.

Emilia bends her head again over her sewing and doesn't answer. She knows what she's said is not ridiculous, though she also knows it is not an insurmountable argument. An unknown poet can make his own name — perhaps even *her* name — by hitching verses cleverly to another man's work. The same can be said of a new play. It happens all the time.

But she knows in her heart she won't try it. She might write anonymously, but she has newly claimed her face, scrubbed bare of paint, and doesn't want to relinquish her naked name. Besides, if such poems achieved any success, claiming the marketful of readers who'd devoured Will's own sonnets, someone, sooner or later, would find out what "dark lady" had authored them. And then — the shame of it, for Alphonso, and for herself! And not just because Will had called her "the bay where all men ride." For a worse reason.

Sir Walter was bold enough. He vied with Christopher Marlowe, she thinks. *But I'm not mad enough to court a comparison between my poems and Will's.*

The sonnet is not her best form.

"Anyway, you must do something," Angelica says, coming back in the room and brushing crumbs from her dress. "Strike while the iron's hot."

"I'll muse on it," she answers, wondering what striking a hot iron would mean in her case. Hard to know.

But that night she's inspired to return to her best verses, to fair-copy them once more, incorporating her most recent improvements. The next day she visits Thomas Thorpe.

The street of printers is not much changed since she came there two years ago with her freight of rhymed goods by Will Shakespeare. There is only the addition of a black-garbed zealot who has taken up a position on the corner. He stands on a box, holding the new King James Bible aloft with two hands, exhorting and prophesying for the benefit of all passing

English folk. He says, "God will cleanse this land of its false shrines and its painted saints, that same God that washed us from our sins in his own blood, Revelation one five! God's vengeance will be as thunder and his blood will scour the paint from the heathen and from the idols and leave the godly white as snow!"

He catches Emilia's eye, and she quickly changes her bemused expression to one of enthusiastic agreement. "The sooner the better!" she says, and nods her head vigorously, then scurries down the lane and into the printer's establishment, her manuscript tight under her arm.

"More poems?" Thorpe says happily when he sees her.

"Indeed," she says, looking around her with wonder. He has expanded his shop, has added a press and, by the look of things, several apprentices. "You have profited from the sonnets."

"Yes, I have, and it's a good thing, since it's hard to keep up with damned Barker, who got the license for the new Bible. By *Jesus*, he's wallowing in the profits —" He checks himself, looking abashed. "Well, of course I should not . . . ." He clears his throat and takes a businesslike tone, rubbing his inky hands with a rag. "What have you for me, Mistress Lanier?"

"You have seen this before." She hands him her manuscript. "You praised it, and suggested — hinted, I should say — that you might print it if I changed my name."

"Well, now I think you should change your name to 'Shakespeare's Mistress.' I'd make a thousand copies."

She's grateful he didn't say "Shakespeare's Doxy," or something worse. But then, he wants her business. At least, so she hopes.

He asks, "Have you anything else by him?"

By him. She thinks of their lost child, of her miscarriage a month after her final return to court from the dream of Tichtfield. How many years ago? Eighteen? Twenty? The memory lies buried so deep she'd not even exhumed it for Will during either of their two encounters since, though she still carries the hurt of it like a rock in her belly. While she lives she'll not forget her sharp sense of loss, the feel of the blood running from her. That pain, and, at last, the dull emptiness. *The expense of spirit in a waste of shame, Will? Hear you a tale.* A jest too bitter, that, even for the bleak moment of their last parting in Longditch, when her sour, shrunken heart had weighed in her chest like a block of ice. And of course, he might not have believed her.

Likely he wouldn't have cared a jot.

"Well?" says Thorpe expectantly.

She tosses her head. "I've nothing else by him." No child, no other poem. She's not willing to lie, though she knows to keep the printer guessing on this point might improve her own poems' prospects.

His face falls a little, but he doesn't turn away. He looks again at the first poem in the sheaf of papers. "This might do well," he says slowly. "Cooke-ham. I remember this one. It's in the vein of the new poem, by Jonson, the first in his new collection. Well imitated, this. You know Ben, do you not?"

"What say you?" She feels the blood draining from her face.

"Ben Jonson. I mean his poem on Penshurst, the Sidney estate. Why, I have it here." He fetches a new book marked on its cover with Jonson's self-fashioned seal, the broken compass.

She takes and opens the volume, trembling, and begins to read. In a minute her eyes are brimming with tears. Her own poem still lies on the printer's trestled counter, and she stretches her right hand toward it, instinctively, as a mother might reach to reclaim a child who's slipped from her grasp.

"BEN JONSON!"

He turns. When he sees her he screams and jumps backward, flinging paint from his brush onto the flats, tin thrones, and planks of the Revels workshop. "By Jesus! Is that you?"

"Who *should* it be, you fat whoreson knave? You pickpurse of poems?"

"But what have you done to your face?"

"Nothing! No adulterous art whatsoever."

"Jesus, Mary, and Joseph, get thee to a paintpot."

"Get *thee* to a paintpot, thou lard! Here's one!" She hoists the can of blacking he's been using to coat the night sky on a flat and hurls it straight at his face. Ben is quick for his size, and dodges, but the can hits a post and spatters night everywhere, on the half-painted trees on the flats, on his sleeves, on the hem of her dress, on the scenery notes that lie on the floor. He lets out a wail, but has no time to prolong it. She's got another paint can in her hand, and he is running for the back of the building, with the carpenters and painters and sawyers at the workshop all whooping and yelling like beaters at a partridge shoot. In her pursuit she successively grabs every color she sees, red paint, green paint, blue paint, and a tub of gold glitter from the edge of a shelf. Her aim is not good, but with so many things to throw she hits his broad back now and then, and he's a rainbowed clown by the time he's reached the door. At the last she hurls an inkpot, which finds its target on his posterior, staining his wide new Venetian breeches as he scuttles out into the alley.

"*That's for Penshurst!*" she yells after him. "*You pirate!*"

Back in Longditch it takes her an hour to clean the paint from her skin with witch-hazel and some turpentine from the Lanier workshop. When she's done she's dizzy from the smell of the chemicals. Her dress is beyond saving. She throws it on the hearth for burning, then thinks better of that plan. Strike a flint, and the house might explode. She bundles the garment away for the parish ash-heap.

When she's finally paintless and smelling only faintly alchemical, she sits at her desk in her dressing gown. She's alone. Alphonso has gone for some days to Mark Lane, to the home of his brother, a craftsman overburdened with the demand for instruments for three royal consorts, since the family of their extravagant Stuart king keep separate households. Alphonso can no longer do the delicate work of stringing and cutting, but he can clean wood and tune the instruments. The money's not much, of course; it now barely matches the shillings she still sometimes garners for lessons in lute and virginals. And the price of hay has fallen so far that the old tax stipend hardly covers the lease. The flat fee she took for Will's sonnets will be spent in a year. Bess's gift, the framed lenses, have renewed her ability to patch ladies' clothes, but the gift came only after her clientele had mostly fallen away, and she has never regained all her customers. *Angelica's right*, she thinks. *I had to sell some poems.*

She is lacerated by Ben's betrayal. But now that her red rage has cooled, she strives to see the thing in a hopeful light. Three years ago, Thomas Thorpe wouldn't print her verses. That he will now may owe only to the fact that they are something like Jonson's poem to Penshurst. Ben Jonson has launched a new genre. Ben knows, and she knows, it is *her* genre. She invented it. But what matter, if she can profit by what looks to be the well-made and first imitation of a master? It's the poet's glory, after all: to do what's been done, but do it better.

The only difficulty is, she hasn't done it better.

She looks at the poem before her, there at the front of the book Thorpe gave her in honor of their new contract. It is ten times finer than her Cooke-ham poem, as if she'd made a charcoal sketch which Ben consulted for a rich painting. He has taken her idea of rooting the virtues, the best human qualities, in the very architecture of an English house, the absolute soil of its pathways. But from its very first line, his poem is more natural, more flowing, more redolent of the meditative walks that inspired it. Like Will, Ben has the art to point to what's real by disclaiming what's false. *My mistress' eyes are nothing like the sun.* And Ben: *Thou art not, Penshurst, built to envious show of touch or marble, nor canst boast a row of polished pillars, or a roof of gold.*

She has laid the two poems on her desk side by side, not Will's and Ben's but Ben's and hers. The first lines of "Cooke-ham" now vex her. *Farewell (sweet Cooke-ham) where I first obtained grace from that grace where perfect grace remained.* She had thought to describe grace, to present its picture. But Ben's poem truly *is* graceful.

Her eye returns again and again to two lines.

> *That taller tree, that of a nut was set*
> *At his great birth where all the Muses met.*

Ben, praising the dead poet Philip Sidney, who was born at Penshurst. But what matter which poet? At *his* great birth.

At *his* great birth.

A knock comes on the front door. She rises, pushing up her spectacles, and crosses the floor to undo the latch. She cracks the door an inch, and peers out. Ben is standing on the stoop with a contrite face, holding a covered pan.

She shuts the door in his face. He continues to knock. "Open, my lady cousin! I bear humble pie."

Sighing, she fetches her oil lamp into the parlor and undoes the door. "What *would* you here? Go to your masque at Whitehall. I've not painted."

Ben heaves himself inside and shuts the door with his back. "You have painted *me*. A patched jester I looked at the baths. How they laughed!"

She shudders. "That's a foul place. I hope you did not truly go there."

"But I did. 'Twas too cold for Thames. I paid for hot water and soap, and still I have paint in my hair. Look." He points at his temple.

"'Twill grow out. I know these matters."

"Such public manners you showed today, Emilia. Fie, fie! Such a caterwauling. You screeched like a fishwife, and ruined a week's work for *The Vision of Delight*. You wasted ten gallons of paint. I abhor waste."

"Poetry is truth. Paint murders poetry. You should thank me for wasting paint. Why were *you* prancing about among the machinery with a brush?"

"I must watch how things are done in the workshop, while Master Inigo Jones is seated with fine paper at an oaken desk in a palace room. Rosewater at his elbow for the stained fingertips, as he sits on his arse with his little ruler and compass, sketching rotating fountains and flying elephants and cantilevered staircases held up by mere air, and leaves it to the gods to implement his designs! But there are no gods in Whitehall or Greenwich or Hampton Court. There is only the royal exchequer." Ben is warming to his rant. He wants to gesture, but his hands are still gripping the covered pan, so he stamps his foot, making the floor-planks shudder. "Jones and all be damned! I'll not be shamed another time because various under-fiends in the Revels Office have purchased cracked wood on the cheap for a royal posterior. You see how I am placed? So that props do not break and none heeds my poetry, I must ensure that Jones's ocular marvels are perfect, and none heeds my poetry."

Emilia's still angry, but she's intrigued. She folds her arms and squints at Ben's frowning face. "You are jealous of Jones."

"Admittedly."

"Because all should praise *you* and your verse. All should look at *you*. But poetry should point to something other than its author, and help people see *that* thing, whatever it is."

"Indeed."

"Yes, indeed. This notion came to me today. A poet should not be a spectacle, but a pair of spectacles."

"By God, that's good Emilia."

"Write it down, do. Sell it."

"I need not write it down." Ben cocks his head. "'Tis in my brain now." He crosses to her kitchen, sets the big covered pan on the table, and regards it approvingly. "But you aim to shift the subject, and I will not allow it. We must begin again at the workshop, and work day and night for a week, because of your outrageous intervention. There's a hundred pounds' worth of paint and labor gone into thin air."

"'Tis a piece of audacity to say I owe *you* anything."

"I did not say you owed me anything. Indeed, as you see, I have brought you a gift."

"I can smell what it is. I find the jest in ill taste."

"Pray, *don't* cast those double-word tricks at me. They smack not of art. Ill taste, you say! This we shall prove." He removes the cloth over the pan. "Behold. Will you have a 'description of cooked ham'? Savory pig, well roasted in juice; Fatter than coney, capon, or goose —"

She snaps her fingers, saying, "So, you make sport of me. For five, nay, six years you have watched me struggle to gain some small name as a poet, in hopes of a true public audience. You *advised* me so to do!"

If it is possible to chew pig remorsefully, Ben is the man. He has seated himself before the dish, taken her candle, and lit another, and now he listens gravely, nodding, using his penknife to strip meat from the ham-bone.

"You were my friend," she says.

"Ah."

"More than that, my kinsman!"

"Aye."

"You might have helped me, but instead, you robbed me of verse."

"I did not!" He points his penknife skyward. "You saw a truth, and brought it to light. But truth is a lady who's open to all. Your poem is good. I said so. Then I wrote *my* poem. Ben's poem."

She will not weep before him. She seats herself on a stool, props her elbows on the table, and rubs her eyes with the heels of her hands.

"Try some pig," he said gently. "'Tis very good, cousin."

She remains silent.

He sighs. "Emilia, your poem is excellent, and differs entirely from mine."

"You say it as though yours came first."

"The valedictory note that reigns throughout. The long looking back. Tell me, why did you not write in the past tense?"

Sullenly, she says, "I chose the present tense because of my view of what poetry does, or should do."

"Ah, tell me this."

"Fancy doesn't recount, it suggests. 'Suppose we see it this way.' I invite the reader to consider things in another light. 'Say it be like this.' The present tense is —"

"The tense of the possible, and not of the finished and changeless. I see!"

She warms to him a little. "That is also why I call it 'a' description of Cooke-ham and not 'the' description of Cooke-ham."

"This is striking, Emilia, as is your conceit of the nightingale, and the mingling of psalms with Philomela's myth. Enviable. I'd seen nothing like that before, and I did not copy it. I do not copy. To imitate is not to copy. The conclusion of my poem is wholly other than yours."

It is true. "To Penshurst" veers into the satire for which Ben is famed and which he can write like no one else, launching a jibe at women's lightness, then sailing skillfully out of danger. The harsh note is sounded only to highlight its sweet opposite, the chastity of Lady Sidney, mistress of Penshurst. He ends then by commending her children. The young Sidneys bless their mother, renew their father. They are living poems in which all can read their parents' goodness.

That was clever of Ben. Laying the groundwork for two generations of patronage.

"I went to Thomas Thorpe after I washed your foul paint from my frame," Ben says. "I went to speak in favor of your poem. But he was printing it already."

She will not show him her pleasure at this. "You might have gone before," she says resentfully. "Last year. Or last month."

"I wished to create a market."

"Oh, *stow* this blather!" She drops her hands hard on the table. "Why are you in my house? I have no more poems for you to —"

"Melly." He takes her wrist, and she stops in surprise. He has often seized her, or tried to, but has never called her this name before. "Please, Melly. If I were free, and if *thou* wert free from thy tin-foil husband —"

"Are we theeing and thouing?" She would make light of his heavy gaze, but she can't. His eyes are dolorous, pregnant with sorrow and passion. She won't look at his grief. She's too tired of her own.

"Melly," he repeats. "Body of me, I do love thee. When will we lie together?"

"*Never.* You'd pox me." She says it with a smile, though the thought of the pox truly frightens her. She has heard there are different kinds, and one, after all, is killing Alphonso.

"I will not pox you. I am hale, and will be faithful." He kisses her wrist.

What is this? He is Ben, only Ben, her comfortable, maddening cousin. Can a man's mere desire flatter her blood?

"Go away," she says. "You would crush me like a moth. I will not."

"When, Melly, when? You are a woman past compare."

"Past compare with Lucy, Countess of Bedford?"

"A shining sun, but one that would bake a man, bake him like a pig, and she looked at him closely. Not like thee, my melancholy nightingale. My moonlit bird."

"Come back tomorrow."

"And find the door locked. You whore!"

She explodes with laughter. "Because I *won't*? You're naught but a male strumpet, yourself."

"And you are a slattern of sonnets. I offer you true faith. Can you love this face?"

"Not at all."

"You, the discarded hoddy-doddy of my second-rate rival! Your dearth of judgment renders you tedious. You dare refuse me!"

What is happening to her? For the second time in a month, she is laughing so hard she can barely speak. Tears spill from her eyes. Instinctively she reaches up to wipe the skin underneath, thinking her kohl must be smearing, until she remembers she isn't wearing any.

"Hoddy-doddy!" she says, gasping for air. "Hoddy-doddy! What is that?"

"Emilia."

The voice is not Ben's. It comes from behind her shoulder, and she turns to look. She has left the door unlatched, and a man is standing in the doorway.

Alphonso, she thinks, and rises, but even as she stands and steps toward him she knows it's not her husband. Alphonso has not stood this straight in years, though the man has his voice.

The visitor steps into the circle of light. It's her brother-in-law, Innocent Lanier. All laughter falls from her face when she sees his expression. Behind her Ben is pulling himself to his feet.

"Innocent." She thinks, *Not this. Not now.* But then, what would have been a right time? "Innocent, speak. Where is he?"

28

Alphonso lies on a pallet in a room adjacent to his brother's workshop. He has fallen while turning a lathe to hollow a flute, and has cut his hand badly, though the wound is only a symptom, not the main cause of his inertia. Tess, Innocent's wife, has wound a thick bandage around his thumb and two other fingers, so the bleeding is stayed. But he lies distracted, muttering about untuned shwarms and cornets and sackbuts and lutes, calling for pegs and a brush to clean his recorder. He is shaking, his arms and legs trembling so hard that the blanket Tess keeps placing over him slips again and again to the floor.

"Leave the blanket, Tess. He isn't cold." Emilia strokes her husband's brow. "He shakes all the time. 'Tis the palsy." She will not say, *'Tis the pox*. She doesn't know how Tess would take it. Emilia's seen pox in Southwark near the Globe, in a woman who sat outside the door of a notorious stew called the Winchester Goose. Ben had gestured bluntly with his head as they walked past, on their way to a new play by John Marston that he'd persuaded her to see. "A sad advertisement. I know not why they let her sit there. She's for Bedlam in a day." The poor woman's tremors, and the blank look in her eye as she held out her bowl to be filled, were identical to Alphonso's, lying there on his pallet.

She'll not take him to Bedlam. She helps him sit, hires a carriage, and brings him home.

It takes Alphonso eighteen months to die. He sleeps much of the day, and when he's awake he lies or sits holding this or that instrument, though he can no longer really play one. He says little. When he talks, it is nothing to the purpose: the vague articulations of a dream, a memory of consort melodies, tunes mixed with words. He hums and moves his fingers. "The E flat. The coda. The *rest*." Once she hears him murmuring fragments, lines she herself remembers from a play of Will's which they possess in quarto and have read together many times. "Know my stops," says Alphonso. "Pluck out the heart of my mystery."

Emilia changes his bedclothes, empties his jordan, washes his wasting body, and cleans his teeth with fresh cloths. She cooks soups and broths and feeds him with a spoon when he can barely raise his head. Though she could never sing sweetly, she sings to him, caressing the strings of her lute. He lies gazing at her, listening intently, letting expressions of bliss or pain wash over his face, and now and then closing his eyes. He's a man who knows how to be sung to.

There is some money. Though the fee for the sonnets is now nearly spent, the stipend from the hay exchange continues, and she has the new sum from Thorpe for her own book of poems. People are buying the book. She hears from Angelica and Bess that it's made people talk. Folk speak of a new kind of poem, a study of the English country house, an admirable form, seen in Jonson, and in a new author, a woman named Lanier.

"Seen in a new author, a woman named Lanier, and in Jonson," Emilia corrects. But after so long with so little, she's satisfied.

The guests these days are a revelation. Alphonso is visited by players from the Globe and the Fortune, by seedy dicers he's befriended in the suburbs, and by out-of-work mercenary soldiers from the Irish campaign, one of whom sips constantly from a bottle and tells filthy jokes. A group of court musicians come, including Henry Carey the younger. The tall young man looks down humbly at the floor the whole time he's in the house, and pats Alphonso's hand in parting. *Well,* Emilia thinks. *Where's the father in that?* Some neighbors who scarcely know Alphonso come to call, and sit with him, then with her. Her neighbors, the Jack Hornes, appear, bringing a gift of costly Indian pepper from Master Horne's last shipment of imported spices. Mistress Horne has never fully recovered from the loss of her children in the plague year, yet she's brave enough to expose the new child in her belly to the air of Alphonso's room, which Emilia does her best to keep sweet, burning candles and strewing herbs and opening windows in defiance of the sickroom custom. Angelica comes weekly as well, donating bits of whispered news regarding new fashions seen in Blackfriars, and new entertainments.

"There was another Emilia," she says, "in a play by your Will."

"He was never *my* Will," Emilia says, sighing. "What am I now? A pirate?"

"A handmaiden to a shrill shrew who tries to save a baby from a lion."

Emilia laughs softly. "She tries, or the shrill shrew tries?"

"Both of them try."

"Master Shakespeare put a real baby on the stage?"

"It was a rag doll wrapped in a dish clout."

"Do the shrews save it?"

"Nay. It's put out into the wilderness. But it lives, of course. It's rescued by a man in a bear suit, or some such thing, I could hardly follow the plot. It was mad. Then the child grows up and comes back to rule a kingdom."

"O, I see. The baby is royal."

"Is there any other kind of lost baby?"

"Not at Blackfriars." Emilia puts on Alphonso's old voice. "Fairytales! Simply the *only* plays for the modern stage."

"I mean to tell him about it."

"He'll not hear you, I fear. But tell him anyway."

There are dutiful visits from relatives, hers and Alphonso's, Bassanos and Laniers. These people sit by his bed, look grave, and struggle to mask their disgust and their fear. "Come back with your instruments," she pleads, and the best of them do. They sit and play with perfect harmony, recorder and cornet and lute in consort. *L'amor Dona Ch'lo Te Porto*. He cannot control his facial muscles now, but his tremors still when they play.

One day she comes in from burning refuse in her yard and hears Ben Jonson upstairs, reading. He has let himself in and walked up the stairs. She stands stock still, straining to hear. Ben is saying, "Written on the occasion of my first son's departure from this life, though never printed." She hears the rustle of papers, and Ben begins. His voice, reading his poetry, is not bombastic, as when he played the grieving father on the stage, but surprisingly mild and conversational, even sweet. "*It is not growing like a tree, in bulk, doth make man better be, or standing long an oak. In small proportions we just beauties see, and in short measures life may perfect be.*" Ben clears his throat. "A just metaphor for a man of music, that one." Papers rustle again. "Now. What think you of a psalm?" Emilia stands listening for many minutes, before she tiptoes into her study and softly shuts the door.

What is their marriage?

The two of them have shared pheasant and fine wine in Whitehall; salt-herring, penny radishes, and small beer in Shoreditch and South-wark. They've laughed, scrimped, and squabbled enough this twenty-odd years to pass as true lovers, a thing distinct from two lovers in a son-net. He once called her child his. She has made his name hers.

Is wedlock a prison or a refuge? What makes a marriage real? She thinks of Ben, living far from his wife in leased rooms and friends' houses, outstaying his welcome with patrons in the country. "I am wed," he tells her. "And yet I am not." Was it even true, what he'd said of his wife — that she would not share his bed? Or was this some shrewd Jonsonian fiction? Ben was a poet, which both he and Emilia thought should mean "truth teller." But she has known the other side of poetry, the colored stain on the glass.

At least music can't lie, she thinks, tuning her lute for Alphonso.

Ben, it seems, knows about Will's sonnets, and her sale of them. In the wake of his semi-contrite visit the night of Alphonso's collapse, she has bit by bit told him everything, spilled and dribbled her whole history as she has always wanted to tell it to someone, in the very *way* she has wanted to tell it, which is gratifying. She could never have done this in such son-nets as Angelica proposed she write. She's described to Ben precisely her pain, her passion for revenge, and how it is all, in the end, a little more comical than not. Ben's been rejected "by better women than you *or* Will Shakespeare," he says, and she sees in his eyes that he knows — what? How it felt to intuit, in a flash, that a longed-for lover had come to her after so many years not from need and desire, but from shrewd calcula-tion? To reclaim his property?

"Yes, but it wasn't like that, Melly," Ben says, in the gentle voice he so rarely uses, in the voice she heard reading verses and psalms to Alphonso. "How is it you don't see? Any man would desire you. *Any* man. He only wanted to protect his wife."

His wife.

Emilia has seen Anne Shakespeare once, the last time she saw Will, which was not in her house, but a year later outside Blackfriars, where the King's Men had just begun routinely playing, despite puritan neighbors' objections. She had come in a carriage with Bess to hear a tragedy, and they were waiting for their driver to pass a patch of muddy road before stepping out. Through their coach's small window she suddenly spied Will helping a woman descend from a coach not ten yards from theirs. It was too late to look away, though she'd sat back and taken care Will didn't see her. Behind Will stood a young woman who resembled him, who might have been his daughter. The woman stepping from the coach was plump, and fiftyish, and uncomfortable in what looked like a fire-new high-crowned hat. As the maid behind him laughed, Will knocked on the high bonnet as if it had a door, saying, "Hi! Ho! Anyone? Anyone?"

"Get you *off*," the woman said, in the midlands accents Emilia had grown used to thinking of as Will's alone. The woman raised a gloved hand to straighten her absurd headgear. "'Tis bad enough you make me wear it at all." Her voice held a thousand notes, or one note with a thousand inflections: impatience, longsuffering, affection, forbearance, amusement. Love.

That is what I wanted from him, Emilia thought, on the carriage ride home, when the play was done, while Bess busily scribbled notes in her commonplace book. *That.*

She could never have had it, that *something* the stout Stratford woman clearly shares with the man. In Will's presence, back when he loved her — had he loved her? — Emilia had wanted so desperately to keep pace with his wit that, of course, she hadn't been able to do it. She can match Ben's wit, as she could Alphonso's in the old days, because she doesn't care whether she matches it or not. So goes love, if that's what it is.

She wonders whether Will has read her poems. There, he might find a part of her she always kept hidden in conversation. What does he think of the verses, if he knows them? She dislikes that she can't help caring.

Now, in the quiet of her parlor, with Alphonso asleep above her head, she thinks again of that scene between Anne and Will Shakespeare. *It was* her *forgiveness he spoke of that morning, upstairs in my bed,* she thinks. *I was not the woman who could wondrously forgive, but the one he needed forgiveness* for. *Perhaps only one of the ones.* The knowledge falls into place like the last piece of a puzzle. It hurts, even stabs, but does not, to her surprise, revive her rage or her hatred against him, or against the wife she's always thought of as a cipher or blank, unworthy of a jealousy she's harbored, instead, against golden Henry Wriothesley. She feels neither of those emotions now, not hatred, not jealousy. Instead, there wells up in her a deep, face-burning shame. Something comes loose in her, and she starts to weep hard, heart-shaken tears, soaking the sleeve of the dress she holds before her eyes, then the small pillow she lifts from the settle. She has thought marriage nothing, an empty form. She's lain with men whose wives seemed to her only the shadows those men cast behind them. But Will has said it through a play, has he not? Wives have sense. They have galls, and grace. As well as some revenge.

Anne Shakespeare's short appearance in Blackfriars courtyard was enough of a gauge. Emilia has no doubt she witnessed a woman fully capable of revenge, should she be inclined to commit it.

Ah, God, I've had enough, she thinks, collapsing on the settle and holding the damp pillow to her face, and laughing in spite of herself. She lets her arms fall and hang. *If the blow ever comes, let it fall on Will, or on Henry Wriothesley. Not on me.*

She tosses the pillow in the air, wipes her face with her drenched sleeve, and grimaces. Anne and Will. She won't worry. They looked to be at some point in their story when revenge was foregone or concluded, a thing of the past. She may as well accept that she, Emilia, will never know what that story is.

They bury Alphonso in the churchyard at St. Clement Danes. The week after his death, Emilia visits the exchequer's office in London to collect their stipend from the hay tax. She is told that the grant is no longer hers. Her husband has bequeathed it to his younger brother, Innocent Lanier.

She flies to the house in Mark Lane and raps angrily on the door. No one answers, but she hears the clack of tools and the buzz of a saw from the workshop behind, and knows Innocent is in there. She moves to an open window and calls out. "Lanier! What have you done with my money?"

Innocent puts down the viola he's stringing and walks to the window. He tries to pull the shutters closed, but she blocks them with her elbow. "*You!* You took his hand and signed his name to a contract! When he was out of his mind!"

"The stipend belongs to the Laniers." Innocent is still pulling at the shutter. Tess has come up behind him. "It is ours, Melly," she says. "It should by rights be ours."

"It is *mine!*"

"Will you yell in the street, bawdy baggage?" Tess hisses, leaning her face out the window and holding it inches from Emilia's nose. Emilia spits at her and walks from the place.

She hastens back to her house, and sits, nearly panting with fear. *Think. Think.* She writes to Bess Cary, and sends a message to her brother-in-law, Edmund Tanfield. *Calm. Calm.* She schools herself to a wait.

Edmund comes to see her the next day. With him she revisits the exchequer's office. After an hour spent examining the contract, her brother-in-law looks at her bleakly. "The stipend is clearly in the Laniers' gift."

"Am I not a Lanier?"

"Had you a son, the tax would pass to him. As it is, I am likely to win you no more than a settlement, if I threaten your brother-in-law with some cumbersome suit. The contract Innocent devised merely bolsters his case. In law, the stipend's his."

Nevertheless, Edmund registers a plea on her behalf, *gratis.* Papers are sent to be served in Mark Lane. Three hours later, Innocent appears at her house with a woodcutter's tool and a hammer. This time it's Emilia who locks the door and jeers from a window. "What will you do with that, brother? Touch my house and you'll be clanking chains in Newgate, for a melody. I've witnesses." Edmund's and Angelica's heads appear in the window next to hers. Two doors down, Master and Mistress Jack Horne stand with arms folded on the stoop before their house, looking grimly and purposefully at Emilia's angry guest.

In the end, Innocent grants her eight pounds to drop the case. "'Tis more than a judge would have given you," Edmund tells her. But eight pounds won't even see her through the year.

She receives a letter from Bess Carey. The Viscountess Falkland has written the queen on her behalf. Emilia dresses in her best blacks and walks four miles to Denmark House on the Strand, where the queen resides. There Queen Anne receives her, sitting in state among three of her ladies, herself in jewels, and all of them in face-paint. On the queen's left, gray-haired and thick-waisted, sits Anne Morgan Carey Montgomery, who divides her time now among the Stuart Court and her second husband's manors in Scotland and Kent. Anne Morgan looks once at Emilia, then turns away and gazes out the window.

Emilia kneels and pleads her case: her husband's long court service, her many years as his helpmate. She has read Homer and scripture with Anne Clifford, a lady held in high esteem at court. She thinks to make a modest living tutoring young women in the great authors, to form a dame school, a petty academy for girls. She only begs a small stipend in her husband's remembrance, to make a start. She thinks, as she speaks, of the four thousand pounds Anne of Denmark spent on *The Masque of Blackness*. Queen Anne hears her to the finish, then bids her retire to the hallway while she considers the matter. She speaks with her ladies, whose advice she routinely solicits. Emilia sits, hearing the buzz of several voices, and one raised above the others, respectfully but earnestly soliciting the queen. In ten minutes comes the reply, delivered in writing, by a gentleman pensioner who has stood guard outside the door, watching her with sympathy. No stipend will be forthcoming to Emilia Bassano.

"What can I do?" Ben spreads his hands. "My state is greatly reduced of late. My last comedy is hated, by me most of all. I applaud your notion of a school for young ladies, if scripture is discussed, though young girls and Horace . . . . Well. But the king has not yet reimbursed me for *The Golden Age Restored*, and can you think what the gilding for its stage-shrubs cost? I am whoring myself right and left, a play here, a poem there, ah, but, wait, wait!"

Emilia will not wait. She is running from Ben's paper-strewn Blackfriars rooms in disgust and despair.

The next day, however, a package appears on her stoop. She pulls off its brown paper wrapping. Underneath lies a leathern box. Inside that box sit twenty gold angels. Folded next to the coins is a page torn from a printed text of Jonson's *The Silent Woman*. One line of dialogue is marked with a pen: *A new foundation, sir, here i'the town, of ladies, that call themselves the Collegiates.*

Thank you, O Ben, she prays. *Thank you.*

29

With the money Emilia leases a larger house in the thriftier, working man's parish of St. Giles in the Fields. She gives Mumbleclutch to the Hornes, transports what moveables she owns that are fit to keep — an iron bedstead, her small desk, her scarred dining table — and shops with Angelica for bargains on Cheapside. The new house's parlor makes a schoolroom. Bess Carey pays a joiner to craft stools and a big table.

Angelica visits, bringing with her a painting. It's a framed Italian oil whose canvas stretches nearly a yard wide and two feet high. Its picture is the infant Moses swaddled and sleeping in a basket while his anguished mother releases the little reed vessel into the river. Emilia thanks her sister profusely for the gift, but stops short of giving it central place in her large front room. She hangs baby Moses on the far wall, keeping the middle spot between the windows for her scene of the oak tree and the brightly lit house.

Angelica is vexed. She asks, "What do you admire so much in that picture?"

"'Tis not the artist's skill. The painting's journeyman work, anyone can see that. But I feel that I recognize . . . it."

"It? What? The house? Is it so much like Cooke-ham?"

Emilia stands with her hands folded before her, gazing semi-beatifically at the familiar oil. "Partly the house, but also the tree. There was a tall tree at Cooke-ham, though I think that tree and even Cooke-ham House were . . . . I know not how to say it. *They* reminded me of something, too. Another house, another tree."

"Where?"

Emilia shrugs. "I don't know."

"And you think you know the road, too."

"The road, yes, perhaps. Though I'm less fond of the road."

"Why?"

Emilia moves closer to the small painting and points. "You see how it narrows as it moves up the hill? It closes in. It makes my throat feel tight when I look at it. I feel I'm coming to the end of it."

Angelica bursts out laughing, and Emilia turns. "What is the jest?"

"You. You're so *wise*. But you're looking at the thing backwards. Here. Stand here." Angelica maneuvers Emilia to the left so she stands directly in front of the frame. "Where do you stand in the road now?"

"I am . . . ." Emilia frowns.

"Stop thinking. Only answer. O, never mind, I'll tell you. You're here, at the *other* end of the road, where it widens into the world. This world, the real one, where we are. The point on the hill is where you *started*, not where you're bound. When you look at the path rightly it is opening, not closing. Then you turn around, and you are always walking out of the painting. It's a question of proper perspective."

"O, *proper perspective*." Emilia wrinkles her nose with disdain. "Mistress, you may know how to spend twenty florins on a Flemish import, but you know nothing of art."

"La, la. And *you* look at everything backwards. Buy some spectacles for *that*."

"*So* witty."

"I'm not trying to be witty."

"I doubt not that's for the best."

Angelica slaps Emilia's arm. Emilia treads on Angelica's toe, then says, "O, forgive me, I thought you were behind me, because I see everything backw — *ow!*" Angelica has seized her arm and now twists it behind her back until Emilia shrieks for mercy. Released, Emilia falls on the settle, beginning to laugh. "Where does a lazy cow like you get such strength?"

"Hoisting babies," Angelica says placidly, sitting down beside her.

Emilia winces barely perceptibly. *Move on.* "I *will* forgive you for this," she says with good humor, "because it is Moses." She rubs her elbow. "Very apt for a schoolroom. Biblical subjects, to teach young women how to behave."

"Yes. Send those little ones down the river, and free your time."

"Into the bulrushes, all."

"Then, for the writing instruction —"

"Papyrus for that."

"— followed by gymnastics and wrestling."

"*You* for that."

Angelica sinks slowly leftward until her head meets Emilia's shoulder, where it rests. "Do you like the Moses painting, truly, Melly?"

"I do, Angel." Emilia pats her sister's hair. "It is wonderful. Though I will always love my oak tree best."

Before Angelica leaves, the two stand briefly together on the front stoop. Emilia splashes a ladleful of well-water on the ground of the dooryard, saying, "I christen this place 'Acorn Court'."

One day a horse-drawn cart stops before the house. A rider dismounts and begins to unload some crates. The Lady Anne Clifford has heard of Emilia's venture and has sent fifty books. Emilia is overwhelmed with gratitude and joy. She buys more books at the printers' and stationers' stalls in and around Paul's Yard. For the first time in her life she has money enough, because every six weeks, like clockwork, a new gift of ten angels arrives at her door. The money is delivered by taciturn messenger from its anonymous source. She purchases slates, copy-books, hornbooks, chalk, and a few penknives to sharpen quills.

One day Bess Carey and Angelica appear together at Emilia's new door with a caped, hooded captive. At least, she looks like a captive, since Bess and Angelica have each got her hooked by an arm. With their free hands they rap, and when Emilia admits them they rush their companion to the settle and tear off her cape.

"Look!" cries Angelica, pointing to the face of the young girl who sits passively between them. The lass looks to be thirteen or fourteen. Her skin is heavily caked with powder, her lips reddened, her eyes lined with smeared kohl. Her pale blonde hair streams over her shoulders, much in need of a combing. Under the wool cape Emilia glimpses her low-cut gown, which is spun of fine cloth, but ripped, soiled, and tawdry. The girl looks curiously around her, showing no alarm. "Look! Look!" repeats Angelica, shaking her finger.

"Look at what?" Emilia's been dusting, and she stands with her hands on her hips, a clout bunched in her fingers, staring at her guests. "Are you mad? Have you stolen a *person*?"

"Rescued, rather!" says Bess Carey. "We were down at the Fortune, hearing Beaumont's *Maid's Tragedy,* and there she was. Angel saw her first, and was off like a shot to get her. I came after, and threw my cape over her head, and we bustled her out, a perfect team, with everyone hooting and pointing like they thought it was part of the play. She went

along cheerfully. God knows what behavior she's used to. And here she is!
I never knew Kate Pettigrew, but Angelica says —"

"She's the image of Kate! Can't you see?"

Emilia comes closer, squats, and raises the girl's chin. Indeed, there's
a likeness in the eyes, and the cheekbones, to Angelica's old cosmetics-
mad roommate, but . . . what of it? "You knew her better than I, Angelica,"
she murmurs.

"She's her mother's very glass."

"Are you Kate Pettigrew's daughter?" Emilia asks the girl, still holding her chin.

The eyes of the young woman swim into focus. "I am Kate Pet-
tigown's daughter," she says simply.

Emilia looks at her shrewdly.

"Don't be mistrustful, Melly," says Angelica. "Not everyone speaks well."

"Did you know my mother?" the girl asks shyly. "Kate Pettigrow?"

"Pettigrew."

"Yes. Poor mama!"

Emilia examines her face again. Indeed, there's a striking resem-
blance. "'Poor mama,' you say?" She frowns worriedly. "And you say 'Did
you know her.' Where is Kate Pettigrew?"

The girl begins to respond, but Angelica breaks in. "She died of
plague, Melly, the year we lost Odilia. She has told us the tale. We never
found Kate because she'd moved to the Shoreditch liberties, where we
never thought to look."

Emilia puts her hand to her mouth and sinks to her knees. "O," she
says. "I am sorry. Why didn't we?"

"Because we were idiots. We thought she would always be in Southwark,
where you first saw her, as though she didn't know how to cross a bridge.
And she left poor Emilia in a brothel, to be brought up to the trade —"

"Poor *who*?" Emilia looks back at the girl. "Is your name Emilia?"

The girl nods.

"Well." Emilia rises, pulls a stool from the wall, and sits, still holding
her dustrag. "I know not what to say."

"Can we keep her? She says she's healthy, still a virgin, she says —"

"Oh, tush and tilly-valley. Whether she is healthy or no matters not.
If she's fallen, she'll be a virgin reborn after a year with me."

"That's the formula," says Angelica in a practical tone. She stands up.
"Have you anything to eat?"

"Wait! What am I to do with her?"

Bess leans forward with excitement. "We will teach her her letters."

"Will you two fill my schoolroom by kidnapping? Who's to pay for her keep?"

"This one will have a Falkland scholarship." Bess smiles broadly. "My lord husband won't know; I'll put the expense up to a Christmas gown or two."

Emilia eyes the quiet girl, who now sits with her eyes cast down. "But does she want to come here?"

"What does it matter what she wants?" snaps Angelica. "She's going to be a scholar. Now, do you have anything to eat?"

"Mistress . . . Em. We'll call you Em." Emilia looks pointedly at her namesake. "Do you want to be a scholar?"

Em raises her eyes and looks appreciatively about the room, noting the heavy oaken furniture and the paintings on the wall. "Yes, madam," she says. "I do."

Emilia throws up her hands. "Then she'll lodge upstairs. Our scholarship girl. And her first lesson will be how to scrub off face paint." She lifts her rag, then grimaces at it. "Angelica, fetch my oil of cloves, and a fresh clout."

30

Em is as docile and placid as Angelica is contentious. At her new home in St. Giles she learns quickly to speak fair terms instead of fairground terms, to drop her London canting talk, to keep herself clean, to help in the kitchen, peeling carrots and onions and stirring stews and scouring pots. She takes pleasure in burning her soiled fripperies in the small courtyard behind the house, and affects the sober fashions of the godly. It takes Emilia some time to recognize that Em is imitating her own style of dress, which the years have seen modified to plain flounce-lessness and muted colors.

Em starts laboriously to study her alphabet. Seeking more students, Emilia and Bess write letters to fifty London ladies. Most, if they write back at all, express disdain at the prospect of girls sitting in grammar school. Some of the women cannot read or write themselves, and dictate their replies through secretaries, saying they do not perceive the advantage. A few profess insult at the suggestion that their daughters be tutored by a notorious London whore.

"Do they mean me?" Bess asks. "Or you?"

"Perhaps neither of us. Word may have gone round that Ben Jonson's in the game."

"Let us write to tradesmen's wives. We have set our sights too high, and hit only the dizzy and senseless."

It will be simpler, at any rate, to seek day students. The two women canvass the neighborhood and meet face to face with coopers and blacksmiths, greengrocers and shoemakers, and their daughters and wives. Viscountess Bess wears the costume of grandeur, all velvet and silks. She's the patron. Emilia wears white puritanical caps, and dangles her spectacles from a chain.

One adolescent girl with an ink-smudged cheek pokes her nose into the kitchen to hear her parents haggle with Emilia over tuition price. The father's a glass-blower named Cleveland. The mother remarks, smiling, as they settle on terms, "We'll be glad to have Grace-of-the-Epiphany out from underfoot several hours of the day. She moons about, and the lads trip over her. It's dangerous at a furnace."

"Good," says Bess Carey. "Get her out of the house. Out, out."

"You'll teach scripture daily?" asks the father with a worried look. Emilia nods vigorously.

By the fall of 1614 Emilia has enrolled ten pupils, who range in age from ten to fourteen, with Em and Grace-of-the-Epiphany at the older end of the scale. Five mornings a week she leads her charges in prayer, scripture, and review of the English catechism, then tutors them in reading and basic accounts. Five girls whose wealthier parents are musically minded stay an hour after dinner twice a week, for instruction in playing the lute. To her surprise, Em shows both an interest in and talent for lute-playing, and soon knows enough to guide the novices in fretwork.

Emilia is frank with her charges' parents. She does not know Latin well enough to call herself a pedagogue. But what matter? The great Latin writings have all been Englished. Once they've mastered their letters and can read simpler texts, the girls can absorb Homer in Chapman's translation, Ovid in Golding's, Plutarch in North's. Emilia does not venture to teach modern tongues, either French or Italian, but together they read Francis Bacon on methods of learning, then Montaigne on cannibalism, thumbs, and compassion, in essays put forth in their own native language by the polyglot John Florio.

My dear old tutor is translating him. Wriothesley's voice floats through a hedge, from the other life that was Tichtfield.

She arrives at the notion that her students should write essays in imitation of Bacon and Montaigne; that they should expand the notes in their commonplace books to express their own ampler thoughts, on virtue, on families, on travel, on music. On Ovid and Chapman. On Bacon and Montaigne themselves. At first the girls blink. They have never before been asked to do aught but recite. When they start to write, they summarize, poorly or well, the thoughts of the authors they've read. "An excellent beginning," Emilia says. "Now, proceed toward dialogue. To imitate is not to copy. Talk back to these authors."

She writes her own essays, and reads them aloud to her pupils. *On Faces.* "We all have our own separate faces. Yet do we share one face, as siblings may appear distinct but all resemble a parent. And that parent is a king, for our face is God's."

Faces. Her girls are plain or pretty. Their cheeks glow with a youth her own glass can scarcely recall to her memory. At times she thinks, with a sorrow long-dulled, of Odilia's bright eyes and soft skin. The baby girl laughs, eternal April in her mother's heart. Bess has two children now, and Angelica three. Nearly past childbearing age, and a widow alone, Emilia has passed without willing it from mother to mere aunt. No matter. She is her own tree, will be her own branches. Let her leaves and her acorns be lessons and writings and thoughts. Each day she greets her shining, borrowed daughters and thinks, *You be my fruit.*

They read Tacitus, absorbing the bloody history of Rome. The girls are enthralled by the ancient historian's accounts of plotting and menace, the graphic descriptions of family treachery and debauched emperors' reigns of terror. The most ink-smudged of the girls, Grace-of-the-Epiphany Cleveland, is asked by her neighbor the vintner to describe her study. Grace recounts with gusto to the vintner the most scandalous details of the murderous tales of Tiberius, Augustus, and Empress Livia.

The next day Emilia is charged to appear in a week's time before a local judge in the court of common pleas. She is charged with practicing black arts and papist proselytizing.

What?

She is ready when the date arrives. Edmund Tanfield, now thick-waisted and fortyish, will stand as her advocate. He's enjoined her to silence. "I will speak for you, Melly. Fear nothing. The man's an ignoramus, and the judge will know it. He's Andrew Gannet, a wise man and a learned. I knew him at Gray's."

When the day of judgment comes she looks about her in the courtroom and sees interested neighbors, a few friends, some seekers of thrills. Most who have come are middle-aged women, sharp-eyed, greying and dowdy. She realizes suddenly that she is one of them.

She stands to hear the charges read. They end, ". . . witchcraft and papistry. How do you plead?"

"Which charge should I answer?" asks Emilia.

"They are essentially the same." The judge wears a white skull-cap, as does Edmund. His voice is dry. He repeats, with an encouraging hint of weary irony, "They are the same charge."

"Not guilty of either, then, my lord."

After this the vintner testifies at length, doing his best to paint his neighbor blacker than black. The sum of his opinion is that Emilia Lanier is a necromancer and a bawd, a former paramour, or so he has heard, of the magician Simon Forman, and she is teaching her students how to paint poison on figs. "She is partly Italian," he adds, as evidence. "I judge her unfit to be tutor to the children of St. Giles."

"If you be my accuser, pray cease to be my judge," says Emilia softly, but loud enough for the judge to hear.

Edmund pinches her arm. "Silence!" says Judge Gannet, though he looks less perturbed than bemused.

The vintner points at Emilia. "I call her an infamous witch! Hers is no *dame* school, but a *damned* school!" Clearly he has worked out this piece of cleverness well in advance. He looks slightly crestfallen when it receives only scattered applause.

Are we children? thinks Emilia, though she keeps her mouth shut. *Where does he think he is? Wales? Worse, Scotland? Ah, to be guilty of so many real sins, and so harshly arraigned for nonsense!*

The man is shouting now. "Ask her what black angel sets her on! By whose example and influence does she practice her arts? By what spirit?"

"Down, you!" yell Angelica and Bess from the gallery.

The judge hushes them all, and invites evidence controverting the charge. Edmund rises. He gives an account of his client's record of good citizenship, her payment of taxes, the commendations of her pupils' parents, her virtuous widowhood. Before this, her years of married chastity. *True, for aught he knows,* thinks Emilia.

Then Edmund unfolds a letter. It is stamped with the broken compass, the seal of Ben Jonson that appears on the frontispiece of all his printed writings. Ben's been told of the case by hired rider's swift post during a "poet's walking tour" of the north, as he makes for the home of another hoped-for patron.

Edmund reads. Ben describes in detail the curriculum of the prestigious Westminster grammar school where he studied his trivium under the tutelage of the renowned Richard Mulcaster. What was the course? Homer, Ovid, Tacitus. Point by point, the course resembles Emilia's, but for the fact that the boys of Westminster read all their texts in Latin, "*a language thought by many (though not by the author of this missive, who is well schooled and, as touches the Greeks, self-schooled, in the Ancients) to be a papistical tongue which, for all its glories, is secondary to the English which Mistress Lanier most virtuously reads and employs. As for her own papistry, this charge is for a jest and a mockery. The woman has not in her life traveled more than ninety miles from London Bridge. Myself having been briefly seduced by the Old Faith, and knowledgeable in it (though happily restored these past eleven years to the English Church, and a regular attender of the same, as the parish records relative to the congregation of St. Anne's, Blackfriars, will prove), I can most amply testify to her ignorance of all Catholic mysteries. Indeed, I have seen her tie a plucked chicken's legs with a rosary. It was not, to be sure, her rosary, nor the rosary of anyone she knew. It was not my rosary."* There is more in this vein, nearly four pages to come, but the judge waves a hand and begs Edmund to rest his defense. Edmund does so.

"I may dismiss these charges, or convene a jury," says Gannet. "Mistress Lanier, have you any word to add?"

Edmund is gripping her elbow tightly. She shakes her head. The judge looks at her for a long moment, then says, "Bid the recorder note that the woman is silent."

No. Emilia shakes off Edmund's hand and stands. "My lord."

"*Melly,*" Edmund whispers urgently, tugging her sleeve, but Emilia barrels on. "Before this letter was read, my accuser posed a question. He asked by what power, what influence, what inspiration and spirit, I acted and taught. I am briefer than Master Ben Jonson. But I do have a word, one word, in answer."

The judge's expression is tolerant. The folk in the court audience look enthralled. What will she say? "God"? "Justice"? "Wisdom"? "Mercy"?

This is an old place of justice, and, as it happens, the vestrymen who maintain it have not yet found the time to replace the old Tudor arms above the judge's seat with those of the Stuarts. She glances briefly up at the Tudor emblem, and notes, from the corner of her eye, that most of the watchers in the court follow her gaze. She takes a breath. "When I am asked by whose inspiration I, a woman, may so boldly live, my word is this. *Elizabeth.*"

She knows she has gambled well when she sees the spark of instinctive reverence jump in the old judge's eyes. She sits. Her brother-in-law pats her hand cautiously.

She casts her eyes briefly to the right, and sees that, despite the equivocation, her true meaning's been well understood by the Elizabeth who matters most to her. *Yes. You.* There's a bright, grateful smile on the face of Edmund's sister, Bess Carey.

31

Late April of 1616, a week past St. George's Day. The hollyhocks and the apple trees are in bloom in the fields of the London suburbs. *From you have I been absent in the spring.* The word has come south with the waters of Avon and Leam, been ridden overland from the rivers' tributaries, traveled with boatmen southeast from the Windrush to the Thames.

Emilia hears it from Angelica. Her sister still dwells in the town, and though she's now a busy mother of four, she still sometimes visits the Fortune, the Blackfriars playhouse, and the Globe. She gets news. Emilia is alone in her kitchen when her maidservant brings in her sister's letter. It is chilly dawn, with the fire yet unkindled, and the back garden's riotously musical. After years in the heart of Westminster Emilia is learning, finally, to distinguish the chirps and warblings here in the slower, greener streets of St. Giles in the Fields. She stands still in her kitchen, her eyes closed, and parses birdsong. The mockingbird, with its changeable tune. The shrill lapwing, shielding its young from the silent, gliding hawk. The jay's raucous complaint, and the robin's brief note. The high, sweet trill of the lark.

She opens her eyes, unfolds Angelica's letter, and reads. Two sentences only scar the page. She trembles a little, then stills, and lays the letter on the buttery bar, among shavings of apples and Valencia orange peels and eggshells she's not yet swept away. *That thou among the wastes of time must go.*

In a week it is May, and folk are gathered in her house. She has lit her parlor with twenty tapers and hung a small, shielded candelabrum that was given to her by Angelica on the anniversary of her first arrival here. She's prepared her lessons for the morrow, a less time-consuming activity than before, in the years since her quasi-ridiculous trial.

Then, Judge Andrew Gannet closed court by tossing out the spurious accusations, as Edmund had predicted, but her antagonist's charges did her some damage notwithstanding. His witchery slander was for laughter, but some of Emilia's female neighbors later wished to inquire more deeply into the story the man had raised of her one-time liaison with that alchemical gentleman Simon Forman, and they did so. The tale gathered force and weight, and some parents, now thinking her virtue a whitewash, removed their young maids from her school.

A few hard-headed mothers were and remain as unfazed by this scandal as they were by Tacitus' tales of the Empress Livia. Were not both ancient history? These practical parents see something in Emilia to admire — something, indeed, they might wish their daughters to absorb, in some small measure — and they continue to send her their female offspring. She now tutors girls in groups which expand and contract with the season. And she has an assistant in Em, who still lodges with her, and teaches the youngest pupils their letters, sitting patiently with them among hornbooks and styluses and abecedariums.

The decline in the demand for her services made Emilia angry with fortune at first. But she has found, in the end, that the freed time is a blessing. She has gone back to her reading, her desk, and her pen. She writes copiously, though no printer — not even Thomas Thorpe, who's so profited by her in the past — has proved willing to print a series of essays composed by a woman. *Essays*? Does she have, perhaps, some more poems? She does not. Thorpe is dismayed. The writings she's given him to read do not even concern themselves directly with scripture, or with any subjects that might be thought religious in the usual sense, and thus fit for a woman's quill.

"*On Falseness in Poetry,*" he says, thumbing her pages and raising an ink-stained eyebrow. "*On Solitude. An Inquiry into the Treatment of the Mad.* And this. *On Divorce.* Body of me! Lady, the censor —"

"Would not lift a finger against you, were my name Jonson, or Bacon."

"But it isn't." He looks at her in sympathy for her misfortune. "It is not."

She finds she can laugh at his refusal. Her diminished school, the narrowed road, now reduced to a point, that her life in print has become — neither of these shrinkages finally trouble her as they might have. The money helps. For a mystery and a blessing, she is still in regular receipt of the monthly sum from her benefactor, three years after her loss of Alphonso. With this and her small income from teaching, she lives. She does not go much into the world, but then, a world has begun to come to her. Her house is filled weekly with friends who arrive eager to discuss the things *they* have written.

There's Bess Carey, whose tragedy of Mariam has now been printed, with her woman's name, in concession to the world, reduced to initials on its front page. "And it *will* yet be played," she insists. A group reads the tragedy's parts aloud in Emilia's parlor. One of Emilia's former pupils, now nearly grown, listens and takes notes. It's Grace-of-the-Epiphany Cleveland, the glassblower's daughter, now betrothed, for a wonder, to the slandering vintner's apprentice. She is drafting a bloody play about the Julio-Claudian emperors, to her young man's delight, and to the horror of his master. Lady Anne Clifford, Emilia's beloved Nan, comes regularly to St. Giles in the Fields. She has learned Greek, and brings her work in progress, a blank verse translation of *Oedipus the King*. She is struggling with the passage that recounts infant Oedipus's abandonment to death by exposure, and his rescue by the homely shepherd. She needs some advice, and gets so much she covers her ears.

The writings shared here are eclectic. Inspired by Emilia's imitations of Montaigne, Edmund Tanfield is drafting a series of speculations on law and life. "On the Blushing Barrister," Emilia teases. "On the Irrepressible Female Client." Sometimes Edmund brings Angelica when a comedy's to be read, and sometimes he brings Jack Donne.

They are no velvet coterie of elegant court authors, no Sidney and Raleigh and Queen Elizabeth. *We are an acorn court,* thinks Emilia one day, as she bends to plant an oak spoor in her garden. Like her ring of pupils, her circle of writing friends widens and shrinks, changing size from this week to that. Yet the circle persists.

Ben Jonson sniffs. He consorts with his own tribe of poets and playwrights in the Apollo Room of the Devil's Tavern, near Temple Bar. "How doth thy Cockatoo College?" he asks her routinely. But after she tells him Jack Donne has made an appearance, Ben brings himself, more often than not. When he comes, he is always the last one to leave.

So here they are joined on this night, a circle of mourners, come to grieve the passing of the swan, the soul of the age. Lighting the candles she's placed about the room, she thinks of that other life, of her blood's heyday, when love was poetry and poetry love and both seemed a portal to eternity. Has the globe shrunk, or has she? She is glad, at any rate, that she's come to this point, a natural perspective from which she can see and speak of *him* as he was, a falcon to her, the silk-spinning moth. He is hers as much as he's anyone's now. She can best possess him by sharing.

They sit in a ring. She chooses the place below the painting of the road and the oak. She remembers the lines from Ben's Penshurst poem.

> *That taller tree, which of a nut was set,*
> *At his great birth where all the Muses met.*

They turn the pages of quartos they've bought over the years in the city. There are new ones this week; the bookstalls can't keep them in stock. But the texts these people own are older, and more worn. Some, brought by Ben, are handwritten promptbooks of plays that have not yet been printed. They read. Hamlet's speech to the players, which gets them all arguing. Bottom's portrayal of Pyramus, which has them all laughing. Juliet's love-smitten prayer, which leaves them all sighing.

Prospero's farewell.

The table is littered with bone-filled plates and half-empty glasses of Rhenish. Young Em has climbed the stair to her bed in the attic. The rest of Emilia's guests have gone home, save Ben, who lounges on the settle.

"You have blurred, Ben," she says, as she trims another wick. "Or is it my eyes again?"

"Nay. I am foggy indeed." Ben is raising each of the glasses within his reach and draining them in quick succession. "This that I do will fuzz my form beyond all delineation. But I cannot tolerate waste."

"What of *your* waist? Must we tolerate that?" She leans to take a glass from his hand, then delicately extricates herself from his hand-grip on her wrist.

"When, Melly, thou shrew? When will we disport ourselves in amorous dalliance, til such time as the cock doth crow? Or wilt thou still whorishly deny me?"

"I would deserve the name of whore indeed, if I lay with such a *ben*-efactor."

"*Imprimis*, I am no one's benefactor. *Secundus*, I ab-*whore* superfluous word-play. It was what I liked least in him."

She sighs as she picks up a cushion. She holds the pillow to her breast like a shield and perches on the arm of the old settle. "Tell me, Ben. What is it like to have your work spoken to a thousand sets of ears? And read everywhere?"

"Those are two distinct cases. For the first: a loathsome horror. Lines butchered by actors. Pied silken dolts in boxes who laugh in the wrong places."

This is Ben's old refrain. Usually she nods in sympathy, but now she shakes her head. "He did not find it so."

"No." Ben is quiet. Then he asks, "Do you envy him?"

"I do. I have *always* envied him. I envy his line. I envy his luck. And I envy his audience. Me, I have felt barren, like some . . . I know not what. I am weary of comparisons. A leafless tree, say. Or else a Bedlamite, jabbering to myself in a windowless cell. None regards me."

"Let me pause to wipe mine eyes. There, now I'm better. Was it not you who said once that an author should not be a spectacle, but a pair of them? What a good saying that was! But do you believe it? Do you write so folk will see something true, or so they will see *you*?"

She buries her face in the cushion. In a muffled voice, she says, "Ben, you as much as anyone know that whatever I said, it is always both ways. Every author wants not just to see, but to be *seen*."

"I knew one who didn't care about being seen. But he's dead. Three weeks now."

She lifts her face. "Yes. He, golden he. The man trod a jeweled path. I myself have had only losses — now, *stop*." Ben has covered his face with his hands and is pretending to weep. His broad shoulders heave with mock sobs and groans. "Ben, you do not *listen*."

"You lie. I *always* listen." Ben drops his hands. "I say he's dead. Are you? No. So who, between you pair, is the lucky one?"

She meditates on this.

Ben stretches and yawns, saying, "And aye, your man was not always lucky. He had losses, before."

"What losses had the King's Man?"

"Five shillings staked to me at the hazard in the Mermaid Tavern. He always paid his debts, but if you touched him for a loan, well, you'd sooner get a fart from a dead man." She laughs, but Ben suddenly frowns. "Do you know what galls me the most? He was not afraid of me. Whom do you think he envied?"

"Kit Marlowe, once on a time."

Ben emits a noise that's half-grunt and half-bark. "Marlowe was no threat to Will. Had he lived, he'd only have written the same tragedy over and over. No. Shakespeare feared John Marston."

"You mean that skeleton?"

"Not Skelton, he's long dead. *Marston*."

"Yes. The skeleton."

"You know him?" He throws her an interested glance. "He is bony, yes. *And* a fearless and colorful scribe, I'll confess. But oh, how it put coals in my belly to see *him* eaten up in envy of John Marston!"

"He felt envy." Emilia feels somehow cheered by this intelligence. "Then he thought himself rivaled."

"Thought it, and was." Ben draws himself up proudly, then sags on the settle again. "And as for losses, well, he lost his only son."

She stares. "Lost a *son*? I never heard of it."

"There are many things you haven't heard of, I think. You are a little blinking worm, hiding in your chrysalis. Will did not publish his misfortunes. Not directly."

"How did it happen? When?"

Ben shrugs. "Long ago. Some twenty years gone. The poor lad drowned in the Avon. His father was away at the time, lightly stepping the Kentish earth with his traveling player-brethren."

Emilia slides from the arm of the settle to its seat. Ben reaches to touch her dress. Distracted, she pushes his hand away. She is glad now, very glad, that she never told Will she'd been pregnant, once, with his child, but had lost it. As she'd lost the father.

I did not know him, she thinks. *I never knew him at all.*

"Melly."

She glances at Ben, who is watching her a-squint through eyes as dark as hers. "Mark me," he says. "The moth spins its silk without knowing why it spins. It spins because it must. When it stops spinning, it dies."

This is interesting. "Is it so?"

He flicks his hand. "So, you interrogate me, like a Star Chamber judge. I won't swear to it, no. I think it an elegant possibility, this conceit of the silkworm. Articulated in the *present tense*, for the approval of Emilia Bassano Lanier."

She feels a rush of warmth for this outrageous mountain of a man, who remembers four years afterward a brief comment she made on a single evening. A comment on poetry. Has anyone ever seen her — not seen through her, but *seen* her — as completely as Ben? She almost hugs him, but stops herself. She doesn't know where it would lead. Or rather, she does.

"Here's the point, Melly," he goes on. "You must never stop writing. You see, he stopped. Then he died."

She presses her sleeve to her eyes, and looks through one curtainless side window at the black night outside. "Writing. Sometimes it seems a mere distraction."

"From what?"

"This slow decay."

"Let us weep together. I'll start."

She laughs. "You lack feeling."

"No. But you are too melancholy, Melly." His voice is gentle. "My nightingale. A portrait of anguish. But do not despair. You will find your readers. They are finding you."

"Fit audience, though few." She pulls her handkerchief from her sleeve and blows her nose.

He lets his head fall back against the settle's frame and watches her through slitted eyes. "Play the lute for me," he says after a moment, in a slurred, sleepy voice. "Sing. Sing. Heigh-ho."

"I cannot sing." She rises and kisses the top of his head. "Thank you, Ben. For the money."

"I ne'er gave you aught. I have told you," he mumbles. "A cockatoo college."

The candles are sputtering. One has gone out. Ben starts to snore. She takes off his shoes and hoists his legs onto the settle. There he lies, his bulk inert under her oil landscape of the house, hills, road, and tree. She remembers the old fantasy of her Tichtfield days: a ring of black-clad friends, all solemn, yet all smiling, each with a book, talking, nodding, listening intently to one another, seated beneath the wide leaves of a towering oak.

She slides again onto the settle and places Ben's big feet on her lap.

Here I am, Will, she thinks. *Here we are.*

32

B ut the world opens up like a road.

In the waning of that year, when the leaves hang yellow from the elms, Emilia sits again on the settle and watches the fire. Dusk has fallen, and she is alone in a dusty house. She's half-asleep, gazing on the hearth's glowing ashes, blinking at the sparks until they begin to seem something less or more than what they are, like an artist's painting of embers, signifying age.

Idly, her fingers stroke the letter that lies in her lap. It came three months ago, and she has unfolded and read it so often its creases are tearing. It is written in what seems the hand of a barely literate child.

"The age of miracles is past," preached the pastor last Sunday, at the parish church of St. Giles in the Fields. That church stands at the site where John Oldcastle, a Bible-reading Lollard, was burned two hundred years ago by the papist authorities for claiming this very same thing. She once saw Oldcastle glorified in a play. He was a Protestant saint, if Protestants had saints, who derided weeping statues and holy wells and magical cures. Burning, he had called through the smoke, "The age of miracles is past!" But were the pastor and Oldcastle wrong?

The letter says,

> *Mistress Lanier. I do not blame your passes with my husband Will. It is long ago and hees dead. As a grace to him I vowed to send this message he spoke to you on his deathbed, indeed when he could barely speke and could rite nothing more. He sayed: Forgive me, Emilia, my second wonder.*
>
> *Anne Hathaway Shakespeare*

When she first got the missive, in August, she spent hours exploring the possible meanings of the reported sentence. A slurred request uttered by a dying man who could hardly talk at all. "Emilia, my second *wander*"? Henry Wriothesley being the first to tempt Will from chastity? Or, "Emilia, my second *wounder*," after Henry? Or after Anne? Or "my *second-wounder*," the slut who made him waste his precious minutes? Each night the week after the letter came she lay awake turning Will's words in her brain, tapping them with a mental hammer, considering all things they could be made to signify, worrying the last thing he ever spoke to her just as she'd once worried each syllable of those cursed sonnets. Finally, as exhausted as amused by the absurdity of it all, she gave up. Now she's chosen to believe what is, after all, most likely: that after more than three decades of marriage, Anne Shakespeare knows what her husband said. It makes sense to accept the transcription of that blunt woman whose own paragraph holds no double meanings or half-hidden suggestions, but walks its message from Stratford to London as directly as a cart-horse to market, saying no more nor less than what is intended. And that is, forgiveness at the beginning, and forgiveness at the end.

He has begged her pardon.

And has called her a wonder, to boot.

As are we all, she thinks dreamily now, considering Henry Wriothesley, whose very face radiated light, and Walter Raleigh, now back in the Tower for some fresh irreverence, writing bitter poems and pleading for liberty just once more to sail the Atlantic, to find El Dorado, still bearing new worlds in his sea-green eyes. *Wonder*. And Ben Jonson, who, braving all mocks, has this year brazenly printed his plays for learned readers in a folio and called them *Works*. Ben is a wonder, as was indomitable Queen Elizabeth, and Baptista Bassano, whose true religion was music, and Alphonso, who knew how to play and how to listen. And Bess Carey, that kind, pen-waving virago. *A marvel*. And maddening Angelica, and lion-hearted Penelope, and mild Em Pettigrew, and even valiant, debauched Henry Carey, to say naught of every pock-faced or beauteous noble or beggar she's ever passed on a London street. *Wonders, all*. That was what Will knew.

It is no low praise, then, to be singled out from this mob of miracles, if only to be put in second place. *My second wonder*. True. Even when she was his lover she played second fiddle with Will, coming behind someone or something, and knew it. So she welcomes, at last, the explicit designation, committed to paper, no less. It has a loud finality, like an enchantment breaking or a second shoe dropped. To her surprise, Anne's message has made her feel free, even glad.

This is also a miracle.

Now, these days and nights, she doesn't study the letter, but keeps it as a kind of totem, a comfort or charm. She likes to have it near her, tucked in her clothing, near to the touch of her hand. The piece of paper rounds and completes her, or better to say it reminds her that she is complete. She is thinking of writing a reply to Anne. If she does, she too will send one page only, and stain it, above the name "Emilia Lanier," with only two words. *Thank you.*

She folds Anne's letter and tucks it into her belt. The gesture reminds her of another paper she carried near her body for years, never knowing why she did so: the woodcut given her by Penelope, with its trick sketch of a maid who, viewed askance, becomes an old woman. She hasn't thought of that drawing for decades, though she once puzzled over it so frequently that now, squeezing her eyes tightly shut, its image rises whole before her mind's eye. For an instant, the two profiles appear side by side, together, the girl and the crone, the single pair of faces Will Shakespeare saw.

Then a log in the fire pops, and she starts, and both pictures fall into dust.

Well. No matter. She leans forward to poke the ashes with a fire iron, then relaxes again against the cushions, feeling her lids once more start to droop. She hears a scrabble of mice in the walls, and thinks drowsily, *I need a new cat,* and then, *Em's seventeen, and I should make a match for her,* and finally, *I must light a taper while I can still see.* With a groan she rises, lifts the tinderbox, and strikes the flint just as a rap sounds on the front door. At first, busy with her own clatterings, she's not sure she's heard a knock. But the rap comes again, and so after lighting her candle she moves to peer through the peephole at the shrouded woman who stands on her stoop.

Her looks were never anything next to Emilia's. Henry Carey, Lord Hunsdon, made his last marriage for lands and alliance after his first wife died, while his bride, like her family, sought rank. Whether love had ever sparked between Anne Morgan and Lord Hunsdon, or in Anne's heart alone, is a question Emilia didn't ask herself for decades. When she did, it seemed, as with so many middle-year questions, too late for the answer to matter. The issue was dead and buried, like Hunsdon himself.

So Emilia has long concluded. And yet here is Anne Morgan, like a spectre in some old play of revenge, shedding like grave-clothes her scarf and her cloak. She is sixty or so, her face human and tired. For this private night visit she hasn't bothered to powder herself as she does for the queen's sitting room or a playhouse box, and for the first time Emilia perceives her as something other than a doll assembled out of parts. Paintless, her cheeks visibly sag. Bags pouch beneath her eyes. She is a person.

Emilia folds Lady Anne's cloak and scarf and places them on the settle. In an earlier year she might have been too shocked at this apparition to speak, but since this is a world of wonders, she now knows that if a woman lives long enough, she may see everything: even Lady Anne Morgan Carey Montgomery paying a nighttime call to Acorn Court in St. Giles in the Fields. So she calmly bids her guest be seated. She sits too, placing the taper on a table between them.

Only then does she notice the small silk purse Anne Morgan clutches in her finely gloved hand.

Anne holds the purse out to Emilia and says, "This is for you."

Emilia takes it. She can tell what's inside it as soon as she feels its bulk and weight. But she pulls the drawstrings loose anyway, in the way a player might perform a scripted action. She does it to make things plain, as though God were watching. Inside the purse, the gold of ten bright angels winks in the candlelight.

"You have supplied me." This is a question, not a statement, but Anne merely nods, and so Emilia feels compelled to continue. "All this time. Why?" She asks this even though the ice has begun to form again in the pit of her stomach, as in years long past, at court, when various fears stalked her daily. She has not felt this afraid since the evening she returned to Longditch from a tragic play to see a red cross nailed to her door. "*Why?*" she repeats, not wanting an answer, asking because she must ask, in conformance to some blind necessity.

"I have prayed," Anne Morgan says. "For years. When you came to the queen three years ago, when you begged her for money, I knew I must act."

"And you acted, lady. You persuaded her against me. I heard your voice through the chamber door. It was you, wasn't it?"

"This is what you thought, and I knew you would think it. But I did the opposite, or tried to. I advised her to give you your stipend. To remember your family's long service to the Tudors. But she —" Anne smiles faintly. "I knew the moment I'd said 'Tudor' I had stepped wrong. Good Queen Nan, you see, dislikes mention of a dynasty that is not, strictly speaking, her husband's. She . . . ." She falls silent. No wonder. It's a habit, no doubt. Anne Morgan lives at Denmark House, which, like all royal places, is riddled with spies.

But Emilia has dwelt in the freer air of the city for twenty years, and is in the habit of finishing sentences. She completes Anne's. "She prefers allusions to the majesty of the Stuart line."

Anne Morgan's mouth twists. "I knew not what to do after she rejected your plea. Yet I feared I'd be damned if I did nothing to help you. And so I have." She swallows. "Because of what I did to you."

Emilia's stomach grows colder. She has for so long buried the memories of the knife, the hushed women's voices at the foot of her bed, the kitchen girl's horrid suggestion. Of mad Margery of the matted hair, howling like a wolf in her cell.

But she cannot stop Anne Morgan's voice. Words spill from the woman. Anne twists her hands as she talks. "You cannot *think* how I hated you. I was nothing to him. He only lay with me for duty, never desire. And he wrote you *poems.*"

"Did you think poetry was love?" Emilia whispers, but Anne doesn't hear her. She is rushing on like a brook through a broken dam. "Not that his dalliances stopped when he packed you away with your music man. I'faith, I thanked God for taking him off when he went at last. Dropping off that horse with a clang, all splendid in his foolish armor. I had to bite my lip to keep from laughing. Does that make me horrible?"

"No," Emilia says softly. "*That* doesn't."

"But his time with you was my worst. You, the proud mistress!"

"I wasn't proud to be called a whore."

"Better that than to be pitied. And I could not conceive. I thought I would never conceive. Yet there you were, as big as a house with his child, and Margery come to tell me of it. All at court knew it, just as well as if he'd printed it, bragged of it. He *did* brag of it, I'm certain. I've been told he did. The cock of the walk! That a man of his age could still sire a child! That it wasn't his *wife's* child didn't matter. He was just like his —" She catches herself again, this time raising a hand to her mouth. Her gloves are cherry red.

"So." Emilia's voice is as thin as paper. "You hired Margery to kill my baby." She has willed herself to say it, and now that the thing is spoken, her voice strengthens with anger. "You gave her money to strangle an innocent child, and to say some trash about a cord around his neck. And to kill me as well with too much mandragora, most like."

Anne Morgan is gaping at her, now from behind both cherry-red gloves. "What do you think of me?"

"I know not what to think." Emilia's frame has begun to shake with rage and horror. "I hoped the story was a fantasy, or a nightmare, and now you come to tell me 'tis true."

"It is *not* true. Me, a blithe murderess?"

"We are both that. But you are a worse one."

"What can you mean? I paid Margery. That much is true."

"Paid her for what, if not —"

"To *steal* the brat! To give him to Hunsdon, who brought him to me. The great lord did me *that* service. And then she put it about that your child had died."

Emilia half-rises, thinking she might strike her, then sinks again to her stool. "You tried to *steal* him?"

"I *did* steal him. He was *taken*, not killed. I had a carriage and a wet-nurse at the postern gate."

Now Emilia is clenching her fists so hard her fingers are whitening, turning numb. She feels the floor falling away from under her feet. "O, excellent falsehood!" she hisses. "I know the truth. Margery killed him, and then she went mad. I saw his grave."

"O, you did? I'truth, did you?"

"I . . . ." *Did I?* She thinks of the gravestone Margery showed her, the flat square engraved with the names of Hunsdon's first lost children. *Yours is there, too*, Margery had said. *You can know it, if no one else does.*

"There was no grave," Anne Morgan says. "No burial."

The two women stare at each other for a long moment. Emilia's fingers slacken and fall loose in her lap. At last she speaks in a low voice. "If he didn't die, where did he go?"

"How can you not know?"

And then, like a thunderclap, she does know. She can see it. That horrid, imperious puny, spoiled by his father, ignored by his mother, or rather, by Anne Morgan Carey. Years later, the quiet, weedy, auburn-haired youth who'd tried to keep Danish Anne's wooden throne from

toppling during *The Masque of Queens*. The young man in the scratchy
lace collar, uncomfortable in a lord's box at Whitefriars. The shy visitor to Alphonso's sickroom. He had brought his recorder, that day, and
played a sweet melody.

"He is standing by the coach," Anne Morgan says. "Just outside."

Emilia is silent for so long that Anne reaches toward her and shakes
her wrist. "Emilia! Wake! Do you know, it is he who finally persuaded me
to come."

"He knows, then."

"He heard the rumors."

"What rumors? I heard none. Or not this rumor."

Her visitor raises her red-gloved hands. "Where would you have
heard it? You left court. He was brought *to* it. I lied to him for years. In
the end, I tired of his gadfly questions, and spoke the truth." She says this
proudly, as though she thinks she deserves a prize. But then her voice
drops to a humble register. "You must forgive me. Please."

Something is shifting in Emilia, a heaviness breaking, a thing cracking open, like a rock, or a door. But she cannot go through the door. This
outrageous pirate! The horror of her act demands a volcano or a tempest
of fury, a howl that would drown the cries of Margery, trapped within
the echoing walls of her last prison. *You have unblessed me, Anne Morgan,*
she thinks. *You have stolen from me a child's face, the little hands, the very
name of a mother.*

But she doesn't say any of it. Anne Morgan's first words have seared
her heart. What would *she* say in reply? What *has* she said? That she,
Lord Hunsdon's wife, was a laughingstock, a barren stale, and Emilia
helped make her so. What is age for, if it grant no perspective? She was
little more than a girl at the time of Morgan's humiliation, but she is now
too old to pretend she played no part in it.

"We must forgive each other," she answers at last. It is all she can
manage to say.

The two women sit in silence, until the candle flickers and threatens
to leave them darkling. Emilia rises to trim the wick. When she returns
to her stool Anne Morgan says suddenly, "That young man is the king of
England, by rights. The last living son of the son of Henry the Eighth. I
mean, the lines of all other royal by-blows having . . . petered out." She
speaks it lightly, as though the remark were not treason because it is so
clearly a jest. Still, Emilia detects a flash of old ambition in her eyes.

Then Anne Morgan laughs. "But lineage counts for little these days. So much for the father's grandeur. Young titled Henry will not settle anywhere. He hobnobs with players, and toots the recorder. He writes."

"Ah," says Emilia. "But that is lineage, too."

Anne nods, conceding the point. "But this is not all. He has sailed to Virginia with Lord De la Ware, and got his hands dirty building log houses there. 'Perhaps I'll go back,' he says on his return. Marry, perhaps he'll take you, now!"

"Take me to *Virginia?*"

Anne shrugs. "They'll soon be in sore need of dame schools there."

"You're mad," Emilia says feebly. "I've never been anywhere. What would *I* do amongst the painted savages?"

Anne throws up her hands. "How should I know? I understand neither of you. That young man could govern a thousand acres of the best land in England, and spend all his days hunting stag, but he'll none of it. Would you believe it? He wants to come here. He has heard of your circle." Anne leans toward her, holding out her hands in supplication. "Will you meet him, Emilia?"

Emilia draws back. "No!"

"But you must." Seeing her expression, Lady Anne adjusts her wording. "Will you not?"

"I will not." Her son? What son? She has not even had the naming of him. What would she say to him? Let him exist, and there an end. She stands. "Lady, I am . . . grateful for your patronage." *Am I?* "But now, you must leave me."

Anne Morgan rises and takes her cloak. "Tell me, what did you mean, 'We are both that'?"

"What?"

"You said we were both murderers. What did you mean?"

"I . . . . What? I don't know. What did I mean?"

"I have flustered you. My news has been a shock."

Emilia's laugh is as brittle and sharp as breaking glass. "How not?"

Anne steps toward her. "Then you truly had no inkling."

"None!"

This retort is gunfire, splitting the air. *Will* she not go? But Anne Morgan stands, shorter than Emilia by half a head, now gripping her hostess's elbow. "He is waiting," she says. "Outside, by the coach. Let him in."

Emilia shakes her head. "He is too late a year. You may tell him."

"Lady, whate'er you think of me, whate'er I have done, the fault was none of his making."

Emilia can't bring herself to voice her fear, which is this. She's deprived the youth of a father, and left him an orphan in the wilderness of the court. She doesn't know this boy, this man. How can she claim or love him?

As she stands immobile, posing the question, Anne Morgan makes a sound of impatience and briskly goes out the door. It is a full minute before Emilia bestirs herself to follow, to drop the latch against all new-comers, all further accidents and surprises. She has tarried too long. The young man is already there, mounting her steps just as she reaches the doorway, doffing his cap. His enthusiasm overwhelms his bashfulness. He takes the candle from her hand and raises it, so that his face and hers are illuminated.

"Do you see!" he says excitedly. "I *knew*! When I first saw you near, with Master Lanier, after that mad *Masque of Blackness*, when the tables collapsed — you know, something is always collapsing — then I said to myself, *That is she.*"

She stares at him and says nothing. *O silent woman!* But her hands talk, rising unbidden to touch with tentative fingertips his shaven chin, his cheek, his auburn thatch of hair. He looks like Margaret Johnson, and Baptista, and Angelica, and even, very slightly, Alphonso. But his eyes are her eyes.

There's a noise on the stair behind her. The young man raises the candle higher, and his eyes widen. "Holy Saint George! Mother mine, do you keep heavenly messengers in your house?"

Emilia tears her eyes away from him, following the track of his gaze. Visible through the open door, Em Pettigrew is standing halfway down the stair holding a candle of her own. She looks ghostly, dressed in a loose gown, her hair falling free over her shoulders. Her face is fresh and bare. She has come to see what the fuss is about. She looks silently at the young man, then drops her eyes modestly, turns, and glides back up to her dormer room.

"*Give me a look, give me a face, that makes simplicity a grace . . . .*" young Henry murmurs. Then, almost guiltily, he turns his face back to Emilia. Even by the single flickering flame, she can see that he's blushing. "My good mother," he says humbly, and casts his eyes down like Em just did. Emilia can't help it. She laughs.

And then, right there on her stoop, like a good son, he kneels. He places the candle on the stoop, then takes her wrist gently and presses her palm to his face. "I'm like you, am I not?" he says as he looks up at her. "A very mirror!"

She stares down at him, amazed by everything. Does she see another country in his eyes? Or is it a place she knows? "The description is just," she murmurs, suddenly shy. "Though I confess I never noted it before."

"It's that you never looked at me." He corrects himself. "You did, though. Anne Morgan showed me. You were watching us at Whitefriars once, from a nobles' box, where you sat with your friend."

"Yes. What friend?" She struggles to remember the scene.

"The lady Elizabeth Carey. You glanced at me. But you did not know what you were seeing."

"Ah." She feels the salt tears in her eyes. She tries Penelope's old sob-stemming trick, the one that never worked for very long, tipping her head back at an angle and furiously blinking. Above her small corner of London the skies are crowded with stars. How can a winged soul stay housed in a breast all alone, and not fly up to shine among them? She puts a hand to her chest as though to restrain her heart. "I think you are right," she says, past the catch in her throat. She looks down again, and sees him still kneeling. "I did not know what I saw, or what I sought. And you, sir?"

His eyebrows rise as her father's used to when he piped a high note, as though he were surprised at his own success. Then he frowns in puzzled thought, looking, again, like her mother. "Did I know what I *sought*? A question to be asked. Well. Music, and to be a player, and the ocean. And the New World, and a pure angel."

She smiles her Mona Lisa half-smile. "You'll find no stainless angels in this house. Nor, to speak truly, in this whole wide world, be it the old one *or* the new."

He gives her a crooked and radiant grin. "Then no matter. Only give me your blessing."

So, laying her palm flat on his head, she blesses him, being angel enough for that.